THE LAST WITNESS

A NOVEL

JOEL GOLDMAN

Find out more about Joel Goldman at http://www.joelgoldman.com

Follow his blog at http://www.joelgoldman.blogspot.com

Sign up for his newsletter at http://www.joelgoldman.com/newsletter.php

Follow him on Twitter http://twitter.com/#!/JoelGoldman1

Follow him on Facebook at http://www.facebook.com/joel.goldman

Contents

Dedication

For Aaron, Danny, and Michele—the greatest kids ever.

CHAPTER ONE

Jack Cullan's maid found his body lying facedown on the floor of his study, his cheek glued to the carpet with his own frozen, congealed blood. When she turned the body over, fibers stuck to Cullan's cheek like fungus that grows under a rock. His left eye was open, the shock of his death still registered in the wide aperture of his eyelid. His right eye was gone, pulverized by a .38-caliber bullet that had pierced his pupil and rattled around in his brain like loose change in the seconds before he died.

"Shit," Harry Ryman said as he looked down on the body of the mayor's personal lawyer. "Call the chief," he told his partner, Carl Zimmerman.

Harry knew that Jack Cullan wasn't just Mayor Billy Sunshine's lawyer. He was a social lubricator, a lawyer who spent more time collecting IOUs than a leg-breaking bagman for the mob. For the last twenty years, getting elected in Kansas City had meant getting Cullan's support. Anyone doing serious business with the city had hired him to get their deals done.

Harry guessed that Cullan was in his early sixties, dumpy from years spent avoiding physical exertion in favor of mental manipulation. Harry squatted down to examine Cullan's hands. They were smooth, unlike the man's reputation. Cullan had a Santa Claus build, but Harry knew the man couldn't have played St. Nick without asking for more than he ever would have given.

Harry had been a homicide detective too long to remember ever having been anything else. He knew that the chances of solving a murder dropped like the wind chill after the first forty-eight hours.

1

If time weren't a powerful enough incentive, a politically heavy body like Jack Cullan's would push his investigation into warp speed.

He gathered his topcoat around him, fighting off the cold that had invaded the study on the back side of Cullan's house. The windows were open. The maid, Norma Hawkins, said she had found them that way when she arrived for work at eight o'clock that morning, Monday, December 10. The heat had also been turned off, the maid had added. An early winter blast had locked Kansas City down in a brutal snow-laced assault for the last week. Cullan's house felt like ground zero.

"The chief says to meet him at the mayor's office," Zimmerman said, interrupting Harry's silent survey of the murder scene.

"What for?" Harry asked, annoyed at anything that would slow down the investigation.

"I told the chief that somebody popped the mayor's lawyer. He told me to sit tight, like I was going someplace, right? He calls back two minutes later and says meet him at the mayor's office. You want to discuss it with the chief, you got his number."

Carl Zimmerman had grown up fighting, sometimes over jabs about being a black man with a white man's name, sometimes to find out who could take a punch. He and Harry had been partners for six years without becoming close friends. Harry was older, more experienced, and automatically assumed the lead in their investigations, a batting order he knew that Zimmerman resented. That was Zimmerman's problem, Harry had decided. Zimmerman was a good cop, but Harry was a better one.

Harry wanted to get moving. He wanted to interview the maid, figure out how long Cullan had been dead before she found him, and backtrack Cullan's activities in the hours before he was murdered. He wanted to talk to everyone Cullan had been with during that time. He wanted to search Cullan's home, car, and office for anything that might lead him to the killer. The last thing he wanted to do was run downtown to promise the chief and the mayor that they would solve the crime before dinner. The next-to-last thing he wanted to do was deal with the chip on his partner's shoulder.

"Here," Harry said, tossing the keys to Zimmerman. "You can drive."

CHAPTER TWO

Lou Mason read about Jack Cullan's murder in Wednesday morning's *Kansas City Star* while the wind whipped past his office windows overlooking Broadway. In the spring, Mason would open the windows, letting the breeze wrap itself around him like a soft sweatshirt on a cool day. Wednesday morning's wind was more like a garrote twisted around the city's throat by Mother Nature turned Boston Strangler.

The story of Cullan's murder was two days old but still front-page news. The reporter, Rachel Firestone, wrote that Cullan had been at the center of an investigation into the decision of the mayor and the Missouri Gaming Commission to approve a license for a riverboat casino called the Dream. The Dream had opened recently, docked on the Missouri River at the limestone landing where nineteenth-century fur traders had first thought to build the trading post that became Kansas City.

Cullan's client, Edward Fiora, owned the Dream. Whispers that Cullan had secured the Dream's license with well-orchestrated bribes of Mayor Sunshine and of Beth Harrell, the chair of the gaming commission, had circulated like tabloid vapor, titillating but unproved. The reporter had dubbed the brewing scandal the "Nightmare on Dream Street."

Mason put the paper down to answer his phone. "Lou Mason," he said. When he'd first gone into solo practice, he'd answered the phone by saying, "Law office," until one of his clients had asked to speak to Mr. Office.

"I need you downstairs," Blues said, and hung up.

Blues was Wilson Bluestone, Jr., Mason's landlord, private investigator, and more often than Mason would like, the one person Mason counted on to watch his back. Blues owned the bar on the first floor, Blues on Broadway. He never admitted to needing anything, so Mason took his statement seriously.

Mason double-timed down the lavender-carpeted hallway, past the art deco light fixtures spaced evenly on the wall between the offices on the second floor. One office belonged to Blues, another to a PR flack, and a third to a CPA. They were all solo acts.

He bounded down the stairs at the end of the hall, bracing one hand on the wobbly rail, his feet just brushing the treads, making a final turn into the kitchen. The cold urgency in Blues's voice propelled him past the grill almost too fast to catch the greasy scent of the Reuben sandwiches cooked there the night before. A sudden burst of broken glass mixed with the crack of overturned furniture and the thick thud of a big man put down.

"Goddammit, Bluestone!" Harry Ryman shouted. Harry hated bars and Blues too much to pay an early morning social call, especially on a day that would freeze your teeth.

Mason picked up his pace, shoved aside the swinging door between the kitchen and the bar, and plunged into a frozen tableau on the edge of disaster. Blues stood in the middle of the room surrounded by Harry Ryman and another detective Mason recognized as Harry's partner, Carl Zimmerman, and a uniformed cop.

The beat cop and Zimmerman were aiming their service revolvers at Blues's head. Another uniformed cop was on his knees next to a table lying on its side, surrounded by broken dishes, rubbing a growing welt on his cheek with one hand and holding a pair of handcuffs with the other.

Blues and Harry were squared off in front of each other, heavyweights waiting for the first bell. Harry's dead-eyed cop glare matched Blues's flat street stare. In a tale of the tape, it was hard to pick a favorite. Though half a foot shy of Blues's six-four, Harry had a solid, barreled girth that was tough to rock. Blues was chiseled, lithe, and deadly. Harry carried the cop-worn look of the twenty years he had on Blues.

No one moved. Steam rose off the cops' shoulders as the snow they had carried inside melted in the warmth of the bar. The wind beat against the front door, rattling its frame, like someone desperate to get inside. Blues was spring-loaded, never taking his eyes from Harry's.

Mason spoke softly, as if the sound of his voice would detonate the room. "Harry?" Ryman didn't answer.

The uniformed cop on his feet was a skinny kid with droopy eyes and a puckered mouth who'd probably never drawn his gun outside the shooting range and couldn't control the tremor in his extended arms.

Carl Zimmerman was a compact middleweight who held his gun as if it were a natural extension of his hand, no hesitation in his trigger finger. His dark face was a calm pool.

The solidly built cop Blues had put on the floor had gotten to his feet, his block-cut face flush with embarrassment and anger, anxious for redemption and ready to take Blues on again. He took a step toward Blues, and Carl Zimmerman put a hand on his shoulder and held him back.

"You're going down, Bluestone," Harry said.

"I told your boy not to put his hands on me," Blues answered.

"Officer Toland was doing his job and I'm doing mine. Don't make this worse than it already is."

"Harry?" Mason said again.

"This doesn't concern you, Lou," Harry answered, not taking his eyes off Blues.

"That's bullshit, Harry, and you know it."

Harry Ryman was the closest thing Mason had to a father. He and Mason's aunt Claire had been together for years and had been unconventional surrogates for Mason's parents, who had been killed in a car accident when Mason was three years old. Blues had saved Mason's life and was the closest thing Mason had to a brother. Whatever was going down didn't just concern Mason. It threatened to turn his world inside out.

Harry said to Blues, "I'm gonna cuff you. Everybody gets cuffed, even if we have to shoot them first. You remember that much, don't you, Bluestone?"

Blues looked at Mason, silently asking the obvious with the same flat expression. Mason nodded, telling him to go along. Blues slowly turned his back on Harry, disguising his rage with a casual pivot, extending his arms behind him, managing a defiant posture even in surrender. Harry fastened the handcuffs around Blues's wrists and began reciting the cop's mantra.

"You're under arrest. You have the right to remain silent. Anything you say can and will be used against you in a court of law. You have the right to an attorney. If you cannot afford an attorney—"

"I'm his attorney," Mason interrupted. "What's the charge?"

Harry looked at Mason for the first time, a tight smile cutting a thin line across his wide face. Mason saw the satisfaction in Harry's smile and the glow of long-sought vindication in his eyes. He had always warned Mason that Blues would cross the line one day and that he would be there to take him down; that the violent, self-styled justice Blues had employed when he was a cop, and since then, was as corrupt as being on the take. As much as Harry might have longed to make that speech again, instead he said it all with one word.

"Murder." Harry held Mason's astonished gaze. "Murder in the first degree," he added. "You can talk to your client downtown after we book him."

Mason watched as they filed out, first the two uniformed cops, then Carl Zimmerman, then Blues. As Harry reached the door, Mason called to him.

"Who was it, Harry?"

Harry had had the steely satisfaction of the triumphant cop when he'd forced Blues to submit moments ago. Now his face sagged as he looked at Mason, seeing him for the first time as an adversary. Harry thought about the battle that lay ahead between them before responding.

"Jack Cullan. Couldn't have been some punk. It had to be Jack Fucking Cullan." Harry turned away, disappearing into the wind as the door closed behind him.

CHAPTER THREE

Mason scraped the crystallized snow off the windshield of his Jeep Cherokee. The cast-iron sky hung low enough that he half expected to scrape it off the glass as well. His car was parked behind the bar, a reminder that covered parking was the only perk he missed from his days as a downtown lawyer. The Jeep was strictly bad-weather transportation. His TR6 was hibernating in his garage, waiting for a top-down day.

He drove north on Broadway, a signature street of rising and falling fortunes Kansas City wore like an asphalt ID bracelet. From the lip of the Missouri River on the north edge of downtown to the Country Club Plaza shopping district, forty-seven blocks south, Broadway was high-rise and low-rise, professionals and payday loans, insurance and uninsurable, homes and homeless, the Big Man and the Little Man elbowing each other for position.

Mason wondered how Blues had been linked to Cullan's murder. As far as he knew, they had never even met. Maybe something had happened between them when Blues was a cop, something that led to Cullan's murder years later. Mason dismissed that as unlikely. Blues didn't carry grudges for years. He settled them or expunged them.

It was possible that Cullan had surfaced in one of the cases Blues had handled as a private investigator, as either a target or a client. Blues didn't talk with Mason about his cases, unless he needed Mason's help.

Before he bought the bar, Blues taught piano at the Conservatory of Music. Cullan hadn't seemed the type to take up music late in life, and teaching someone the difference between bass clef and treble clef wasn't likely to drive Blues to murder. At his worst, Blues would tell a student to play the radio instead of the piano.

Harry Ryman was right about one thing. Blues had his own system of justice and he didn't hesitate to use violence to enforce it. For Blues, violence was a great equalizer, leveling the playing field against long odds. Few people would use it, even those who threatened it. The threat without follow-through was weak, a shortcoming Blues couldn't abide. Blues wasn't casual about violence, though. He wielded it with the precision and purpose of a surgeon using a scalpel.

Blues and Harry were partners when Blues was a rookie cop and Harry was the veteran who was supposed to teach him about the street. Harry was by the book and Blues wrote his own book. Their partnership, and Blues's career as a cop, ended six years earlier when Blues shot and killed a woman during a drug bust. Internal Affairs gave Blues the choice of quitting or being prosecuted. He quit.

Harry had warned Mason against working with Blues, predicting that Blues would go down one day and that Harry would be there, waiting. Blues shrugged when Mason told him what Harry said, refusing to talk about the case that had fractured their relationship.

Saying that Harry and Blues hated each other was too simple an explanation. Harry and Blues shared a wound neither man could heal. Whenever the three of them were together, Mason felt like he was on the bomb squad, trying to guess whether Blues or Harry would go off first.

CHAPTER FOUR

"Sergeant Peterson," Mason said, reading the desk sergeant's name tag, "I'm Lou Mason. Harry Ryman brought Wilson Bluestone in a few minutes ago. I'm Bluestone's lawyer."

Peterson was reading *USA Today*. He looked at Mason over his half-glasses, sighed his resentment at Mason's intrusion, dropped his paper, and picked up the phone.

"He's here," he said and hung up, returning to his paper.

A civilian police department employee materialized and escorted Mason to the second-floor detective squad room, pointing him to a hard-backed chair. The squad room reflected the uninspired use of public money—pale walls, faded vanilla tile, and banged-up steel desks covered with the antiseptic details of destroyed lives.

Mason waited while the crosscurrents of cops and their cases flowed around him. He'd been here before, waiting to be questioned and accused. An ambivalent mix of urgency and resignation permeated the place. Cops had a special sweat, born of the need to preserve and protect and the fearful realization that they were too often outnumbered. That sweat was strongest in homicide.

Homicide cops took the darkest confessions of the cruelest impulses. They sweet-talked, cajoled, and deceived the guilty into speaking the unspeakable. The more they heard, the more they were overwhelmed by one simple truth: there were more people willing to kill than they could stop from killing. Sterile statistics on closed cases couldn't mask the smell of blood and the taste for vengeance that clung to homicide cops like a second skin.

Justice was supposed to cleanse them, but the pressure to make an arrest could wash justice down the drain. Even a good cop like Harry Ryman wasn't immune. If he was going to save Blues, Mason knew he had to slow down the clock.

Saving Blues also meant taking on Harry Ryman. Mason could remember the days when Harry used to pick him up by his belt loops and swing him up over his shoulder like a sack of potatoes. And Mason could remember the day he graduated from law school and Harry bear-hugged him with a father's pride. Easing his grip just enough to see Mason's face, Harry told him how to navigate the uncertain waters that his clients would take him through.

"Just do the right thing. You won't have any trouble knowing what it is. The only hard part is doing it."

Life was never more complicated than that for Harry. He interrupted Mason's memories.

"You can see him now. He's in number three. No one will be watching or listening. And don't worry about it being my case. Just do your job and I'll do mine."

Blues was standing at the far end of the room staring into a mirror, his burnished-coppery skin, straight black hair, and fiery eyes muted under the exposed fluorescent tubes that hung from the ceiling.

"You're not that good-looking," Mason told him.

"I get prettier every day. It's a two-way mirror and this room is wired for sound."

"Harry said that no one is watching or listening."

"You believe him?"

"I believe that he's not that stupid. If they want you for this murder, they aren't going to fuck it up like that."

"Don't count on it."

Mason thought about Wally Sutherland, his first criminal defense client. Wally's one-thing-led-to-another encounter with a woman he'd met in a bar ended with his arrest for attempted forcible rape. When Mason visited him in jail, he cried for his wife, his mother, and God, in that order. Mason had never seen Blues cry and didn't expect he ever would.

"Did they question you?"

"Nothing official. Harry tried to make it like old times. Good old Harry stroking me, telling me how much easier it would be just to get the whole thing over with. His partner, Zimmerman, tells him to hold off until you got here. Harry says to Zimmerman that I'm too smart to fall for any tricks, especially since I had been such a smart cop, saying that he was just reminding me of what I already knew."

"Harry playing good cop with you is—"

"Stupid. Ryman's done everything but put a bounty on my ass, and he thinks he's gonna talk me into confessing because he's such a damn nice guy. Bullshit."

"What do they have on you?"

Blues leaned over the oak table that separated him from Mason, planting both hands firmly on the surface.

"First things first. Can you do this?"

"What do you mean, can I do this? You've seen the law license hanging in my office. I'm an official member of the bar. Murder cases are a walk in the park. Besides, at the rate I'm charging you, I can't afford to take long to get you off. I'll go broke."

Blues didn't laugh or smile. His face was a death mask. "I'm not asking you about the lawyer piece. You're as good as anybody I've ever seen. I want to know, can you do this?"

Mason understood the question. "Harry isn't the issue. He's not looking at the needle. You are."

"Ryman doesn't just think I killed Jack Cullan. He wants it to be me. Cops who want somebody found guilty know how to make that happen."

"Not Harry. He's hard. He probably does want it to be you, but Harry plays it straight. He doesn't know any other way."

"We get to court, Ryman's on the stand—can you take him on, carve him up, make the jury want to blame him instead of me? Can you tell the jury that Harry Ryman doesn't know his ass from third base and hates his old partner enough to send him to death row even if I'm innocent? Can you go home and tell your aunt Claire when all this is over that it was just business?"

Mason had asked himself the same questions as he drove downtown. Hearing Blues ask them reaffirmed the advice Harry had given him years ago. Knowing the right thing to do was easier than doing it. Since Harry was the lead on the investigation into Cullan's murder, his testimony would have an enormous impact on the jury. Blues's life might depend on Mason's ability to turn the case into a trial of Harry and his investigation rather than a trial of Blues's innocence.

Mason realized another troubling aspect of Blues's questions. The criminal justice system was sometimes more about criminals than it was about justice. Innocent people were convicted for any number of reasons. Cops who planted evidence. Lazy defense lawyers. Jurors who believed that only guilty people got arrested, especially if they were black or brown. Being innocent wasn't always enough.

That's why nothing scared Mason more than an innocent client. The gangbanger, the embezzler, the jealous spouse turned killer, all knew in their gut that they'd do the time. They knew that after their lawyer turned every technical trick he had, the system would beat them. The odds favored the house.

Innocent people didn't understand any of that. They were just innocent. End of story.

"I'll do whatever it takes to beat this. Harry doesn't expect anything less. He won't cut either one of us any slack, and he'll get none from me. Now, tell me what they've got on you."

CHAPTER FIVE

Blues hesitated a moment, then nodded and sat across from Mason.

"Jack Cullan came in the bar last Friday night, about nine o'clock."

"You knew him?"

"He tried to hire me once. He wanted me to take pictures of a dude playing hide the nuts with the wrong squirrel. I took a pass."

"How long ago was that?"

"Not long enough that he didn't recognize me when he came in the bar. When he paid for the drinks, he told me that I should have taken the job since it paid better than bartending. I told him it didn't pay better than bar owning."

"Was he alone?"

"Opposite of alone. He was with a fine-looking woman, early forties, my guess."

"Did you get her name?"

"Not at first. Before she left, she gave me her card. Her name was Beth Harrell."

"As in Beth Harrell, the chair of the Missouri Gaming Commission?"

"Not likely that there's more than one Beth Harrell who'd be out clubbing with Jack Cullan."

"I can't believe she was out anywhere with Cullan. They've been all over the front page of the *Star*. She's got to be out of her mind to be out with that guy."

"Maybe that's why she threw a drink in his face."

"Okay. You want to take this from the top or just play catch-the-zinger?"

"You're the one asking the questions. I'm just the defendant."

"Start talking or I'll give you up to the public defender."

"Don't tempt me. I was on the bar. Pete Kirby, Kevin Street, and Ronnie Fivecoat had just started their set. Weather's so bad, the place is dead, but they were killing it, really cooking."

Mason had heard the trio before, Kirby on piano, Street on bass, and Fivecoat on drums. He'd have happily gone anywhere to hear them play.

"So Jack Cullan and Beth Harrell are out on one of the worst nights of the year and pick your place to get warm? How does that happen?"

"People with money come into my place, I try not to ask them if they're lost. I served them drinks and didn't pay any more attention to them until she stands up and douses him. Cullan's old and fat, but that old, fat man jumped up and popped her with the back of his hand. Knocked her on the floor."

"And you couldn't just tell them to take it outside?" Mason asked.

"Would have been the smart play. But I don't like it when fat old men slap women around. I grabbed Cullan from behind before he could smack her again, and that little prick scratched me like a cheap whore before I squeezed the air out of him."

Blues showed Mason the scabs on the backs of his hands.

"Was that it?"

"Almost. I told Beth Harrell that she should press charges against Cullan. She said that wasn't necessary, that they'd just had a misunderstanding. She was very cool about the whole thing. Gave me her business card, like that was some kind of permission slip for getting punched in public."

"And then they left?"

"Yeah. Cullan was upright and pissed. He promised me that my liquor license would be gone in a week."

Mason knew that Blues wouldn't let the threat go unanswered, and he waited for him to finish the story. Blues looked at the two-way mirror. "You sure they aren't listening in on this?"

"Not if they want to see you strapped to that gurney with a needle in your arm. What did you say to Cullan?"

Blues sighed, looked at the mirror again, and then back at Mason. "I told him that if he tried jacking with my license or ever came in my bar again, I'd twist his head off and stuff it up his ass."

"Well, that was memorable and stupid. What happened to being the strong, silent type?"

"Cullan is used to getting in the last word, shoving people around, pimp-slapping women. No way he walks out of my place like he owned it."

"Blues's Law. What about afterward? What did you do after you closed the bar?"

"Home, man. By myself."

"So you fought with this guy, he threatened you, and you threatened him back. If I know Harry, he's already talked to Beth Harrell and Kirby, Street, and Fivecoat. That makes four witnesses to your threat. And you don't have an alibi. Can't blame him for liking you for the murder. The coroner probably found skin and blood under Cullan's fingernails. It's too early for Harry to have linked you to that, but when he does, he's going to like you even more."

Mason pushed back from the table and stood.

"Where are you going?"

"Talk to Harry and find out what else he's got."

"Aren't you forgetting to ask me one thing?"

"What's that?"

"If I did it?"

Mason shook his head and smiled. "I never ask. Besides, you would have told me. Blues's Law."

Blues smiled for the first time. "I guess you can do this."

"That I can," Mason said.

CHAPTER SIX

Mason found Harry squeezed into his desk chair, talking on the phone and rolling his eyes.

"Yes, sir," he said. "I'm glad it's all over too, Mr. Mayor. Goodbye, sir."

Harry put the phone down and motioned Mason to pull up a chair, pointing at a cup of coffee he'd poured for him.

"Did you forget to tell the mayor about the trial?"

Harry was pushing sixty, with half-gray sawdust hair, a soft-squared face, flat on the top and round on the sides. His bulk was more muscle than fat, and his hands were like catchers' mitts.

"That's like the next election. Mayor Sunshine will worry about that tomorrow. Today he'll tell the public that the case has been solved and make it sound like it was his collar."

"I never saw a politician get so much out of his last name. Anybody who can campaign on the slogan 'Let the Sunshine in Kansas City' with a straight face wouldn't break a sweat solving a murder."

"The people elected him. William 'Billy' Sunshine. His Honor the Asshole."

Mason sipped and grimaced. He was an occasional coffee drinker, never quite developing an appreciation for the bitter brew.

"Get yourself some cream and sugar," Harry said. "Make it sweet like when you were a kid. You'll like it better that way."

Mason set his cup down, wondering whether Harry intended his remark to be a gentle paternal reminder of their long relationship or just idle chatter. There would come a time when he'd have to tell

Harry that their relationship was irrelevant to this case. He wasn't looking forward to that moment.

"It's fine. The mayor been pushing you guys pretty hard?"

Mason intended the question to sound casual, even innocent—more concerned about Harry than about the implications for the rush-to-judgment defense he was planning for Blues.

Harry gave him a wise smile. "Lou, I'm going to handle this case like every other one. It doesn't matter to me that Bluestone is the defendant or that you're his lawyer. I'll tell you what you're entitled to know and that's it. Everything else you can get from the prosecutor in discovery."

Mason felt like the little boy again. First Harry told him how to drink his coffee, and then he told him that he's not so clever after all.

"Fair enough," Mason said. "Tell me what I'm entitled to know, but don't leave anything out, because it won't be fun for either one of us if I find out the hard way."

Harry shuffled through a stack of reports on his desk, humming under his breath until he found the one he wanted. He put on a pair of gold-rimmed glasses and studied the report.

Mason had been a spectator to many of Harry's cases, listening to his take on the bad guy of the month, his no-good defense lawyer, and the ballbusting judge, always marveling at Harry's command of the nitty-gritty. Harry didn't miss much, and he forgot even less.

Mason had no doubt that Harry knew everything about Cullan's murder by heart and could recite it backward in his sleep, his pretense of unfamiliarity a dodge meant to encourage Mason to underestimate him. He figured Harry was doing it more out of habit than out of any expectation that Mason would take him lightly. Harry put the papers back on his desk along with his glasses.

"Housekeeper found the body when she came to work on Monday morning around eight o'clock. She had a key. The alarm was off, which surprised her because Cullan was never home when she got there and he always left the alarm on. She had the code. Said he ate breakfast in Westport every morning with a bunch of his cronies."

"Where did she find him?"

"On the floor in his study with a .38-caliber bullet hole in his right eye. Your client was a good shot."

"Or the killer was just lucky," Mason said, not taking the bait. "Did the coroner fix the time of death?"

"That part is a bit tricky. The killer turned the heat off and opened the windows in the study. You could have hung meat in there. The cold temperature makes it tough to determine the time of death. Coroner says that it could have been any time from Friday night to Sunday night."

"That's a lot of ground to cover."

"Maybe. But we detectives like clues, and we found some good ones."

"Don't make me beg, Harry."

"Too soon for that. Begging comes during the sentencing phase. Cullan's bed was made, hadn't been slept in. The housekeeper says she made the bed on Friday. The Saturday, Sunday, and Monday newspapers were on the driveway, and the Saturday mail was in the box. Best bet, Cullan was popped on Friday night. Your client wasn't as smart as he thought."

"Any signs of forced entry?" Mason asked, ignoring Harry's jab. "No."

"How did you get to Blues?"

"We traced Cullan's movements last Friday. His secretary, Shirley Parker, kept his schedule. Shirley says that he was in meetings all day and that she had made reservations for dinner for two at Mancuso's."

"I assume his secretary knew who he was having dinner with."

"You assume right. Cullan had dinner with Beth Harrell. She's the one who's head of the gaming commission. So we talked with Ms. Harrell. She said that she and Cullan went to dinner and then stopped at Blues on Broadway to listen to Pete Kirby's trio. She wasn't real busted up about Cullan."

"She used Kirby's name?"

"Yeah. So what?"

"You've got to be a hard-core local jazz fan to know Pete Kirby's trio. That's all. Did she tell you anything else?"

Harry grinned. "That's all she told us the first time we talked to her. Kirby and his guys gave us a blow-by-blow on the fight she and Cullan had at the club and how Bluestone broke it up. My favorite part was when Bluestone threatened Cullan."

Harry hadn't said anything about the scratches on Blues's hands. Mason didn't know whether Beth Harrell or the musicians hadn't noticed the scratches, or whether Harry was holding out on Mason, waiting for him to raise the subject.

"So you went back to Beth Harrell and jogged her memory?"

"Early morning is a good time to question people. She didn't have her makeup on yet, and the bruise Cullan had given her was just turning yellow. She said she didn't tell us about the fight because it was too embarrassing, but she did say that Bluestone scared her more than Cullan."

"Why was that?"

"Because Cullan was old and mean but she could handle him. When Bluestone threatened Cullan, she didn't think anyone could handle him."

"None of that places Blues at the scene."

"We're working on that. Try this for starters."

He tossed Mason the coroner's report, Mason's stomach sinking when he found the information he knew would be there. Blood and tissue had been found under Cullan's fingernails. According to Blues's police department personnel file, the blood type found under Cullan's fingernails matched Blues's blood type.

"DNA match will take a while, but we both know it's his blood," Harry said.

"C'mon, Harry. You talked to four witnesses who saw Blues grab Cullan from behind to stop him from beating up Beth Harrell. Cullan scratched the backs of Blues's hands. He's still got the marks. You've got to do better than that."

Harry didn't hesitate. "None of the witnesses saw Cullan

scratch your client's hands. They only saw him squeeze Cullan until his eyes started to bug out."

"That doesn't change a thing. They just didn't see the scratches. I'll bet none of them told you that they looked at Blues's hands afterward and didn't see any scratches. Because you didn't ask them that question. Did you? Your case sucks without something that puts Blues in Cullan's house Friday night. Tell me what you've got, Harry."

CHAPTER SEVEN

Harry listened as Mason turned up the volume, his blank expression giving no clue whether Mason's antagonism bothered him, whether he had the evidence Mason was demanding, or whether he'd even heard a word Mason had said. Harry waited until the silence pressed down as heavily as unspoken bad news.

"I've got enough that the prosecuting attorney was happy to sign the arrest warrant. He says he might ask for the death penalty. Your client's first court appearance is tomorrow morning at nine in associate circuit court."

"This isn't a death-penalty case. It's barely a murder-one case. Even if your take on Blues is right—and it's not—you've got him killing Cullan because Cullan pissed him off. That's murder two on a good day. Where are the aggravating circumstances that would make it a death-penalty case?"

"You'll have to get that from the prosecutor in discovery. His orders, not mine."

Mason knew better than to press. Harry never deviated from the chain of command.

"So who drew the short straw in the prosecutor's office?"

Leonard Campbell, the prosecuting attorney, limited his court appearances to accepting high-profile plea bargains and trying cases with dead-certain guilty verdicts. He was more of a politician and bureaucrat than he was a trial lawyer. Mason assumed that he would assign one of his senior deputies to Blues's case.

"Campbell says he's going to try the case. Nobody here believes that. He may sit at the counsel table so the TV cameras can get a good shot of him, but Patrick Ortiz will be lead."

Mason had been up against Ortiz enough times to appreciate his plodding, understated style, which could lull a defense attorney into careless mistakes. Juries responded to him, seeing him as one of them. He was a regular guy who just talked to the jury, making the complex simple, explaining why the alibi was just a lie. He had the highest conviction rate of anyone in the prosecutor's office and was always the lead prosecutor in death-penalty cases.

"I've got some other things to go over with Blues. Let me know when I can get a set of the investigative reports, or are you going to make me wait for discovery?"

"I told Campbell you'd want that. You can get them tomorrow morning. In the meantime, I'd like to get a swab from your client's mouth so we can run the DNA test."

"Let's see how things go in the morning, Harry."

"You can agree or we can get a warrant. Either way, it doesn't matter to me. We won't have any trouble finding your client. Just tell him that when the judge imposes a sentence, he'll ask us if Bluestone cooperated or made life difficult."

Mason was tired of Harry's pinpricks. "I know you've had a hard-on for Blues since the two of you were partners. Don't use this case to get even. Blues's life is on the line, and you're too good of a cop to make it personal."

Harry fired back. "Is that what you think? That this is personal? Well, let me tell you something, Lou. It's damn personal! Your client killed an unarmed, innocent woman and walked away. He killed Jack Cullan last Friday, and if he thinks he's walking away this time, he's wrong. Murder is about as personal as it gets, and I take it real personal that I didn't nail the son of a bitch the first time."

Harry's rant attracted the stares of the other detectives jammed onto the floor. Mason looked around the room. They all knew about Blues and Harry. Though cops never liked it when one of their own was busted, Blues was no longer a brother behind the shield.

"You won't nail him this time either, Harry. I won't let you."

CHAPTER EIGHT

"You don't look like a lawyer who just convinced the cops to let his client go home," Blues said when Mason returned to the interrogation room.

"The case Harry told me he has against you doesn't worry me. It's the one he wouldn't tell me about that should worry both of us."

Mason had always been impressed at Blues's ability to occupy a room. Though tall and muscular, he wasn't always the biggest man, but when he was backed up, he grew a foot higher and wider with the menace he promised.

"You got something to say, Lou—just say it."

Mason let out a long breath. "Okay. Blood and tissue were found under Cullan's fingernails. They checked the blood type against the blood type in your police department personnel file and got a match. They want a swab for DNA testing."

"So what. He scratched me. Who else's blood could it be?"

"None of the witnesses in the bar saw Cullan scratch your hands, but they will testify that you threatened Cullan."

"So I'll testify."

"You know what they call a defendant who testifies? Convict. I told Harry that his case still sucked unless he could put you at the scene."

Blues stared at Mason, hands on his hips. "You told him his case sucked? That's strong. I'll bet he gave up right then."

"Almost. I asked him what else he had, and he said it was enough for the prosecuting attorney to consider asking for the death penalty. He said you got away with murder once before and that he's not going to let you get away with it again."

Blues turned away. Mason expected the news to knock him back. Instead, Blues gathered himself, straining as if he would break out of the interrogation room by sheer will.

"What do you think?"

"I think a lot of clients hold back information from their lawyers. They want to look their best, their most innocent, especially when they're not. Shit, half of them probably undressed in the dark on their wedding nights so they wouldn't disappoint their spouse." Mason paused. "I think Harry's case sucks unless he can place you at the scene. I need to know if he can."

Blues paced once around the small room, stopping with his back to the two-way mirror, and folded his arms against his chest.

"I wasn't there and I didn't kill Jack Cullan."

"I'll be sure to mention that to the judge. You'll be arraigned tomorrow morning in front of an associate circuit court judge, who will set bail. I'm guessing bail will be no less than a quarter million and maybe as much as half a million."

"The judge won't grant me bail."

"Hey, give me some credit. You've got substantial ties to the community. You're not a threat to anyone else. Carlos Guiterriz will bond you out. The bar will be more than enough collateral. You'll be out by lunchtime."

"You don't get it, Lou. Charging me with murder one and threatening me with the death penalty is a power play to make me take a deal. Somebody wants me to go down for this, and keeping me in the county jail until trial will be the next card that gets played. Make an ex-cop spend the winter in the general prison population, and see how long it takes him to find religion. If I don't roll over, they hope I'll get shanked before the trial. The last thing I'll hear is, 'Enjoy your stay at the Graybar Inn.'"

"Harry wouldn't do that."

"Oh, Harry would do it, except it's not up to Harry. He's just carrying water for the chief, or the prosecuting attorney, or whoever doesn't want my case to go to trial."

"This isn't the Conspiracy Hour. Cullan was connected to everybody in town, but he would have had to own everybody—the police, the courts, and the mayor—everybody for you to be right. Plus he's dead. All the IOUs he held have been canceled."

"How are you going to prove I'm innocent?"

"Find out who killed Cullan."

"You'll have to peel the layers off of his life, read every one of those IOUs."

Mason nodded, grabbing the thread that held Blues's fears together. "Cullan was probably killed by someone who wanted to cancel an IOU and who won't mind if you take the fall. If Cullan owned half the people the *Star* claims he did, there will be plenty of pressure to keep your case from coming to trial. Otherwise, I'll hang every dirty piece of laundry I can find in front of the jury to convince them that someone else did it."

"That's why I won't get bail. Remember something else while you're out there stirring up this shit pot."

"What's that?"

"The killer won't mind killing again to make sure I go down."

CHAPTER NINE

Associate circuit court judge Joe Pistone's courtroom was on the eighth floor of the Jackson County Courthouse, a neoclassical monument to the durability of public works projects built during the Depression. It was on the east side of downtown, across the street from city hall, another monument cast from the same mold. Police headquarters, an uninspired squared fortress, was one block east on Locust. The three buildings, all hewn from Missouri limestone, formed Kansas City's triangle of legislative, judicial, and executive order. The courthouse was eight stories and police headquarters was six. City hall loomed over both of them at thirty stories. The branches of government may have been equal on paper, but the daily grind of governing required considerably more people and space than public safety or justice.

Mason passed through the metal detector in the courthouse rotunda, hurrying up to wait for the elevators. The job of operating the courthouse elevators had been one of the last county patronage jobs to succumb to modern technology. Since the courthouse opened in the 1930s, loyalists at the bottom of the political food chain had been rewarded with the stupefying opportunity to sit for hours at a time on a small stool and bounce the elevators from floor to floor. Over the years, they had perfected a herky-jerky stop-and-go technique that left most passengers gasping when the doors opened at their floor. When the ancient elevators and their equally ancient operators were replaced, the county installed new elevators that ran smoothly, but slowly enough to drive even the most exercise averse to use the stairs.

Associate circuit court was the home of rough justice. Rules of evidence and procedure were loosely applied to hasten the endless passage of collection, landlord-tenant, and traffic cases through the system. The judges carried the same honorific title as their circuit court brethren, though many lawyers treated them behind their backs like minor leaguers. The one exception was the criminal defense attorney whose client stood before the judge seeking bail in an amount the defendant could make. At those moments, the lawyers meant it when they called the judge "Your Honor."

Reporters had gathered outside the courtroom, creating a media gauntlet. Mason ignored the questions they tossed in his path, smiling politely without answering until Rachel Firestone stepped in front of him. He recalled her tenacious pursuit of him in the aftermath of the bloody demise of his last law firm, Sullivan & Christenson.

"Listen," she had told him. "This story is going to be written whether you like it or not. You are the story. Talk to me."

"Not interested," Mason had told her. "Too many people are dead. Let them be."

Rachel wrote the story, quoting his refusal. She sent him a copy with a note saying she hoped he liked it and asking him to call her. Mason threw the note and the article away.

She had short-cropped dark red hair, alabaster skin, and dancing emerald eyes. Her trim, athletic build matched the nervous energy she radiated like a solar flare.

"Welcome back to the meat grinder," Rachel said. "Care to talk?"

"No."

"Wrong answer. I'll give you another chance later," she said before pushing her way into the courtroom and a seat directly behind the prosecutor's table.

Joe Pistone's legal career had been spent in associate circuit court, the first twenty-five years as a lawyer and the last fifteen as a judge. He had white hair, a thin face, and shoulders that were hunched like those of a man who'd spent his life ducking trouble.

He rarely looked at the lawyers or the litigants, keeping his head down and the cases moving.

Judge Pistone's courtroom was small enough to be crowded if more than a handful of people were present for a case. When there was a docket call for first appearances in criminal cases, the courtroom shrank as the jury box was filled with defendants dressed in orange jailhouse jumpsuits, their hands and feet shackled.

There were two counsel tables, one for the prosecution and one for the defense. The pews behind the rail that separated the lawyers and judge from the public were filled with family members of defendants and victims who divided themselves like the bride's side and the groom's side.

Inexperienced lawyers who didn't arrive in time to sit up front wedged themselves into any empty space they could find, while the veterans hung around the judge's bench as if they were at a local bar. Toss in the media pack and the courtroom was standing room only when Patrick Ortiz made his way to the prosecution's table, trailed by two assistants.

"Morning, Patrick," Mason said, extending his hand.

"Lou, good to see you," Ortiz answered, shaking Mason's hand without conviction.

Mason was six feet tall, with a hard, flat body kept in shape on the rugby field and a rowing machine he kept in his dining room. Ortiz was a head shorter and had the irregular rounded shape of someone whose diet was limited to foods that end in the letter *O*. Mason sat on the edge of the prosecutor's table, a friendly adversary chatting up the opposition.

"I'm here on Wilson Bluestone."

"So I've been told. These are for you," he said, handing Mason a copy of the police reports. "You'll get the rest in discovery."

"I'll keep that in mind," Mason answered as he skimmed through the pages.

"Sign this," Ortiz said, and slid a single sheet of paper toward Mason.

Mason picked it up. It was a consent form authorizing the state of Missouri to obtain a DNA sample from Wilson Bluestone, Jr. Mason signed it and handed it back to Ortiz.

"You want to talk about a plea, come see me this afternoon," Ortiz told him.

"My client's only plea is innocent. I don't expect you to agree to release him without bail. How much are you looking for?"

"No bail. That's what I'm looking for."

Before Mason could respond, three deputy sheriffs led Blues into the jury box. After a night in jail, clad in Day-Glo orange with his hands and feet manacled, he looked like a flight risk and a danger to the public.

They made eye contact. Mason shook his head, telling Blues all he needed to know about the prosecutor's position on bail.

CHAPTER TEN

Judge Pistone made his entrance as the bailiff called the courtroom to order.

"Good morning, Counsel," the judge began. "We'll take the video arraignments first."

A projector mounted on the wall directly above the table for defense counsel beamed a six-foot-by-ten-foot image on the opposite wall. The picture was grainy and washed-out. The audio was a beat behind the image, and the transmission speed was somewhere between real time and slow motion. The proceedings had the look and feel of justice administered in the middle of a bad dream.

Each defendant appeared on-screen, an oversized head shot that magnified every tremor and twitch. The last defendant was a young boy Mason guessed was barely twenty. He tried to retreat from the camera, his lips quivering as he tugged at his chin. The judge read the charge and the maximum sentence for the offense.

"You are charged with forcible rape, a Class A felony for which the maximum penalty is life in prison."

The boy whipped his head up at the camera, his mouth gaping at the judge's words.

"Do you have an attorney?" The boy shook his head. "Very well. The public defender will come see you."

The picture disappeared. Mason had the feeling the boy was as lost as the image that had been on the wall.

"The next case is State of Missouri v. Bluestone," Judge Pistone announced. "State your appearances, Counsel."

Patrick Ortiz stood and announced, "The people of the state of Missouri appear by Patrick Ortiz, deputy chief prosecuting attorney."

Mason followed. "The defendant appears in person and by his counsel, Lou Mason. We're ready to proceed, Your Honor."

"Very well, Counsel," the judge said without looking up. "The defendant will rise."

Blues stood from his seat in the jury box. Mason could hear the faint etching sounds of the courtroom artists.

Judge Pistone continued. "The defendant is charged with the crime of murder in the first degree in the death of Jack Cullan. Does the defendant understand the charges or wish to have them read?"

"We'll waive the reading of the charges, Judge. We'd like to discuss bail," Mason said.

"What's the state's position, Mr. Ortiz?" the judge asked.

"The people oppose bail in this case. The defendant is a former police officer who was forced to resign because of a shooting death that violated departmental rules on the use of deadly force. He has an extensive history of violent conduct. Though we acknowledge his ties to the community, he's both a flight risk and a danger to the public."

"Mr. Mason?"

"Your Honor, my client is entitled to bail. He owns a business that will be shut down if he's not there to run it. Everything he owns is tied up in that business and he's not about to run out on that. Mr. Ortiz is correct that the defendant is a former police officer. He's wrong about the defendant's history. He's never been charged with or convicted of any crime. The state's evidence in this case is as thin as yesterday's soup. While the victim was a high-profile member of the community, the court should reject any pressure to deny my client bail."

As soon as the judge looked up for the first time that morning, Mason knew he'd hit the wrong nerve.

"Mr. Mason, if you have any basis for suggesting that someone is attempting to improperly influence this court or that I would be susceptible to such attempts, now is the time to share that with me."

The color rose in Mason's neck. He refused to look at Ortiz, who, he was certain, was smiling wide enough to suck down a bag of Doritos. He couldn't look at Blues.

"I didn't mean any reflection on the court, Your Honor. All I meant was that the state is pushing a lot harder on my client than they would in any other case with this kind of evidence. Whatever the reason for that, it's not sufficient to deny bail."

"You can take that up with the circuit judge who gets assigned to this case. Bail denied. We're adjourned."

Mason was beginning to believe that Blues was right. Even though he had roused Joe Pistone's slumbering judicial dignity, the decision on bail had already been made. Mason's gaffe had given the judge all the cover he needed.

He weaved through the media throng, making his way into the hallway that connected to the judge's chambers. It was the route by which Blues would be taken back to the county jail. He caught up to the sheriff's deputies and Blues just as they were getting onto the elevator.

"Mind if I get a word with my client?" Mason asked one of the deputies.

"Make it fast. This ain't a parade," the deputy said.

Mason pulled Blues by the arm as far from the deputies as he could without getting them too excited.

"Listen, I'm sorry about what happened in there, but I don't think it would have made any difference."

"It's cool, man," Blues said. "Like I told you, they're going to try to squeeze me."

"We'll get another chance in front of the circuit court judge. Ortiz can either ask for a preliminary hearing or take the case to the grand jury. I'm betting on the grand jury. That way he doesn't have to tip his hand. The grand jury meets every other Friday. The next session is a week from tomorrow. Once you're indicted, we can ask the circuit court judge to set bail."

"I've got a better idea. Don't ask for bail. If we don't fight for it, they can't hold it over me. Spend your time finding out who killed Cullan, not writing motions the judge is going to turn down anyway."

Mason studied Blues for a moment. "You won't have any friends inside."

Blues gave Mason a broad grin. "You'd be surprised how easy I make friends. There's just two things you need to worry about besides winning my case."

"What?"

"First thing is you got to find somebody to run the club. Try Mickey Shanahan. He's the PR guy whose office is next to yours. He's always behind on his rent. Tell him he can work it off behind the bar."

"Okay. What's the second thing?"

"You're on your own. Don't get dead. They'll throw away the key to my cell."

CHAPTER ELEVEN

Mason found Patrick Ortiz talking to the assistant prosecutors. They stopped talking when Mason approached, the younger lawyers looking away to hide their smirks.

"You were way out of line with that shit about Blues being forced to resign from the police department," Mason said. "You know that there's no way in hell that comes into evidence. Except now it will be the lead on every newscast and plastered on the front page. You must want me to file a motion to move the trial out of town so my client can get a fair trial."

"I'm not going to tell you how to try your case. Bluestone already shot one person to death. That may not be admissible to prove he killed Jack Cullan, but it's sure as hell relevant to the sentence he's going to get and whether he should get bail."

"Forget about the bail. You're lucky that Blues is more patient than I am. He'll take the county up on its offer of hospitality until the trial."

Ortiz's assistants lost their smirks, but Ortiz maintained his poker face. "As long as he's prepared to sit for a while, maybe he'd like to talk about a plea."

"Is that how you pump up your conviction record? Squeeze the hard cases until they plead and take the chumps to trial? The only plea my client is going to make is innocent. Be sure to tell that to whoever is yanking your chain on this one."

CHAPTER TWELVE

Mickey Shanahan's office was smaller than Mason's and didn't have any windows. It did have a lot of posters. Mostly from political campaigns. Mickey didn't have a desk. Instead, he had a card table and four chairs.

When Mason knocked on the open door, Mickey was straddling one of the chairs, his back to the door, wadding up pages from the morning paper and tossing them at a basketball goal, making the swish sound regardless of whether he made the shot.

Mickey had been a tenant for six months. Mason liked his scrappy attitude but couldn't figure out how he made a living. Blues told him that Mickey had graduated from college a couple of years earlier, worked for a big PR firm in town, and then decided to go it alone. That was when he signed a lease with Blues. Mason had yet to see a client walk into or out of Mickey's office and wasn't surprised that Mickey was behind on his rent.

"Hey, Mickey. What's going on, man?"

Mickey glanced over his shoulder, beamed when he saw Mason, and scrambled to his feet.

"You're asking me?" Mickey picked up the front page of the newspaper with the two-inch headline announcing *Ex-Cop Arrested for Murder of Political Boss*. "I should be asking you. No, I shouldn't. I should be telling you to hire me to handle the PR on this case. I'm telling you, this case, win or lose—and don't get me wrong, I'm pulling for you and Blues—this case can make you in this town; Blues too, if you win. It's all about how you spin it."

Mickey had an unruly shock of brown hair that fell across

his pale Irish forehead. He could pour nutrition shakes down his throat with a funnel and still be invisible when he turned sideways. He was a finger-tapping, pencil-twirling, punch-line machine, all revved up with no place to go.

"I'll keep that in mind. In the meantime, Blues wants you to run the club for a while. The judge wouldn't let him out on bail. He says you can work off the back rent you owe him."

"Outstanding!" He crossed the short distance to the door and gave Mason a fist bump. "Outstanding!"

"I'll tell Blues you said so," Mason told him. "Do you know what to do?"

"Haven't a fucking clue, man. But no one will know the difference. That's why they call it PR!"

He raced down the stairs, and Mason retreated to his office, stepping over and around the files, clothes, and junk scattered on the floor and furniture, remembering his aunt Claire's theory of the relationship between men's stuff and available space.

"No matter how much crap a man has," she told him when she visited his office, "he will fill every available inch of open space. Put him in a smaller office with just as much stuff, and the stuff shrinks to fit. Add a hundred square feet and his stuff will spread over it like a rising tide."

Bookshelves lined the wall on either side of the door. Client files were crammed into the shelves on one side and books filled the other. More files, a rugby football, and a pair of sweats competed for room on an overstuffed corduroy-covered sofa on which he'd spent more than a few nights.

A low table and two chairs in front of the sofa formed a seating area. Mason dropped his topcoat on one chair and his suit coat on the other.

A four-foot-by-six-foot dry-erase board enclosed by burnished oak doors was mounted on the wall opposite the sofa. The inside panels of the doors were covered in cork. A rolled screen was mounted above the dry-erase surface. Mason was a visual thinker. He kept track of ideas, questions, and answers by writing them in different colors on the dry-erase board. He pinned notes he wrote to himself onto the cork surface. He studied his board until order emerged from the chaos, and when a problem was solved, he erased it.

His desk sat in front of the exterior wall in a three-sided windowed alcove, flanked on one side by a computer workstation housing a combination printer, fax, scanner, and copier and on the other by a small refrigerator that was usually empty except for a six-pack of Bud. Mason didn't have enough room or business to support a secretary. He gave thanks every day to his eighth-grade typing teacher, who had threatened to hold him back if he didn't learn to touch-type.

A faded Persian rug covered the center of the hardwood floor, a gift from Claire, who said the place needed a little class.

Mason opened the doors to the dry-erase board, picked up a red marker, and began writing. Next to Jack Cullan's name he wrote *victim/fixer* and the questions *Who's afraid of Jack?* and *Who wins if Jack dies?*

Switching to black, he wrote *Blues—at the scene?—connection to Cullan?*

Still using the black marker, he wrote on the next line: *Harry—why so certain about Blues? Who's pushing Harry?*

He wrote Beth Harrell's name in blue, adding—*why with Cullan?*

His last entry was in red—*who else?*

CHAPTER THIRTEEN

Rachel Firestone knocked on Mason's door and opened it without waiting for an invitation. He was at his desk, reading the police reports. He looked up, instinctively turning them over.

She looked first at Mason and then at the board before she even said hello. Mason couldn't prevent her from reading everything he'd written, so he pretended not to care rather than give her the satisfaction of thinking she'd seen something she shouldn't have.

"I don't suppose there's any point in asking you if you had an appointment."

"I don't suppose there was any reason to ask for one since you'd just tell me no."

"Can't argue with that. How about I just tell you no anyway and you leave?"

"Give it up, Lou. I'm on this story and you're on this case. We can't avoid each other. It won't be that bad. You'll get used to me. You'll probably even get a crush on me, make a stupid pass, and I'll break your heart and make your testicles shrivel like raisins."

Mason took a good look at her as she posed for him, hands on her hips, her chin punched out at him in a devilish, take-your-best-shot angle. She was luminescent, inviting, and somehow unattainable. Mason felt a surge that had been dormant since he'd broken up with Kelly Holt, the woman who had investigated the murders of his former partners. It was the jolting combination of need, desire, and unexpected opportunity. He'd dated a few women since Kelly, but the only connection he made with them was glandular.

"And why would you do that? The testicles part, I mean."

"Can't be helped, Lou. I'm gay. I'm a boots, jeans, flannel-shirt-wearing, short-haired lipstick lesbian, and I'm a knockout in a simple black dress I keep in my closet for special occasions. If women got me the way guys do, I'd be fighting them off."

"That would do it," he conceded as his rising sap retreated to its roots. "Thanks for sparing me."

"Not a problem. I like getting that out of the way up front. Fewer complications," she added as she picked up the football and made a place for herself on the sofa. She tossed the ball back and forth between her hands, frowning at its odd feel.

"It's for rugby."

"That's a hard-hitting game. You play?"

"Not as much as I used to. I'm getting a little old to dive into the middle of a bunch of maniacs going after the ball. I'll take you to a game in the spring," he offered without understanding why.

"Great. I'd like that," she said with a smile that filled him with regret. "So Beth Harrell was with Jack Cullan the night he was killed," Rachel said, pointing to Mason's board.

"You heard that too?"

"Yup. I tried to talk with her, but she keeps her door locked. Any idea why they were out together?"

Mason hesitated. He felt as if he were walking on an active fault line with Rachel that could cleave open and swallow him at any moment. She was beautiful, flirtatious, and completely unavailable. She knew she had him off balance and was enjoying his disadvantage.

"I think we need some ground rules."

"So do I. Here's freedom-of-the-press rule number one. Everything's on the record unless you tell me in advance that it isn't on the record."

Mason shook his head. "Here's defense-lawyer rule number one. Nothing is on the record unless I say so. Rule number two—burn me and I'll cut you off at the knees."

Rachel folded her arms over her chest. "You're just angry about the lesbian thing. Hey, it wasn't my idea. A girl doesn't get to choose. Not that I'm complaining."

Mason got up and started to close the doors to the dry-erase board.

"Okay, okay," she told him. "Nothing is on the record unless you say so."

"Good. I don't know why they were at the bar, but I think she'll tell me."

"Why?"

"First, because I'm not going to print it on the front page of the newspaper in a story accusing her of being a crook. Second, I can put her under oath and make her tell me, and third, we know each other."

"How?"

"I took ethics from her when she taught at the law school. I was a first-year student and it was her first semester teaching. We hit it off pretty well, but I've only run into her a few times since I graduated. Alumni functions and that kind of thing."

Rachel nodded. "Is your client guilty?"

"No."

"How do you know?"

"He told me so."

"That's not good enough for an acquittal."

"It's good enough for me. All I have to do is figure out who did kill Jack Cullan. The cops are done looking. Any suggestions?"

"I've been chasing Jack Cullan for three years. He was into everything important that happened or didn't happen in this town. Want to get elected? Go see Jack. Want to cut a deal with the city? Need tax increment financing? How about the concessions at the airport? Go see Jack. He always delivered the goods."

"How did he do it? Where did he get that kind of influence?"

"Cullan invested in the long term. Long-term relationships and long-term IOUs. One day, the city wakes up and peeks out from under its covers. Only the view is from Jack Cullan's back pocket. I've been picking up threads. I can't get anyone to corroborate it, but I'm convinced that Cullan took a page from J. Edgar Hoover's playbook."

"Files filled with secrets?"

"On everyone who is anyone."

"You said you couldn't corroborate that. What makes you think it's true?"

"The same thing that makes you think your client is innocent. I can feel it."

She picked up the red marker and wrote *Cullan's Secret Files* on the board.

"Anyone who was in those files may have had a motive to kill Cullan," Mason said. "And the rest of them would give anything to make certain the files stayed secret. The easiest way for that to happen is to make certain Blues is found guilty."

"I'll make you a deal. You find the files first, I get the exclusive. I find the files first, I'll let you see them before I go public."

"Deal. Why so generous?"

"Let's just say that I'm a sucker for good-looking rugby players. In fact, I'm dating one now. She's fabulous. I'll be in touch," she said as she left.

CHAPTER FOURTEEN

Mason finished studying the police reports without finding any daggers to throw at Harry on cross-examination. He had been as thorough as Mason had expected.

The crime scene had been preserved, none of the evidence contaminated. Photographs were taken from every angle, fingerprints lifted from every surface, and a meticulous search had been made for footprints and fibers that didn't belong.

The contents of the house had been inventoried and double-checked against Cullan's homeowner's insurance records. No valuables were missing and there was no sign of forced entry. Cullan had opened the door to someone who had come there for one reason—to kill him.

The maid passed a polygraph exam and thirty people at a family reunion in Omaha confirmed her alibi that she was out of town when Cullan was killed.

Beth Harrell and the musicians at the bar gave statements that established Blues's motive. And Blues didn't have an alibi.

The case had shifted from catching Cullan's killer to proving that Blues was guilty. If none of the witnesses saw Cullan scratch Blues's hands during their scuffle at the bar, he would have to take the stand in his own defense. No matter how certain he was of Blues's innocence, Mason knew that was a high-stakes gamble. Patrick Ortiz would come in his pants at the prospect of taking on Blues.

There was nothing Mason could do about any of the evidence the prosecutor already had against Blues. He wouldn't make the mistake of trying to win the case on the prosecution's ground. Instead, he'd have to find the killer.

He stared out the windows, listening to the icy wind swarm over the city, slip-sliding through weak spots in brick and mortar, seeping into cracks and faults, sucking out the warmth. He imagined that Jack Cullan had been that way, wrapping his own cold fingers around the weak spots in other people's hearts until they became brittle and broke in his hands.

The warmth in his office was small comfort. He'd be out in the wind soon enough, playing catch-up with Oritz. The prosecutor was way out in front.

Mason wouldn't get any help from the people who'd been under Cullan's thumb. Though each would light a candle for the killer and ask God to reserve a special place in hell for Cullan, they'd let the wind sweep Blues away.

Mason picked up the black marker. Beneath his question *who else?* and Rachel Firestone's note about Cullan's secret files, he added the names of Ed Fiora, Billy Sunshine, and Beth Harrell. All three were tied to Jack Cullan. It was all he had.

Mason began with what he knew about each of them. Ed Fiora owned the Dream Casino. Though he'd passed the gaming commission's background checks, Rachel's newspaper stories had him only a sham corporation or two removed from his leg-breaking days.

Billy Sunshine was a charismatic mayor who'd steal your vote and your wife with equal aplomb. He was glib and charming, a native son with the ethos of a carpetbagger. More than anything else, he was ambitious. He'd been elected by a wide margin to a second term and, by law, couldn't run again. The mayor had all but announced he would challenge Delray Shays, the black incumbent congressman, in the next election. Local wags had it that the casino scandal was the only thing holding up the formal announcement. When last asked about it, the mayor said he'd let the people of the Fifth Congressional District decide.

Beth Harrell was the piece of the puzzle that didn't fit. Ed Fiora was a thug posing as a gaming entrepreneur. Billy Sunshine was the poster boy for mamas not letting their babies grow up to be politicians. Beth Harrell was the good queen.

Mason remembered her from law school. She was only five years older, having practiced for two years after graduating before becoming a professor. She had dark blond hair that dangled above her shoulders, softening her bold walk. Her body was trim, her lips full, and her eyes said, "Authorized personnel only." She carried her beauty with the experience of someone used to taking advantage of it and wary of those who would.

All of which made the class she taught the most popular one offered. Mason resisted the temptation to sit in the front row with his tongue hanging out like his less subtle friends. He worked hard in her class, and she rewarded his effort with a good grade and a friendly handshake whenever they ran into each other over the years.

Beth's reputation as an expert in ethics had brought her to the attention of the governor. When the previous chair of the gaming commission was convicted of accepting kickbacks, the governor turned to Beth to restore credibility to the commission. The license for the Dream Casino was the first major piece of business for the commission after she took over. Mason found it hard to believe that she had stepped over the line.

Mason had learned from Harry that it was much more effective to question a witness when he showed up unexpectedly. Rachel Firestone had proven the point earlier in the day.

He doubted that the ambush interview would work with the three people on his list. He'd have to cut through a layer of muscle to get next to Ed Fiora, and a regiment of bureaucrats guarded the mayor. He doubted that Beth Harrell had a gatekeeper, but he knew better than to just drop by. Even in law school, she demanded that students make an appointment to see her outside of class.

He called Fiora's office and was told that Mr. Fiora would be unavailable until the next millennium. The mayor's scheduling secretary said that he didn't have an opening until after his term expired. He left a message for Beth Harrell. She just didn't call him back.

CHAPTER FIFTEEN

Mason checked on Mickey Shanahan before leaving for the night. It was past eight and Mickey was behind the bar, giving directions to Pete Kirby's trio as they set up. Pete looked at Mickey like he was a blind man directing traffic. Mason decided to take a crack at Kirby's memory.

"Hey, Pete, how you doing, man?" Mason said.

Pete Kirby was short and squat, like a fireplug. He played the piano with the enthusiasm of a man whose natural rhythm was eight to the bar.

"Everything's cool, Louie, my boy. How's my man Blues?"

Kirby was the only person who called Mason Louie, a list Mason wasn't anxious to expand.

"He's doing fine, Pete. I understand you were playing Friday night when Jack Cullan came in."

"That's right, I was. Me and the boys wouldn't have stuck around since it was such a shitty night and the joint was empty, but we figured, what the hell, we'll play a set for Blues. Then Cullan comes in with this good-looking broad and the next thing I know, the two of them are playing Frankie and Johnnie."

"Blues tells me he busted up the fight."

"That he did. Blues grabbed that old man like he was gonna pile-drive the cat right into the goddamn ground. Don't pay to tussle in Blues's joint," Pete added with a deep laugh. "No, sir, it don't."

"I hear Cullan fought like a cat too. Scratched the hell out of Blues's hands."

Kirby tugged at the corner of his beret and stroked his goatee, measuring his response in a firm meter.

"Like I told the detective, I didn't see any of that. Now, you lookin' like your woman just run off with the drummer makes me wish maybe I had, but I just didn't see none of that. Sorry, Louie."

"Don't worry about it, Pete. It's not important," Mason said and left.

The parking lot behind the bar was covered in old asphalt that had given birth to potholes big enough to swallow women and children. Blues was an easygoing landlord who believed in deferred maintenance. Mason stepped around the craters, afraid that if he fell into one, no one would find him until spring.

His car was parked at the back of the lot; the front end aimed at the alley behind the bar. Though there was a curb between the lot and the street, Mason planned to ignore it. Otherwise, what was the point of driving a Jeep?

The wind had calmed from its all-day shriek to a steady howl strong enough to rake tears from the corners of Mason's eyes. Fine crystals of sleet tattooed his face like asteroid dust. Blues's deferred-maintenance program extended to the parking lot floodlights, which had been burned out since Thanksgiving. The lights were off in the building across the alley, and the sky had been buttoned down with blackout clouds. Moonlight couldn't have found its way to Mason's dark patch even if it had a GPS.

A pair of high-beam headlights opened up on him as he reached his Jeep, the lights coming from a car parked near his, the sound of its engine muffled by the wind. Heavy boots ground sand and salt into the pavement as a man bigger than Mason's Jeep stepped from the shadows.

"Car trouble?" Mason asked, still unable to make out the man's features.

When he didn't get an answer, Mason's internal wind chill hit bottom. His new best friend stepped in front of the headlights, casting a nightmare's silhouette. He was wearing a full-length topcoat and a fedora jammed low on his brow, which covered his face but not the frozen gray breath leaking from his mouth like poison gas.

Mason reached for his car door, hoping to put some steel between him and the man, but he was too slow. In the next instant, the man grabbed Mason and spun him around, pinning his face flush to the side of the Jeep, the frozen surface burning Mason's jaw.

Mason stiffened, trying to leverage his hands against the Jeep and drive his hips and back against the man, but the side of the Jeep was too slick and the man was too huge. He leaned in hard and close to Mason's face. The wet wool of his topcoat smelled like a dog left too long in the rain, and his breath tasted of coffee, cigarettes, and licorice.

"You get one chance, you understand that?" the man said.

"Right. Sure. One chance. That's easy enough."

"Your client's gonna get an offer. Make sure he takes it."

"What kind of offer?"

The man jammed his knee into the small of Mason's back, sending a paralyzing jolt through Mason's kidneys.

"The only offer that will keep him and you alive. Got that, smart boy?"

"Got it," Mason managed through clenched teeth.

The man released his grip and Mason crumpled to the pavement gasping for air. When he looked up, the man and the car were gone.

CHAPTER SIXTEEN

Mason crawled out of bed Friday morning feeling as if he'd slept in the middle of a rugby scrum. The blow he'd taken to his back had scrambled his internal organs and hardened his soft tissue. He was relieved that there was no blood in his urine. His kidneys had been shaken but not stirred.

Ed Fiora was the only person Mason knew who had been involved with Jack Cullan and had a charge account at Thugs R Us. When Mason called the Dream Casino the day before and asked for Fiora, his call was transferred to an enthusiastic telemarketer named Dawn.

"This is Dawn. May I make your dream come true today?"

Mason had told her, "Absolutely, Dawn. Just connect me to Ed Fiora."

"We have a fabulous special offer today. I can sign you up for the Dream Casino's free Super Slot Ultra-Gold New Millennium Frequent Player Bonus Point card. It's personal and confidential."

"So is my business with Mr. Fiora."

"Just swipe your card through the card reader on any of the Dream's fabulous slot machines, and each time you pull the handle, you'll receive, absolutely free, ten bonus points. You can redeem your bonus points for fabulous prizes, beginning with two nights at the Dream's Riverboat Casino Resort in Lake Winston, Mississippi, for only twenty-five thousand points. Isn't that fabulous?"

"No, Dawn, it isn't. Fabulous would be not spending two minutes in Lake Winston, Mississippi. Fabulous would be you putting down your script, listening to me, and connecting me to

Mr. Fiora. That would be really fabulous."

Dawn sputtered into the phone, caught somewhere between tears and ticked off. "One moment, please."

The next voice Mason heard was all New Jersey bent nose. "Sir, do we have a problem here?"

"Who's this? One of Frank Nitti's boys?"

"This is Carmine Nucci, guest relations. Who the fuck is this?"

"You're making that up, aren't you, Carmine? I mean your name's not really Carmine and the accent is phony. This is like part of the entertainment. Am I right?"

Mason was certain that none of it was made up. Not Dawn. Not the bonus points, and not the threat laced through Carmine's voice like battery acid.

"Hey, pal. You want to make jokes, call Comedy Central. You want an Ultra-Gold slot card, we'll give you one. You want to bust my girl's chops, I'll stick this phone up your ass you come around here."

"How many bonus points is that?" Mason asked, hanging up before Carmine could reply.

Mason called back, this time asking for the business office, identifying himself as a lawyer, and asking to speak with Mr. Fiora concerning a criminal matter. Three underlings later, none of whom sounded as if they'd ever left Nebraska, Mason spoke with a woman whose name was Margaret who said she was an assistant to Mr. Fiora.

"My name is Lou Mason. I'm an attorney. It's very important that I speak with Mr. Fiora about a criminal matter."

"May I tell Mr. Fiora what the nature of the matter is?"

Mason couldn't tolerate people who didn't take their own calls, who hired other people just to answer the phone calls transferred to them by other people who'd been hired for the same purpose, only to ask the caller the nature of the matter. He pictured Margaret sitting at her computer, scrolling down the list of criminal matters that would be worthy of Ed Fiora's attention.

"You may tell Mr. Fiora that the nature of the matter is the murder of his lawyer, Jack Cullan, and what he might know about it."

"I see," Margaret said with more disappointment in Mason than concern for her boss. "I see," she repeated as if the words had cured her astigmatism.

"So, if you'll just connect me to Mr. Fiora, I'm sure he'll want to talk with me."

"Oh, I'm so sorry, Mr. Mason, Mr. Fiora is not available."

"And when will he be available, Margaret?"

"I don't believe that he will ever be available, Mr. Mason. I'm so sorry."

"Margaret, you aren't even close to sorry. You aren't in the same zip code as sorry. Sorry would be that Mr. Fiora had a terrible accident on the way to the office, was rushed to the hospital for emergency surgery, but can work me in this afternoon. That would be sorry. This is just a mistake. A big mistake. You tell Mr. Fiora I said so."

"If you insist, Mr. Mason."

Mason replayed his conversations with Dawn, Carmine, and Margaret as he settled into his rowing machine and slowly began easing the kinks out of his back. He set the digital readout for ten thousand meters and gradually lost himself in the soothing repetitions of the stroke.

The seat slid backward with each leg drive and rode forward with each pull of his upper body. He imagined that he was sculling downriver, the ripple of his lean wake cutting the water as he slipped unnoticed through the morning's enveloping mist.

A quick look around reminded Mason that he was in the middle of his dining room and that his rowing machine occupied the space that had been home to a table that seated eight. Not long ago, the Kansas City auxiliary of the Chicago mob had reduced the table, the chairs, and the rest of his worldly possessions to a pile of broken legs, glass, and splinters. It was their way of saying he shouldn't have taken work home from his last law firm, Sullivan & Christenson.

Mason lived on the money his homeowner's insurance company paid for the loss of his personal possessions, using part of it to pay the expenses for his childhood friend Tommy Douchant's lawsuit. By the time Mason settled Tommy's case and could afford to refurnish the house, he didn't want to. Instead, he bought only the things he needed, which turned out to be the only things he wanted.

He finished his row. The mist, the lake, and the ache in his body were gone. "Plan your row and row your plan" was the rower's creed. He hadn't followed that simple rule when he tried to reach Ed Fiora. Instead, he'd smart-assed his way into a one-punch knockdown that underscored what to expect if he insisted on not getting the message.

After downing a bottle of Gatorade, he went outside for the morning paper. The wind had moved on to punish some other part of the country. A light cover of snow crunched under his feet. The subzero air was bracing. His dog, Tuffy, a German shepherd–collie mixed breed, joined him on the short walk to the end of his driveway. Her blond and black German shepherd colors were layered through her winter coat in a collie's pattern, complete with a pure white thatch under her chin.

Tuffy raced through the front yard, nose to the ground, sniffing for anything interesting. She found nothing and followed Mason back into the house, where the phone was ringing.

"Hello."

"It's Rachel Firestone. What did you think of my story?"

"What story?"

"Don't tell me you don't get the paper. The story is on the front page, above the fold."

"I just brought the paper in," he said. "Give me a minute."

Rachel's story recited Judge Pistone's refusal to grant bail to Blues and Mason's implied charge that unknown persons were applying pressure to get either a conviction or a plea bargain that would close the case of Jack Cullan's murder as soon as possible. It tied Ed Fiora, Mayor Sunshine, and Beth Harrell into a tight circle around Cullan's body and speculated aloud whether any of them would cooperate with Lou Mason in his defense of Wilson Bluestone, Jr., against a first-degree murder charge and possible death penalty. Fiora, the mayor, and Beth Harrell declined to comment.

"You left out one thing," he told her.

"What?"

"Off the record."

"Fine, fine. What?"

"I think Fiora commented privately," he said, telling her about his parking lot encounter.

"Holy shit! Did you call the cops?"

"What for? There were no witnesses. I couldn't ID the guy or the car. Besides, I wouldn't expect to get a sympathetic response. The cops are more likely to look for a cat stranded in a tree than for someone who kicked my ass. And I don't want to read about that in tomorrow's paper. I'll figure some other way to get to Fiora. I don't think he'll respond well to being accused in the paper of ordering someone to assault me."

"My editor would be even less interested in getting sued. Did you have any luck with the mayor or Beth Harrell?"

"Nope. I figure the mayor is the most likely to respond to bad press. I think Beth Harrell will see me because I was an irresistible student."

"Don't sit by the phone. You'll grow old. Listen, the mayor is speaking at the Salvation Army Christmas luncheon at the Hyatt today. I understand that the baked chicken is to die for."

"Any chance you'll be stalking the mayor along with me?"

"You can bet on it."

CHAPTER SEVENTEEN

Mason's first stop was the Jackson County Jail, a redbrick building on the east side of police headquarters. The exterior was perforated by longitudinal rows of rectangular windows big enough to satisfy court-mandated quality-of-incarceration living standards and small enough to make certain the inmates stayed there to enjoy them.

The receptionist was a civilian employee who wore olive slacks and a pale blue shirt with epaulets on the shoulders to give the ensemble an official appearance. Her bleached blond hair was pulled back tight enough to raise her chin to her lower lip, freezing her mouth in a scowl, though she might have just made an awful face as a child and it froze that way.

According to the tag on her blouse, her name was Margaret. He rejected the likelihood of a conspiracy by the World Federation of Margarets to make his life miserable but clenched his smart-ass impulse just in case.

"Good morning," he told Margaret. "I'm Lou Mason and I'm here to see my client, Wilson Bluestone."

He handed her his driver's license, his Missouri Bar Association membership card, and one of his business cards.

Margaret scanned Mason's card collection like a bouncer checking for fake IDs. "You didn't sign the back of your bar card. I can't accept it without a signature," she said, handing the bar card back to Mason.

Mason felt the first wave of intemperance ripple through his back and neck. He resisted the urge to vault the counter separating them and smiled instead.

"Of course. Sorry about that," he said as he signed his name and handed the card back to her.

Margaret held the bar card alongside Mason's driver's license, comparing the two signatures like a Treasury agent looking for counterfeit twenties.

"Bar card is expired. Can't take an expired bar card. You should have paid your dues."

She handed the bar card back to Mason. He gripped the counter with both hands to keep them from her throat and decided to appeal to her sense of reason.

"Margaret, consider what you're saying. The bar card only means that I'm a member of the Missouri bar. It's a form of identification. There's nothing in the law that requires me to belong to the bar association or even be a lawyer to visit an inmate. Now, it happens that I am a lawyer and I have a client who's locked in a cell upstairs who is entitled to the effective representation of his chosen counsel. If he's deprived of that representation because you won't let me see him, the judge will have to dismiss the charges. My client happens to have been charged with murder, which most people think is a pretty serious deal. So why don't you call the prosecuting attorney and tell him that his case is going to get dismissed because you, Margaret, are refusing to let me see my client because my bar card has expired?"

"Jeez. Are you a tight-ass or what? I'm just doing my job here. Pay your damn dues like everybody else."

"Trust me, Margaret. I've paid my dues. Now, open up."

Mason passed through a series of security checks that fell one pat down short of a body-cavity search and was ushered into a cramped room divided by a narrow countertop that served as a table. A reinforced double pane of glass cut the room completely in two. A circular metal screen was mounted in the glass, which allowed conversation to be heard on both sides.

Mason stood, pacing in the small room until Blues entered through a door on the inmates' side. They looked at each other for a full minute. Mason saw a defiant man, ramrod straight, ragged coal black hair hanging over his tawny brow, piercing eyes searching Mason for good news. Blues touched his closed fist to the glass, holding it there, Mason returning the gesture.

"They're going to offer you a deal."

"I won't take it."

"I know that."

"How do you know they're going to offer me a deal?"

Mason couldn't tell Blues what had happened in the parking lot. If Blues knew that taking a deal would protect Mason, he might agree. Mason assumed that whoever had sent him the message was counting on his relationship with Blues as one more source of pressure that would bring this case to a quick conclusion.

"Patrick Ortiz invited me to his office to talk about it. I turned down the invitation. Are you ready to ride this thing out?"

"All the way. I'm innocent and I'm not going to let somebody railroad me. Besides, no matter how many of them there are, you and me got them outnumbered."

Mason smiled at the vote of confidence. "This case is hot and it's going to get hotter. You watch yourself in there."

Blues chuckled. "Man, you forget one thing. All those brothers and white-trash crackers in there are afraid this crazy Indian will scalp 'em in their sleep. No one is going to fuck with me. Not more than once."

"Be cool, Blues. The case they've got against you isn't worth a shit. Don't give them one they can make."

"I hear that."

They touched their fists against the glass again, and Mason pushed a button signaling the guard that they had finished their meeting.

CHAPTER EIGHTEEN

When Mason got back to his office, he listened to a message from his aunt Claire telling him to meet her for lunch at the Summit Street Cafe at noon. It wasn't an invitation. It was an order. She wasn't much for protocol.

Mason assumed that she wanted to talk about Blues's case. If he was caught in the middle between Harry and Blues, she was caught between him and Harry. Though she wouldn't see it that way. She was one of the few people Mason knew who meant it when she said, "Let the chips fall where they may."

He had time until lunch so he searched the *Kansas City Star*'s Web site for Rachel Firestone's articles about Jack Cullan's murder, noting that there had been three other murders during the same span, none of them getting the same coverage and none of them generating any fanfare or outrage. Mason knew why.

Kansas City knows murder. Any town that began as a river trading post called Old Possum Trot knows killing. Any town that claims Jesse James as a wayward son and commemorates the Union Station Massacre knows how to let the lead fly. Any town that has convulsed with riots and raised a generation of hopeless hard cases who expect to die before they're twenty-five knows the sweet agony of death.

Put a million and a half people—white, black, brown, yellow, rich, poor, faithful, faithless, doped, dependent, and demanding— in the rolling river country of the heart of America and they'll find endless ways to kill. Put it in the papers and on the news with candlelight vigils for the funerals of infants. Watch as TV reporters stick microphones in mourners' faces asking how does it feel and the people will search themselves for shock while keeping a head count, a steady drumbeat of death, ahead or behind last year's pace.

But take the life of a mover and a shaker, of one to whom it's not supposed to happen, someone who holds all the cards, someone who gives more dispensations than the pope and holds more markers than the devil. Well, that's showbiz. The mayor grieves the victim and denounces the guilty. The chief of police reassures an anxious community with a quick arrest, and the prosecuting attorney promises justice swift and certain.

Rachel Firestone reported it all. Her prose was concise, her tone neutral, and her facts straight. Only the headlines above the stories announced an agenda. They painted the crime, the victim, the accused, and the supporting cast with a broad brush dipped in sensational ink to capture mind share and market share in a media-saturated world. *Kingpin Murdered*, screamed the headline in Tuesday's paper. Wednesday's lead promised *Police Close to Arrest*, and Thursday's paper trumpeted *Ex-Cop Arrested for Murder of Political Boss*.

None of the stories added to Mason's knowledge of the case. He ran a search for articles on the Dream Casino, printed them, and began reading.

Missouri had been a late entrant in the sweepstakes for gambling dollars. Bible Belt morality had kept the casino interests out of the state for decades, though Kansas City had been a wide-open town from the beginning of the twentieth century through Prohibition. Gambling had flourished in speakeasies all over town, particularly along the Twelfth Street strip from Broadway to city hall. Tom Pendergast had been the boss in those years, running his empire of influence and muscle under the guise of a concrete business.

A coalition of clergy, political reformers, and the IRS had brought Pendergast down, and Kansas City settled into a long period struggling with its lingering reputation as a cow town, unable to compete with the temptations offered on a grander scale by bigger cities.

The gaming people had seen opportunity on the Missouri and Mississippi Rivers. They sold the state legislature on a scam that would have shamed even Professor Harold Hill with its Music Man audacity.

They promised gambling on riverboats reminiscent of Mark Twain's paddleboats; two-hour cruises with five-hundred-dollar loss limits to ensure that no one would lose the rent money. To prove they were good citizens, they offered to fund programs for problem gamblers and suggested that their tax revenue be dedicated to education. The legislature doubled down and took the bet, offering the voters an amendment to the state's constitution legalizing riverboat gambling on the Missouri and Mississippi Rivers. The voters couldn't wait to cash in.

The first boat in the Kansas City area came to an unincorporated area north of the city. To the surprise of everyone but its owners, the Army Corps of Engineers ordered that the boat remain docked because of the hazards of navigating the Missouri River. With a sigh of regret heard all the way to their banks, the other casinos built their facilities on huge barges, digging moats around them that were fed by rivers to meet the legal requirement that the casinos be riverboats.

The legislative scheme was complex, having been drafted by lawyers with help from the casinos' lobbyists. Like any successful partnership between regulators and those they regulate, the law appeared tough but was actually more malleable than a politician's oath to do what's right.

The Missouri Gaming Commission was established to oversee and regulate all gaming activity. Each city retained the right to issue licenses to casino operators, subject only to the gaming commission's approval of the qualifications of the owners. Rules prohibiting ownership by convicted felons and other unsavory individuals were window dressing to distract attention from the real horse-trading that accompanied the grant of licenses.

The competition for Kansas City's license had been fierce. Four casino operators had expressed interest in obtaining a license from the city. Each put together their own team of local supporters and business partners that had as its singular purpose getting the mayor's blessing. Some had been subtler than others, giving ownership interests to black and Hispanic businessmen who carried a message of diversity and economic opportunity to the mayor. Others offered sizable campaign contributions to the mayor and city councilmen.

Mayor Sunshine announced the appointment of a blue ribbon commission to recommend which of the contenders should receive the sole license Kansas City intended to grant. It was the mayor's way of remaining above the fray and gave him plausible deniability of any effort to influence his decision.

Of equal importance to the selection of the casino operator had been the selection of the site for the casino. Kansas City's river frontage afforded several possible locations, each of them privately owned. The owners of those sites joined in the free-for-all, anguishing over whether to choose between aligning with a particular casino operator and waiting to see if their site was selected. The wrong move could cost them millions.

When all the coalitions and alliances were formed, when all the political contributions were deposited, and when all the promises that would be broken were made, the blue ribbon commission recommended to the mayor that he grant the license to Galaxy Gaming Co.

Galaxy was a publicly traded company with casinos in Las Vegas, Atlantic City, and three other states that had approved riverboat gambling. Galaxy formed a joint venture with three prominent black businessmen and two labor unions whose local presidents were Hispanic. It pledged $250,000 to the Kansas City chapter of Gamblers Anonymous. Galaxy signed a ninety-nine-year ground lease, contingent on getting the license, with the owner of the site the Army Corps of Engineers had designated as its first choice for a 150,000-square-foot floating barge. Three city councilmen and Congressman Delray Shays backed the Galaxy proposal.

The mayor thanked the commission members for their efforts, praised their hard work, and then bestowed the license on Ed Fiora and the Dream Casino. He announced that the casino would be docked at the limestone ledge that had once attracted eighteenth-century traders and trappers to pull in and build the trading post that grew into Kansas City. That site, he noted, was owned by the city and would be leased to the Dream Casino, turning an unproductive historical footnote into a new source of revenue for the city.

The owners of the losing casinos had shrugged their corporate shoulders, accustomed to the game of chance they played in cities throughout the country. A few local investors in the losing companies cried foul, more aggrieved by the loss of the money they were convinced they would have made than by any misplaced sense of civic outrage. In time, they had let the matter drop and gone in search of the next good deal.

Rachel Firestone didn't let the story drop. She dogged the Missouri Gaming Commission, the mayor's office, and the Dream Casino until she found the one thing that tied them all together. Jack Cullan. Cullan had represented Ed Fiora and led the behind-the-scenes efforts to win approval of the Dream's application. Before that, he had been treasurer of Billy Sunshine's two successful campaigns for the office of mayor.

Though she hadn't found evidence of a direct relationship between Cullan and Beth Harrell, she cited highly placed confidential sources intimating that Harrell had been improperly influenced in her decision to approve the license for the Dream Casino.

She traced the flow of money from Ed Fiora to Billy Sunshine. Though her most recent article intimated at a quid pro quo, she fell short of an outright accusation. She quoted the U.S. attorney as not finding sufficient evidence to take the case to the grand jury, making it sound as if he was part of the cover-up.

Trying to find a connection between Cullan's murder and the Dream Casino reminded Mason of a game of three-card monte. The game was a con, not a game of chance or skill.

The dealer dealt three cards, one of which was the ace of spades.

The dealer then turned the cards facedown, and the gambler bet that he could keep track of the ace as the dealer shuffled the three cards at lightning speed. When the dealer finished shuffling, the gambler pointed to the card he believed was the ace. If the dealer wanted the gambler to win a small pot and keep playing until he lost a big one, the dealer would let the gambler win. The trick was to distract the gambler while the cards were being shuffled so that the dealer could replace the ace with another card, hiding the ace in his clothes.

The dealer worked with a partner who bumped the gambler, offered him a drink, or otherwise pulled his attention away from the dealer just for an instant. Mason looked at the notes on his board, the newspaper stories, and the police report. He wondered who was hiding the ace of spades and who was trying to keep him from finding it.

CHAPTER NINETEEN

Claire Mason had practiced law by herself for thirty years, waging battles for those who had no one else to fight for them. Whether her battles were hopeless or hopeful, she won enough of them to keep going.

Many of the bedrock businesses and institutions in town had been her target at one time or another. One of her favorite tactics was to buy a single share of stock in a company just so she could attend the shareholders' annual meeting. During the question-and-answer session, she would ask the CEO if he preferred that she just file a class-action lawsuit against the company since he was obviously too busy to return her phone calls.

She was seated when Mason arrived for lunch, her heavy winter coat draped across an empty chair. It was dark olive, impervious to nature's elements, and looked as if it were designed for a Prussian Cossack, a sharp contrast to his navy pinstripe suit, white shirt, and red-and-navy-striped tie.

"You look like you're dressed for a job interview," she told him as he sat down.

"Interview, not job interview. I need to talk to the mayor about Jack Cullan. His staff won't work me into his schedule, so I'm going to work him into mine."

"When God said let there be light, he didn't mean Billy Sunshine."

"Not one of your favorite politicians?"

"Favorite politician is an oxymoron. Billy Sunshine has the distinction of being both an oxymoron and a regular moron."

"I take it you didn't vote for him."

"To the contrary. The politicians that disappoint me the most are the ones I vote for. I always feel like a sucker afterward. Billy Sunshine was smart, charismatic, and wanted to do all the right things for the right reasons. Revitalize downtown, pump private investment into the East Side and fix the potholes on every street, not just the mayor's. He wanted to unite the people who lived north of the river with the people who lived south of Seventy-Fifth Street, neither of whom believed they lived in the same city. He wanted the Hispanics on the West Side to have a bigger role in city government since they were the fastest-growing minority in the city. He wanted to pull the public schools out of the black hole the school board had thrown them into."

"And you're disappointed he didn't do all of that?"

"Don't be cute. Half that stuff is impossible and the rest is just too hard for mere mortals. That's not the point. He made the promises, got the job, and sold out quicker than a whore on Saturday night."

"Sold out to whom?"

"Anybody with the price of a vote or a sweetheart deal or a zoning variance or whatever else a big campaign contributor was shopping for."

"Are you saying he took bribes?"

"Maybe. Probably not cash in a brown paper bag. It's usually not done that way. It's more often money that gets funneled to friends or family who get hired by somebody as a favor to somebody who wants a favor, that kind of thing. The mayor ends up with friends who owe him favors and pay him back with big campaign contributions or hidden interests in deals."

"How do you know all this and why isn't it on the front page of the newspaper?"

"I know it because I represent the people who get screwed in these deals. The business owner whose building gets condemned for some new high-rise, or the schoolchildren who can't read by the time they're in the eighth grade but are smart enough to figure out how to shoplift, sell dope, and get knocked up. And it's not in the newspaper because everyone knows it and no one can prove it."

"Rachel Firestone thinks she can, at least on the Dream Casino."

Claire studied Mason over her half-glasses. "Since you're short on time, get the lentil soup. They serve it in a bread bowl. It's perfect for a cold day. You probably skipped breakfast, so you need something hearty."

Mason smiled at his aunt, surprised that she had dodged the subject of the Dream Casino. She never pretended to replace his mother after her death, though she loved him as well as any parent could have and still worried about him.

"I know you didn't invite me to lunch to make sure I'm eating right. I figured you wanted to talk about Jack Cullan's murder, not local politics."

"Good for you. No beating around the bush."

Their server interrupted them with a laconic rendition of the daily specials. They ordered the lentil soup.

"I talked to Harry. We'll do our jobs, and whatever happens, happens. It'll work out."

"Don't kid yourself. There's not much chance this is going to work out. At least not for us. One of you, or both of you, will end up bloodied by the other. Blues may end up in prison for the rest of his life. Or worse, so there's not much that's likely to work out."

"What do you want me to do? Walk away? Let somebody else defend Blues?"

She glared at him as if he'd forgotten everything she'd ever taught him.

"Sometimes things don't work out. Sometimes they can't. Sometimes those are the things that have to be done no matter what. You'll live with it and move on, but you won't quit. Don't talk to me about the case. Don't apologize or rationalize to me or to yourself about what you have to do. Just do the best damn job."

Mason didn't have an answer, though he had questions. He wanted to ask Claire about Jack Cullan, since she must have crossed paths with him more than once. He wanted to ask her if

Harry was capable of pushing a bogus case against Blues just to even a score. More than anything, he wanted to ask her what had really happened between Harry and Blues. Instead, he watched her as she pretended to study the paintings on the wall behind him. His aunt never minded silence, believing it preferable to boring conversation. This silence was uneasy.

The server deposited their soup, steam rising from the bowl mixing with the tears brimming in Claire's eyes. She turned away, red eyed and red faced.

"Damn the work we do!" she said, shoving the bowl away from her. She stood, grabbed her coat, and left without another word.

Mason let her go, knowing better than to follow or argue. He ate his soup while he thought about her rendition of Billy Sunshine's promises for a diverse city. The Summit Street Cafe was on the West Side, the urban West Side, barely south of downtown and slightly west of the revitalized Freight House District, where art galleries, coffee shops, and lofts converted to condos were in vogue. West Side meant Mexican restaurants and bakeries and neighborhoods where extended Hispanic families lived in row houses lining an entire block.

Kansas City was dotted with ethnic pockets like the West Side. Decades earlier, Italian immigrants had settled in the North End. Though later generations had moved south to the suburbs, enough had stayed to preserve the identity of the area.

The East Side was called the urban core, code words meaning where the black people lived. It had the highest crime rate, the highest unemployment rate, and the worst schools. It was the recipient of the most lip service, campaign promises, and hand-wringing at city hall.

Midtown was a rough square bounded on the north by the Plaza at Forty-Seventh Street, on the east by Holmes Road, on the south by Seventy-Fifth Street, and on the west by State Line Road, the divider between Missouri and Kansas. It was home to the city's power elite. Private schools made the dismal public schools irrelevant. Homes in Sunset Hills above the Plaza, where Cullan lived, and along Ward Parkway fetched seven figures. Fashionably fit white men and women jogged along Ward Parkway, comfortable in the belief that their lives were the ones the city was referring to when it claimed to be the most livable city in America.

His aunt Claire's house, the house Mason had grown up in and later received as a wedding gift from her, was located in the heart of midtown between Ward Parkway and Wornall Road, two blocks south of Loose Park. Claire had made it one of her missions in life to expose Mason to the entire city lest he grow up thinking that everyone was white and drove a Land Rover.

Though they were Jewish, she had taken him to a black Methodist congregation, telling him that no one had the best corner of religious real estate. She took him to the City Union Mission to serve Thanksgiving dinner to the homeless, and then took him on a driving tour of the city's underbelly, where they found those who wouldn't come to the mission and gave them blankets and box dinners.

"You're damn lucky, that's all," she told him after they'd completed their deliveries one particularly cold Thanksgiving when he was ten years old. It had rained all day, the kind of cold, relentless rain that erodes any trace of warmth hidden in the body. Their last stop had been a tarpaper shanty built into the side of a bridge abutment. A man and a woman lived there, although it was difficult to tell which was which. They both had greasy brown hair plastered to their heads with dirt and rain that had blown into their makeshift shelter. Their eyes were hollow, their cheeks splotched with broken blood vessels, and the few teeth they still had were yellow and rotted.

"Why?" Mason asked her. "Because we don't live under a bridge?"

"Partly. Mostly because you're an upper-middle-class white male and this country doesn't like anything better than that. Just don't confuse luck with brilliance. Don't think because you were born on third base that you hit a triple. Do something with your life that makes a difference for someone beside yourself. Otherwise, you'll never score. You'll just die on third base."

Mason envied Claire for her passion to do the right thing, fight the good fight. He had looked for the same spark in his own practice, first in a small firm that represented injured people, then in a big firm that protected people's money, and now in his own practice, where he just protected people. He'd found the spark. Now he just hoped it wouldn't start a fire that consumed everyone he cared about.

THE LAST WITNESS

CHAPTER TWENTY

Mason was lousy at big social functions. He was no good at being a hail-fellow-well-met or assuring a new face that he was damn glad to meet him while the new face looked over his shoulder for a better deal.

He stood at the back of the Hyatt Hotel ballroom and listened as the mayor sang the praises of the Salvation Army. The speech had been written for him, but he made the words his own. He had the connection gene in his DNA that linked him to his audience, erasing any suggestion that both he and they were just going through the motions.

Billy Sunshine had been the quarterback for the Kansas City Chiefs, retiring after winning the Super Bowl on an eighty-yard bootleg as time expired. He announced his retirement and his candidacy for mayor the day after the ticker-tape parade. Women swooned at his chiseled good looks and men got teary eyed when he told football war stories on the campaign trail.

Even his critics conceded that he was more than another jock with a Super Bowl ring. He was bright, earnest, charming, and irresistible. Dogged by scandal, his cleats replaced with feet of clay, he pretended not to notice as he worked the crowd. No one else in the ballroom noticed either as he wove another football memory into his remarks, earning warm laughter and enthusiastic applause.

The ballroom was packed, at least a thousand people by Mason's estimation, each table festooned with a placard identifying the corporate sponsor that had paid for lunch. Sponsors who wrote big enough checks watched their names and company logos scroll across a video loop projected above the head table.

Mason was Jewish, making Christmas a bystander holiday. His aunt Claire raised him on Jewish ethics, adopting as her personal creed the commandment to heal the world, while discarding the rituals and holidays as little more than historical relics. He wasn't observant, though he occasionally acknowledged a spiritual itch in the back of his soul he wasn't certain how to scratch.

"The gentiles sure know how to throw a party," Rachel Firestone said.

He was so caught up in the mayor's speech that he hadn't noticed her until she tugged on his sleeve.

"Let me guess. You're a Jewish lesbian."

"Damn straight! Though I'm not. Too bad you can't take me home to your mother."

"More than you know. She would have wanted me to marry a nice Jewish girl, just not one who also wanted to marry a nice Jewish girl."

"Oops. A past-tense mother is not a good thing. Sorry."

"Don't worry about it. She and my father were killed in a car wreck when I was three. My aunt Claire raised me."

"Sounds like a feature story. Not my beat. What's your plan to get to the mayor?"

"I was planning on waving a five-dollar bill over my head and whistling. What do you think?"

"That only works with the hookers on Independence Avenue. The mayor's price is higher. See that woman standing over there next to the door to the kitchen?"

Mason followed the aim of Rachel's extended hand, fixing on a dark-haired woman in a severe gray suit standing next to the kitchen door, watching the mayor and her watch, and tapping her foot against the thick carpet.

"Who is she?"

"Amy White, the mayor's chief of staff. She ran Sunshine's last campaign and is planning his run for Congress just in case he doesn't get indicted."

"What's her story?"

"The usual political prodigy. Savvy, loves politics, and thinks Sunshine will take her a long way if he can stay out of jail."

"Savvy enough to keep me from asking the mayor, in front of God and everybody, if he knows who killed Jack Cullan?"

"With one hand tied behind her back. Take your best shot."

Mason winked at Rachel. "No time like the present."

He weaved his way around the tables, ignoring the turned heads and murmurs that followed him. Last year, his picture had been in the newspaper and on television for weeks, accompanied by a media chorus flogging the deadly demise of his law firm, Sullivan & Christenson. He refused to play the celebrity, adding an unintended angle to the story. Rachel's latest article on Cullan's murder identified him as Blues's attorney, reminding readers that he had been a suspect, killer, and hero in the Sullivan & Christenson case.

The mayor finished his remarks and made his way toward Amy White. Mason was on course to intercept him. The buzz increased as people sensed that something was about to happen that would make their $150-a-plate lunch worth the price of admission.

Amy White was the first hurdle Mason had to overcome. She had auburn hair that fell against the base of her neck, dark-rimmed glasses giving her unlined face a serious cast, her gray suit covering a slender build.

She watched as he approached, not flinching, her intense gaze more curious than concerned. Those closest to the scene surged a few steps closer, not wanting to miss anything. Billy Sunshine reached Amy a half step ahead of Mason.

"Merry Christmas, Lou," the mayor boomed loud enough to be heard at Santa's North Pole workshop and grasped Mason's hand. "Glad you could make it. I want to talk with you about Jack Cullan's murder. You've got a job to do. I understand that. But Jack was a good man and a good friend. He deserves justice and his killer deserves the maximum punishment the law allows. I know you want that as much as you want to help your client."

Amy White permitted herself a small smile, satisfied that the TV cameras had captured the moment. She tilted her head toward the doors to the kitchen. Sunshine took his cue, cupping Mason's elbow, leading him through the kitchen, stopping at the service elevator.

"You're as good as people say you are, Mr. Mayor. You saw me coming the whole way," Mason said.

"A good quarterback has to be able to pick up the blitz."

"And it helps to have a good defensive coordinator."

"Amy is the best in the business. You've got five minutes. Don't waste them and don't darken my door again. You do and I'll tell the press that you're harassing me. You can call me to testify at the trial if you think I've got anything to say, but you won't hear anything different then from what I'll tell you now."

"I'll have a lot more than five minutes at trial."

Sunshine looked at his watch. "Four minutes. I hope you're better in court."

"Let's make it the two-minute drill. Did Jack Cullan ever represent you?"

"Yes. On private matters that are protected by the attorney-client privilege."

"Did he bribe you to approve the license for the Dream Casino?"

"No. One minute."

"Who killed him?"

"According to the police, your client. Thirty seconds. Time for one last play."

"What's in Jack Cullan's secret file on you?"

Sunshine didn't answer. His involuntary glance at Amy and the twitch in his eye told Mason he'd scored.

"Maybe you don't know," Mason said. "I guess you'll find out in court. Merry Christmas."

CHAPTER TWENTY-ONE

Mason was parked on the third level of the Hyatt's covered parking garage. Melting snow laced with dirt and debris gave the garage a dank taste, like a flooded basement. As he turned the key in the ignition, Amy White rapped a gloved hand on the front passenger window, opened the door, and slid in beside him.

"If you lost the mayor, don't look at me. I left him with you."

"Cute. We need to talk."

"I tried that. It didn't work too well."

"I'm sorry about what happened in the hotel. Blame me, not the mayor. I read Rachel Firestone's article in today's paper. She practically accused the mayor of trying to railroad your client onto death row. I had a feeling you might show up at one of the mayor's public appearances since he wouldn't see you at his office. I handled it the only way I could without having another incident."

"Wouldn't it have been a lot easier to make an appointment?"

"The mayor's schedule is so tight I can barely get in to see him."

"That's bullshit. You just hoped I didn't have the balls to nail your boss in public. I've got to hand it to you, though. You guys were ready. Made it look like I was at the top of the mayor's Christmas list."

"I can put you there."

She arched an eyebrow and cocked her head to one side. It wasn't exactly a come-hither look. She didn't strike him as the kind of woman who would wet her lower lip with her tongue and open her thighs a provocative inch or two to make an offer he couldn't refuse.

"Of course you can. In return for what? My firstborn male child?"

"Nothing so dramatic. Besides, Rachel Firestone would just write a story that the mayor had fathered another child out of wedlock."

"She really gets under your skin, doesn't she?"

"No. She just creates work for me to do. The mayor has done tremendous things for this city, and she can't stand that."

"Save it. The mayor isn't George Washington or even George Bush. He won the Super Bowl and should have gone to Disney World instead of city hall. I thought he'd be more interested in who killed Jack Cullan since they were so tight."

"The mayor believes that the killer has been caught. But he wants to be fair to your client. He's opposed to any rush to judgment."

"You can't possibly believe that, and even if you do, you can't possibly expect me to believe it. If half of what Rachel Firestone has written about your boss and the Dream Casino is true, the odds are two to one that Cullan's murder is tied to that deal. We both know the best thing that could happen to the mayor is for my client to be convicted or plead guilty before Cullan's secret files end up on the front page of the *Star*."

"Do you have the files?"

"What do you think?"

"I think if you did, they would already have been on the front page."

"And you can't let that happen, can you? If I keep the mayor out of my case, will he name a street after me?"

"The mayor had nothing to do with Jack Cullan's death. There's no reason to throw mud at him. That won't save your client."

"Finding the killer will save my client. If the mayor wants to stay above the fray, I need his help. I need to know the whole story about the Dream Casino."

"The mayor can't help you. Even if he wanted to, I wouldn't let him. But I'll help you on one condition. If you find Cullan's files—

assuming they really exist—I want to see the mayor's file before anyone else. If there's anything in it that will help your client, use it. If there isn't, I get the file and you agree that you never saw it."

Amy was the second person to make him an offer if he found the files. Like the deal he had made with Rachel, this one could also help Blues.

"Okay. You've got a deal. Now tell me about the casino."

"Sorry to disappoint you. There's no story there. The casino deal is clean. The U.S. attorney, the prosecuting attorney, and the gaming commission have all blessed it. Ask me something I really can help you with."

"That doesn't mean the deal was clean. It only means they couldn't prove anything. When was the last time you spoke with Jack Cullan?"

"Last Friday night, but that won't help your client."

Mason leaned toward her. "Let me make that decision. Besides, I'd rather know the bad facts now. Finding out in court ruins my day."

Amy pressed her back against the passenger door and took a deep breath.

"Okay. Jack called me at home Friday night. It was late, about midnight. He told me that he wanted a copy of the liquor license for a club called Blues on Broadway and he wanted to know all about the owner."

Mason felt the inside of the Jeep shrink as the case against Blues got a little tighter.

"What else did he say?"

"He told me that the owner had roughed him up and that he was going to shut the bar down, teach him a lesson he wouldn't forget. I told him that I'd get him the records on Monday morning."

"Is that a service the mayor's office routinely provides?"

"Favors are what I do. It wasn't illegal to provide him with records that are available to anyone who wants to walk into the office of the director of liquor control."

"Do the police know about this?"

"Yes. I told them when they came to see the mayor about Jack. I hadn't had a chance to request the records before we found out that Jack had been killed."

"How did you find out about Cullan?"

"The chief of police called the mayor and said he had something important to discuss. He came to the mayor's office around ten o'clock Monday morning with a couple of detectives."

"Harry Ryman and Carl Zimmerman?"

"That's right. The mayor was very upset. In spite of what you might think, Jack and the mayor were really close. The mayor cross-examined the detectives as if they were on trial. He told them to keep him informed of the progress of the investigation."

"Which means keep you informed?"

Amy nodded. "I'm paid to be his eyes and ears."

Amy's story added credibility to Cullan's threat that he would punish Blues for interfering in his fight with Beth Harrell.

"Could Cullan have gotten Blues's bar shut down?"

Amy shrugged. "Depends on what he came up with. Jack had a lot of influence, but he wasn't king."

Mason decided to switch gears. "Do you know Ed Fiora?"

Amy gave him her cocked-head look again. "Yes, I know Ed Fiora and the mayor knows Ed Fiora."

"Do you know any of the people who work for him?"

Amy hesitated. "A few."

"How about a big guy, roughly the size of New Jersey, with breath that smells like licorice?"

Amy frowned. Mason assumed that she wasn't trying to decide whether she knew him. Rather, he figured she was deciding whether to give him up.

"Tony Manzerio," she said at last. "I met him at Fiora's office. He sits outside the door like a guard dog. Ed must give him licorice instead of dog treats. Why do you ask?"

"Can't tell the players without a program. I'll let you know if I find the mayor's file."

"I'm counting on you," Amy said.

CHAPTER TWENTY-TWO

The door to Mason's office had a slot in it for mail delivery. He scooped Friday's delivery off the floor, tossed it on the sofa, and opened up the dry-erase board. Using a green marker, he drew a short line down from Ed Fiora's name and added Tony Manzerio's name to the board. He wrote Amy White's name in parentheses next to the mayor's name and underscored Rachel's reference to Jack Cullan's secret files.

His conversation with Amy had convinced him that Cullan's files did exist. He couldn't decide whether the files were the motive for Cullan's murder or the reason for the determined effort to railroad Blues—or both.

The words he'd written on the board didn't suddenly come to life and rearrange themselves into the answers to his questions. It was, he reminded himself, a dry-erase board and not a Ouija board.

He found an envelope buried in the stack of mail from the Jackson County prosecutor's office marked *Hand Delivery*. It contained a motion filed by Patrick Ortiz asking the court to set a preliminary hearing in Blues's case and an order signed by Judge Pistone setting the hearing on January 2. The judge's order was not a surprise, but Ortiz's motion made as much sense as folding with a full house when no else had placed a bet.

There were a number of steps in the life of a criminal case once a suspect was arrested. The first was the arraignment, which was to officially inform the defendant of the charges against him and to set bail.

The next step was for the prosecutor to establish that there was probable cause to believe that a crime had been committed and that the defendant had committed it. The prosecutor could meet that burden by presenting the case to the grand jury and asking for an indictment. Or the prosecutor could ask the associate circuit court judge to hold a preliminary hearing, at which the state would present its evidence and ask the judge to bind the defendant over for trial. If the judge found the state's evidence sufficient, the case would be assigned to a circuit court judge for trial.

The grand jury met in secret. Witnesses could be subpoenaed to testify and forced to appear without a lawyer to represent them. Taking the Fifth Amendment was the criminal equivalent of a scarlet letter. Hearing only the state's side of the case ensured that the grand jury would issue whatever indictments the prosecutor requested.

A preliminary hearing was public. The defendant had the right to attend and listen to the case against him, and his lawyer had the right to cross-examine the state's witnesses and present evidence of his client's innocence. Prosecutors hated preliminary hearings because they were forced to show too many of their cards to the defendant. Secret justice was more certain.

Patrick Ortiz would rather rip out a chamber of his heart than give up the grand jury. He didn't care about politics or appearances. He fought the battles and let his boss take the credit. Leonard Campbell was a politician first and a lawyer last. He must have made the decision to give up the grand jury, and Mason knew why.

Rachel Firestone's article, and the media frenzy it had launched, had forced Campbell's hand. He needed to use the preliminary hearing to defuse Rachel's accusation that Blues was a victim of political expediency.

The date of the hearing meant that Mason would be working on New Year's Eve instead of celebrating, though he didn't mind. He didn't have anyone to kiss at midnight, and now he had an excuse to skip the sloppy embraces of people he didn't know at parties that he didn't want to attend alone.

New Year's Eve was an annual take-stock moment for Mason,

demanding an honest appraisal of where he'd been and where he was going. The best New Year's he'd ever celebrated had been the first one with Kate. They'd been married a month and were still giddy. She'd surprised him with tickets to Grand Cayman, a second honeymoon before they'd finished paying for the first one. They danced as if they were possessed, shouted and laughed with strangers, and marveled at the magic in their lives. Minutes before midnight, Kate led him onto an empty beach glowing with the reflection of the moon and stars, where they had made love as the New Year dawned.

Three years later, she left him, telling him she had run out of love for him. It was a concept he couldn't understand. Love wasn't like oil, he told her. You don't wait for the well to run dry and start digging someplace else. Unless you were Kate.

Since then, Mason had done his share of digging, though his relationships had proved too shallow or fragile to last. He was glad to use work as an excuse to skip New Year's Eve and the annual audit of his personal account.

CHAPTER TWENTY-THREE

Mason capped his evening with another ten-thousand-meter row across his dining room, his strokes rough, his timing off. Blues's case had the same effect, both making him sweat.

His punctuated his ragged breathing with deep grunts each time he hauled the rowing handle deep into his belly. Tuffy, not liking what she saw, paced back and forth, ears up and tail down. He finished as the doorbell rang, mopping his face and neck with a towel as he staggered to his feet.

His house was fifty years old. The front door was a massive arched slab of dark mahogany set into an entry vestibule with a limestone floor. When he opened it, a woman was standing on the stoop, head down and her arms bundled around her. He didn't recognize her until she raised her chin. It was Beth Harrell.

He'd last seen her at a bar association lunch or law school alumni dinner—he couldn't remember which, only that it was a couple of years ago. Sophisticated, beautiful, and playful, she was also the smartest person in the room, a combination that drew people to her. In law school, everyone wanted to take her class, the guys so they could drool and the girls so they could learn how to be more like her, traits that made her and Billy Sunshine soul mates.

As she stood in his doorway, bowed by the winter wind, something was missing. The certainty that the world was hers had vanished. Her eyes flickered and her lips were pressed in a tight half smile.

"Beth?" She nodded. "Come on in before we both freeze to death."

Mason closed the door as she pulled off her gloves, rubbing her hands along her arms and then pressing them against her face to warm her frozen cheeks. Her body shook with a final shiver.

"Thanks. I don't remember when it's been so cold."

She unzipped her coat. Tuffy trotted to her side, sniffed her, and planted her front paws on Beth's stomach. Beth stroked the back of her head. Satisfied, Tuffy dropped her paws, circled behind Mason and lay down.

"My dog is shameless and will give herself to anyone who scratches her behind her ears."

"Love and loyalty should be so easy to come by."

Mason knew that the only reason Beth Harrell would come knocking at nine o'clock on a Friday night cold enough to freeze her face off was to talk about Jack Cullan and Blues. Figuring that she chose the time and place so that no one would know, he decided to let her get around to Cullan's murder in her own time.

"Can I get you something to drink?"

"That would be great. Something hot would do the trick."

Mason led her to the kitchen. Tuffy figured out where they were going and raced there ahead of them.

"I've got tea. Never developed a taste for coffee, so I don't keep it in the house."

"Tea would be good, perfect."

Mason boiled a cup of water in the microwave, and a few minutes later they were seated at his kitchen table. Beth stirred her tea, pressing the tea bag against the side of the cup. Mason drank from a long-necked bottle of beer and pressed the cool glass against his neck.

"I read about you in the paper last year. That thing with Sullivan & Christenson," she began. "We didn't teach you that in law school."

"We've both been in the papers. All things considered, I prefer the comics."

"Amen to that."

A faint patchwork of crow's-feet and laugh lines had crept onto her face since he was her student, changes she wore well. She was five years older than him, a gap that mattered then but was now a distinction without a difference.

"Was it difficult?" she asked him.

"Was what difficult?"

"Killing that man. The article in the newspaper said that he would have killed you if you hadn't. I suppose that made it easier, but it still had to be a hard thing to do."

Mason had come to understand the reluctance of men who'd gone to war to discuss their battles. Heroes were for bystanders. Soldiers killed so that they could live. That's what he'd done, and he'd found no glory in it.

"That's all old news. I left you a message yesterday. You could have just called back. I would have come to your office."

"I was out of town. When I got home this evening, I read the paper and saw you and the mayor on the news. I decided a house call would be more private. I live at the Alameda Towers and the press has practically camped out in the parking lot."

"How did you get past them?"

"Our building is connected to the Intercontinental Hotel. I parked in the hotel garage and walked through the hotel. The press can't get past my doorman and they haven't figured out my secret entrance."

"Gee, that's a better setup than having Alfred and the Batcave."

Beth laughed. "You were always good at that in law school. I used to watch you with your friends. You were always the one who made everyone laugh."

Mason grinned. "If you were watching me, you know I was watching you. If only I'd have known."

Beth shrugged. "I was your teacher, but I wasn't dead."

"Is it too late for extra credit?"

"It's too late for that, but I hope it's not too late for you to help me."

CHAPTER TWENTY-FOUR

Mason drained his beer and carried it to the sink. He leaned back against the counter and studied her.

She had drawn him in with a mix of vulnerability and flirtation that he found engaging, flattering, and, under other circumstances, irresistible.

"The governor appointed you because you were an expert on ethics, on right and wrong. You know who my client is and why I called you. When this case is over, I could represent you. But not now."

"I'm not asking you to be my lawyer. I know better than that."

"Then what do you want?"

"Protection."

"From who?"

She crossed the room to him, stopping within arm's reach, trembling, begging to be held without saying a word. Mason clamped his hands on the counter's edge.

"Protect you from what?" he repeated.

She dipped her head, looked away, and then turned her back to him.

"You're right. I shouldn't have come here. My office would have been better."

"Maybe not. If you tell me who or what you're afraid of, I may be able to help you. But you realize the position we're both in here."

She stiffened and took a deep breath and went back to her chair. "Let's stick to your business. I'll take care of mine. Why did you call?"

Mason didn't press. He wasn't looking for more complications.

"Good enough. Tell me about last Friday night. Why were you out with Jack Cullan?"

Beth straightened, her posture saying she was ready to get down to business. "He asked me out. We're both single. He was a very interesting man, well read and charming when he wanted to be."

Mason heard the words but didn't believe them. "You're telling me that in the middle of a scandal over whether Cullan had you in his back pocket, he asked you out on a date and you said yes? Are you nuts?"

Beth clasped her hands, setting them on the kitchen table. "I'm forty-three years old. I've been married and divorced twice and I have no children. I don't even have a damn dog! Men call me the Ice Queen behind my back, and that's the nicest thing they say. So when Jack Cullan asked, I said yes. There's no crime in that."

"There's no sense in it either."

"All the official investigations went nowhere. Rachel Firestone is the only one beating the scandal drum, and no one was paying any attention. We would have had a pleasant evening and no one would have written or said anything about it. We didn't even talk about the Dream Casino or any other gaming commission business."

"If it was all so pleasant, why did you throw a drink in his face?"

She took a breath. "I said that Jack could be charming. He could also be crude, especially when he asked me to spend the night with him. I told him I wasn't interested and he called me a cock teaser, among other things."

"That's it? He called you names?"

She reddened. "No. He threatened me. He threatened to ruin me."

"How? I've heard that Cullan collected dirt on a lot of people. Did he have a file on you?"

"He didn't say and I don't know. I haven't led a perfect life, but I never took a bribe. He just said he would do it, that I wouldn't see it coming, and that no one but the two of us would know that it had been him. That was too much. I've had two husbands who tried that crap on me, and I wasn't going to put up with it from him."

"So why didn't you press charges?"

"Having dinner with Jack and going to that bar afterward was a nonevent. Filing criminal charges against him for assault would have been a media circus. No, thanks. It was better to chalk it up to one more bad judgment about the men whose company I keep."

Mason took the chair next to hers. "The owner of the bar is my client and my friend. He goes by Blues. He saved my life and I'm trying to save his."

"I'm not sure I can help you."

"Let me decide that. You threw your drink in Cullan's face and he came after you."

"He grabbed me, yes."

"And Blues pulled him off of you, right?"

"Yes. Yes, he did."

"And that's when Cullan scratched the back of Blues's hands. Am I right?"

Beth thought for a moment and shook her head. "I'm sorry. I was pretty upset. I just don't remember. All I do remember is Jack telling your client that he was going to put him out of business."

Mason gave her time to say more, but she didn't. "Okay. What happened after you left the bar?"

"Jack took me home. He dropped me off. He didn't apologize and I didn't invite him upstairs."

"Did you stay home the rest of the night?"

She stood and circled the table. "My God, Lou! You're asking me if I killed him?"

"I'm doing my job. I'm sure the police asked you the same question."

Beth glared at him. "I expected that from them but not from you."

She headed for the door, picked up her coat, and jammed her arms into the sleeves, twisting a scarf around her neck. "I didn't kill him. I'm sorry I went out with the son of a bitch, but I didn't kill him. And, I'm sorry I came here tonight."

"I'm not sorry. I don't want it to be you."

"Neither do I," she said and left.

Tuffy went into the living room, climbed into her dog bed, turned around three times, and lay down. Mason joined her on the floor, scratched behind her ears, and thought about the last two days.

His working theory was that Cullan's murder was linked to the Dream Casino deal, a theory that led to three suspects—Ed Fiora, Billy Sunshine, and Beth Harrell. Fiora refused to talk to him but sent Tony Manzerio to deliver a message. The mayor played politics and sent Amy White to plead his case. Beth Harrell made a house call, asking for his help without offering anything in return.

Though she was long on motive and short on alibi, Mason meant it when he told her that he hoped it wasn't her. He slipped his hand under Tuffy's face and aimed her head at his.

"What do you think? Can I save Blues and still get the girl?"

Tuffy raised her paw and pushed his hand away, then pawed him again until he resumed scratching behind her ears.

"It's all about you, isn't it? Well, at least you're honest about it."

CHAPTER TWENTY-FIVE

Patrick Ortiz called Mason on Monday morning, asking Mason to meet him and Leonard Campbell at eleven.

"What's the occasion? You guys ready to surrender, or what?"

"Eleven o'clock," Ortiz answered, and hung up.

Mason didn't think they were ready to surrender. He did think they were ready to negotiate, or at least make the offer that Tony Manzerio had encouraged him to take during their slow dance in the parking lot.

He wasn't looking forward to getting an offer Blues wouldn't take. Telling Blues about the offer was the easy part. Telling him that Manzerio had threatened both their lives if Blues didn't take the offer was the hard part. Blues wouldn't take the deal to save his own life, but he might do it to save Mason's, and that was a debt Mason didn't want on his books.

Mason liked representing defendants. He just hated being on the defensive. He slapped his hand on his desk, taking his frustration out on an inanimate object that stung his hand in return. *That's solo practice,* he thought to himself. Even his desk gave him a hard time.

Mason signed in at the receptionist's desk when he arrived at the prosecutor's office, printing his name, address, and telephone number and the name of the person he'd come to see. Four other people were already waiting. Two of them were dressed in lawyer's uniforms, thumb-typing on their BlackBerrys. The other two were an elderly man and woman, the man clutching a brochure on how to avoid home-remodeling scams. From their ruined looks, Mason concluded that they had waited too long to take the advice.

The receptionist was a young woman with big hair and long fingernails painted bright yellow. She kept her back to him while playing solitaire on her computer and talking on her headset, saying "Get out!" and "You go, girl!" as if that was the limit of her vocabulary. Had her name been Margaret, he wouldn't have stayed. Fortunately, according to the nameplate on her desk, her name was Tina, so he stuck it out.

"Damn this piece of shit! Not you, girl," she said into her headset. "This damn computer. Beats me every damn time. I give up. Someone's waitin' on me anyway."

She scanned the sign-in sheet, pressed a speed-dial button on her phone, and announced Mason's arrival. Moments later, Campbell's secretary, an attractive woman with dark hair and a lavender skirt that had been spray-painted onto her heart-shaped bottom, appeared and told him to follow her. He wanted to tell her to slow down. She ushered him into Campbell's office with a small flourish of her hand and held his eyes as he nodded his thanks.

Patrick Ortiz was seated in a chair on the visitors' side of Campbell's ornate walnut desk. Campbell stood behind his desk, the phone to his ear. He motioned to Mason to take the chair next to Ortiz and squeezed his thumb and forefinger together to indicate that the conversation would be a short one.

Mason remained standing, smiled at Ortiz, and shook his hand. They didn't speak. Mason had nothing to say, and Ortiz was being deferential to his boss.

Mason looked around the office. There were law books on one wall that Mason was confident Leonard Campbell had never opened; pictures of Campbell with various local dignitaries on another; and Campbell's framed law school diploma on a third. Mason examined it closely to be certain that Campbell's degree wasn't from the Columbia School of Broadcasting. He was annoyed to learn that he and Campbell had gone to the same law school, though Campbell had graduated twenty-five years earlier.

Campbell finished his phone call, hung up the phone, and greeted Mason.

"Good to see you, Lou!"

He was a trim, well-kept man nearing retirement, a neat white mustache penciled in above his upper lip. He shook Mason's hand with both of his, the left clamped over the right in a firm commitment of fellowship that Mason took as a sign that Campbell was about to screw his lights out. Claire had once warned him that the two-handed shake was the male equivalent of a woman's air kiss, a gesture of phony intimacy and a warning to keep your hand on your wallet and a close eye on your virtue.

"Nice to see you too."

"Have a seat."

"I don't think I'll be here that long."

Campbell gave him the toothy grin he reserved for voters. "You might change your mind after you hear what we've got to say."

"I'm listening."

"Patrick tells me that we've got your client dead to rights. No sense in putting the taxpayers through an expensive trial. We've got a proposal for you. Let your client put this whole thing behind him, do his time, and start over while he still has something to look forward to."

"Patrick is too good a lawyer to have told you that you've got my client dead to anything. Your case sucks."

"Your client's skin and blood were found under the victim's fingernails. The victim threatened to shut his bar down, and your client responded by threatening to kill him. And, he doesn't have an alibi."

"My client stopped Jack Cullan from beating the crap out of his date. The rest is trash talk. You can't even put my client at the murder scene. The only deal you should be offering me is a dismissal and an apology in return for a promise not to sue your ass."

Campbell smiled again and nodded at Ortiz.

"We can put him at the scene," Ortiz said.

Mason looked at Ortiz, knowing he wouldn't bluff on something like that. It would be too easy for Mason to call him on it.

"What have you got, Patrick?"

90

"Your client's fingerprints on Cullan's desk in the study where the maid found his body. Still think my case sucks?"

Mason refused to be baited. He needed to talk to Blues. "I'm obligated to convey any offer you make to my client. You're still a long way from home on this case and we all know that."

Campbell chuckled. Mason wanted to sew his lips shut.

"We'll accept a plea to second-degree murder and we won't make any recommendation on the sentence. Your client will probably be sentenced to twenty years to life and be paroled in seven years."

"That's not much of a deal. Even with the fingerprints, second degree is the worst that he's likely to be convicted of on your best day in court. This isn't the kind of deal that will make anybody lose any sleep if we turn it down."

"This is our best and only deal. It's on the table until the preliminary hearing. After that, we go to trial. Believe me, this deal is in everyone's best interests."

"Including yours? Is that what Ed Fiora told you?"

Campbell's face purpled, his eyes narrowing. Ortiz jumped in before he could answer.

"You're way out of line!"

"We'll see. In the meantime, be careful you don't step in your boss's shit bucket."

CHAPTER TWENTY-SIX

Twenty minutes later Mason was in a visitor's room at the county jail with Blues.

"They found your fingerprints in Cullan's study. On his desk."

Blues showed no emotion. He didn't curse and he didn't deny.

"Did you hear what I said? Patrick Ortiz told me they found your fingerprints. They can put you in Cullan's house the night he was killed."

"I wasn't there."

"Fine. I'll tell them that. I'm sure they'll just throw the fingerprints out. That will take care of everything."

"I wasn't there that night or ever."

Mason studied Blues as he spoke. There was no artifice, no subtle tics borne of a liar's stress. There never had been with Blues. Mason couldn't think of a single time that Blues had ever lied to him. About anything. Blues knew it would do him no good to lie now. Just as it would do Ortiz no good to lie. They couldn't both be telling the truth.

Mason shrugged. "I don't know. Maybe the forensics people just made a mistake. It wouldn't be the first time."

"If that's supposed to make me feel better, it doesn't. I told you they want me for this. They've got to make it be me."

"I don't buy it. I don't care what happened between you and Harry. I don't buy it."

"Doesn't matter if it is Harry. You've got to go after all of them. If you don't, I'm a dead man."

Mason sighed, feeling the walls close in on him as if he were the prisoner. "Campbell offered you a deal. Second degree, no recommendation on sentencing, out in seven years."

"No."

"I know. I told Campbell that was the worst that you would get in a trial. Campbell said it's the best deal you'll get and that it's off the table once the preliminary hearings starts."

"No deals, Lou. Tell Campbell to go fuck himself. Tell him today—now. I don't want that punk bitch to believe I'm even thinking about it."

Mason called Patrick Ortiz after he left the jail. "My client says he'll take a pass on your deal."

"Have a nice life," Ortiz said, and hung up.

"Yeah," Mason said to the dead phone. "Whatever is left of it."

CHAPTER TWENTY-SEVEN

New Year's Eve fell on a Monday. No one had tried to kill him since Blues had turned down the prosecutor's plea bargain. Mason didn't know whether that was just luck or whether thugs took off the week between Christmas and New Year's.

He sat at his desk late in the afternoon gazing out the window onto Broadway. It was a slate-gray day, the sky nearly the same color as the pavement. It was hard to tell where one ended and the other began. Black ice made of frozen slush and grime was pocketed along curbs and buildings. It hadn't snowed in two weeks, but it hadn't been warm enough to melt the hard-core remnants of the last storm.

The week before, Mason took Mickey to visit Blues so they could discuss the plans for New Year's Eve. Mason explained to Mickey that he could go by himself, but Mickey declined, telling Mason that jail was a place you should never go without someone who knew how to get you out.

"I've got a terrific idea for New Year's," Mickey told Blues.

Blues raised his eyebrows, doubting whether Mickey was capable of such a thought.

"It's a bar," Blues said. "I've got Pete Kirby's trio booked already. I've lined up extra bar and kitchen help. All you have to do is keep the booze and the food moving."

Mickey waved both hands in protest. "No, no, no. You've got it all wrong. This is an opportunity, a huge opportunity. We bill the night as a benefit for your legal defense fund. It'll be a knockout."

He looked back and forth at Blues and Mason, who both shook

their heads. "No fund-raiser," Blues said.

"Not a chance," Mason added.

"Okay, okay. Plan B. You guys will love this. We do a murder mystery. You know, hire actors to stage a murder. Involve the people in the bar in solving the crime. Plant clues, stuff like that. Reveal the killer at midnight. I'm telling you guys, it will be fantastic!"

Blues had pressed his hands against the glass separating prisoners and visitors like he wanted to reach through and strangle Mickey.

"Just say hello to the people when they come in, take their money, and don't fuck it up."

Mickey overcame his anxiety of going to the jail by himself, shuttling back and forth, pleading with Blues to approve one scheme after another. Blues finally told him that if he came back again, the guards would arrest him.

Today, Mickey called Mason a dozen times with last-minute pleas to approve one off-the-wall idea after another. Mason had said no to the first ten and hung up on the last two.

He spent the rest of the day going over his notes for the preliminary hearing. He didn't think Patrick Ortiz would reveal anything more about his case than was necessary to convince Judge Pistone to bind Blues over for trial. The evidence of Blues's fingerprints at the scene would be more than enough.

Mason had listed the witnesses he expected Ortiz to call on the dry-erase board. The maid would testify that she had found Cullan's body. The coroner would testify to the cause of death. Beth Harrell or Pete Kirby would testify about the fight at the bar and Blues's threat. Harry Ryman would testify about his investigation. A forensics investigator would testify about the fingerprints.

Mason had no evidence to work with. The last two weeks had yielded nothing that changed the core facts of the case. Judge Pistone would find probable cause to believe that Blues had murdered Jack Cullan. The press would have a field day, its monstrous appetite satisfied for the moment. Leonard Campbell would smile into the cameras on the courthouse steps and boast about doing the people's business. The image made Mason want to puke.

The phone rang again. He let it ring twice before picking it up.

"Listen, Mickey," he said. "Just do it the way Blues told you. It's not a carnival."

Rachel Firestone said, "What's not a carnival? Who's Mickey and what did Blues tell him to do? Are you planning a New Year's Eve jailbreak? Tell me what time and I'll get a photographer over there."

"Shit. I told him not to call me at work. You reporters are too clever. I knew you'd figure it out."

"I'll make certain it's front-page, above the fold. All seriousness aside, what's going on?"

"Mickey is running the bar while Blues is on vacation. He's been driving me crazy all day wanting to turn it into the Circus Maximus for New Year's. I figured it was him."

"Sorry to disappoint you."

"You didn't. What's on your mind?"

"New Year's Eve. What else? You have any plans?"

"It's against my religion. Besides, what happened to your girlfriend the rugby player?"

"Fear of commitment."

"Hers or yours?"

"Mine. I figured you would be the perfect date. I'm on the rebound and I don't like guys. Who could be safer for a girl at the peak of her vulnerability?"

"You make it sound irresistible, but I think I'll pass. I'm not in a party mood."

"I haven't told you about the party yet. You might change your mind."

"Okay, where's the party?"

"The Dream Casino. Invitation only and I've got one. Does your tux still fit?"

Mason perked up. He doubted that Ed Fiora would talk to him about Cullan's murder, but he figured it couldn't hurt to ask. The worst Fiora could say was no. The preliminary hearing was in two days and Mason needed something. He couldn't think of any reason not to try and get it from Fiora, except for Tony Manzerio. Mason didn't think Fiora would whack him in the middle of his casino on New Year's Eve in front of hundreds of witnesses.

"I don't own a tux, but I've still got my bar mitzvah suit. Will that be formal enough?"

"Perfect. I'll pick you up at nine o'clock."

CHAPTER TWENTY-EIGHT

Rachel rang Mason's doorbell at exactly nine. He finished smoothing out the knot in his tie before he opened the door.

"Man-O-Manishewitz!" Mason said.

Rachel swirled into the entry hall wearing a full-length mink coat. She slipped one arm effortlessly out of her coat, letting it slide down the other into a pile on the floor, revealing an off-the-shoulder, above-the-knee, black sheath that clung to her body as if she were born with it on. Hands on her hips, she bumped to the right, then grinded to the left, the light reflecting off the diamonds and gold on her wrist, ears, and neck.

"Am I not fabulous?"

"Fabulous doesn't come close. You're going to break every heart in the place. The men will die because they can't have you and the woman will hate you because they don't know they're the only ones with a chance."

"Trust me. The right ones will know."

"What? You have a secret handshake?"

"Can't tell you. That's what makes it a secret."

"How do you afford all this glory on a reporter's salary?"

"I'm different."

"Why? Because you're gay?"

"No, because I'm rich. Let's go."

Casinos are built on the myth that luck lies in the next roll of the dice; the optimism that prosperity is in the next card and not just around the corner; and the greed of human beings dying to spend the rent money to cash in on something for nothing. Casinos sell euphemisms by the pound. Gambling is gaming. Blackjack dealers are buddies, and losers are high rollers.

But the house is not a home. Mason had represented a string of people who'd put their faith in hitting on sixteen and hit the skids instead. Some went home and beat their wives and kids. Some stole from their employers to cover their losses. Some went to liquor stores to buy something to make them forget, stealing it instead.

Mason didn't blame the casinos. They didn't round people up at gunpoint and make them empty their pockets. The casino owners, from the entrepreneurs like Ed Fiora to the shareholders of the publicly traded companies like Galaxy, knew there was a lot of money to be made in the stuff of dreams. Winning big was the American dream writ large.

The lobby of the Dream Casino was carpeted in deep red and gold, the walls papered in a soothing creamy shade, and the whole area lit by cascading floodlights. Above an arched entryway to the casino, images of demographically correct winners were plastered on the wall. Three couples—one white, one black, one Hispanic—were locked in ecstatic embraces as poker chips rained down on them. The casino's slogan made the point. "Take a Chance! Make Your Dream Come True!"

Mason and Rachel joined the crowd of people thick with fur coats and jewels. Her eyes glittered more than her diamonds, and her red hair shimmered like woven rubies. He shook his head, mourning the loss of Rachel to heterosexual men, himself in particular.

Hidden fog machines spewed white clouds in the path of the partygoers, creating a mystical sensation as they entered the casino. They might not have been walking into a dream, but the effect was like passing into another world.

"Can you believe this?" Rachel asked Mason once they emerged from the clouds. "It's a hundred and fifty thousand square feet; one of the biggest casino floors outside of Vegas and Atlantic City. Look at the people!"

Thousands were jammed hip to elbow as far as Mason could see.

Rachel may have had an invitation, but judging from the crowd, everyone else in town had one too, except for him. The crowds around the tables were so deep that the players had disappeared from view. The only open areas were in the pits, where pit bosses patrolled under the watchful eyes of the hidden cameras that ran the length and width of the casino.

Every person who entered a casino was videotaped from the moment he or she arrived until the moment he or she left. The only places that cameras weren't allowed were the bathrooms, and security guards checked them on a regular basis.

Rachel said, "I'm going to check my coat and wander. I'll meet you back here at midnight. Have fun."

There was a bank of slot machines to his right, each one singing out its electronic siren call. Bells and whistles begged the players for more money. Women wearing thousand-dollar designer dresses sat on stools in front of the slots, padded gloves on their right hands to avoid calluses from pulling the handle, plastic buckets in their laps to collect their winnings, whooping and hollering as the slots paid off.

Mason plunged into the crowd. He nodded and smiled at a few familiar faces and pretended not to notice those who stared at him a little too much.

A woman planted herself in his path, her platinum hair piled as high as her dress was cut low. The breasts of a well-endowed twenty-year-old poured out of her gown, the rest of the woman a good thirty years older. He tried to look away, but the press of other bodies around them made it impossible.

"Got 'em for Christmas, so might as well unwrap 'em," the woman told Mason as she cupped her hands under her breasts. Her speech was slurred and her stride was unsteady, her breasts the only things keeping her anchored.

"Deck the halls."

"Deck this, sweetie," she told him as she grasped his groin, laughed, and moved on to find her next grope.

Mason wedged himself into a blackjack table long enough to

win two hundred dollars, giving up the chair before it turned cold. He sliced his way through the crowd until he reached a wall of private poker rooms. Tony Manzerio, wearing the largest tuxedo ever made, stepped out of the room to Mason's left, forcing the crowd to go around him and trapping Mason against the wall.

Mason's shirt collar lost a size when Tony flashed the gun tucked in the shoulder harness under his tux jacket and motioned Mason into the poker room.

"Need a fourth for bridge?" Mason asked.

"Move your ass, wise guy. Mr. Fiora wants to talk to you."

"Lucky me. I didn't even have an appointment."

Mason walked past Tony, straightening his jacket with a studied nonchalance. Tony shoved Mason between the shoulder blades. Mason spun around, ready to shove back.

"Hey," Tony said with a shrug. "Your collar was messed up. I was just straightening it."

"Perfect. A hood with a sense of humor. Your mother must be so proud."

Mason stepped inside the poker room as Tony closed the door behind him, staying outside.

CHAPTER TWENTY-NINE

The room was six sided. A poker table in the same shape stood in the center, covered in green felt. Stacks of hundred-dollar chips surrounded a dealer's shoe filled with four decks of cards.

Ed Fiora was standing at the bar on the back wall. He was in his fifties, slicked-back hair, square chin, and a nose that had been broken more than once. He was skinny, not one intimidating muscle on his body. All his power and all his menace were in the two dead pools that passed for his eyes.

"So Tony found you."

"Not easy in a crowd like that."

"Not hard either. Video cameras picked you up when you came in with that bitch from the newspaper. What's her name? Rachel something?"

"Firestone. Rachel Firestone."

"Yeah, Firestone. You banging that broad? I hear she don't dig guys."

"If you're such a big fan of hers, why did you send her an invitation?"

"You think I made up the list? My PR people did that. They invited everyone with a pulse but you. You, I didn't invite."

"I'd hire new PR people."

Fiora measured him. "You're a smart guy, aren't you? Tony says you're always wising off. Offended him. Made him think you weren't listening."

"Is that why he's standing guard outside the door? To make sure I listen?"

Fiora poured himself a drink and took a sip, waving one hand at the door. "And to make sure nobody bothers us."

"He's a multitasking marvel."

"You don't give up, do you?"

"I don't respond well to structure. What do you want?"

"I thought you were the one who wanted to ask me questions."

"You'll just lie to me. I'll wait until you're under oath. Then I'll let you commit perjury."

"Perjury! Bullshit! I got nothing to lie about."

"Then why are you trying so hard to make my client plead guilty to something he didn't do?"

"Who says he didn't do it? Him? You? So what? He should take the deal the DA offered him. Everybody will be better off. Including you. Did you explain that to your client?"

"He wasn't moved. He figures if you kill me, he won't have to pay my bill."

"You keep up the jokes, Mason. Just remember all the laughs when it's over."

"What makes you think Jack Cullan's files will stay hidden just because my client pleads guilty? If those files are so valuable, someone will find them. Then what will you do?"

Fiora set his drink on the bar and walked slowly around the table until he was nearly on top of Mason. Fiora gave up more than half a foot and thirty pounds to Mason, but standing in front of him, eyes blazing, Fiora couldn't have cared less. He knew, as did Blues, that violence leveled all kinds of playing fields.

"Any motherfucker digs up dirt on me, I'll bury him with it. You got that?"

Mason was tired of being pushed and pulled by cops, politicians, and thugs.

"Sure. Now I've got news for you. Any motherfucker who threatens me, my client, or my dog better have more than an ape guarding his door. You got that?"

Fiora ran his tongue over his lips, pushed it around the inside of his mouth, and reached his hand inside his tux jacket. He pulled out a gun and rested the end of the barrel on Mason's chest.

"You got more balls than sense."

"Helps in my line of work." Mason pushed the gun away. "Happy New Year."

He opened the door and tapped Tony on the shoulder. Tony turned sideways so he could see his boss. Fiora nodded and Tony stepped aside for Mason.

"Hey, Mason. You find those files, come see me. We'll do some business."

"I don't think so."

"Don't be stupid. You'll live longer."

"Doing business with you? Not likely," Mason said, and headed back into the crowd.

CHAPTER THIRTY

Mason retreated to one of the many bars that ringed the gaming tables, ordered a beer, and watched the crowd from his stool. He added Fiora's name to the list of people who wanted him to find Cullan's files for them. He could live with the deals he'd made with Rachel Firestone and Amy White but wasn't willing to bet his life on a deal with Fiora.

A band of cheerleaders surrounding a craps table screeched as someone ran a hot streak even hotter. The shooter was the celebrity of the moment, mistaking a statistical anomaly for good looks, charm, and wit. Anything was possible while the dice were hot. A collective moan rose from the hangers-on and side betters when the shooter shot craps. His last reward was a few claps on the back as people shifted their loyalties and hopes to the next shooter, welcoming him with a joy and rapture usually reserved for tent meetings.

Mason caught a glimpse of Rachel now and then. Once she was taking her turn at rolling the dice, basking in the instant adoration of her own good luck. Not long after, he saw her huddled with another woman, a lanky brunette in a black pantsuit and open tuxedo shirt, sharing full-throated laughs and long looks. Mason had assumed that she was on the prowl for a story, not companionship. Instead, he realized, she was using the night to lose herself in the anonymity of the crowd and give free rein to impulse. Tomorrow, no one would remember.

Just after eleven thirty, Billy Sunshine arrived and began working the crowd. Amy White hung at his side, whispering the names of contributors who sought him out. She scanned the crowd, looking for opportunities or trouble. Her eyes caught Mason's for a moment, and her calculus was quick as she steered the mayor in the opposite direction. Mason tipped his bottle toward her in a small salute, acknowledging her good call. If she saw his gesture, she ignored it.

Thousands of balloons were gathered in nets suspended from the cavernous ceiling. Confetti cannons were aimed in a crossfire pattern to blanket the crowd. Scoreboard-sized digital clocks were mounted throughout the casino, counting the final minutes until midnight down to the tenth of a second.

Two of the clocks were visible from the bar. A drunken duo sitting next to Mason were arguing whether one clock was faster, settling the argument with a twenty-dollar bet on which would strike twelve first.

Mason set his bottle on the bar and turned to the two gamblers, who were studying the competing clocks with watery-eyed concentration.

"Hey. I saw a clock on the other side of the casino next to the roulette wheels that was a minute ahead of those two."

"No shit?" they asked in unison.

"No shit. There's a guy standing under it giving five-to-one odds that it hits midnight first."

"Damn," they said, and left their unfinished drinks to cash in on Mason's tip.

The bar was near the back of the casino. Mason decided to make his way to the front to be certain he was there at midnight to meet Rachel. He stood and waited a moment, trying to get his bearings. The casino was designed to obliterate all points of reference except for the tables and slots. There were no windows and, except on New Year's Eve, no clocks.

The noise level was rising to near deafening. Slot machines trumpeted new winners with bleating air horns. Piped-in music throbbed overhead with an orgasmic Latin beat. The craps tables erupted in roars as one good throw followed another. Even the blackjack players, notorious for their semicomatose poker faces, were high-fiving one another. The joint was jumping.

A sliver of the crowd parted in front of Mason as a woman cut through their ranks. People peeled away from her path as if she pushed them aside, or so it seemed to Mason, when he recognized her.

Beth Harrell, clad in a shimmering silver gown cut halfway to her waist, her head thrown back, was walking toward him. She was holding a mink coat over her shoulder, a string of lustrous pearls roped around her neck, a sly smile creeping across her face. He didn't move.

"Happy New Year, Lou," she said.

"I'm counting on that."

They stood for a moment, inches apart. She was probing. He was wondering. In a room of stunning women, she could have stopped the clocks with a single look. She handed him her coat, turned her back, and pressed herself against him as she slipped her arms into the sleeves. The sensation of the fur and her body against his was electric.

Beth faced him again, closer than before. Her perfume was heady. "Walk with me."

He followed her through an exit onto the outer deck. Heaters mounted along the wall glowed red, cutting the night's chill as they made their way along the dimly lit deck.

"Some riverboat," Mason said.

Beth laughed. "It's a barge permanently docked in a moat filled with water from the Missouri River. If the state legislature says it's a riverboat, that's good enough for me."

"And me."

She slipped her arm through his as naturally as if they'd been doing it all their lives. "I didn't expect to see you here."

"Into the belly of the beast. Ed Fiora wouldn't return my phone calls, so I decided to come see him."

"Alone?"

"Sort of. I came with a friend, but we're not together."

"Good," she said, emphasizing her satisfaction with a slight squeeze of his arm.

"How about you? Are you flying solo too?"

"I'm afraid so. Not many men are anxious to be seen with me these days, especially since my last date didn't live through the night."

"I suppose that would scare some guys away."

They had reached what was, in the mind of a fanciful architect, the prow of the boat. It was an elongated triangle that reached out over the Missouri River, ten feet wide at its base, narrowing to a couple of feet at its farthest point and enclosed by a four-foot wrought-iron rail. Pale blue Christmas lights strung along the rail provided the only illumination. They walked out onto the end of the prow and leaned on the rail as the chill breeze blew off the river.

"How about you, Lou? Are you afraid of me?"

He shook his head. "I don't scare so easy."

Beth eased her back against his chest and he slipped his arms around her middle. She covered his hands with hers, neither talking, until fireworks launched from the parking lot announced the arrival of the New Year. Tracers of red and streaks of blue arced high into the sky. Green and white clusters exploded overhead, raining glowing cinders into the swiftly moving current twenty feet below.

Beth rolled in Mason's arms, her lips brushing his. "Don't let me scare you." She pressed herself against him, kissing him softly, tentatively.

She pulled away for an instant, long enough to let him see in her quivering lips how much she wanted him, to let him feel the surge of need in her body for his.

Mason was lost in the moment, intoxicated with her taste, a series of small shudders building like shifting fault lines in his groin and belly. In that split second, he saw all that he wanted and all that he could lose and let her go.

"I'm sorry, Beth. I'm truly sorry. Maybe when this is all over, but not now."

The fire went out of her face as swiftly and coldly as the fireworks when they hit the water. She stepped back toward the deck, wiping her mouth with the back of her hand.

"Well, that's one way to start the New Year. Humiliate myself like a horny middle-aged broad who can't get laid."

"Don't do that, Beth. You're better than that."

"Am I?"

She didn't wait for Mason's answer, leaving him alone at the end of the prow.

CHAPTER THIRTY-ONE

Mason stayed where he was, perched like the lookout on the *Titanic*, staring across the Missouri. The wind was brisk, but he wanted to give Beth time to leave the casino without another embarrassing encounter.

She had locked onto him like a heat-seeking missile. She couldn't have known he was at the casino, let alone where to find him, unless someone told her. Only Ed Fiora could have done that. The more intriguing questions were why he'd pimp her out like that and why she'd let him do it.

He looked at the river, surprised at how far out over the black, swirling water the prow extended, when he heard a sharp crack, like a firecracker, and felt something ricochet against the railing, knowing but not believing it was a bullet. He whipped around in time to see a muzzle flash from the shadows of the deck, another bullet pinging off the rail.

He couldn't have been more exposed if he were doing backflips naked down Broadway. Two more shots careened around him, sending him crashing back and forth in the corner of the prow like a pinball and showering broken Christmas lights at his feet.

Stay where he was and the shooter would find him. Run and he'd catch a bullet. The river was his only option. Crouching and coiling his legs, hands gripping the wrought iron, he vaulted the rail, letting go as a bullet singed his side.

He hit the river at an angle, slapping his face on the water before the current swept him under. The icy water flash-froze him, his hands going numb as he fought to get out of his jacket, afraid it would drag him down. Kicking ferociously, he managed to break to the surface, gasping for air and treading water, trying to get his bearings.

The casino was already a hundred yards behind him, grim testimony to the swift current that had carried him to the center of the river, the bank too far away to think about. Swimming across the current would exhaust him before he got close, so he tried to cut it at an angle. That would keep him in the water longer but give him a better chance of reaching shore if he didn't freeze to death first.

He pressed one shoe against the other, slipping it off, doing the same with the other to give him a better kick. The cold was toxic, his arms and legs growing heavy, each stroke harder than the last. He was getting light-headed, the bank a distant blur.

Weariness crept into his bones and muscles until he couldn't lift his arms or summon more than a weak flutter from his legs. He was going to drown, and in that moment he smiled, the prospect somehow peaceful, the end of his struggle welcome. He closed his eyes and slipped beneath the water.

A raspy chopping sound stirred him as hard steel banged against his spine, caught his collar, and yanked him to the surface.

"Gotcha!"

Rachel Firestone dropped the fishing gaff she'd used to snag him, slipped her hands under his shoulders, and hoisted him over the side of the small boat, the effort putting her on her butt. Mason was facedown, half in and half out of the water. She rose to her knees, grabbed him by the belt, and dragged him the rest of the way into the boat, falling backward again and pulling him on top of her.

She squirmed out from under him, rolled him over, and opened his mouth, making certain his airway was clear, doing chest compressions until he coughed up river water and started breathing.

"When I told you to meet me at midnight, this is not what I had in mind," she said.

When Rachel got Mason to dry land and into her car, he refused to let her take him to a hospital. "I don't want to explain to an emergency room doc what happened," he said through chattering teeth. "Somebody will call the cops; then the press will get ahold of it."

"Fine. You'll probably catch pneumonia plus ten different diseases from the crap in the river, and it looks like you've been shot," she added, pointing to a red stain on the left side of his tuxedo shirt. "And in case your brain completely froze while you were in the water, I am the press and I've already got ahold of this story."

"You forgot our deal. Everything's off the record unless I say otherwise."

Rachel rolled her eyes. "Men are too dumb to live."

She draped her mink coat over him. "Take off your clothes."

"Does this mean you've changed teams?"

"Not in this lifetime. I just don't want you to freeze to death in my car. Makes a lousy obituary."

She drove and Mason did as he was told. The heater and the fur coat restored the feeling in his hands and feet by the time they reached his house. He got another chill when he saw an unfamiliar car parked in front.

"Don't worry," Rachel said. "She's a friend of mine."

Rachel's friend turned out to be a doctor who made house calls before sunrise on New Year's Day. She had a soothing, confident touch as she palpated and prodded him, not once asking him what had happened. He followed her instructions to take the hottest shower he could stand, after which she dressed the wound in his side, gave him an injection of antibiotic, and left samples of more antibiotics, to take over the next five days.

Mason dressed in sweats and heavy wool socks before coming downstairs to thank her, only to find that she had left. Rachel was alone in the kitchen, sitting at the table with two large mugs of steaming tea.

"Where's your friend?" He sat at the table and took a sip from his mug. "I didn't get to thank her."

"I thanked her for you."

"She didn't even tell me her name."

"You didn't need to know it. "

"Why? Is that another secret of the sisterhood?"

Rachel slapped her hand on the table, shaking her mug so that tea spilled onto the table.

"Damn you, Lou! I drag your ass out of the river before you drown and find you a doctor in the middle of the night on fucking New Year's Eve so that you don't have to go the hospital, where you belong, and you've got to crack dyke jokes."

Mason raised his hands in surrender. "I'm sorry. She was terrific. You redefine terrific."

Rachel grabbed a dish towel from the kitchen counter and wiped the tea that had spilled from her mug.

"Yeah, well, she is terrific and she couldn't exactly send a bill to your insurance company."

"I am suitably humbled. Tell her the door swings both ways. Make sure she knows where to find me if she needs me."

"I'll do that. Now, tell me what in the hell happened out there."

"Off the record?"

Rachel threw the dish towel onto the table in surrender. "Off the record."

CHAPTER THIRTY-TWO

"It was about a quarter to twelve and I was coming to look for you when Beth Harrell appeared out of the crowd like Moses parting the Red Sea. She asked me to take a walk with her."

"And since you are cursed with a penis, you had no choice."

"Jealous?"

"Of her? Not a chance. She's not my type."

"You don't give a guy any hope, do you?"

"Get this through your testosterone-drenched brain. No guy has any hope with me."

Mason sighed. "You have made me a believer. So Beth and I take a walk. We end up out on the end of the prow. She snuggles up, the rockets red glare, and she makes a pass at me."

"A beautiful woman comes on to you and you decide to jump into the river. Are you sure you're not gay?"

"You should live long enough to find out. In spite of what you might think about the curse of the penis, I turned her down. It wasn't pretty. She's got a fair dose of self-loathing inside that perfect body. She left and I gave her a good head start. The next thing I know, someone is shooting at me. The river was my only way out. How did you find me?"

"I guess it's time for my little confession." Mason's eyes widened. "No, you moron, I didn't shoot you, but that's starting to look like an attractive option."

"Latent heterophobia?"

"More like overt smart-ass phobia! Ed Fiora sent a bunch of invitations to the newspaper. I took one so that I could ask you to go. I threw you in just so I could watch what happened. I didn't think you could resist going after Fiora. I thought I could get a good story." She looked down and away, a red stain creeping across her checks. She wiped a tear from the corner of her eye. "I'm really sorry."

Mason let out a long, slow breath. "You didn't make me come with you and you didn't make me go out on that prow with Beth Harrell. But you did save my life, and that should balance anybody's books. How did you manage that?"

Rachel looked up. "My God, you are a mess of a human being! You come on to any woman with a pulse, you can't go two minutes without being a smart-ass, and you forgive way too easily."

"Makes you want me for a brother, doesn't it?"

"Yeah," she said softly. "It really does." They sipped from their mugs for a moment. "I saw Tony Manzerio fetch. I want to hear all about that, by the way. Then I just kept my eye on you. When you went outside with Beth, I went out another exit, figuring I could get close without being seen."

"You saw what happened?"

She shrugged. "I'm in the voyeur business. When she left, I was going to hustle back to the front of the casino and wait for you. Then I heard the shots and saw you jump in the water. I'd been to that casino a lot and I knew there was a boat tied up at the pier. There wasn't time to call the Coast Guard. I ran for the dock, which wasn't easy in this body condom I'm wearing. The rest is commentary."

"Did you see who was shooting at me?"

Rachel shook her head. "All I know is that it wasn't coming from my side of the deck. Whoever it was couldn't have been much of a shot. It would have been hard to find an easier target."

"Unless the shooter wasn't trying to hit me. Maybe the idea was to get me to jump, let the river do the rest."

"I still don't understand why you wouldn't go to the hospital and let the police take care of this."

Mason didn't say anything. He drained the rest of his mug and set it down on the table.

"Yes, I do. I am so dumb sometimes. You don't want to involve Beth Harrell in another scandal. You think she might really have something that you want."

"I do, but it's not what you think. You were watching me all night, but I don't think Beth was. The casino has video cameras everywhere, and Fiora monitors them. That's how Tony Manzerio knew where to find me. If Fiora had me on videotape making love under the stars with a key witness against my client, the court would kick me out of Blues's case in a heartbeat. When that didn't work, he went to plan B."

"Then the whole thing is on videotape. The shooting, everything."

"I'll take odds that those tapes are gone by now. I have to find out what's going on between Ed Fiora and Beth Harrell."

"Of course. You'll drop by, talk about old times, and she'll spill her guts."

"Something like that."

"This I've got to see."

"Sorry. No press. Don't pout. You'll still get your exclusive when it's all over. There is just one thing you may want to think about."

"What's that?"

"If Fiora saw Beth and me on videotape, he saw you too. I'd be very careful."

"Happy New Year to me," Rachel said.

CHAPTER THIRTY-THREE

Mason didn't know whether Beth Harrell would see him, but he liked his chances when the doorman at her building turned out to be named Jim and not Margaret.

He hadn't slept, too jazzed by his near-death experience. Unshaven and carrying bags under his eyes that been packed for a long trip, he didn't look like someone on the guest list for a New Year's Day breakfast. And it was seven a.m., too early for company. Jim squinted at him, ready to tell him that they didn't have a public restroom.

"Would you tell Beth Harrell that Lou Mason is here to see her?" Jim hesitated. "It's okay. We were together last night and I've got something I promised I'd return this morning on my way home."

Jim's raised eyebrows said he didn't believe a word of it, but he called Beth on the house phone, telling her she had a guest. "I'll send him right up, Ms. Harrell."

Riding the elevator, Mason wondered if she would tell him the truth and whether he'd recognize it if she did. She was a witness and suspect in Jack Cullan's murder and a possible conspirator in the attempt to kill him. She was also beautiful, troubled, and borderline irresistible, a combination that made him want to hold her close and keep her at arm's length at the same time. Rachel would have told him to leave his penis in the car.

She answered the door wearing a long white robe, tied loosely at the waist, and nothing else, finger combing her tousled hair.

"It's a beautiful morning." Mason said.

"The best so far this year."

She stepped aside, inviting him in, closing the door after him. She leaned against the door, letting her robe fall open for an instant before gathering it around her.

"If you've changed your mind about last night, I'm afraid I have too," she said. "I behaved very poorly. I hope you're not too disappointed in me."

It was the most contradictory rejection and apology Mason had ever received. The more he learned about Beth, the less he understood her. The more he saw of her, the more he wanted her.

"We need to talk. You should get dressed first."

Beth waited a fraction of a minute, letting him reconsider, nodding when he didn't. "Of course. I'll only be a minute." She left a renewed chill behind as she disappeared down a hallway.

The minute she promised turned into thirty. While he waited, Mason explored her apartment. There was a portrait in the living room of a brooding young girl set in shadow, her long blond hair hanging loosely over a thin white gown, open at the neck. The girl's fingers were wrapped in strands of her hair, her lips half open with wistful longing. Her features were soft, her eyes both dreamy and sad. The artist had captured an ache that reverberated throughout the girl, as if she'd seen her future and wished she could turn from it. He realized that the girl was Beth.

"I was fifteen. My mother was the artist," Beth said from behind him. "She painted portraits while my father took his secretary on business trips. She told me how he had cheated on her since before I was born but that she couldn't afford to leave him. Then one day, he left her. She said she wanted to paint me while I was still young and no one had crushed my heart like he had crushed hers."

She was dressed and had brushed the kinks out of her hair but wasn't wearing any makeup. She still looked beautiful, but for the first time, she also looked brittle, as if one more jolt would fracture her. The girl in the painting had seen her future.

"You said we needed to talk," she reminded him. "What about?"

"Why did Ed Fiora send you to find me last night?"

"Why do you think?"

"Then he did send you?"

"You won't consider the possibility that I was there alone, that I saw you and wanted to be with you?"

Mason hesitated, choosing his words. "I did consider that. It may even be true, but it's not the entire truth."

"A concession to your ego and my weakness, Lou?" He didn't answer. "It would be less humiliating if it weren't true at all. Then I'd just be a victim instead of a fool and you might be willing to help me."

"I can't help you if I don't know the truth, and I may not be able to help you even then."

She walked over to the painting. "My mother wasn't a prize either. She was cold and aloof, even toward me. She put her feelings in her paintings, stroking her brushes instead of my father and me. My father needed constant reassurance that he was wonderful and wanted. They made each other's weaknesses worse."

"It's a little late in life to be blaming dear old Mom and Dad, isn't it?"

Beth folded her arms over her chest. "You bet it is. I just got some of the worst from both of them, and I ended up looking for love in all the wrong places."

"That song has been covered by a lot of people."

"Listen, this isn't easy. I was so determined not to screw up like they did. I put everything into school and my career. I graduated first in my class, got a job with a top firm, went back to teach law school, got appointed to the gaming commission. I did everything right in public, but I made some bad choices in private."

"Including taking a bribe to approve the license for the Dream Casino?"

She shook her head. "No. I really thought Fiora's application was the best one. The key to it was the lease with the city for the location at the landing. It was the best deal for the taxpayers."

"What about Fiora's background?"

"We checked him out every way possible. He's rough around

the edges, but we found no compelling evidence that he was dirty."

"Then why the scandal?"

Beth looked at Mason, her lips pursed, then made her decision. "Fiora bribed the mayor. Jack Cullan set it up through a secret ownership in the Dream Casino."

"Can you prove that?"

"I heard enough whispers that I was going to have the gaming commission investigate it. I think we could have made the case."

"Why didn't you?"

"I didn't have time. Jack invited me to dinner. I assumed he wanted to ply me with liquor to find out where our investigation stood. I agreed to go because I thought I might learn something."

"Did you?"

"Yes. I learned what it was like to be offered a bribe. He let me know that I would be well taken care of if the investigation just went away."

"You turned him down?"

"I told him that we couldn't discuss commission business and he let it drop until we got to Blues on Broadway. Then he brought it up again. Only this time he threatened me."

"With what?"

Beth sat down on a sofa, sinking into the cushions. "I told you that I had made some bad choices. One of my husbands was the worst. I let him take some photographs of me." She dipped her head, bit her lip, and looked away. "Doing some things." She rubbed her palms across her eyes. "Jack said that he'd bought the pictures from my ex and had given them to Ed Fiora. He promised to get them back from Fiora if I played ball. That's when I threw my drink in his face."

Mason didn't know whether he should drop to one knee, take her hand in his, and promise to avenge her honor, or twist her arm until she agreed to take a polygraph test.

"That doesn't explain last night."

Beth took another deep breath and sat up straighter. "No, it doesn't. I was at the grocery and this huge man comes walking down the aisle and dropped an envelope in my cart. I thought it was an accident. Then I saw my name on the envelope. There was an invitation to the party inside and a copy of one of the pictures and a note that said Mr. Fiora looks forward to seeing me at the party. So I went."

"Did you keep the invitation and the picture?"

"No. I almost got sick right there in the grocery store. I burned them when I got home."

"What happened when you got to the party?"

"Fiora's moose found me. God only knows how in that crowd. Fiora told me where to find you."

"And the rest?"

Beth rose from the sofa and walked to the floor-length windows at the front of the room, her hands balled into fists. She banged them against the glass, pressed harder, and turned to face Mason.

"The little prick told me that since I liked being in pictures so much, he wanted to get some of you and me together. He told me to go find you and use my imagination. He said he'd be watching."

Mason thought about their embrace, her kiss, and his rejection of her. "What did you do after you left me out on the prow?"

"I got out of there as fast as I could, came home, and got drunk."

He stared at her, hoping to peel through the layers she was wrapped in and find something or someone he could believe.

"Right after you left, someone tried to shoot me. I had to jump into the river to get away. I got shot anyway and nearly drowned."

Beth's hands fluttered to her mouth and she let out a long, low moan as she slid into a heap on the floor. He reached for her and she pulled him toward her.

"Lou, you've got to believe me. I didn't know. It wasn't me. I'm begging you to help me. Get those pictures for me. I want my life back."

They stayed that way for a time, neither of them saying anything. Mason left without making a promise he didn't know whether he could keep.

CHAPTER THIRTY-FOUR

On Wednesday morning Leonard Campbell swept into Judge Pistone's courtroom for the start of the preliminary hearing as if it were the Oscars, stopping every few feet so that the press could take his picture, giving each reporter and photographer a hearty smile and a thumbs-up. He plopped his briefcase on the prosecutor's counsel table, pulled out an empty legal pad, and surveyed the courtroom like a commanding general, shooting his cuffs and snapping off a crisp nod to the press corps.

Patrick Ortiz arrived a few moments later, along with two assistants, one of whom pushed a two-wheel handcart loaded with bankers' boxes. The other assistant carried two-foot-by-three-foot enlargements of photographs of the murder scene and the victim, the autopsy report, and the results of the tests conducted by the forensics lab. They ignored Campbell and the media, emptying their boxes and setting up the files and exhibits they would use throughout the preliminary hearing.

Court was scheduled to begin at nine o'clock. Mason spent the previous hour locked in a cramped, windowless witness room, little bigger than a walk-in closet, telling Blues about Tony Manzerio, Ed Fiora, and his New Year's Eve swim. Blues was wearing the one suit he owned. Brown, worn at the elbows, and too tight across his shoulders, it was still a step up from a jailhouse jumpsuit.

"I should have told you about Fiora sooner, but I was afraid you'd try and break out of jail just so you could kick his ass," Mason told him.

"I might have done that. I think you were more worried that I'd take the deal to save your bony white butt."

Mason scribbled a bad sketch of the prow of the Dream Casino and laughed. "Yeah, I suppose that's right."

"Well, guess what? I'm not taking a fall for you or anybody else, and you know that. So why are you telling me now?"

"You understand street-war strategy better than I do. That's what this is. The trial may only be a side skirmish. I need your help tying all this together. I can't do my job if I keep you in the dark."

"In that case, get me bailed out of here. I can't do either one of us any good inside."

Mason said, "Pistone is going to bind you over and deny bail again. Our best chance is with the circuit court judge we draw for the trial. In the meantime, I'll try to find you a new suit."

Mason opened the door, and two beefy deputies on the Dunkin' Donuts diet plan approached Blues to escort him to the courtroom. Blues dropped his right shoulder and gave them a head fake like a running back looking for a seam, cackling when they grabbed for their guns and then blushed like schoolkids when they realized he was pimping them.

"Careful, now, boys. I'm a dangerous man," Blues said, sticking the needle in a little deeper.

One deputy cursed under his breath and the other nodded in vigorous agreement. A third officer joined them, and the three of them huddled outside the room while Mason and Blues waited. The largest of the three deputies stepped into the room, flanked by his comrades.

"We're gonna let your little joke go this time, big man. Don't fuck with us again or it's gonna be a rough ride back up in the elevator. Got me?"

"Lighten up, Deputy," Mason said. "He was yanking your chain and you just threatened him in front of his lawyer. That elevator gets stuck and you'll be on the other end of a civil rights charge faster than you can sing 'We Shall Overcome.' Got me?"

The deputy turned on Mason, his hand on his nightstick. "You tell your client we don't play games here."

Mason looked at Blues. "No games or they'll put you in time-out."

The deputies shepherded Blues through a side door into the courtroom. Mason followed, glad to have avoided the press. Blues took a seat at the defendant's table, the deputies occupying the row of chairs directly behind him.

Mason sat next to Blues, his chair covered in worn vinyl and thin padding. It swiveled and rocked, but Mason couldn't get comfortable.

The judge's bailiff, a stern-faced, middle-aged black woman, entered the courtroom through the door to the judge's chambers.

"Judge Pistone says that if he sees a camera in the courtroom, he'll add it to his collection. Pregame festivities are over. All rise! Hear ye, hear ye, hear ye! The Associate Circuit Court of the Sixteenth Judicial District is now in session before the Honorable Joseph Pistone. All persons having business before this court draw nigh and pay attention. Court is now in session."

Everyone stood as Judge Pistone shuffled up the two steps to his seat behind the bench, elevated above the masses to remind them of the power of the court. They all waited for his permission to sit down. Without looking up, he offered a dismissive wave.

"Be seated."

CHAPTER THIRTY-FIVE

Mason glanced around the courtroom as the door opened from the hallway. Harry Ryman and Carl Zimmerman slipped inside and leaned against the rear wall. Harry and Lou looked at each other, both trying not to reveal anything. Harry tipped his head at Lou, who responded with the same sparse gesture.

Mason found Rachel standing in the corner on the opposite side of the back wall from Harry and Zimmerman. They exchanged winks and smiles, comforting gestures, while the judge recited the name of the case and his instruction for the attorneys to state their appearances.

Leonard Campbell rose from his chair, buttoned his suit coat, and stepped to the podium in the center of the courtroom.

"The people of the state of Missouri are represented by Leonard Campbell, prosecuting attorney, and Patrick Ortiz, deputy chief prosecuting attorney. We are ready to proceed at the court's pleasure, Your Honor."

Campbell turned on one heel, struck a confident, serious pose for the crowd, and resumed his seat. Patrick Ortiz hated showboats and adopted Judge Pistone's head-down posture, pleased that the next time Campbell got up it would be to go to the bathroom.

Judge Pistone raised his eyes at Mason, who stood.

"Lou Mason for the defendant. We're ready. I've got a preliminary matter that I'd like to take up before we get started."

"Proceed."

"There are a lot of people in the courtroom, Your Honor. Some of them may be witnesses. I recognize Detectives Ryman and Zimmerman, who investigated this murder, and there may be some others. I'd like to invoke the rule that prohibits a witness from being in the courtroom prior to testifying."

"Mr. Campbell?" Judge Pistone asked.

Patrick Ortiz rose in Campbell's place. "We've got all our witnesses sequestered except for Detective Zimmerman. He's our first witness, and I guess he's just a little anxious to get started."

Ortiz's explanation drew soft laughter from the packed house, establishing his usual easygoing connection to his audience. There was no jury in a preliminary hearing. Only the judge would make the decision whether to bind Blues over for trial. Ortiz didn't need all the boxes or the blowups to make his case for Judge Pistone. He understood that the reporters in the courtroom would tell everyone who read a paper, listened to the radio, or watched television how overwhelming the state's evidence was. That message would reverberate with the people who would become the jurors who would decide this case. He also knew that Mason would pay close attention, gauging the gamble between trial and plea bargain, between a crapshoot for freedom and a date with a deadly needle.

"What about Detective Ryman?" the judge asked.

"We don't intend to call Detective Ryman to testify. I don't know what Mr. Mason's plans are."

Mason was surprised at Ortiz's decision to keep Harry off the stand. He wondered if Harry had asked to take a pass to avoid a confrontation with him, or whether it had been Ortiz's idea. Either way, Mason knew Harry wouldn't help his defense of Blues.

Mason said, "I don't intend to call Detective Ryman and I have no objection to his presence in the courtroom."

"Very well, Counsel. The rule is hereby invoked. No witness will be permitted in the courtroom until after he or she has testified. I expect the lawyers to enforce the rule by keeping a close eye on who comes and goes. Don't expect me to take roll. If you let somebody slip in, it's on you. Any opening statement, Mr. Ortiz?"

"Yes, Your Honor. Even though this is a pretty cut-and-dried case, I'd like to put the evidence in context for the court and let you know who you are going to be hearing from."

Mason was glad that the state had the burden to prove its case. He understood that was why the prosecutor got to go first at every stage of the preliminary hearing and trial—first to make an opening statement, first to put on witnesses, first to make a closing argument. But Mason couldn't stand going second. Sitting on his hands while Patrick Ortiz did his this-defendant-is-so-guilty-why-bother-with-the-trial routine was worse than having a tooth pulled slowly.

"How about you, Mr. Mason?"

"Your Honor, I'm certain that Mr. Ortiz believes that all of his cases are cut-and-dried, that the police only arrest the guilty, and that we could save a lot of tax dollars if we just skipped all this trial stuff. Fortunately, the Founding Fathers decided not to leave it up to Mr. Ortiz, or me or you, to decide innocence or guilt in this case. The jury will make that decision. I'll save my opening statement for the trial."

Mason didn't want to admit that he had nothing to say at this point in the case except that the prosecuting attorney was taking orders from Ed Fiora to offer Blues a plea bargain. He could add that Amy White wanted Mason to find Jack Cullan's secret file on the mayor even though she assured him that it had nothing to do with the murder. He might mention that someone had tried to kill him after he refused to play ball with Ed Fiora. He could describe how Fiora had blackmailed Beth Harrell into trying to seduce him and that she had asked Mason to get back the blackmailer's blackmail so she could seduce him, for her own reasons. None of which, he would have to admit to Judge Pistone, he could prove any more than he could prove that Blues was innocent. So instead, Mason took a shot at Ortiz's understated arrogance and sat down.

"I would suggest that both counsels save their editorial comments for the press, except I'm imposing a gag order. No one connected with this case will discuss it in public outside of this courtroom. When we're done here, this case is going to be assigned to a circuit court judge. I don't want the first motion filed by the defendant to be one moving the case out of the county because there's been so much publicity the defendant can't get a fair trial. Now, let's get to it. Mr. Ortiz, you may begin."

"Excuse me, Your Honor," Mason interrupted. He stood, hands raised, underscoring his regret at delaying the proceedings again. "I'm certain you didn't intend to prejudge this case, but your comments suggest that you've already decided to bind the defendant over for trial. If that's so, I'm compelled to ask that this case be reassigned to another court."

Judge Pistone glared at Mason. "The last time you were before me, Mr. Mason, you practically accused me of being pressured to deny your client bail. I invited you to prove such and you declined. Now you are suggesting that I have prejudged the case against your client. Tell me? Is it your desire to be held in contempt by this court? If you are, I shall be happy to oblige you."

"Not at all, Your Honor. I'm certain that you misspoke when you said that this case was going to be assigned to a circuit court judge. That will only happen if you bind the defendant over for trial. You can't know until you hear the evidence whether you will make that decision. I didn't want to leave that impression on the record without bringing it to the court's attention. Perhaps you'd like the court reporter to read back your comment."

Mason was willing to dig a deep hole because Judge Pistone had made up his mind, and, just like Ortiz, Mason had more than one audience. The judge had just testified on behalf of Blues in the court of public opinion. Mason had given the press a different lead than one about Blues's guilt. They could now write a story about how Mason had trapped the judge with his own words, continuing Rachel Firestone's theme that Blues was getting the bum's rush. The judge wouldn't hold Mason in contempt since that would elevate Mason to martyr status for a wrongfully accused client. Instead, the judge would have to swallow hard.

Judge Pistone, known for his disinterested demeanor, was eye-popping mad at Mason and gripped the edge of the bench as he fought to keep his self-control. He wouldn't risk asking the court reporter to read his comments aloud.

"Thank you for bringing to my attention what was clearly an unintended and unfortunate choice of words. I assure you that I have the highest regard for the presumption of innocence. If you have any doubt on that score, you may request another judge. Is that your desire, Mr. Mason?"

Taking hits from the court to deflect attention from his client was a defense attorney's high-risk, don't-confuse-me-with-the-facts ploy that meant one thing: the defense attorney didn't have dick. Having played the card, he let it go.

"Not at all, Your Honor. As you said, let's get to it."

CHAPTER THIRTY-SIX

Patrick Ortiz ambled to the podium, a rumpled, overweight everyman who knocked back a few brews on the weekend, watched sports, talked about women, and sent men to death row.

"Your Honor. I agree with Mr. Mason about one thing. It's not his job or mine to judge the facts. It is our job to tell you what the facts are. But don't make the mistake Mr. Mason did. You are the only judge of the facts at this point in this case. Before a jury is asked to decide the defendant's guilt, you are asked to decide whether there is reasonable cause to believe that a crime was committed and that the defendant committed it. If you find that there is probable cause to believe those things, then you must bind the defendant over for trial.

"Mr. Mason seized on an innocent misstatement by the court to suggest that you have prejudged this case, although he knows that you haven't and wouldn't. Mr. Mason has his own reasons for trying to keep our attention away from the facts and away from his client. When the state has finished presenting its evidence, listen closely to hear if Mr. Mason denies any of the facts we present to you. Listen to hear if he offers any other explanation for who shot Jack Cullan in the eye with a .38-caliber pistol. Listen to the silence from Mr. Mason, because that's all you will hear.

"I told you that this case was cut-and-dried. Tell me if I'm wrong. Jack Cullan was found murdered on Monday, December tenth, by his housekeeper. He'd been shot to death. Mr. Mason won't deny that. The preceding Friday night, Mr. Cullan and Beth Harrell had been customers at a bar owned by the defendant called

Blues on Broadway. Mr. Cullan and Ms. Harrell quarreled. The defendant intervened and fought with Mr. Cullan. Afterward, the defendant threatened Mr. Cullan with physical harm if he interfered with the defendant's liquor license or came back to his bar. Four witnesses, including Ms. Harrell, will testify at trial to the fight and the threat. Mr. Mason won't deny that.

"Blood and tissue belonging to the defendant were found under the fingernails of the murder victim. The defendant's fingerprints were found in the room in which Mr. Cullan died. The defendant has a history of violent conduct, including shooting to death an innocent and unarmed woman while he was a police officer. The defendant has no alibi. Mr. Mason won't deny any of that.

"There is more than enough evidence to bind the defendant over for trial on the charge of murder in the first degree. I call that a cut-and-dried case and make no apology for it. I wonder what Mr. Mason calls it."

CHAPTER THIRTY-SEVEN

Patrick Ortiz presented his evidence in a smooth procession of well-prepared witnesses, finishing at five o'clock. Mason did not call anyone to testify.

Blues remained impassive throughout the long day. When Dr. Terrence Dawson, chief of the forensics lab, testified that Blues's fingerprint had been found in Cullan's study, Blues reached over to Mason's legal pad, writing *bullshit*, pressing hard enough with his pen to cut through to the next sheet of paper.

Judge Pistone said that he would deliberate in his chambers before announcing his decision. When he returned fifteen minutes later with renewed pep, Mason concluded that he had used the time to go the bathroom and have a cup of coffee.

The judge ordered that Blues stand trial on the charge of first-degree murder in the death of Jack Cullan and that he continue to be held without bail. He added that the case had been assigned for trial to Judge Vanessa Carter and that Judge Carter had set the case for trial beginning Monday morning, March 4.

Everyone stood while the judge made his exit. Leonard Campbell clapped Patrick Ortiz and his assistants on their backs, straightened his jacket, and left, looking for the nearest microphone. Ortiz packed his briefcase and shook Mason's hand, telling Mason that he'd done a good job. It was the standard empty praise of an adversary who'd won the day, Mason grinding his teeth as Ortiz delivered the bromide.

The three deputies surrounded Blues again while one handcuffed him. Mason pressed into their circle and tapped fists with him.

"Today was their day, man," Mason told him. "Tomorrow will be ours."

Blues nodded. "Get 'em," he said, and left with his escort.

Mason looked around the empty courtroom. On paper, no one could have found fault with what had happened there. The state had met its burden of proof. Even he conceded that. No appellate court would overturn Judge Pistone's ruling, even though Mason was convinced the judge had decided the case before breakfast.

The system had worked, except for one thing. Mason was certain that Blues was innocent. That realization had led him to another conclusion. He would have to find justice for Blues outside the courtroom.

Now, hours later, worn with fatigue, Mason stared at the notes he'd written on the dry-erase board, replaying the few points he'd scored during cross-examination of the prosecution's witnesses, looking for leads.

Carl Zimmerman testified first. He was an experienced witness, directing his answers to the judge, who sat upright in his chair, watching Ortiz and Zimmerman play catch with softball questions. Mason wasn't surprised that Judge Pistone had abandoned his usual head-down disinterest. Murder had that effect on people.

Ortiz took Zimmerman through each step of the investigation, beginning with the call he received from the dispatcher about a hysterical woman claiming to have found her employer shot to death. The woman turned out to have been Norma Hawkins, the housekeeper. Mason started his cross-examination with that description.

"Norma Hawkins told the dispatcher that Mr. Cullan had been shot to death. Is that correct, Detective?"

"Yes, sir."

"The body was found facedown and hadn't been moved when you arrived at the scene, correct?"

"That's right. The uniformed officers who arrived at the scene first secured the area. The housekeeper said that she hadn't touched anything in the study."

"No gun, bullets, or shell casings were found at the scene, correct?"

"Correct."

"In fact, when you arrived at the scene, you didn't see anything that told you Mr. Cullan had been shot. Isn't that correct, Detective?"

Zimmerman stiffened as he saw the high hard pitch coming. "I suppose that's correct, Mr. Mason. But, there's no question that Mr. Cullan had been shot."

"Yet, somehow, Norma Hawkins knew that Mr. Cullan had been shot. That's what she told the dispatcher. True?"

"Well," Zimmerman said, stalling for a better answer than the one he had, "I don't know what she told the dispatcher. I could have heard him wrong."

"There is another explanation, isn't there, Detective?"

"What's that, Mr. Mason?"

"Norma Hawkins shot Mr. Cullan."

"Objection!" Patrick Ortiz said. "The question calls for speculation. There is no evidence that Norma Hawkins committed this crime. She's an innocent woman who doesn't deserve to be smeared by Mr. Mason."

"The police and the prosecution rushed to judgment in this case," Mason shot back. "They picked their suspect at the beginning and disregarded any other possibilities."

"Sustained, unless you've got better evidence than that," Judge Pistone said. Mason didn't.

Norma Hawkins was the next witness. She was a slightly built white woman in her late thirties whose rough hands and sloped shoulders testified to the hard work she did and the hard life she led. Norma spoke slowly and softly, in the upstairs-downstairs tradition of domestic help, describing her daily routine at Jack Cullan's house. Then Ortiz asked her about finding the body.

"What happened when you came to work on Monday morning, December tenth?"

Norma leaned forward in the witness box and clutched the

hem of her dress. "Well, it was like I told the detectives. The alarm wasn't on, so I figured Mr. Cullan was still home. He usually wasn't there when I got to work, so I'd have to turn off the alarm. He gave me the code 'cause he knew he could trust me, you know. I been cleaning people's houses since I was fifteen. Everybody gives me their alarm codes. I never had any trouble till that morning."

"What did you find when you went inside the house?"

"First thing I noticed was that it was freezing in that house. I kept my coat on, it was so cold. I went looking for Mr. Cullan to find out why the furnace wasn't working, and I found him lying facedown on the floor in his study. I turned him over and could see that he was dead. I called 911."

"Did you know that he'd been shot?"

"I saw blood. I didn't know what else to think."

Ortiz placed the enlarged photograph of Jack Cullan's body on an easel. Cullan was lying facedown in the photograph, a dark pool of blood seeping around his head and out into the carpet.

"Does this photograph accurately depict what you saw when you entered the study?"

Norma trembled and turned away, nodding her head. "He was a good man, always treated me fair."

"No further questions," Ortiz said.

CHAPTER THIRTY-EIGHT

Mason leaned the photograph facedown and out of sight against the front of the jury box. Ortiz had used it for the press, not Norma Hawkins.

Norma had explained why she had assumed that Cullan had been shot, and Mason knew he wouldn't get anywhere chasing the slim chance she had killed him. Instead, he waited for Norma to gather herself before probing gently on cross-examination about minor matters, more for the purpose of blunting the emotional impact of the photograph than anything else.

Norma admitted that Cullan often forgot to set the alarm. It was a small thing, but Mason knew that credibility was built on a foundation of small things. The more he could chip away at it, the more likely it would crumble.

Pete Kirby, resplendent in a dark green suit and cranberry vest, described the fight in the bar. When he quoted Blues's threat to tear Cullan's head off and stuff it up his ass, a ripple of laughter cut through the audience, causing Judge Pistone's bailiff to rise and glare the offenders into silence. Kirby admitted on cross-examination that he hadn't taken Blues's threat seriously.

"Yeah, it was jive," Kirby said. "Except with Blues, it was real serious jive. The man was making a very heavy point."

Dr. Terrence Dawson, the forensics examiner, was the last witness. He was a thin man with a sharply angular face who had risen through the ranks of the police laboratory over twenty years to become the director of forensic science. He explained on direct examination how he had matched Blues's blood and tissue samples to those found under Cullan's fingernails and how he had matched Blues's fingerprints to one that had been lifted from the corner of the desk in Jack Cullan's study.

"Dr. Dawson," Mason began, "I assume that other fingerprints were found at the scene besides the ones you claim belonged to Mr. Bluestone?"

"Yes. That's quite common."

"I'm certain that it is. Whose prints did you find?"

"The victim's and the housekeeper's, of course."

"Anyone else's?"

Dr. Dawson glanced at Patrick Ortiz. Mason also looked at Ortiz, who had suddenly become interested in a stack of papers on his table.

"There were a number of fingerprints found throughout the house; most of them were too smudged or incomplete for identification," he said after Ortiz failed to help him by objecting to Mason's question.

"But not all of them, right, Doctor?"

"That's correct. We were able to identify fingerprints belonging to Ed Fiora and Beth Harrell. We matched them with their fingerprints on file with the Missouri Gaming Commission."

"Where in Mr. Cullan's house were those fingerprints found?"

"Mr. Fiora's fingerprints were found in the kitchen. Ms. Harrell's fingerprints were found on the headboard of the bed in Mr. Cullan's bedroom."

Mason felt like a boxer wearing cement shoes. Patrick Ortiz had spent the entire day dancing around him, landing jabs to his midsection and uppercuts to his chin. Mason had been unable to get out of his way. Dr. Dawson had sucker punched him without knowing it. The press would draw every salacious inference possible about the relationship between Jack Cullan and Beth Harrell. Mason couldn't blame them. The image of Beth in Cullan's bedroom crowded his own memory of the embrace they had shared. He didn't have room for both.

The assignment of Blues's case to Judge Carter had been the last kidney punch of the day. Judge Carter, a former prosecutor, was a conservative Republican with a reputation for harsh treatment of criminal defendants, an African American woman with ambitions to become a federal judge. Mason was worried that she would use Blues's case as a stepping-stone.

Mason studied the dry-erase board. In the last three weeks it had become a jumbled patchwork of lawyer's graffiti. He drew red circles around the keywords and phrases—*Cullan's secret files—pictures of Beth—blackmail by Fiora—Blues's fingerprints—Harry and Blues—why kill me?*

He was convinced that the identity of the killer lay within those scraps. The last of them, the question about whether he would live or die, shook him more than he cared to admit. Maybe it was the late hour, or maybe it was just that he didn't have Blues to watch his back this time.

He went down the hall to Blues's office. The bookshelves, file cabinet, and desk were all gunmetal gray. The floor was bare hardwood and the walls were decorated with a calendar. A digital electric piano sat against one wall. When Blues played, it was like decorating the room with a bucket of rainbow paint.

Mason pushed the piano away from the wall and used a key Blues had given him to open a small safe hidden in the floor. He lingered over the contents of the safe, his hands sweating as he fought with himself. Shivering at the too-recent memory of the river's cold grip, he reached into the safe and picked up the gun Blues had given him a little over a year ago.

"It's a .44-caliber semiautomatic with a nine-shot magazine," Blues told him. "Fits in a holster that goes in the middle of your back. Wear a jacket or a loose shirt over it and no one will notice."

Mason had barely survived the death of his old law firm and, along the way, had shot a hired killer named Jimmie Camaya, who was supposed to have added Mason to the law firm's obituary list. Camaya had been arrested but later escaped. Blues had convinced Mason that he should carry the gun for his own protection. Mason had reluctantly agreed, and Blues had taught him how to handle the gun. After a few months, he returned the gun to Blues.

"I'm not going to spend the rest of my life walking around waiting to shoot it out with someone who's probably forgotten all about me. I'm a lawyer, not a gunslinger."

"And this isn't Dodge City," Blues said. "It's Kansas City, but you've got a real talent for pissing off people who don't know the difference. I'll keep the gun for you. My money says you're going to need it sooner or later."

Now, alone in his office with his gun and holster, he wished he had a corner man to patch him up, rub him down, and shove him back into the ring when the bell rang for the next round. Blues was his corner man, and Mason needed him. Bone weary, Mason lay down on his sofa and let it wrap its arms around him.

CHAPTER THIRTY-NINE

Mason woke to find his aunt Claire sitting in one of the chairs next to the sofa. She was reading the newspaper and sipping coffee from a stainless-steel mug. The coffee's aroma was strong enough to wake the dead.

"You didn't answer your phone at home last night or this morning, so I thought I might find you here," she said.

Mason sat up, running his tongue over his teeth, stretched his arms and legs in a spread-eagle salute, and flopped back onto the sofa. He felt trampled.

"You didn't consider the possibility that a beautiful woman had taken me home to comfort her?"

He pushed himself to his feet and stumbled toward the dry-erase board.

"Have you looked in the mirror? Anyone who picked you up would take you to the nearest shelter. Make that the nearest animal shelter. And don't bother with your board. I've been here long enough to read it and the newspaper."

Mason changed course for the refrigerator next to his desk. He was surprised to find a bottle of orange juice.

Without looking up from her newspaper, Claire said, "You're welcome. By the way, the next time you decide to sleep in your office, lock the door and don't leave a gun sitting on your desk. Put it under your pillow like all the other action heroes. Just don't shoot yourself in your sleep. That would be pathetic."

Mason gulped half the bottle of orange juice before taking a breath and wiping his mouth.

"Any more advice?"

"Sorry, I'm fresh out."

Claire read the newspaper, and Mason looked out the window, watching the morning sun glance brightly off the windows on the building across the street. She folded the paper and dropped it on the table in front of the sofa. The headline shouted back at her— *Ex-Cop Bound Over for Murder.*

"So," she said with as much neutrality as she could muster, "someone is trying to kill you again. That's why you have a gun. Who is it this time?"

Mason drained the last of his orange juice, banking the empty bottle off the wall and into the wastebasket.

"Don't know."

Mason marveled at his aunt's capacity to listen to the most outrageous stories of abuse told to her by her clients without betraying a hint of her own outrage. She explained that her clients had enough emotion invested in their problems without seeing their lawyer lit up as well. He was glad that she employed the same detached interest as he told her about his riverboat adventure.

"You could talk to Harry."

"Not this time. You were right. It's too complicated."

"Can I help?"

Mason considered her offer. His love for her was as unconditional as hers was for him. She was his anchor, his reality check. She never waited for him to ask for her advice or help. She gave it whether he wanted it or not. That she had come to check on him, not demanded that he call Harry, not called Harry herself, and only gently berated him, underscored how delicate the situation was.

"There's too much going on here that I don't understand, and I don't want to be the last one to figure it out. The key players couldn't be more connected if they were inbred. You could fill in one branch of the family tree for me. Tell me what happened between Harry and Blues."

"Why is that so important?"

"Harry thinks Blues got away with murder six years ago. He's using this case as payback. I think somebody knows that and is using Harry to make sure Blues is convicted. I can't go to Harry unless I know what happened."

Claire studied the headline in the newspaper, deciding what to do. It was a silent sound bite, incapable of telling the whole story. Yet it was enough for most people, and all that many would read or remember. She realized that wouldn't be enough.

"Harry and Blues had been partners for a couple of years. Harry had taught Blues at the academy, helped him along when he first got on the street, and recommended him for detective when Blues took the exam. Harry always said that Blues had the best instincts of any detective he'd ever seen but that he also had one of the worst weaknesses."

"He used violence too easily?"

"It wasn't just that. The violence came too easily to Blues. He didn't get worked up or enraged. He just did it and went on. Harry didn't know why. He worried that Blues had a dead spot that made it too easy to kill. It scared Harry because he didn't want Blues to get it wrong. Someone would die."

"So why didn't Harry wash him out at the academy? Why promote his career and take him on as his partner?"

"I met Harry for the first time at the Nelson Art Gallery. He was sitting on a bench in the Chinese Temple in front of the statue of the Water and Moon Bodhisattva. The Bodhisattva was a Buddhist god that was supposed to protect the faithful from catastrophe. That's what Harry does. That's why he became a cop. That's why he took Blues on as his partner. He'd seen men who had that dead spot, and he thought he could keep it from happening to Blues."

"That doesn't explain what happened with the shooting."

"It was a drug bust. They had an informant who claimed that some Colombians had brought in a substantial quantity of cocaine and were setting up shop on the East Side. Blues was the first one through the door of the apartment. The Colombians were waiting for them. Blues and Harry both would have been dead if they hadn't been wearing Kevlar vests. Two of the Colombians were killed."

"I remember when it happened. Harry wouldn't talk about it, but it was all over the newspaper. The woman Blues shot was a prostitute who had a gun."

"She was in the back of the apartment. Blues went room to room. He heard a noise. It was Harry's nightmare come true. Blues said he thought the girl had a gun, but she didn't, though she wasn't innocent either."

"Who was she?"

"She wasn't a prostitute. She was the daughter of a very wealthy man who used her father's money as seed capital for her drug business. She hired the Colombians to bring in the cocaine. The father settled for Blues's badge rather than have the story made public. And there was some question about whether the father knew where his money was going."

"That's a pretty tough story to cover up."

"Not if your lawyer was Jack Cullan."

Mason came out of his chair. "Harry and Blues went along with the cover-up?"

"They didn't know. She didn't have any ID on her. Later, Harry and Blues were fed the prostitute story. The Internal Affairs investigation was kept quiet. Blues was given a choice to resign or be prosecuted. It was a bluff that worked because no one wanted to hang the department's dirty laundry in public, including Harry and Blues. Blues took the deal."

"How do you know what happened if Harry and Blues don't know?"

Claire gathered her coat, finished her coffee, and stood, facing Mason.

"I represented the wife when she divorced her husband six months later. He told her what had happened, and she couldn't spend another moment under his roof. She told me."

"What she told you was confidential. Why are you telling me?"

"The purpose of the attorney-client privilege is to protect the client. My client committed suicide last month. The privilege didn't do her much good."

143

"Did you tell Harry?"

"Yes. I told him this morning. I should have told both of you sooner. I'm sorry."

"What did Harry say when you told him?"

"He thinks Blues found out that Jack Cullan had cost him his badge and had been waiting for a chance to get even. He thinks Blues used the incident at the bar with Beth Harrell as cover."

"That makes no sense. Blues has been charged with the murder, not Beth."

"Harry says that Blues got careless when he left a fingerprint in Cullan's study. Otherwise, Beth Harrell would have been the number one suspect. Harry thinks Blues is using you to get him off. Harry says that you'll try to convince the jury that Beth Harrell killed Cullan."

"That's a hell of a risk for Blues to take."

"Harry says that a man with a dead spot takes risks no one else would consider."

"Does Harry know that you've told me all of this?"

"He asked me to tell you. He's afraid that Blues will take you down with him. He wants you to convince Blues to take a plea."

"I'm Blues's lawyer, not his coconspirator. How can Blues take me anywhere except to the poorhouse when he doesn't pay my fee?"

Claire walked over to Mason's board, picked up the black marker, and drew a large circle around Mason's question *why kill me?* "Someone knows the answer to that question, Lou. Don't take too long to find out."

CHAPTER FORTY

Mason decided it was time to connect the dots instead of waiting for someone else to draw the picture for him. He'd spent the last three weeks scrambling to get ready for the preliminary hearing even though the outcome was a foregone conclusion. The trial was in sixty days, and he would have to use that time to make something happen, beginning with getting Blues released on bail.

He called Judge Carter's chambers to request a bail hearing. He was surprised when the judge's secretary informed him that Judge Carter would send out an order that day setting a hearing for the following Monday, January 7, at eight o'clock. Shortly after he hung up, his fax machine rang and whirred as the judge's order arrived. He was reading the order when Mickey Shanahan knocked at his open door.

"This is not a good look for you, Lou," Mickey told him. "You've got to be perma-pressed and lightly starched, wrinkle-free, know what I mean, man? No worries. Everything is cool. That's what the people expect. This I-spent-the-night-in-a-Dumpster look isn't going to cut it. Listen to me. It's all about image."

"Turn around." Mickey hesitated. "Turn around now."

Mickey saw the gun on Mason's desk, blanched, and did a quick pivot. "I'm just trying to help, for chrissakes. That's no reason to go ballistic, man."

Mason walked over to the dry-erase board and closed the cabinet doors. He was tired of people walking in and reading his mind.

Returning to his desk, he picked up the gun, balanced it in his palm, and shoved it into the holster. It felt like a prop, not a part of him. He couldn't decide whether to put it away or put it on. The fear he'd felt the night before had receded as he hid the attempt on his life behind the closed cabinet doors. He shook his head at the image of himself as a heat-packing action hero. Carrying a concealed weapon was the road to Palookaville, the punch line to a bad joke. He put the gun in a desk drawer, slamming it shut loudly enough to make Mickey jitterbug in the doorway.

"Dude! Give a guy some warning that you're gonna make him piss his pants for saying hello."

"At ease. About face."

Mickey peered over his shoulder at Mason, taking care to look for the gun, before turning completely around.

"Hey, you still look like shit. You know that, man. That's not good, not good."

"I'm not interested in your fashion advice. How good are you on the Web?"

Mickey brightened as if he'd just added a thousand gigabytes to his game. "A Web site is just what you need. I can have it up for you by the end of the day."

"I don't want a Web site, Mickey. I want every word ever written about Ed Fiora. Can you do that?"

Mickey locked his fingers together and stretched his arms out. "Any six-year-old can do that in his sleep. I can do better than that."

"How much better?"

"Asset search, bank accounts, anything you want. There are no secrets anymore. Everyone's life is floating in cyberspace, waiting to be bought or sold."

"Do it."

"Does this mean I'm on the team?"

Mason thought for a moment, hoping he wasn't making the wrong choice, not just for him but for Mickey.

"Sure."

"Do we get T-shirts? T-shirts would be cool. Great way to build the brand."

"Only if we win," Mason said.

A shower and a shave later, Mason parked in front of what was once the People's Savings & Loan Building on the corner of Twentieth and Main. The bank had owned the six-story building until it went under during the thrift crisis in the 1990s. Jack Cullan bought the building and moved into a second-floor office.

Many law firms spent lavishly on impressive entrances to their offices, with carefully designed logos, nameplates, and eye-catching art, one local firm bragging that the paneling in its office had been made from a rare tree found only in the Amazon rain forest. Mason appreciated the simple inscription painted on the solid oak door to Jack Cullan's office—*Attorney.*

Shirley Parker looked up from her desk as Mason closed the door behind him. She had a buoyant, upswept hairstyle that had been fashionable decades ago but was now a silvery-blue-tinted artifact. She was a stout woman with stiff posture and disbelieving eyes, going through the motions because she didn't know what else to do.

"Yes, may I help you?" she asked.

"My name is Lou Mason," he said, as if that would be explanation enough.

"I'm Shirley Parker, Mr. Cullan's secretary."

Mason wasn't certain where to start. He guessed that Shirley had been Cullan's secretary long enough to know his secrets and how to keep them and wouldn't surrender them just because her boss was dead.

"I'm the attorney for Wilson Bluestone."

"Yes. I know who you are."

She gave no hint whether she cared who he was or whether she resented him, as she must have hated his client.

"I'm sorry for your loss."

It was a clumsy gesture, and Mason regretted he hadn't been more sincere, though Shirley was gracious.

"That's very kind of you."

Mason looked around, nodding. The furniture in the outer office was nearly as old as he was, though it had fewer nicks and scratches. Framed prints from a Monet exhibit hung on the walls. A stack of unread magazines sat on a corner table at the junction of a short couch and a chair.

"It must be difficult closing up a law practice under these circumstances. I imagine you've been going nuts trying to get clients placed with new lawyers, files transferred, and all those other things."

"Yes," was all she said, not agreeing or disagreeing.

There were only a handful of papers on Shirley's desk, no more than would have come in the mail on an ordinary day. Her computer screen was on CNN's home page. The phone hadn't rung since Mason walked in.

He realized that there were no storage cabinets, no places to keep client files or the secret files. Maybe Shirley had already transferred the clients and their files and was just coming in each day to open the mail until there was no more mail.

"It looks like you've pretty much cleaned things up. You must have already shipped out the client files."

Shirley didn't respond, waiting for Mason to say something that warranted another polite acknowledgment.

They smiled at one another for a long minute, neither speaking until Mason quickstepped past her and opened Cullan's private office. He was through the door before she could try to stop him.

CHAPTER FORTY-ONE

"You can't go in there!" she said, and was on his heels before he could turn on the light.

The office was a mirror of Mason's, down to the oversized sofa with shoes and clothes strewn across the cushions and a refrigerator parked next a desk littered with papers. Mason was certain that Shirley had removed anything confidential, leaving the rest in the grief-driven hope that Cullan would walk through the door one day as if nothing had happened.

Shirley stood in the doorway, arms folded across her chest. Mason took a step toward her. She didn't back up.

"Where are they, Shirley?"

"Where are what?"

"Your boss's secret files. The dirty pictures and other trash he collected all these years."

"I don't know what you're talking about."

"Sure you do. How long did you work for Jack? Twenty years, thirty years? You had to know about the files and you had to know where he kept them."

She didn't flinch. "I'll have to ask you to leave."

"Of course you do. That's your job even though your boss isn't here to tell you. Maybe you didn't know what he was up to. Maybe he liked you well enough not to make you an accessory to blackmail, extortion, and racketeering. All things considered, you'd be better off helping me now than answering all these questions in court, under oath."

"As I said, Mr. Mason. I don't know what you're talking about.

Please leave now."

Mason stopped in front of a black-and-white photograph of an old man and a young boy. They were shaking hands in front of a barbershop, the barber's pole framed between their outstretched hands. It was on a wall covered with photographs of Cullan with politicians and celebrities, but he didn't recognize either the man or the boy.

"Who are they?"

Shirley sighed, her hands hard on her hips. "I'm going to call the police if you don't leave now."

Mason raised his hands in surrender. "Okay, I'm convinced. Just tell me who's in the picture and I'll leave. That can't be a state secret."

"Very well. The young boy is Mr. Cullan. The other gentleman is Tom Pendergast. Now, please leave."

"No kidding? Tom Pendergast. When was this taken? Last question, I promise."

"I'll tell you on your way out." She locked the door to Cullan's office and ushered him out into the hallway. "Nineteen forty-five," she said.

Back in his car, Mason looked up at the window to Cullan's office. For an instant, he thought he saw Shirley Parker lingering in the shadows, but then dismissed the image as a trick of the sun against the glass and his own creeping paranoia.

He started to pull away when he saw a barber pole bolted to the wall of a building across the street. The barbershop, and the rest of the block, was vacant, but the photograph in Cullan's office and the barber pole triggered his memory of a story his grandfather told him.

Tom Pendergast ran Kansas City during Prohibition and after, ruling with a velvet hammer Cullan must have envied. He was ruthless to some, generous to others, handing down decrees and handing out favors from an office above the abandoned barber shop across the street from Cullan's office.

Mason's grandfather, Mike, had gotten his start in the wrecking business when Pendergast had given his blessing to his grandfather's plan to salvage the scrap from the construction of Bagnel Dam at the Lake of the Ozarks and sell it. Afterward, his grandfather had gone to Pendergast's office to pay the man his respects and a cut of the profits. Pendergast had accepted the gratitude but not the cash, and Mason's grandfather had been on his way, though his patron eventually went to jail for tax evasion.

By 1945, when the picture had been taken, Pendergast had been released from jail, his organization lay in ruins, and he had only a short time to live. The young Jack Cullan couldn't have known or cared about Pendergast's background. It must have been pure coincidence that he shook hands that day with the man whose career he would emulate. Looking back years later, Cullan probably saw it as a portent, his first step on a well-trod path.

CHAPTER FORTY-TWO

There was a small diner, another relic from pre-fast-food times, one block south on Main. It was the last building on the east side of the street and offered a handful of parking spaces in a lot on the south side of the building. Mason pulled into the parking lot and called Mickey Shanahan.

"Law offices of Lou Mason. To whom may I direct your call?" Mickey said.

"Are you auditioning for a job as a receptionist too?"

"No job too small, no duty too great. Pay me soon; it's been a week since I ate."

"I'm not surprised. Your shtick is from hunger. While you're cruising the Internet, go to the county's Web site and check property ownership records for 2010 Main. In fact, check the ownership records for that entire block. The west side of Main between Twentieth and Twenty-First. Call me back when you've got something."

The Egg House Diner was a twenty-four-hour restaurant with a counter that seated eight and a row of booths along the front window, none of which were occupied when Mason picked one. A man of indeterminate age, wearing layers of soiled clothing and a strong odor, sat at the counter, stirring a cup of coffee. A large black plastic bag, stuffed to its limit, lay on the floor at his feet.

Mason chose a booth that gave him a clear view of the vacant barbershop. He picked up a menu that had more stains than entries. A few moments later, a flat-faced woman with dull eyes and thin hair, wearing a lime-green-and-white-striped waitress uniform, brought him a glass of water and took his order for a turkey sandwich. He took the first bite when his phone rang, the caller ID telling him it was Mickey.

"What do you have for me?"

"The whole block is owned by New Century Redevelopment Corporation except for 2010 Main. Shirley Parker owns that building. Her name mean anything to you?"

"Yeah. It means I'll be out the rest of the day."

Mason spent the afternoon in the booth at the Egg House Diner. The man sitting at the counter did the same. The waitress, used to customers who spent little, talked less, and stayed forever, left him alone. He watched the traffic on Main Street, waiting for Shirley Parker to jaywalk from the People's Savings & Loan Building to the barbershop across the street.

He wasn't good at sitting and waiting. He lacked the patience for a stakeout, though he wasn't certain whether sitting in a restaurant qualified. He figured a real stakeout meant sitting in a dark car, drinking cold coffee, peeing in a bottle, and scrunching down in the front seat whenever someone drove by. He was just killing time in a dumpy diner, kept company by people who had no place else to go.

After a while, he retrieved a yellow legal pad from his car and tried to reproduce the notes from his dry-erase board. He wrote the names and the questions again, adding order and precision to the notes without finding any new answers. He drummed his pen against the pad until the vagrant at the counter silenced him with an annoyed look. No one else came into the diner.

At three o'clock, he ordered a slice of apple pie and a cup of coffee to be polite. He picked at the pie and stirred the coffee, then told the waitress to give it to his counter companion. The man gave him another annoyed look but didn't send the snack back to Mason's booth.

By five o'clock, clouds had moved in, hastening the transition from dusk to dark. Headlights blinked on, slicing the gloom on Main Street as people began making their way home. As if on cue, the man at the counter grunted at the waitress, hoisted his plastic bag over his shoulder, and left, giving Mason a final silent stab on his way out the door.

A pair of city buses, one northbound, the other southbound, stopped at the corner of Twentieth and Main, momentarily blocking his view. When the buses pulled away, he saw Shirley Parker jostling the lock on the door to the building that housed the barbershop. He waited until she was inside before leaving the diner, trying to remember when he'd had his last haircut.

CHAPTER FORTY-THREE

The door to Shirley Parker's building opened into a long, dark hallway that led to the back. Bare wooden stairs to the second floor narrowed the passage. No one was in the hall when Mason stepped inside. He stood still for a moment, listening, hearing nothing.

A door to his right would have opened into the barbershop had it not been lying on its side, propped against the wall as an afterthought. The shop was empty except for an ancient barber chair tilted in the reclining position, as if its last occupant had come in for a shampoo and shave. Steel bars had been bolted to the storefront window frame, a stark concession to the uneasy plight of an abandoned building made too late to save anything but memories.

A naked lightbulb at the top of the stairs cast shadows at Mason's feet. The silence was broken by the sound of shoes scraping overhead. Shirley Parker was upstairs in Tom Pendergast's old office.

Mason had spent the afternoon in the Egg House Diner betting that Jack Cullan had hidden his secret files in Pendergast's office, the irony of using his hero's headquarters too delicious to pass up. Putting the ownership of the building in Shirley Parker's name was a thin dodge, arrogance mistaken for cleverness—a common weakness of bad guys. Superman never would have put Jimmy Olson's name on the deed to the Fortress of Solitude.

Mason had also bet that his questions had unnerved Shirley Parker, forcing her to conduct her own stakeout of the barbershop to confirm that Mason didn't try to break in. When he didn't, she still couldn't resist checking on the files to be certain he hadn't somehow sneaked past her.

Breaking and entering was a Class D felony, not an upward career move for most lawyers. Mason convinced himself that he was neither breaking nor entering; he was simply making a business visit knowing that Shirley was inside. Besides, he had no intent to commit any crime on the premises, at least not at that moment. He just wanted to talk with Shirley Parker.

As he stood at the foot of the stairs, the plan that had made so much sense as he sat in the booth at the diner now struck him as foolhardy. Shirley had refused to answer his questions in Cullan's office during normal business hours. Popping up like the Pillsbury Doughboy in Pendergast's office after hours wouldn't loosen her tongue. She would call the police, and the files would disappear overnight.

His insight produced Plan B, and in that moment he understood the curious reasoning that landed his clients in jail. It was a mix of overstated need, self-justification, and unfounded optimism that he could pull something off that a rational person would never consider.

Uncertain exactly when and where he had crossed that line, he was confident that it really was a good idea to hide in the basement until Shirley left the building, then search Pendergast's office until he found the files. Tomorrow morning, he would serve Shirley with a subpoena for the files, and then sit back and watch Patrick Ortiz marvel at his resourcefulness.

His eyes adjusted to the dark as he felt his way along the hallway, soon coming to the backside of the stairway, where he found a door that he hoped led to the basement. Taking care not to aggravate squeaky hinges, he nursed the handle until he felt it release, then eased the door open just enough to slip through. Probing the black space with one foot, he confirmed his guess about a basement and stepped down onto the first stair, pulling the door closed behind him, sweating in spite of the cold that crept up the stairs.

He spent twenty minutes on the top stair until he heard Shirley coming down from the second floor. He opened the basement door a crack to make certain he would hear her leave, taking comfort in Shirley's unhurried gait and unbroken march down the stairs and out the door. She didn't hesitate as she would have if she had heard or sensed his presence.

Mason waited another five minutes before heading upstairs. Shirley had turned off the light at the top of the stairs, and Mason didn't want to take the chance that she was watching from across the street for a light to come on, leaving him to feel his way along the wall with his hands. If he could have seen his feet, he would have kicked himself for not bringing a flashlight.

He found the door to Pendergast's office and was relieved that Shirley had left it unlocked. The office was darker even than the stairwell, as if it had been sealed. Recalling that there was a double window overlooking Main Street and that he'd seen blinds on that window when he'd looked up from his car, he felt his way to the street side of the room to peek through the blinds. When his fingers found smooth drywall all along that surface, he became disoriented, so uncertain of direction that he circled the room twice as his mouth dried up in a blind man's panic.

On his second pass, his knuckles brushed against a switch, flicking it on. He leaned against the wall, squinting until his pupils stopped dilating. The double window had been covered, the blinds still in place, so that the outside world would see the window, unchanged and unopened—but a window nonetheless. Inside, the light was captive, unable to illuminate the secrets behind the walls.

The room was empty. Mason imagined Pendergast sitting behind a desk, dispensing favors or broken legs as the moment required. He envisioned a couple of overfed cronies in snap-brimmed fedoras, smoking sour cigars, giving witness and protection to Pendergast's patronage practice. He thought of his grandfather, genuflecting with a humble "Thank you, Mr. Pendergast." There were no reminders of those times, no photographs on the walls, not even outlines in the dust on the floor where the furniture had been.

There was a sliding panel built into the wall, which Mason guessed would have been behind Pendergast's desk, because that would have given him a straight-on view of each supplicant or sucker who crossed his threshold. A circular groove had been cut at one end of the panel into a finger hold with which to pull the panel open. A lock had been added directly above the groove. Mason tried it without success, not surprised when it didn't yield.

There were no lock picks or crowbars lying on the floor, so Mason used his shoulder to loosen the lock. It gave on the third try, splintering the wood. He shoved the panel back along its track and stepped into a walk-in closet lined with wooden file cabinets. Expecting the drawers to also be locked, Mason yanked on the nearest one, almost falling over when it spilled into his arms.

The names on the files should have read *Pay Dirt*. Instead, they were labeled with the names of the rich and powerful, including Billy Sunshine, Ed Fiora, and Beth Harrell. He didn't have time to read them before his career as a second-story man ended like a scene from a late-night rerun.

"Police! Freeze! Put your hands where I can see them, and turn around real slow!"

CHAPTER FORTY-FOUR

Mason left the drawer gaping open and did as he was told. A cop aimed his service revolver at Mason from the doorway. Mason could see Shirley Parker peering around the cop, her eyes drawn in beady satisfaction.

"I'm unarmed."

There was no point in telling the cop that this was all a misunderstanding, that he hadn't really done what he'd so clearly done. He expected to be arrested and was more interested in not getting shot.

"Up against the wall, legs and arms spread wide."

Mason complied again, flinching as the cop ran one hand down his sides, up his legs to his crotch, under his jacket, and around his middle.

"Okay. You can turn around now."

The cop was tall, square shouldered, and vaguely familiar until Mason read the name beneath his badge, James Toland. He was the cop Blues had decked when Toland had tried to put cuffs on him, Mason understanding the impulse. He waited for Toland to pull out his handcuffs, read him his rights, and end his career. None of which happened.

Shirley Parker stepped past them and into the closet, conducting a quick inventory. Toland broke the silence.

"Do you want to press charges, Miss Parker?"

"There doesn't seem to be anything missing. You can let Mr. Mason go."

Toland looked like a kid whose Christmas had been canceled.

"Must be your lucky day, pal."

Mason felt his blood start circulating again as he realized why Shirley had granted him a reprieve. He might have been guilty of breaking and entering, but she was sitting on the mother lode of blackmail, which would make her the next front-page defendant. Whatever Shirley intended to do with the files, exposing their existence wasn't an option.

She stepped back into the room, her face bleak and ashen. She knew she was in over her head. She had gone through life doing what Jack Cullan had told her to do, maybe nursing a quiet love that was never noticed or returned, resigned to her life at his side, loyal and lonely. She'd been angry and afraid enough at Mason's intrusion to call the cops, but she'd outsmarted herself and could only let him go.

Mason had more questions for her that he was certain she wouldn't answer, but he couldn't resist the most obvious.

"How did you know I was here?"

"There's a motion detector on the stairs. Satisfied, Mr. Mason?"

"Completely. I'll be back in the morning with a subpoena for those files, so take very good care of them tonight. You've got enough problems without adding a charge for obstruction of justice."

Mason hurried back up the street to the Egg House Diner, checking over his shoulder to see when Shirley Parker and Toland left the building. He'd just slid into his booth when they emerged. Shirley locked the door, pulling a steel bar across it that he hadn't noticed before.

Toland watched her cross the street back to the People's Savings & Loan Building before climbing into his squad car and driving away. Mason waved as Toland passed the diner, pleased with his escape and happy for Toland to know that he was still keeping his eye on the files.

A second shift had come on duty during his absence. A waiter had replaced the waitress, and a homeless woman seated at the counter had taken the place of the homeless man. Though he couldn't be certain, Mason suspected that the waitress and the homeless man had simply traded places. The waiter's pale skin looked even paler against his two-day growth of beard when he shoved a glass of water across Mason's table. Not wanting to push his luck, Mason ordered another turkey sandwich. The woman huddled inside her tattered overcoat and scarves as if she were in a cocoon for the winter.

"Give her some dinner and put it on my check," he told the waiter.

The waiter returned to the counter, leaned over to the woman, and spoke too softly for Mason to hear. A moment later, the woman shuffled off the stool, gave Mason a poisonous glare, and disappeared down Main Street. The waiter shook his head as if cursing himself for not knowing any better. Mason had tried taking a page from his aunt Claire's book, only to realize that it was now a different book, titled *No Good Deed Goes Unpunished.*

Mason didn't trust Shirley Parker to leave Cullan's files where they were until he showed up with a subpoena the next morning. He didn't know whether there was another entrance to the barbershop, and he couldn't watch both Shirley and the barbershop all night. Nor was Mason thrilled at the prospect of spending the night in the diner, pissing off homeless people. The simplest solution was to make a deal with the prosecutor. Mason would tell Ortiz about the files in return for Ortiz's promise to share the contents with him. Ortiz would track down Judge Carter and get a search warrant before Shirley Parker had a chance to move the files.

Mason's deal with Ortiz would cancel the ones he'd made with Rachel Firestone and Amy White and more than disappoint Ed Fiora, but that couldn't be helped. He called Ortiz, not surprised that he was still working long after most county employees had gone home.

"Patrick Ortiz."

"Patrick, it's Lou Mason. I've got a great deal for you."

"Too late. I told you the plea bargain was off the table if we went to the preliminary hearing."

"Forget the plea bargain. I'm going to make you the hero in

this case. Jack Cullan was blackmailing Beth Harrell and a lot of other people, maybe including the mayor. I've found the files he kept on those people."

"So you're calling to report a crime committed by a dead man?"

"I'm calling to tell you to get a search warrant for those files so you can prevent them from disappearing. Those files are evidence in Cullan's murder. The killer is probably someone Cullan was blackmailing."

"Your client is the killer. Did Cullan have a file on him?"

"I don't know. Listen to me. Cullan's secretary has those files squirreled away in Tom Pendergast's old office on Main Street. She's an accessory to Cullan's blackmail. She knows that I know about the files, and if you don't get a search warrant for them tonight, they'll be in a shredder before sunrise."

"Sorry, Lou. I'm not going to bother Judge Carter tonight on a bullshit story like that. You want to take it up with the judge tomorrow, give me a call. I've got work to do."

CHAPTER FORTY-FIVE

Mason wanted to throw his phone across the room. Instead, he called the homicide division, hoping that Harry Ryman was working late. Carl Zimmerman answered instead.

"Carl, it's Lou Mason. Is Harry around?"

"Nope. He had to go see a witness, a guy he's been chasing for a couple of weeks. What's up?"

Mason hesitated. He intended to tell Harry the entire story and ask him to help babysit Cullan's files until Mason could talk to the judge in the morning. He even hoped that Harry would send a couple of uniformed cops to sit outside the barbershop all night. Mason didn't know Zimmerman well enough to ask for a favor like that, but he didn't have another choice. He decided to keep his story simple to convince Zimmerman that there was a good reason to help him out.

"Jack Cullan was blackmailing Beth Harrell. He kept secret files on her, the mayor, and Ed Fiora, plus a lot of other people. I've found Cullan's files but I can't get to them. The prosecutor won't ask Judge Carter for a search warrant tonight. If we wait until tomorrow, the files could be gone. I know you're convinced that my client killed Cullan, but there's a good chance something in those files will prove he didn't. I need your help to make sure nothing happens to them."

"Where are the files?"

"In Tom Pendergast's old office above the barbershop at Twentieth and Main."

"Anybody there now?"

"No."

"Who else knows about the files?"

"Cullan's secretary, Shirley Parker. That cop, Toland, who was with you when you arrested Blues, knows that there's something in that office, but I don't think he knows what it is."

"Where are you now?"

"In a diner up the street from the barbershop."

"Sit tight, Lou. I just caught a case on a dead body in Swope Park. I'll meet you when I'm done with that. It may take me a couple of hours, but it's the best I can do."

"Thanks."

A couple of hours passed, and then another. Mason tried Harry's number again without any luck. He called the dispatcher, asking her to contact Harry and tell him to call Mason. When Harry didn't call, he left the same message for Zimmerman. He called his aunt Claire, who told him that she hadn't spoken to Harry all day. The waiter was eyeing Mason like he should start charging him rent for the booth when Mason's phone rang.

"Harry?"

"It's Zimmerman. What's going on?"

"I'm growing old in this diner. I think the waiter is about to add me to the menu."

"Leave him a big tip. I'm stuck in the park. Stay where you are and wait for me."

"Right," Mason said, having decided in the same instant that he couldn't wait any longer.

Mason left a ten-dollar tip for a five-dollar meal and went to his car. His ex-wife had once given him a tool kit to keep in the trunk. It was one of the first indications that they didn't know each other as well as their glands would have liked. Mason's tool of choice to fix anything was a hammer he could use to beat whatever was broken into submission. The rest of the tools were for guys who knew the difference between a flat head, a Phillips head and a blackhead. He found a small flashlight, grabbed the hammer, and got ready to commit his second felony of the night.

CHAPTER FORTY-SIX

Mason made his way to the alley that ran behind the barbershop, looking for a back door or a window, knowing that he had to be faster than the cops if he tripped the motion detector again. Clinging to the shadows in the alley, he hoped that Shirley Parker hadn't already taken Cullan's files out the back door, sticking him with a great case of he said, she said.

The possibility left Mason with a thin sweat and a twisted gut by the time he reached the rear of the barbershop. Sweeping the flashlight across the wall, he heaved a deep breath mixed with relief and frustration when he discovered there was no rear door or rear window on the first floor. There was, however, a second-story window next to a fire escape with a ladder that ended well beyond his reach.

There was a Dumpster in the alley a few yards away. Mason shoved it across the uneven pavement until it was beneath the ladder. Climbing on top, he reached for the ladder, finding himself still a foot shy of the bottom rung. He stuffed the flashlight and the hammer into his belt and backed up to the edge of the Dumpster. Measuring the short step to the wall, he took a running step and launched himself at the ladder.

The cold iron froze against Mason's hands as he held on to the bottom rung, gaining purchase with his feet against the brick wall. He pulled himself up, his breath coming in sharp gasps, until his feet found the bottom rung. A moment later he was on the catwalk beneath the window, certain that he was about to be caught in a cross fire of searchlights while some cop demanded that he throw down his hammer before they opened up on him.

The window was locked or nailed shut. He shined his flashlight through the glass and could make out the top of the stairs. He hoped the motion detector was at the bottom and not at the top.

He pulled off his sweater, using it to muffle the hammer, broke the window, and climbed inside, broken glass crunching under his shoes, assuming that he had set off the motion detector. He had no more than a couple of minutes to grab the files, get out, and make up an alibi.

He left the light in Pendergast's office off, feeling less exposed in the darkness. The flashlight beam glanced off something shiny in the center of the floor that Mason didn't remember seeing a few hours earlier. Dropping to one knee, he picked up a white, quarter-sized campaign button with the words *Truman for Senator* in blue. Tom Pendergast had been Harry Truman's political godfather.

He aimed his flashlight at the walk-in closet, certain that someone had dropped the button on the floor while removing other more current political souvenirs. He traced the flashlight beam up to the lock he had broken, when he was flattened by a blast that shattered the panel door, opened the floor like an earthquake, and dropped him into the barbershop.

He slammed into the outstretched barber chair, bounced off onto the floor, and crawled beneath the chair while fire and debris rained from overhead. The explosion was loud enough to scramble the eggs at the Egg House Diner, but Mason was deafened by the blast before his brain could register the sound. Though he was stunned, he understood how life turned on such small moments as bending down to pick up a button. Had he been standing, the panel door would have cut him in two when it blew out from the wall.

Mason ran his hands over his scalp and face, checking for wounds too fresh to hurt, finding a trickle of blood from a cut above one ear. He pulled off his shirt to cover his mouth and nose against the acrid smoke that had enveloped him.

The initial wave of debris had settled into fiery heaps feeding flames racing up the walls. He staggered to his feet, giving a quick and futile pull to the steel bars covering the barbershop window. The glass had blown out into the street and the cold air tasted sweet even as it fueled the fire.

Cars stopped on Main Street, and passersby stood in front of the People's Savings & Loan Building, pointing and screaming at him to get out in voices that he imagined more than heard. He agreed with their advice even if he couldn't find a way to take it.

The flames were engulfing the outer walls of the building. Mason glanced up through the hole in the floor above and saw that the fire had eaten through the roof, obliterating the stars with billowing smoke. He could feel his clothes heating up as if they were about to ignite.

Gagging into his shirt, he made his way to the front door, cursing Shirley Parker and the bar that she had locked into place like a coffin nail. Any thought of escaping out the window the way he had come in vanished with the stairs that were crackling like seasoned kindling as the fire roared down on him.

Ducking to stay as close to the ground as possible, he stumbled down the hallway to the basement door. Covering the door handle with his shirt, he pulled the door open, yanked it closed behind him, and bolted down the stairs, grateful for the pocket of cool air in the basement. He leaned against the rough cement wall and slid down to the floor, gasping and wondering how long it would take the fire to burn through the first floor and bury him.

His question was answered a moment later. The stairs to the second floor collapsed into the basement, carrying the fire with them.

Mason jumped to his feet, looking around at blank walls that now glowed with a deadly orange like one of Dante's chambers. Smoke rolled across the ceiling, shrinking the basement. In the far corner, he saw a half-open chest-high door and raced over to it.

Shirley Parker lay on the floor, propping the door open. Mason knelt alongside her, feeling for a pulse in her neck and wrist. Her eyes were open, unseeing and untroubled by the smoke. A dark stain above her left breast was still damp with blood. Mason now understood Norma Hawkins's certainty that Jack Cullan had been shot.

The door led to a tunnel. Ducking inside and crouching under the low ceiling, Mason felt his way, counting his steps to gauge the distance. Fifty paces later, the tunnel ended against a locked door. Bracing his arms against the walls of the narrow shaft, Mason kicked at the door until its hinges surrendered, letting him into another basement.

He took a few deep breaths and went back into the tunnel, bent over and trotting until he reached Shirley's body. The heat and smoke from the fire rolled through the tunnel. Mason hoped the flames wouldn't follow. He pulled Shirley's body back to the other basement, closing her eyes and laying her down against the floor. There was no peace in her soft features.

The basement was filled with framed and unframed paintings, stacked against the walls. There were two stairways, one that led to the first floor and another that led to a door with a small window in its center. Mason trudged up the second stairway and opened the door into the alley behind the barbershop. It took him a moment to realize that the tunnel had passed beneath the alley.

He saw firemen running up the alley carrying a hose. A fire engine blocked the entrance to the alley, its red and white lights cascading across the pavement. Two paramedics raced toward him from the south end of the alley, waving and calling to him. Reaching him, one put her arms around him to hold him up while another peered into his eyes.

"Hey, buddy!" one of the paramedics mouthed. "Are you all right?"

"Yeah," wondering whether the paramedic could hear him if he couldn't hear the paramedic. "There's a woman's body down there," he added, not certain whether he was whispering or shouting.

He opened the door and pointed down the stairs. The paramedic who had been holding him up led him toward an ambulance while her partner went back for Shirley Parker.

CHAPTER FORTY-SEVEN

The police had blocked off traffic on Main Street except for emergency vehicles. The spectators who'd been first in line in front of the People's Savings & Loan Building had been herded a safe distance away. Two fire department pumper trucks were pouring heavy streams of water into the burned-out shell that had been Pendergast's office. Local television stations had dispatched live crews to the scene. Cops, firefighters, reporters, and rescuers did their dance.

No one noticed Mason and his paramedic escort when they first emerged from the alley and made their way to an ambulance parked half a block south of the barbershop. By the time the paramedic had persuaded Mason to get inside the ambulance so she could examine him, he'd been picked up on the media's radar. Reporters clustered around the ambulance, jostling for an angle. Rachel Firestone squeezed through and sat down next to him. The paramedic started to order her to get out, but Mason said she could stay.

His hearing was gradually coming back, first a dull roar of unfiltered noise, then a steady ringing like a flatlined heart monitor, and then voices.

"I let you out of my sight for five minutes and you get into trouble!" Rachel told him. "Look at you. You're a mess!"

"I forget. Are you my big sister or little sister?"

"I'm just a sister, and you're still a mess. What in the hell happened?"

Before he could answer, Carl Zimmerman waded through

the throng of reporters, trailed by a uniformed cop and the police department's director of media relations, who politely but firmly ordered the reporters back behind the police line.

"You too, Miss Firestone," Zimmerman told her. "You'll get your shot at him if there's anything left worth having, but we get to go first."

"Detective, do I look the kind of girl who'd settle for sloppy seconds?"

Zimmerman didn't let his cop face slip. "I wouldn't know."

Rachel gave Mason a peck on his ash-stained cheek. "Save something for me."

Zimmerman glared at Mason. "You are one dumb-assed motherfucker, you know that? I don't know whether to arrest you or just throw you back into that fire and save Harry Ryman the trouble of kicking your tail into next week."

"You hold him down and I'll kick him," Harry said as he joined his partner.

Mason looked at both men and then at the paramedic. "Am I in any shape to have my ass kicked?" he asked her.

"In your condition, you probably won't even notice. I get the impression that you deserve it, but don't call me when they're finished. I'm not interested in repeat business." Turning to the detectives, she added, "He'll be black and blue and shitting soot for a week, but he's all yours."

Mason climbed out of the ambulance as Harry and Zimmerman each took him by an arm.

"Am I under arrest?"

Harry answered. "Not until we figure out all the things to charge you with. Let's get a cup of coffee first."

Mason groaned as they led him to the Egg House Diner. "Too bad this place didn't blow up."

The waiter gave Mason his I'm-not-surprised look as they slid into a booth, Mason on one side facing Harry and Zimmerman. The homeless woman was back at the counter and giggled into her coffee cup as she exchanged a wink with the waiter.

Mason caught his reflection in the window. His face was camouflaged with soot; his hair was spiked with blood. He was draped in a thin blanket the paramedic had given him, his pants blackened and torn. He understood the homeless woman's laughter. She looked better than he did. He wondered if she would offer to buy him dinner.

The waiter brought them three glasses of water. "Turkey sandwich?" he asked Mason.

"Two coffees, black," Harry said. "What do you want Lou?"

"Nothing. I've had enough."

"Why didn't you wait for me, like I told you?" Zimmerman asked.

Mason had an answer that was good enough for him, though he doubted it would satisfy Harry and Zimmerman.

"Cullan's files were the key to his murder. If I couldn't get my hands on them, I couldn't prove you guys were wrong about Blues. Ortiz hung up on me when I asked him to get a search warrant. The two of you were fighting crime. I was afraid someone would get to them before you were finished, so I went after them myself. Turned out I was right. Someone blew them up or stole them and made it look like they were blown up."

"You better rethink that bullshit when the judge asks you to show remorse," Zimmerman said.

"For what? Breaking and entering?"

"That's chump change," Zimmerman said. "I suppose you're going to tell us that Shirley Parker invited you down into that basement so you could pop her?"

Mason looked at Harry, not believing what he was hearing. "Get real. You can't possibly think I shot Shirley Parker."

"Who said she was shot?" Zimmerman asked him, enjoying the role reversal from Mason's cross-examination.

"Good for you, Carl. I had that coming. Maybe the killer just threw the bullet at her."

Harry interrupted. "Lou, this is serious. Officer Toland reported that he caught you inside that building earlier tonight but that

Shirley Parker refused to press charges. He says that you threatened her. Carl tells you to sit tight, which for you is not possible. You and Shirley are the only ones inside that building when it blows up, and you are the only one who comes out alive. Only Shirley is shot to death, not blown up. How does all that look to you?"

"It looks like head-up-your-ass police work that is a lot easier than figuring out what really happened. Like figuring out who blew up the damn building, who knew about the tunnel to get the files out before they blew up the building, and who would kill Shirley Parker to make sure nobody found out what was in those files."

"You'd been sitting on that building all day," Zimmerman said. "You could have found the tunnel, found the files, and been caught again by Shirley Parker. Only this time she wasn't going to let you off, so you killed her."

"You left out that I also decided to blow my ass up along with the building to hide the evidence of my crime. Harry, if you guys are really looking at me for this, take me downtown, book me, and let's go see a judge. I'll crucify you in court and the media will pick at what's left."

Harry said, "You keep up this cowboy shit, and you won't leave us any choice. Same as Bluestone."

"Okay, I'll be a good boy. But do your job. Check out the slug that killed Shirley Parker. Odds are that the same gun was used to kill Jack Cullan. That will clear Blues."

"We don't need you to tell us how to do our job, Counselor," Zimmerman said. "If you killed Shirley Parker, I'll see to it that you share the needle with your client."

"Carl, you know it's not safe to share needles. Leave the waiter a nice tip."

Rachel was waiting for Mason when he got to his car. He was shivering under his blanket, envious of her warm parka.

"No," he told her.

"No, what?"

"No, I'm not letting you take me home, patch me up, and put me to bed again unless you're in it, and that ain't likely."

"You need to learn to value a woman's friendship for more than her vagina, Lou. It would broaden your horizons immeasurably. How about you take me home, I wait for you to patch yourself up, and then you tell me what happened? After which, you can go to bed by yourself."

"Rachel, you need to learn to value a man's friendship for more than the stories you can squeeze out of him. It would broaden your horizons immeasurably."

"I don't know. Men have so little else to offer."

CHAPTER FORTY-EIGHT

Friday morning, standing naked in front of his bathroom mirror, Mason's body looked as if he'd been tattooed with a Rorschach test. He walked creakily around his house like the Tin Man in search of a lube job, trailed by Tuffy, whose whining and yelping Mason mistook for sympathy until he realized that the dog just wanted to be fed.

He tried rowing but gave up when he started to sink. He took a shower hot enough to parboil his skin, the heat loosening the kinks in his muscles and joints, and got back in bed long enough to read Rachel's article in the morning paper.

She had followed him home the night before, tending to his wounds long enough to extract information she agreed to attribute only to a source close to the investigation.

"I don't want you to think I'm a killer," he told her.

"I don't; a lousy burglar, yes, but a killer, not so much."

"Thanks for the endorsement."

"So who did it? Who killed Cullan, blew up the barbershop, and killed Shirley Parker? And what happened to the files?"

"Like GI Joe says, knowing is half the battle. The other half is proving it. Ed Fiora is the leader in the clubhouse. He may have been happy that Cullan worked his magic on the license for the Dream Casino. But who wants a lawyer with a file that could send him to the federal penitentiary? Plus he's got the muscle. Tony Manzerio probably gets his rocks off blowing stuff up. Fiora killed Cullan—or had him killed—to preserve the attorney-client privilege. Then, he sent Tony to get the files from Shirley and killed her because she was the last of the loose ends."

Rachel chewed on Mason's theory. "Maybe, but killing Shirley is too messy. Threaten her, buy her off, and send her out of town. That would have made sense, but killing her turns up the heat hotter than the fire. Fiora isn't that stupid."

"No plan ever goes down the way it's written. Something went wrong and Tony popped Shirley."

"So Fiora has the files?"

"They ain't at the public library."

"So how do you prove it?"

"Beats the hell out of me."

Her story ran alongside a color photograph of him clutching the bars on the barbershop window while flames danced a pirouette around him. A spectator had taken the photograph and sold it to a wire service, turning a quick profit on tragedy. Mason held the picture up for a closer look as he searched for a trace of courage in his bugged-out eyes and gaping trout mouth.

Rachel wove the Pendergast angle into the story, giving it a gangland flavor that linked two twenty-first-century murders with a long-dead twentieth-century kingpin. She noted the rumored existence of Cullan's confidential files and the suspicion that they contained embarrassing information on the city's leaders, speculating that the files may have been destroyed in the fire or stolen. She described Shirley Parker as a never-married woman with no survivors whose only known employment had been for Jack Cullan, making her life more tragic than her death.

As for him, Rachel played it straight. The caption under the photograph identified him as Blues's lawyer. The article offered no explanation for his presence in the barbershop, noting that he had declined to comment on the record, as had Harry Ryman when she had asked him whether Mason was a suspect in Shirley Parker's murder.

CHAPTER FORTY-NINE

Mickey Shanahan was sitting in Mason's desk chair, his feet propped on Mason's desk, drinking from a bottle of fresh orange juice, when Mason arrived just before ten o'clock.

"Is that my orange juice?"

"Sorry, Lou." Mickey wiped his mouth with the back of his hand. "This woman dropped it off a while ago. Said she was your aunt. Said you should call her so she could chew your ass. Whatever you did, she's, like, totally pissed, man. What's goin' on?"

"First, that is my orange juice. Second, my aunt is probably upset that I got trapped in a burning barbershop with a dead body. Third, when did you move into my office?"

"Sorry again, boss," Mickey said, this time taking his feet off of Mason's desk. "I give on the OJ. But you've got to tell me about the barbershop and the body. That is too much! And you're the one who hired me to check out Ed Fiora. That was yesterday. You left me here without the key. I didn't want to leave the place unlocked and I didn't know when you were coming back, so I stayed."

"All night?"

"That sofa's not bad. And the orange juice is pretty good."

Mickey was wearing the same faded jeans, denim shirt and black crew-neck sweater he'd worn the day before. He had scruffy stubble on his chin, and his unwashed hair looked like it had been finger combed.

"Mickey, where do you live?"

He brushed his sweater, freshening his dignity. "I've got a place not far from here."

"What about clients? I haven't seen a single client in or out of your office in six months. What's up with that?"

"It's been a little slow. I'm expecting things to pick up. This case will give me a big boost."

Mason got a quick picture of a kid barely off the street who thought he had scammed Blues on the office lease and had probably been living at the bar ever since. Mason doubted that Mickey had fooled Blues from the moment he'd said hello. Mason reached into his wallet and took out a twenty.

"I haven't had breakfast. Would you mind picking something up for me? Get yourself something too if you want."

"Hey, no problem, boss. I'll probably stop at home and get cleaned up if that's okay."

"You bet. Did you find anything out about Fiora?"

"A lot of smoke, not much fire. It's all here in a report I did for you."

"Give me the highlights."

"I've covered the public-record stuff, property ownership, lawsuits, stuff like that. The gaming commission files could be the real bonanza."

"Why?"

"I found two things in those records that are the keys to the information universe. Fiora's social security number and bank accounts. It will take some time, but I'll eventually be able to follow the money."

"Is that legal?"

"Hey, you're the lawyer. Do you really want to know?"

"No, I really don't. What's the bottom line?"

"Fiora is a big football fan. Just like the mayor. I did some checking on him too."

Mickey handed him a typed report with printouts attached. Mason thumbed through it, impressed by the level of detail and organization. He reached into his wallet again and handed Mickey two fifties.

"We haven't talked salary yet. This will cover yesterday until we have time to work out the details."

Mickey folded the fifties and stuck them in his pocket with a nonchalance that clashed with the hunger in his eyes.

"Works for me. I'll have to see where I'm at with my other clients before I can commit to anything full-time."

"Sure. I understand. Check your schedule and let me know. I'm probably going to need somebody at least until Blues's case is over. If you're not available, I'll have to run an ad. That's always a pain in the ass."

Mickey pursed his lips and nodded, realizing that they were playing each other. "So what's the story on the barbershop and the body?"

"Buy yourself a newspaper and read all about it. Come to work for me full-time and we'll talk."

Mickey smiled. "Catch you later, boss."

Mason, certain that he would, settled into his desk chair, checked out the traffic on Broadway, and read Mickey's report.

The relationship between Fiora and the mayor was more complicated than a backwoods family tree and was filled with enough smoke that there had to be a fire somewhere. The Dream Casino bought a wide array of goods and services to make dreams come true for its customers, including food, laundry, carpets, paint, security equipment, slot machines, lighting, liquor, and beer.

The Dream had an exclusive contract with a local beer distributor owned by Donovan Jenkins, a former wide receiver for the Kansas City Chiefs who had been Billy Sunshine's favorite target. Jenkins had been a steady supporter of his old quarterback, making modest campaign contributions. A month after Jenkins inked the exclusive deal with Fiora, Mayor Sunshine refinanced the $250,000 mortgage on his house. The mayor's new lender was Donovan Jenkins. Mickey speculated at the end of his report that the mayor wasn't making house payments like regular folks.

Mason picked up his phone and dialed Rachel Firestone's number at the *Star*.

"What do you know about the mortgage on Mayor Sunshine's

house?" he asked her.

"Good morning to you too. Nice of you to call, and you're welcome for last night."

"I'm sure it was as good for you as it was for me."

"As good as it gets. How did you find out about the mortgage?"

"You aren't my only source," he told her. "What do you know about the relationship between Fiora, Donovan Jenkins, and the mayor?"

"Fiora made Jenkins his exclusive beer supplier. Jenkins loaned the mayor a quarter of a million bucks. It's dirty, it sucks, but it's legal. I've talked to the U.S. attorney about it. Jenkins's loan is a matter of public record. Amy White, the mayor's chief of staff, showed me canceled checks for the monthly house payment Mayor Sunshine makes to Jenkins. The interest rate is a market rate. End of story, but I've got something you might be interested in on that tunnel you found in the basement of the barbershop."

"Are you going to make me sit up and beg?"

"Not over the phone. I can't tell if you're really sitting up. I checked the paper's archives. During Prohibition, Pendergast owned a speakeasy that was on the other side of the alley from the barbershop. He built the tunnel so his boys could escape in case the feds raided the joint."

"Who owns the building?" Mason asked.

"Donovan Jenkins. He bought it from Jack Cullan a year ago."

"That's handy. Who does Jenkins lease the space to?"

"An art gallery. They had a big opening last month. It was vacant a long time before that. Care to guess who the last tenant was before the art gallery?"

"And rob you of the pleasure of telling me? Never."

"You are so thoughtful. Would you believe it was the Committee to Reelect Billy Sunshine?"

"Get out!"

"Get in and get in deep."

"Man, is there anybody in this whole mess who isn't in bed with one another?"

"Just you and me, babe. Just you and me."

"Don't you hate being left out?"

"No. Deal with it."

He laughed. "That should be my biggest problem. Thanks again for last night."

"It was nothing. Keep in touch," she added before hanging up.

CHAPTER FIFTY

With Cullan's files either destroyed or stolen, Mason was back at the bottom of the hill, still trying to push the boulder to the top. He would let Mickey continue plowing fields in cyberspace while he dug at ground level.

He logged on to the county's civil-lawsuit database and punched in Beth Harrell's name. Both of her divorce cases showed up. Husband number one was Baker McKenzie. Mason recognized his name. He was the senior partner in the McKenzie, Strachan law firm. Husband number two was Al Douglas, a name Mason didn't recognize. According to Beth, one of her ex-husbands had snapped nasty pics of her and had given them to Jack Cullan. Mason's best idea of the day was to find the exes and ask which one of them was the shitbag.

Mason didn't want to ask Beth which of her ex-husbands was the shitbag because he wasn't convinced that she was telling the truth. If Beth knew he was checking out her story and she was lying, she would backpedal or find some way to distract him, and he wasn't up to being distracted. If she were telling the truth, she would start crowding Ed Fiora's pole position on the suspect track.

He called the clerk of the circuit court to locate Beth's divorce files. The voice-mail system cast him into a menu of choices that he accepted and rejected until a human being answered. When the woman said her name was Margaret, he knew she didn't mean it when she asked how she could help him.

"My name is Lou Mason. I'm a lawyer and I'm trying to locate two divorce files."

"Are they on-site or off-site?"

Mason swallowed. "I don't know. I was hoping you could tell me."

"If they are on-site, they might only be available on microfilm. That would mean that we shipped the hard copy off-site. If the files are off-site and you want the hard copy, it will take one to three business days to retrieve the files from off-site storage. Hold, please," she added before he could respond.

Mason imagined dozens of different torture scenarios for bureaucrats named Margaret during the three minutes and twenty-seven seconds she left him on hold.

"This is Margaret. May I help you?" she asked when she returned to his call.

"Margaret this is Lou Mason. We've already met. I'm looking for two divorce files and I know the on-site, off-site drill. Let me give you the case numbers so you can find out where they are."

"We can't give that information out over the phone. You'll have to come to the clerk's office and sign a form."

He took a deep breath. "Should I ask for you, Margaret?"

"Yes. I'll be at lunch."

Thirty minutes later, Mason cautiously approached the court clerk's office. He was less concerned that Margaret would actually be at lunch than he was that she would be there and he'd end up a suspect in another homicide. He passed through the double glass doors of the court clerk's office. A long white counter laminated with Formica separated Mason from the employees processing the county's civil and criminal cases.

He had concluded from past experiences that they had been trained not to look up unless it was at the clock. It was ten minutes to noon when Mason rang the bell on the counter under the sign that read *Ring for Service*. The woman at the nearest desk raised her eyes at him; her resentment at his interruption shot through her glare.

"I'm here to see Margaret."

She picked up her phone, stealing glances at him until he was certain that she'd called the sheriff's office. She hung up, put the cap on her pen, and disappeared to the back of the office.

Mason waited. There was a large clock on the wall to his right. He watched the second hand sweep around the dial and the incremental march of the minute hand to twelve o'clock high. The other people in the office, as if in response to an inner clock, rose in turn from their desks, vanishing into the depths of the clerk's office.

One woman remained. She walked slowly to the counter, eyeing the clock, timing her advance.

"I'm Margaret."

"I'm Lou Mason. We spoke on the phone. You said I had to fill out a form to request a couple of divorce files."

She reached into a drawer and handed Mason two forms, one for each file. He filled them out and flashed her his best smile when he handed them back to her. He followed her gaze to the clock.

"It's noon. I'm on my lunch break. Come back at one o'clock."

Mason watched helplessly as Margaret carried the forms back to her desk, dropping them on her chair, never looking back.

He returned exactly sixty minutes later. Seventy minutes later, Margaret presented him with both files, neither of which had been off-site or on microfilm. He filled out additional forms to check out the files, which meant that he could take them into a small adjoining room and look at them. He would have to fill out another form to request copies, and he could not under any circumstances, Margaret explained in the severest of tones, remove the files from the clerk's office.

The files were one-dimensional ledgers of dates and dollars, the final accounting of dead relationships. He thought about his own marriage, about the passion and pain that had swept both him and Kate along for three years until Kate called it quits, depriving him of the choice to fight or surrender.

There was no exuberance in the dry recitation of the dates of Beth's marriages and no regret in the hollow entries of the decrees of divorce. It was history without humanity, *irreconcilable differences* code words for hearts empty and broken.

Beth Harrell had married Baker McKenzie shortly after graduating from law school. She was twenty-five and he was twenty-five years her senior. They had met when Beth worked as a summer intern at McKenzie's firm. The marriage had lasted two years. There had been no children, and she hadn't sought alimony or any of his property, asking only for the restoration of her maiden name.

Five years later, she married Al Douglas, an architect fifteen years older than her. She kept her maiden name, and they signed a prenuptial agreement that prohibited either of them from seeking any monetary settlement from the other in the event of a divorce, with the exception of child support if they had a family. Irreconcilable differences had again been diagnosed, like a recurring cancer. The court entered the decree of divorce on their fourth wedding anniversary.

It was impossible to draw any conclusions about Beth's marriages other than that they had had a beginning and an end. What had taken place in the middle was not a matter of public record. Mason would have to ask Baker McKenzie and Al Douglas to find out which of them was the shitbag.

CHAPTER FIFTY-ONE

Mason had learned one thing about celebrity. It cleared a lot of scheduling conflicts. Both Baker McKenzie and Al Douglas agreed to see him that afternoon. He started with McKenzie.

Baker McKenzie was the third generation of McKenzies in the firm his grandfather and Matthew Strachan had founded seventy-five years earlier. None of Strachan's heirs had followed their ancestor in the law, though no later generations of interloping partners had suggested removing the Strachan name from the door. McKenzie, Strachan was the oldest and largest law firm in the city, its bloodlines were the bluest, and its stockings were woven of the finest silk.

Baker McKenzie sat comfortably at the top of the firm, worrying more about his putting stroke than about the firm's clients. He had hidden mediocre legal skills and a civil service work ethic beneath the legacy of his grandfather and father. Mason had run across him once or twice in cases where the client had expected the name partner to show his face. McKenzie had shown it just long enough to make certain he didn't get it dirty before begging off because of pressing matters in the case of *Tee v. Green*. He was a society-page regular, never seen in public without a beautiful woman on his arm.

McKenzie greeted Mason as if they were asshole buddies. "My God, man! How the hell are you? I swear to Jesus that you are turning our profession into one dangerous contact sport."

McKenzie gleamed as if he'd just been washed and waxed, his teeth and hair both bleached to a high sheen. McKenzie was

Mason's height, broad where Mason was lean and fit for his age or any other, shaking Mason's hand vigorously enough to make the point.

He led Mason to his forty-first-floor corner office with a panoramic view of the city.

"You've got a helluva view."

"Hell, I can see from here to next week," he said, laughing at a line he'd used a thousand times. "It's really something during a lightning storm, especially at night. I'm telling you, Lou, it's like standing next to Zeus throwing thunderbolts. It electrifies women of a certain erotic sensibility—like, their nerve endings get supercharged and they've just got to plug something into all that current."

"And I'll bet you know how to throw the switch."

McKenzie took a deep breath, swelling his chest. "I could light up a Christmas tree, my friend."

"I'll bet those are some moments to remember."

"Indeed they are. Indeed they are."

"All that excitement, it must be hard to remember one woman from another. You ever keep any souvenirs?"

McKenzie's boasting gave way to suspicion. "You didn't ask to see me to talk about my love life. What's on your mind?"

It had taken Mason only a few minutes to bait Baker McKenzie and less time to hate him. Mason didn't want him to mistake diplomacy for deference.

"Beth Harrell says she's being blackmailed with some dirty pictures either you or her other ex-husband took and gave to Jack Cullan. If she's telling the truth, that means she's a suspect in Cullan's murder and the ex-husband is a shitbag. I need to know if the pictures are real and I need to know if you're the shitbag."

McKenzie looked out over the horizon for a moment before turning toward Mason, his face besotted with angry blood. He closed the distance between them before Mason realized that he wasn't coming to shake his hand again, and launched a right cross at Mason's chin. Mason couldn't get out of the way, and he spun around once before toppling at McKenzie's feet.

"Dartmouth boxing team, light-heavyweight division," McKenzie said as he stepped over a stunned but conscious Mason and opened the door to his office. "Call maintenance," McKenzie said to his secretary. "Tell them to clean up the shitbag on my floor."

CHAPTER FIFTY-TWO

Al Douglas's office was in a suburban office park surrounded by woods and ringed by a bike path. Banners hung from light poles in the parking lot, depicting festive winter scenes that clashed with the barren trees. Mason sat in his car for half an hour, ministering to his chin with an ice bag he bought at a convenience store, before going inside.

He was prepared to take a more temperate approach to husband number two when Al Douglas looked up at him from a drafting table. Douglas worked in an office without walls, where no one had a private office. Mason assumed that the design was intended to build camaraderie, but judging from the beehive hum that greeted him, it bred whispers and rumors.

"You must be Lou Mason," Douglas said, extending his hand. "Baker called me. He said he'd already taken out your chin but that I could have the rest of your face unless I was the shitbag you were looking for. Let's talk someplace quiet."

Douglas slid off his drafting stool and led Mason into a break room where two other people were huddled over a crossword puzzle. Douglas cleared his throat and waited. The puzzle people took their cue and left, closing the door behind them.

He was round-shouldered, thin on top and thick around the middle. He wore half-glasses that had slid two thirds of the way down his nose. He took off the glasses, letting them drop to his chest, where they dangled from a thin chain that looped around his neck.

"He really tagged you, didn't he? The sucker punch is Baker's specialty. He tried it once with me, but he misjudged how short I am and missed. If he misses the first punch, he's finished. I kicked him in the nuts and he cried like a girl."

Douglas's story about Baker McKenzie was a verbal sucker punch, letting Mason know he wouldn't be intimidated even though he looked like the only thing he'd ever thrown in anger was a fit.

"I'll try to remember that when we have the rematch."

"You really should put some ice on that before you grow a second chin."

"I'll do that. No offense, but you and Baker aren't exactly cut from the same cloth. Baker has two last names and you have two first names. Other than that, I can't see the connection. How did both of you end up married to Beth Harrell?"

"She's a woman of extremes, and Baker and I are at the opposite end of several masculine scales. She tried both ends. The next guy will probably be in the middle. Strong, tough, but likes sunsets. I suppose you want to know about the pictures."

"If you don't mind. Do the pictures really exist?"

Douglas poured a cup of coffee and took a chilled bottle of water from a refrigerator and handed it to Mason. "Here. Put that on your chin, and yes, the pictures are real."

Mason rolled the bottle across his chin. "Did Baker take the pictures?" Douglas shook his head. "You?"

"Neither one of us took them. Beth did. She put her camera on a tripod and used a timer. We were both into adult entertainment and she wanted to shock me, stir me up in some different way. I won't lie to you. It worked. She's a beautiful woman and the pictures were quite graphic. I hadn't gotten off like that since my first *Playboy*."

"Did she do the same thing with Baker?"

"I don't know, but I doubt it. Beth always said that Baker screwed around, but only in the missionary position."

"You sound awfully philosophical for a guy who got dumped. You don't even sound angry with her."

"Guys like me never end up with women like Beth for very long. When she left me, it was like the clock struck midnight and I was back to being Al, the invisible man with the boffo porn collection. Except I had the pictures. So I didn't get mad; I got off and then got even."

Douglas was blasé enough about his relationship with Beth that Mason pegged him for a sociopath interested only in his own needs and indifferent to anyone else. His casual, unemotional vengeance was creepy.

"You gave the pictures to Jack Cullan?"

Douglas smiled. "I sold them. I guess that really makes me the shitbag."

Mason resisted the impulse to shove Douglas's chalky face into the back of his skull.

"When did you sell the pictures to Cullan?"

"You want to hit me. I can tell from the way your jugular vein is throbbing. But you won't do it. I can tell that too. You're stuck with your conventional ethics. That's why people like me are able to do the things we do."

Mason measured his breathing. Douglas was a gut-sucking parasite with a sunny disposition. He bellied up to Douglas, crowding him into a corner. Douglas backed up, his hands shaking, causing him to spill his coffee on the front of his pants.

"You don't know me, Douglas, so don't assume too much. When did you sell the pictures to Cullan?"

"Okay, okay," Douglas said, holding up his hand in protest. "I sold him the pictures a couple of months ago. Satisfied?"

"Barely. If I find out you kept any copies of those pictures, or sold them or gave them away or posted them on the Internet, I'll come back here and turn you inside out."

Douglas found more courage when he realized Mason wasn't going to smack him. "I'd be more worried about Beth, if I were you. I kept the pictures, but she kept the gun."

Mason couldn't tell if Douglas was pimping him, but he couldn't resist the next question. "What gun?"

"Baker gave her a present when they got divorced, since she wouldn't take any money. He told her she should use it with her next husband to get a better settlement. I settled very cheaply."

"Do you know what kind of gun it was?"

"A .38-caliber pistol," he answered with a grin that said he'd just gotten even with Beth all over again.

CHAPTER FIFTY-THREE

Mason's new theory was that Ed Fiora, Billy Sunshine, and Beth Harrell had all killed Jack Cullan, drawing straws to see who would hold him down while one of them shot him. They had such a good time that they played their game again with Shirley Parker. As a theory, it sucked, but it was easier than trying to pick a favorite.

Returning to his car, Mason called his office, curious whether Mickey had ever come back.

"Lou Mason and Associates," Mickey said.

"Associates are young lawyers who are overpaid and underworked. I don't recall hiring any associates. I'm sure I would have remembered."

"Chill out, boss. It's branding, like Coke or Kleenex. Gives the name some flair. Tells people we're going places."

"I catch you playing lawyer, I'll give you some real branding. Understood?"

"No problemo, dude. Hey, you got a call from Judge Carter's administrative assistant, reminding you that she wants to see you and Ortiz first thing Monday morning, eight o'clock."

"The judge's assistant wasn't named Margaret, was she?"

"She didn't say. Why, do you think you know her?"

"Only if her name is Margaret. Are you still following Fiora's money trail?"

"Inside and outside, boss. I may have something for you tonight."

Mason stopped at the jail to talk with Blues. The sheriff's deputy who brought Blues into the visiting attorney room pointed his thumb and forefinger at Mason, dropped the hammer on his imaginary gun, and told Mason he was saving a cell for him.

"Talk inside is that the cops are looking at you for the Shirley Parker thing."

"They can look all they want. Harry knows I didn't do it."

"Who did?"

"Tony Manzerio is my choice." Mason briefed Blues about Cullan's files, the fire, and Shirley Parker. He told Blues about Donovan Jenkins's contract with Ed Fiora and Jenkins's loan to the mayor. He finished up with his visits to Baker McKenzie and Al Douglas.

"You think the same person killed Cullan and Parker?" Blues asked.

"Makes sense. If the ballistics tests show that the bullets were fired from the same gun, you'll be out of here with a refund. I'll check with Harry as soon as I can."

Blues nodded silently, got up from his seat, and knocked on the door, signaling the guard that he was ready to return to his cell. He cocked his fist at his side, making imaginary contact with Mason, who returned the gesture.

Mason worried as the door closed behind Blues. His face never betrayed what he was thinking or what he might do. That unpredictability made him particularly dangerous. Even a rattlesnake rattled before it struck.

Blues had been in jail for more than three weeks, charged with a murder that could take his own life. Mason had looked for signs that he was bending to the grind of incarceration. He had seen none, no tic at the corner of his eyes, no tightening of his mouth, no tremor in his hands. Yet Mason knew that Blues's rage simmered just beneath the surface and that he would make someone pay for putting him behind bars. Mason worried that getting him out of jail might just be the first step down a path that brought him back to the same place.

December's subzero wind chills and snowstorms had given way to a raw January. Each day brought a thin mist or a thicker sleet that whipped and whirled into every body pore and open space. The sun was being held hostage behind a slate-gray sky. It was the kind of weather that kept heads down and chins tucked against chests. By spring, the entire city would need a chiropractor just to stand up straight.

Mason's phone rang as he got behind the wheel of the Jeep, rubbing his hands against the cold.

"Lou Mason," he said, his breath vaporizing before disappearing.

"I didn't think you would answer." It was Beth Harrell. She sounded breathless and shaky.

"That makes us even. I didn't think you would call."

It was a small lie. Mason had expected that one of Beth's ex-husbands, or both, would tell her about his visits. She was the kind of woman who kept a hold on a man long after the last kiss. He wondered which ex-husband had called. Baker McKenzie would call to brag about decking him. Al Douglas would call to hear her cry.

"I'm sorry. Calling you was an impulse, another bad one, I guess."

Her voice triggered a crotch-centered impulse. Beth was a dangerous woman under the best of circumstances, and they were a long way from that ground. Still, she managed to reach inside him.

"Don't apologize. What's on your mind?"

"I'm practically a prisoner in my apartment. If I go out, the press won't leave me alone. I guess I was just feeling lonely and I couldn't think of anyone else to call." She hesitated, waiting for Mason to reply. He didn't. "Bad idea, huh?" she asked in a low, throaty, bad-girl voice.

"Not the best, but I haven't heard many good ideas lately. The last guy you went out with on a Friday night ended up with a bullet in his eye. I don't want to make page one again anytime soon."

"Neither do I. Although I don't think we could top your picture in this morning's paper unless we were caught having sex on Main Street."

Mason laughed, disarmed by her earthy humor. "You haven't

seen my good side."

"Show me. I'll make us dinner. You can park at the hotel and take the walkway across to my building. No one will see you. You'll be safe."

"Give me an hour."

CHAPTER FIFTY-FOUR

Mason had a hard time using the words *safe* and *Beth* in the same sentence, but he had to talk to her about the pictures and about the gun. He stopped at home, showered, shaved, fed the dog, and listened to his messages, including one from his aunt Claire demanding that he call her. He promised the answering machine that he would and left the lights on so that Tuffy wouldn't be left in the dark.

There were two entrances to the hotel's parking garage, one on the north and one on the east. Beth's apartment was in a high-rise on the south side of the Intercontinental. Mason chose the north entrance to the parking garage to minimize the chance that some reporter staking out Beth's apartment would see him.

It took him longer than he expected to find the walkway that connected the hotel and the apartment building, and it was past seven o'clock when he knocked on her door. He heard the sharp clack of heels on hardwood as Beth walked hurriedly to the door, opening it with a sigh mixed with relief and anticipation.

Mason stood in the doorway, deciding whether to cross her threshold. Beth waited, one hand on the door, the other on her hip, wearing black linen slacks and a bloodred silk shirt unbuttoned far enough to get his attention. A sly smile creased her cheeks. She looked like a woman who'd never known trouble she hadn't asked for and who was ready to ask again.

"Come on in, Lou. I won't bite."

"Hardly worth the effort, then," he said as he walked past her.

The entrance hall opened into a living room with a wall of

glass that faced north, looking over the top of the Intercontinental Hotel to the Plaza fifteen stories below, its eight square blocks of shops sparkling in a quarter of a million Christmas lights. Long, tapered candles lit with perfect ovals of yellow flame beckoned from the dining room table. Mellow jazz filled the corners from hidden speakers.

Mason stopped in front of the windows, taking in the view, Beth nestling against his back, her hands on his shoulders, drawing his coat halfway off. He turned toward her and she pushed his coat onto the floor, resting her hands on his chest. He held her arms, not trusting his hands.

"We're alone, if you were wondering," she said.

"That's what worries me." He took her by the wrists and pulled her hands of him. "Get your coat."

Her face reddened as if he had slapped her. "Why?"

"We need to talk, and the chances of keeping our clothes on while we do it are much better outside than inside."

She backed up a few steps, hugging herself. "You are the master of the mixed message. I'm at the end of my rope and you take advantage of me every time we're together. I can't keep playing these games with you."

"That's good, Beth. That's very good. The best defense is a good offense. Let's stay on task. If I can prove that both you and Blues are innocent, you'll only get one message from me. In the meantime, I don't trust either one of us unless we're standing up with our clothes on and it's too cold to take them off."

"I won't go with you," she said, adopting a pout. "You can't make me."

"Would you prefer your own front-page story? I don't have a photograph to go with it yet, but sometimes it's better for the reader to create his own picture. Especially when it's a story of a woman taking nude pictures of herself, then claiming a dead man was blackmailing her with the pictures."

"You wouldn't!" she said, wheeling around, her hands planted on her hips.

"Without pleasure and with regret, I assure you, but I will do it the moment I walk out of here. Rachel Firestone would love to have the story."

"I saw you with her on New Year's Eve. I don't know what you see in a woman like that! She can't love you!" Tears pooled at the corners of her eyes, spilling down past her nose and tracing a wet line along her lips. "Damn you!" she said as she stood crying, her arms limp, her shoulders heaving.

Her world was collapsing around her and Mason was pushing her to the brink. Each time she reached out her hand, he was afraid to take it because he didn't know if she would take him down with her. But for now, he needed her to hold on. He wrapped his arms around her and she muffled her cries against his chest, gathering herself, wiping her eyes.

"God, I'm a mess," she said.

"Not if you like mascara streaks. I understand that's how Kiss got the idea for their makeup."

"Screw you," she said, finding half a smile.

"Let's go for a drive instead."

"Okay. Let me change."

She chose corduroy jeans, ankle-high boots, and a heavy red woolen sweater. She had washed her face and tied her hair back with a bandanna. Not bothering with more makeup, she was scrubbed clean and fresh, indifferent to the crow's-feet and laugh lines she'd left exposed. Relieved of the burdens of tears and seduction, she had a fresh vulnerability that pierced Mason's heart. She pulled on her parka, grabbed her purse, and marched to the door while he stared at her, transfixed.

"Let's go," she said. "I'm not going to spend my whole life waiting for you."

Mason did a lap under the Plaza lights and headed south. Neither of them spoke. When they left the city limits in the distance and the headlights ahead and behind them dwindled to a few, curiosity overcame her.

"Do we keep going until you run out of gas?"

"Not much farther."

A few minutes later, they pulled into the driveway of a farmhouse. Mason got a swift shot of paranoia until a car that had seemed to be following them continued on past the driveway. He got out and walked to the end of the driveway, looking to his west as the car's taillights disappeared over the next hill. Satisfied, he got back into the Jeep and drove around the farmhouse, down a rutted path, and into a small clearing in the woods.

"Let's go for a walk," he told her.

"Are you nuts? In the dark? In this cold?"

"It's invigorating. The Swedish do it all the time. If we had snow, we'd take our clothes off and roll around in it."

Mason grabbed his flashlight from the glove compartment and led her through the woods, back toward the farmhouse, quieting her with hand signals whenever she started to ask a question. Mason could make out the shape of the farmhouse when a pair of high-beam headlights bounced off the front windows and splashed back into the front yard. Mason turned off his flashlight and pulled Beth down to the ground.

Tony Manzerio stepped out of the car, silhouetted by the headlights, and took a quick tour of the grounds. Sound travels farther at night, and in the cold stillness he heard Manzerio invoke ghosts and godfathers in frustration at having lost them. They waited in the woods until Manzerio drove away, and another twenty minutes to make certain he wasn't coming back.

"Okay," Mason said. "Let's go." He helped her up and began walking toward the farmhouse.

"Wait a minute," Beth said. "The car is back the other way."

"We're not going to the car. We're spending the night here."

Mason walked to the back door of the farmhouse and knelt at the stoop, where he found a porcelain jug. He twisted the top off the jug and removed a key. He unlocked the door and returned the key to the jug.

"Lou Mason, international man of mystery," Beth said as they stepped inside. "Whose place is this?"

"It belonged to a former partner of mine who was killed when he got in over his head in a money-laundering scheme. He used to invite me out here. He was a nice man, gentle but weak, and it got him killed. I look after the place for his family, who live on the West Coast. They're waiting for suburbia to get here before they sell it."

"And you feel safer spending the night with me in an abandoned farmhouse in the middle of nowhere than in my nice, warm apartment on the Plaza where we can actually order room service from the Intercontinental Hotel? Don't tell me what drugs you're taking because I don't want any of it."

"I didn't intend to come here, but it looked like we were being followed. I'm not much good at playing hide-and-seek in traffic, so I tried a little misdirection and it worked. I don't know if Manzerio was following both of us or just one of us. There's no point in finding out by going back to either of our places tonight. No one will bother us here."

"What about keeping our clothes on?"

"Trust me. You'll want to keep every stitch on. There's no heat and no electricity."

CHAPTER FIFTY-FIVE

"I am not spending the night in a freezing-cold abandoned farmhouse!"

"It's a long way to anywhere from here," Mason told her. He shined the flashlight around the kitchen, spotlighting a worn butcher-block table and two vinyl-upholstered chairs. "Let's talk first. Then we can decide about spending the night."

Beth stepped toward the back door. Mason cut her off, aiming the flashlight at the chairs.

"Oh, please! You aren't really going to hold me hostage here until I talk. Don't you remember anything from law school? Like kidnapping is against the law? Like coerced confessions are inadmissible?"

"I'm not kidnapping you. You're free to go, but it is a long walk and Tony Manzerio is out there somewhere. Maybe he'll give you a ride. Just tell me the truth about you, Jack Cullan, your pictures, and his files, and then I'll take you home."

Mason held the flashlight in front of him, pointing the beam at the ceiling like a torch, illuminating their faces as if they were sitting at the edge of a campfire. Beth looked at him, her mouth clamped shut, her eyes narrowed, waiting for Mason to call off his parlor game. He tipped his head at the table and raised his eyebrows as if to say he wasn't kidding.

"Okay. You win. But turn off the light just in case Manzerio comes back."

"Good thinking."

He turned the flashlight off and sat in one of the chairs, his eyes adjusting to the dark, moonlight sneaking through a window as Beth rustled in her purse.

"Turn your flashlight on for a second. I've got a surprise for you."

Mason chuckled. "You were supposed to keep your clothes on." He aimed the beam at her chest. She pointed a gun at his. "Does that count as a mixed message?"

"Give me the keys to your car," she said.

"Is that the .38 Baker McKenzie gave you?"

"Give me the goddamn car keys!"

"Or you'll shoot me like you shot Jack Cullan and Shirley Parker?"

Before Beth could answer, Tony Manzerio kicked in the back door, carrying a flashlight bigger than Mason's and a gun bigger than Beth's. Mason jumped to his feet.

"Steady, Batman," Manzerio told him. "I like you a lot better sitting down." Mason hesitated, weighing his chances. "Do it!"

Mason sat down, noticing that Beth was no longer pointing her gun at him. She wasn't pointing it at Manzerio either. Mason didn't know what she had done with her gun or whom she was likely to point it at next.

The momentary silence was broken by the sound of someone kicking the front door off its hinges. Ed Fiora and two men only slightly smaller than Manzerio made their way in the dark to the kitchen.

"Hey, Mason," Fiora said as his two goons flanked him. "It must be hard to tell who your friends are these days."

The goons laughed and pointed their flashlights and guns at him. Mason held his hands up to shade his eyes from the glare.

"Can't tell the players without a program."

"You are right about that."

"Why were you following me?"

"I got something for you that you been looking for. I wanted to give it to you so maybe you'd get off my back. I sent Tony here to deliver it, only he couldn't catch up to you. You gave him the drop, but I figured you stayed at the farmhouse when we didn't see any other cars on the road."

One of the goons handed Fiora a large envelope. He held it in one hand, tapped it against his other, and tossed it onto the table.

"Go ahead, open it."

Mason picked up the envelope, guessing at its contents. Beth hung her head, looking away. He put the envelope back on the table.

"Not interested."

"That's not what I hear. Tony," Fiora said to Manzerio, "Mason's dick has gone limp. Open that envelope for him."

Manzerio stuffed his gun in his pocket and his flashlight under his arm, ripping the envelope open and fanning out pictures of Beth Harrell across the table. Mason kept his eyes on Fiora. Manzerio gripped the back of Mason's head like a melon, pushing his face at the pictures.

Beth was nude in each photograph, legs spread, squeezing and probing her body with her hands in some pictures, using a dildo in others. Her closed eyes and open mouth mimed a staged rapture that looked stag-film phony.

"Not bad for amateur stuff," Fiora said, nodding at Manzerio, who released his grip on Mason's head.

"What do you want?" Mason asked.

"Like I told you, I want you to back off. You think I'm blackmailing this bitch with these pictures. Cullan gave me the pictures after I got my casino license. I never used them except to make sure she came to my New Year's Eve party."

"So forcing her to come on to me while you watched on closed-circuit TV is just taking one of those edges you need every now and then? Is that it? Plus now I'm supposed to believe that you didn't have Cullan whacked so you could get rid of his file on you?"

"I knew all about Cullan's files. They didn't mean squat to me. Cullan couldn't take me down without taking himself down. Hell, I've got my own files. Everybody has files on everybody else. It's like nuclear bombs. Everyone wants them, but none of us can afford to use them."

"Then who killed Jack Cullan?"

"I don't know and I don't care. It wasn't me or my boys. I may rough some chump up that tries to stiff me on a tab at the casino, but I got too good a thing going to whack my own lawyer or anybody else."

"What about Shirley Parker?"

"Not my problem. Not my solution."

"If you are so uninterested in Cullan's files, why did you make me that offer if I found them first?"

"That offer still stands. I knew who I was dealing with when Cullan had his files. I don't know who or what I'm dealing with if somebody else gets them. I got one more tip for you, Counselor."

"What's that?"

"Cut out all that computer shit your wiseass gofer has been doing. I don't understand that shit, but my people tell me that anyone tries to get in my computer records leaves electronic footprints that lead right back to them. I had a little talk with that kid tonight. What's his name? Mickey something or other. By the way, I think you're going to need a new computer."

"You hurt that kid and I'll—"

"You'll what, Mr. Big Shot? Kill me? Give it a rest. Like I told you, I might rough somebody up, but I don't whack anybody. I'm a businessman and I'm done doing business with you. Let's go, boys."

As Fiora turned to leave, Beth whipped her gun from inside her coat and aimed at Fiora. Mason lunged across the table, shoving her gun hand high just as she fired. The bullet lodged in the ceiling.

"Don't shoot! Don't shoot!" Mason screamed as he tumbled on top of Beth and wrestled the gun from her.

Manzerio and the other two goons showered their flashlights on Mason and Beth as they lay in a tangle on the floor. Beth wept as Mason covered her body with his, looking over his shoulder at Fiora and his men.

"I owe you, Mason," Fiora conceded, "but I wouldn't turn my back on that crazy bitch if I was you."

CHAPTER FIFTY-SIX

Mason kept Beth's gun but offered the photographs to her. She shook her head, saying that it didn't matter anymore. She stared out the window on the drive back to town, silent and wiping away an occasional tear.

Beth's gun was a .45-caliber Beretta autopistol, not the .38 Baker McKenzie had given her and not the .38 used to kill Jack Cullan. He decided to hold onto the .45 until he knew what kind of gun was used to kill Shirley Parker.

Mason called Mickey from the car. When he didn't answer, Mason called Harry and asked him to check out a possible break-in at his office and promised to meet him there as soon as possible.

When he parked in the garage at the Intercontinental Hotel, Beth made no move to get out of the car. Mason wasn't certain she could move at all.

"I'll take you upstairs," he offered.

Beth got out of the car without answering and started toward the elevator. He caught up to her, cupping her elbow with his hand, a gesture she ignored. He followed her inside her apartment, turning on lights as she slumped onto a sofa. After making certain they were alone, Mason sat next to her.

He didn't know what to think or feel about her. He didn't understand why she would have taken the pictures, though he did understand why she tried to shoot Ed Fiora and wondered if the same thing had happened with Jack Cullan. Whatever the answers, he was afraid to leave her alone, but he had to make certain Mickey was okay.

"Don't worry," she said, sensing his concern. "I don't need to kill myself. I'm already dead."

"Self-pity is a luxury for someone in your shoes."

She lifted her chin from her chest, focusing her blank eyes on him. "What do you suggest?"

"Start with the truth. How did your fingerprints end up in Cullan's bedroom?"

Beth looked away, biting her lower lip. "You want me to tell you that I was holding on to the headboard while he fucked me doggie-style?"

"I don't care if the two of you got naked and howled at the moon. Just once, I'd like the truth. Did you take those pictures?"

"Yes," she said with a resigned, flat tone.

"Why?"

"According to my therapist, I have a self-destructive tape playing in my head because I had an abusive father and a disinterested mother, so I do crazy things to punish myself."

"Do you believe that?"

"I don't believe anything. That's all an excuse. I did it because I wanted to, not because I know why I wanted to."

"Then why ask me to get them back?"

"After Jack was killed, I was afraid the police would think I did it because of the pictures. I had to get them back."

"Where's the gun Baker McKenzie gave you?"

"I got rid of it after Jack was killed. The paper said he was shot with a .38-caliber gun. My gun was a .38, and I knew that would look bad. I liked having a gun for protection, so I bought the Beretta."

"The police could have run ballistics tests on your gun and ruled it out as the murder weapon."

Beth got up and paced around the living room, finding renewed energy. "I admit I wasn't setting records for clear thinking. I just wanted to get the pictures back and get rid of the gun. I wanted to be a good girl again." She stopped in front of Mason and looped her fingers into the collar of his sweater, pulling him up. "I wanted to be a good girl for you."

She wrapped her arms around his neck, pressed her breasts hard against his chest, and ground her pelvis against his crotch. "You saved me," she murmured as she felt him grow hard.

Mason pushed her away. "What are you?"

She opened her eyes wide and licked her lips. "I'm just a girl who can't say no."

"And I'm not interested in yes," Mason said and left her standing in her living room.

CHAPTER FIFTY-SEVEN

Friday nights were big nights at Blues on Broadway, but business had slowed since New Year's Eve, and the joint was dead when Mason arrived shortly before midnight. Mickey had turned out to be a lousy bartender, and Blues had hired a temp who wasn't much better. Pete Kirby's trio had taken a gig on the road, and Blues hadn't found anyone to take their place. Jazz musicians were used to oddball gigs, but working for someone sitting in jail on a murder rap hadn't proved to be very attractive.

Mason recognized Harry's off-duty car, an old Crown Victoria that had done time as an on-duty detective's ride. Mason made his way through the bar, where three customers were nursing flat beers while the bartender cleaned glasses, a cigarette dangling from the corner of his mouth, dribbling ashes into the soapy sink water.

He took the stairs two at a time, his concern for Mickey quickening his pace. Fiora was in the casino business, but he didn't strike Mason as a man who bluffed very often. He took Fiora at his word when he said that he'd paid Mickey a visit. Mason knew enough about computers to read his e-mail. He had no idea that an amateur hacker like Mickey would leave an electronic trail that could lead to a beating. Mason was mentally calculating Mickey's workers' compensation benefits when he saw Mickey in the hall with Harry and his aunt Claire.

"Harry," Mason said, "is everything all right?"

Harry was wearing a warm-up suit and athletic shoes underneath an open trench coat. Claire was also wearing a warm-up suit under her made-for-the-tundra topcoat. It took Mason a minute to realize that they were wearing identical warm-up suits and that his aunt was wearing house slippers and that her car was not also parked outside. Both of them had a slightly rumpled, just-rousted-out-of-bed look. Mason wasn't certain, but he thought he saw a small hickey on Harry's neck. Mason flushed with a queasy jolt, like a teenager who'd walked in on his parents while they were doing it.

"No, everything is not all right!" Claire snapped. "Someone broke into your office and smashed your computer."

Mason stepped into his office. His computer tower was crumpled as if it had been in a head-on collision, and the top was peeled back as if it had been operated on with a can opener. His monitor was shattered. He looked around the rest of his office, confirmed that there wasn't any other damage, and came back out into the hallway.

"Thanks for coming over, Harry."

"Is that all you've got to say?" Claire demanded. "Every time I turn around, you're this close to getting killed or robbed," she said, pinching her fingers together. "I won't have it!"

Mason hadn't seen his aunt this angry in years. "I'm sorry. I didn't mean to upset you."

"Well, you have, and so has he!" she said, jabbing her thumb at Harry. "It's time you two started working together on this case instead of against each other." Harry and Mason both studied their feet, waiting for Claire's outburst to subside. "I'll wait in your office."

Mickey was grinning so widely that Mason forgot to ask if he was hurt. "I would not piss off that woman anymore if I was you."

Mason put his hand under Mickey's chin, tilting his head upward. "You look good with a black eye, Mickey. It gives you that mature look."

Harry referred to the notepad he always carried. "Your neighbor here, Mr. Shanahan, says he was asleep in his office when he heard a commotion next door. He jumped up to see what was going on and ran into his door and knocked himself out. By the time he came to, whoever had broken into your office was gone. That still your story, Mr. Shanahan?" Harry asked with no effort to disguise his disbelief.

"Yes, sir, Detective. That's my story and I'm sticking to it."

Harry turned to Mason. "Are you satisfied with that story?"

"It'll do for now."

"Good, 'cause it's bullshit and we both know it, but if you don't care, I don't care. At least we don't need anything else from Mr. Shanahan. Let's you and me go have a talk before your aunt makes us take turns walking into the door and knocking ourselves out."

"Don't think for one second that I'm going to clean up that mess for you," Claire said as Mason closed the door behind him.

Mason raised both hands in surrender, knowing better than to get in her way while she still had a head of steam going. Harry picked up the computer tower and peered inside.

"The hard drive is gone. You back up your stuff?"

"Not in the last six months."

"How long you had this computer?"

"Six months."

"You're screwed."

"Is that a professional opinion?"

"Worth every cent of the tax dollars you paid for it. Who did it?"

"Ed Fiora."

"Why?"

"He objected to me checking out his personal affairs."

"Hacking? You couldn't hack yourself. That kid, Shanahan—he do the hacking for you?"

"Yup."

"Fiora probably has somebody who runs security for his computer systems, picked up the hacking, traced it back to your computer. Fiora values his privacy. So why does Shanahan give me that crap about running into his door?"

"He's like all law-abiding citizens. He doesn't trust the cops and he thinks he's doing me a favor."

"Why are you investigating Fiora?"

CHAPTER FIFTY-EIGHT

Mason took two bottles of Budweiser out of his refrigerator and handed one to Harry. Claire gave him a long, threatening look, and he handed her the other bottle, then grabbed another one for himself. He threw his parka over his desk chair, sat down on the sofa, and put his feet up on the low table in front of it. Harry and Claire dumped their coats on top of his, and each took a chair at either end of the table. They raised their beers, Claire drinking the deepest.

"Cullan's murder, Shirley Parker's murder, and the fire at the barbershop were all about one thing—Jack Cullan's secret files," Mason said. "I was looking for a link, something that would tie Fiora to the files and the murders, or at least the other suspects."

"And who might the other suspects be? Assuming, of course, that we don't count your client." Harry asked.

Mason tipped his bottle at Harry. "You assume correctly. His Honor the mayor is on the take. He made at least one sweetheart deal with Fiora that lined the pockets of his old wide receiver Donovan Jenkins. Jenkins paid the mayor back by refinancing his house. That deal may have actually been legal, but I think there's more. That's what Mickey was looking for."

"Who else?"

Mason hesitated, swirling the beer, concluding that he had only one client, not two. "Beth Harrell. She gets the Head Case of the Year award. On the outside, she's a superachiever public servant. On the inside, she's a bad girl who owned a .38-caliber pistol she threw away after Cullan was killed because she thought it would look bad. Especially since Cullan was blackmailing her with dirty pictures."

"Where'd Cullan get the pictures?"

"She took them and gave them to her ex-husband before he was her ex. He sold them to Cullan."

"What kind of a woman would do that?" Claire asked.

"A severely messed-up one," Mason answered. "Beth claims she voted to give the license to the Dream Casino because it was the right thing to do. Then she got suspicious that Fiora had bribed the mayor. She was about to start an investigation when Cullan threatened her with the pictures."

"What makes you think she's telling the truth?" Claire asked.

Mason retrieved the envelope of pictures from an inside pocket in his parka. He dropped them on the table in front of Harry and Claire. "I've seen the pictures. Fiora gave them to me tonight. He was trying to convince me that he wasn't blackmailing Beth and that he had nothing to do with Cullan's or Shirley Parker's deaths."

Harry reached for the envelope, but Claire snatched it and opened it first. "I am never surprised what we will do to get even with ourselves," she said before passing the photographs to Harry.

Harry looked at the photographs without betraying any reaction. "Shirley Parker was killed with a .38-caliber bullet, but it was fired from a different gun than the one that was used to kill Jack Cullan. It sure would have been nice to have a look at Beth Harrell's gun. Where does all this leave Ed Fiora?"

"Fiora says he wasn't worried about Cullan's files because Cullan couldn't take Fiora down without taking himself down. That makes sense. Fiora wants his file before it winds up with someone he can't do business with. That also makes sense. He tried to hire me to find the file for him. That makes sense too. Killing Cullan and Shirley Parker doesn't make sense."

"What about the mayor?" Claire asked.

"Yeah," Mason said to Harry. "Did you ask the mayor if he had an alibi for the time of Cullan's murder?"

"Sure. Right after we asked him for semen samples so we could clear up some open rape cases."

Mason finished his beer in a final swallow. "All I've done in this case is chase my tail. I'm getting absolutely nowhere."

"Maybe you're just digging up a lot of dirt but no killers because your client is guilty," Harry said.

"Maybe. And maybe you and Zimmerman and the prosecuting attorney and the mayor are sweeping a lot of dirt under the rug because you want Blues to be guilty. It's obvious that the mayor was pressuring you to make a quick arrest."

"Sure he wanted a quick arrest. He also wanted a conviction, not a botched case."

"When did you first talk to the mayor about Cullan's murder?"

"Right after we got to the murder scene. I called the chief and the chief called the mayor. The mayor told the chief he wanted to meet with me and Carl, which really frosted the chief."

"Because that made the chief look like he wasn't running the investigation?" Claire asked.

"Exactly. There's more politics in the police department than the Catholic Church," Harry said. "The mayor told me and Carl that he wanted daily reports on the case until the son of a bitch who killed his lawyer was found guilty."

"So you've been on the phone with the mayor every day?" Mason asked.

"Not me and not the mayor. My partner, Carl, is a better politician than me. The mayor told Carl to report to his chief of staff, Amy White. She told Carl he was on twenty-four hour call and his cell phone better be on all the time." Harry laughed. "She's driving Carl crazy."

"There's one thing I don't get," Claire said. "Where did Cullan get all his dirt? I doubt that everyone was as stupid as Beth Harrell. Maybe whoever was supplying Cullan with information decided to go into business for himself—or herself—which meant putting Cullan out of business."

Mason and Harry stared at Claire, slack jawed at her insight. Claire smiled, careful not to smile too much, and set her empty bottle on the table. "I love both of you, but sometimes you are thick as fence posts. Let's go home, Harry, before that beer drowns out what little spark I've got left."

CHAPTER FIFTY-NINE

Mickey walked into Mason's office as soon as Harry and Claire hit the street. "Hey, boss," he said before Mason cut him off with a raised hand.

Claire had come at the case from a completely different angle than Mason or Harry. Both of them had made the mistake of focusing on the explanations that best suited their biases. Harry wanted it to be Blues. Mason wanted it to be someone Cullan was blackmailing. They both wanted it to be easy, and the truth was seldom that easy.

Mason opened the doors to the dry-erase board, wiped out a week's worth of now meaningless notes, wrote *Cullan's source for dirt* in large red letters on the board, and sat in his desk chair. He rocked and swiveled, fingers steepled beneath his chin, then rubbed his temples and thumped his desk with the palms of his hands.

Mickey tried again, "Lou, I've got—"

"It'll have to wait. Have a seat."

Mason shuffled through the papers on his desk until he found the initial police report on Cullan's murder. The dispatcher had recorded the call from Cullan's maid, Norma Hawkins, at 8:03 a.m. Mason remembered that the first cop on the scene had been a uniformed patrol officer. Mason scanned the report for his name, finding it at the bottom of the report. Officer James Toland had arrived at the scene at 8:10 a.m. Harry and Carl Zimmerman had arrived at 8:27 a.m.

Mason was beginning to think that Toland was like the guy who showed up at every major sporting event wearing a rainbow wig and holding a sign that said *John 3:16*. Toland had been first on the murder scene; he'd been at the bar to arrest Blues; and he'd busted Mason in Pendergast's office just in time to prevent Mason from reading Cullan's files. Nobody had timing that good. Not without help.

Mason called Rachel Firestone, tapping a pencil on his knee while the phone rang five times.

"What?" Rachel said, her voice thick with sleep.

"It's me, Lou."

"Whoopee."

"I need you to do something for me. It's important."

"I hope it's important enough to die for because I'm going to kill you if it isn't."

"I want you to check for any reports of a body found in Swope Park on Thursday evening any time in the three hours before the fire at the barbershop."

"Of course. Then I'll run a check for Jimmy Hoffa when I'm done."

"This is serious, Rachel."

"This is the middle of the night. Call me tomorrow," she said, and hung up.

Mason was jazzed. He had a hunch that felt so right it had to be wrong, and if he was right, it could still go down very wrong. He smacked his hands together.

"Okay, Mickey. What have you got?"

"This," Mickey said, holding up a thumb drive.

"And that is?"

"It's a thumb drive with a copy of the bank records of Ed Fiora and the mayor, plus a few dozen money-laundering stops in between that show a steady stream of cash from Fiora to the mayor. The total is around a hundred and fifty thousand bucks. It began a month before Fiora got his casino license and goes right up to last week. I backed the records up just before Fiora and his trolls did a tap dance on my face. I stuffed it down my pants when they busted in here."

Mason jumped out of his chair, pulled Mickey up, and embraced him. "I love you, man!"

"Don't go there, dude!" Mickey pushed Mason away and dusted himself off. "Now what?"

"First of all, you're hired. Second of all, we work weekends. Tomorrow night, we're going to the Dream Casino."

"We gamble on the job?"

"Only for high stakes," Mason said.

CHAPTER SIXTY

Mason was so wired when he got home that he had rowed a two-thousand-meter sprint just to wind down, adding a second sprint for good measure. By the time he took a shower, he was barely able to crawl into bed. The last thing he saw was his clock telling him it was four in the morning.

He was sleeping the sleep of the comatose when his phone rang Saturday morning. He let it ring until the answering machine came on.

"Pick up, Lou. The sun is up and you'd better be," Rachel said.

Mason fumbled for the phone, trying to clear his throat while squinting at the clock. It was eight o'clock. "I'm here," he groaned.

"Good. Paybacks are hell. Why do you want to know about a body in Swope Park?"

"Can't tell you," he said, pulling himself up in bed before collapsing back against his pillows.

"Why not?"

"I may be wrong about something. If I am, no one needs to know. If I'm right, you'll get the story."

"It had better be a good story. I talked to one of the dispatchers who's a friend of mine."

"You mean an anonymous source who gets a turkey at Thanksgiving?"

"I don't bribe people. The paper is too cheap. She's a kindred spirit."

"A member of the lesbian underground?"

"We're everywhere. She said there were no reports of a body

being reported or found in Swope Park on Thursday night or any night for the last six months. What does that tell you?"

"That you may get a hell of a story if I don't get killed."

"Then, don't get killed. I need all the good stories I can get."

"That's it? No Thanksgiving turkey?"

"I'd miss you. How's that?"

"Nice," he told her, and hung up.

Mason rolled over and tried to go back to sleep. He tossed and turned with the uneasy confirmation of his suspicions. He gave up when Tuffy stuck her nose in his face, reminding him that she wasn't operating on his schedule. Her whimper said she was overdue for breakfast and her morning ablutions in the backyard.

While Tuffy was outside, Mason took another shower, hoping that the pulsating hot water would trick his body into feeling fresh and renewed instead of tired and abused. After pulling on faded jeans, a washed-out green sweatshirt, and sneakers, he let the dog inside and poured himself into a chair at his kitchen table, wishing someone would appear and make his breakfast.

Cooking was not one of Mason's skills. He wasn't the kind of man who could scour his pantry for a few disparate leftovers and whip up a tantalizing omelet while whistling classical music and puzzling over what wine works best with a bagel and cream cheese. He relied too heavily on fast food, once prompting Claire to warn him that one day he would drive through McDonald's and the cashier would greet him by asking, "The usual, Mr. Mason?"

Tuffy was pacing around the kitchen, poking her head into nooks and crannies she'd explored countless times, before stopping in front of Mason and pawing his thigh. He gazed down at her, raising an eyebrow as if to ask, what now? She yelped once and trotted to the back door, repeating the ritual she observed whenever she wanted to go on a walk.

"Why not?" Mason muttered. "Maybe we'll find some roadkill for breakfast."

He put on his coat, grabbed a ball cap that he yanked low on his brow, and hooked Tuffy's collar to the leash he kept on a hook by the door.

Mason hadn't paid attention to the day until Tuffy took him outside. The sun had blasted away the grim bedrock of slate-colored clouds that had covered the city like a fossil layer for weeks. The temperature had climbed into the forties but felt even warmer in comparison to recent days. The air was crisp and clear and hit him like a shot of adrenaline. The next thing he knew, he was jogging alongside Tuffy, his jacket unzipped and a thin sheen of sweat lining his forehead. He grinned at his dog, who grinned back before sprinting after a squirrel.

Tuffy led Mason to Loose Park, the city's second-largest park, which was only a couple of blocks from his house. They stopped at the large pond along Wornall Road long enough for Tuffy to say hello to the other dogs that were walking their owners, Tuffy sniffing enough dog butts to last a lifetime. Mason was about to introduce himself to a good-looking woman with a white fur ball of a dog when Tuffy sniffed the dog once and knocked it on its butt. Horrified, the woman scooped up her dog, gave Mason the finger, and marched off in a huff.

A few minutes later, Mason and Tuffy power walked past Beth Harrell's building. He craned his neck skyward, shielding his eyes from the sun, wondering which windows were hers and what she was doing behind her drawn shades. Tuffy wasn't interested in the answer and tugged him along the last few blocks to the Plaza.

Mason tied her leash to a traffic sign outside Starbucks while he went inside for a blueberry muffin and a bottle of water. He shared both with Tuffy, pouring the water into a plastic bowl he borrowed from the cashier.

On the way back, they stopped at the waterfall in front of the Intercontinental Hotel. The waterfall plunged two stories from the pool deck to street level. The fountain had been turned off for the winter, but a heavy layer of ice had built up during the storms of the previous weeks. The sun bore down on the irregular slags of ice, reflecting and refracting across their faults, forecasting the coming meltdown.

From his vantage point, Mason could see west to the entrance to the hotel's parking garage on Ward Parkway. He could also see south, up Wornall Road, to Beth's building, which towered over the roof of the hotel. The juxtaposition of both views crystallized something that had lurked in the jumble of details that this case had become.

He remembered Beth telling him that Cullan had taken her home after the incident at Blues on Broadway the night he was killed. She had said that Cullan had dropped her at the door and that she had stayed inside the rest of the night. Later, she had told Mason that she began using the hotel's parking garage to avoid the press, taking advantage of the walkway between the hotel and her apartment building so that she wouldn't be seen coming or going.

Mason guessed that the security system in her apartment building included video monitoring of the apartment garage. Had Beth gone out again that night, or any night, her departure and return would have been recorded. If she'd used the hotel exit strategy, she could have left undetected.

That scenario, Mason realized, would have left her on foot. He doubted that she would have called a cab to take her to Cullan's house and told the driver to wait outside while she murdered Cullan.

Cullan lived in Sunset Hills, an exclusive area just south and west of the Plaza. The hills were real hills by Kansas City standards, making the round-trip walk from the hotel to Cullan's house a punishing one of several miles, though Beth could have hiked to Cullan's house, killed him, and walked back.

Mason shook his head at the possibility. The night Cullan was murdered had been brutal, with a lacerating wind chill and hard-driven snow. Even a cold-blooded killer wouldn't have made that hike. Unless the killer was convinced that no one else would think she might have done exactly that.

CHAPTER SIXTY-ONE

By the time Mason and Tuffy returned home, the prospect that Beth Harrell had covered the murder of Jack Cullan under a blanket of snow had robbed him of his enthusiasm for the beautiful morning. It also didn't jibe with his growing suspicion that James Toland and Carl Zimmerman had been dirt gofers for Cullan and might have killed Cullan to go into business on their own, as Claire had theorized.

When Mason called Zimmerman to ask for his help preserving Cullan's files, Zimmerman put him off with a lie about working a case involving a dead body in Swope Park. The lie had only one purpose—to keep Mason away from the files until Zimmerman and Toland could steal them and rig the bomb that would destroy the rest.

It was possible that Zimmerman and Toland hadn't known where the files were until Mason unwittingly tipped Zimmerman. Maybe Mason's phone call tipped Zimmerman, or maybe they had known all along, and Mason's call forced them to move the files. Maybe Shirley Parker made one last visit to check on the files and they killed her when she tried to stop them. There were too many maybes, but none of them made Toland and Zimmerman look clean to Mason.

Nor did Mason's suspicions prove anything. It would be difficult and dangerous to make a case against two cops, particularly when one of the cops was Harry's partner. He had gathered from Harry that it was a good partnership, though neither man had embraced the other as a blood brother. Still, they were cops and they were partners, and that was a stronger bond than most marriages.

Mason didn't even know where to begin. He couldn't talk to Harry, who would dismiss his theory as a malicious red herring Mason had fantasized to cast doubt on Blues's guilt. Even worse, Harry would consider it an unholy attempt to drive a wedge between him and Zimmerman and an unethical pitch to discredit their investigation. Mason couldn't go after Zimmerman without painting Harry with the same brush.

Mason's best and only idea was to keep an eye on Zimmerman. He had been to Zimmerman's house once before. Zimmerman lived in Red Bridge, a suburban subdivision in south Kansas City. Mason wouldn't stake out Zimmerman's house. That's what cops and PIs did, not lawyers. Besides, Mason didn't want to pee into a bottle on a cold day, even if the sun was shining.

All the same, a drive-by couldn't hurt. Mason looked at Tuffy. "Want to go for a ride?"

Tuffy ran him over racing to the garage. Mason opened the door to his TR6, and Tuffy vaulted the stick shift, landing in the passenger seat. It wasn't a top-down day, but it was close enough.

For Mason, the TR6 was the last great sports car ever built. He didn't believe it in the squishy way that some people believe that black is a slimming color, or that all good things come to those who wait. He believed it with the same bedrock certainty that Rocky Balboa believed when he told Mrs. Balboa that a man's got to do what a man's got to do.

In Mason's world, BMW, Porsche, and Audi roadsters were for cash-heavy baby boomers willing to overpay for the thrill of the wheel. The Corvette was a contender, but with its powerful engine and oversized tires, it was in another weight class. He conceded that those cars could outperform the TR6, but they couldn't outcool it. The brand name, Triumph, said it all for Mason.

The TR6's raw lines and hard look had captivated Mason the first time he had seen the car. By then, British Leyland had inexplicably abandoned the model, turning each of the ninety-four thousand TR6s it had made from 1969 to 1976 into instant classics.

Mason had never been much of a car guy. He'd always driven whatever he could afford until he couldn't afford to keep it running. He'd never gotten sweaty at the sight of a muscle car, nor had his head been turned by a sleek import. The TR6 was different. It had snagged his automotive heart, lingering there unrequited until he'd succumbed years later, taking advantage of a neighbor's divorce to buy his dream car. It was a British-racing-green, four-speed, six-cylinder, real live ragtop trip.

Tuffy loved the car more than Mason, delighting in the endless scents that sped past her when the top was down and her nose was in the wind. Sitting in his garage, Mason resisted his dog's pleading, doleful eyes to put the top down. A man and his dog both blowing in the wind on a cold winter morning would garner too much attention, no matter how brightly the sun was shining.

As he drove toward Carl Zimmerman's neighborhood, he had a throat-tightening epiphany. He was in over his head in a death-penalty case that was as likely to cost him his life as it was his client's. He needed help, and the one person who could help him the most was sitting in the county lockup. Mason tapped the clutch, downshifted, and opened the throttle. The burst of growling speed came at the same moment as a crazy idea of how he could get Blues out of jail.

Mason circled Zimmerman's block once, relieved that there were no signs of life in the split-level, brick-front house. He circled again, this time stopping at the curb on the street that intersected Zimmerman's. A minivan parked in front of him gave him added cover and a right-angle view of Zimmerman's house, which was in the middle of the block. He turned off his engine and hoped that no one would notice the only classic sports car within miles, even though a sign at the corner read *Neighborhood Watch! We Call the Police!*

Tuffy pawed at her window, and Mason cranked the engine so he could put it down for her. She leaned the upper third of her body out the window and wagged her tail in Mason's face. He knew a bad idea when he had one and said as much to the dog.

"This is nuts. We're out of here."

Before Mason could put the car in gear, a lumbering black Chevy Suburban turned onto his street. Mason blanched when he looked in his rearview mirror and saw Carl Zimmerman behind the wheel. He scrunched down in his seat, racking his memory for any mention that he might have ever made to Zimmerman about owning the TR6.

The Suburban rolled past, slowing for the stop sign at the corner. Mason peeked at the Suburban and saw a collection of young faces pressed against the passenger-side windows, mouths agape at the TR6 and the dog riding shotgun, hanging out the window, relieved that Zimmerman ignored him.

He watched as Zimmerman pulled into his driveway and a half dozen young boys dressed in Cub Scout uniforms piled out of the Suburban, some of them staring and pointing at his car parked half a block away. Carl Zimmerman herded them toward the front door, taking a long look at Mason's car before following his troop into the house.

"Brilliant," Mason told Tuffy. "Carl Zimmerman—homicide detective, Cub Scout leader, and murderer. That's the ticket!"

Tuffy ignored him and pointed her snout into the breeze as Mason headed for home.

CHAPTER SIXTY-TWO

Mason picked Mickey up at nine o'clock, still driving the TR6, counting on the cool to carry into the casino and make them winners. Mickey had told Mason that he was working crowd control at the bar and that Mason should pick him up there instead of at his apartment. Mason was pretty certain that Mickey's apartment was also his office above the bar but saw no reason to tell Mickey. At least, Mason figured, he'd always know where to find him.

Mickey was waiting on the sidewalk when Mason pulled up. "Is there a crowd inside that needs to be controlled?"

"Not unless you count three guys who don't have four teeth among them. If Blues doesn't get out soon, I doubt that any PR campaign will save this joint. It's going to shrivel up and blow away before spring."

"Did you do what I told you?" Mason asked as he pulled into the light traffic on Main Street.

"Piece of cake. I printed out a hard copy of Fiora's bank records, and I put it in your desk just like you told me."

"And what about the rest?"

"That's the part I don't understand. I e-mailed the file to Rachel Firestone just like you told me, but I delayed the actual transmission until ten o'clock Monday morning. What's up with that?"

"It's an insurance policy. We're going to trade the flash drive to Fiora. He'll suspect that we kept another copy of the records, and he'll send someone back to search my office. Hopefully, when he finds the copy you put in my desk, he'll be satisfied. If he doesn't hold up his end of the deal I'm going to make with him, Rachel will get the e-mail with the records. If Fiora comes through, we'll cancel the e-mail."

"And if he tries anything rough, we can tell him about the e-mail," Mickey said.

"That is a very bad idea. If he knows about the e-mail, he can cancel it."

"So what do we do if he tries anything rough?"

"Duck," Mason said.

"I'll try to remember that. Does Fiora know we're coming?"

"Yeah. I called the casino this afternoon and left a message. I'm expecting the VIP treatment."

Mason used valet parking to give Fiora the added comfort of holding his car keys, wanting Fiora to think the odds were all with the house on the game they were about to play. Mason had to press, but not too hard, take risks, but not too great.

Tony Manzerio was waiting for them. He didn't speak, settling for the universal sign language of goons everywhere—a nod of the head that meant follow me and keep your mouth shut.

Mason and Mickey did as they were nodded to do, trailing a respectful five steps behind Manzerio. People moved out of Manzerio's way without being told or nodded. The man was large enough and his eyes were dead enough to trigger the flight side of the survival impulse, Mason catching a few there-but-for-the-grace-of-God-go-I expressions.

They took an elevator marked *Private*, opened a door marked *Authorized Personnel Only*, and walked down a corridor marked *Secure Area*. None of which made Mason feel safe.

Manzerio led Mason and Mickey into Fiora's office. A window looked out over the Missouri River, a black view without dimension or detail. Fiora sat at a poker table playing solitaire.

"Did you search them?" he asked without looking up.

Manzerio didn't answer. Instead, he ran his porterhouse-sized hands up and down their sides, torsos, legs, and arms.

"Nothin'. No guns. No wires."

"Wait outside."

Fiora turned over the facedown cards until he found the one he wanted. Smiling, he ran through the rest of the cards until they were all arranged in order.

"How about that! I won again."

"Odds always favor the house, but cheating takes the suspense out of it," Mason said.

"I'm a businessman, Mason, not a gambler. The craps table is for suckers. I need an edge, I take it. I don't make business a game of chance."

"I like to think of it as supply and demand. The market moves buyers and sellers to the middle, where they can make a deal."

"Your message said you wanted to make a trade. What do I have that you would want?"

"My law practice."

"How could I possibly have your law practice?"

"It's on the hard drive you ripped out of my computer last night. Client files, my receivables, my payables. The works."

"That must be inconvenient for you. What's the matter? Didn't you back your stuff up? I don't know much, but I know that much. I got people working for me that don't do nothing but back shit up."

"Actually, I did back up one thing." He reached into his coat pocket and pulled out the flash drive. "It's not much, really. Just some bank records you might be interested in."

Fiora's eyes hardened. "You're taking a hell of a risk coming to my place offering to trade my records to me. Why don't I just have Tony come in here and take that drive and throw your ass in the river?"

Mason didn't flinch. "You said it yourself. You're a businessman. Buy, sell, trade, but don't take chances. I'm the same way. I was out of line meddling in your business and I'm sorry. Last night, you convinced me that you had nothing to do with Jack Cullan's murder. I don't need to clutter up the defense of my client with extraneous bullshit that the judge won't let me get into evidence anyway. I'm offering you this flash drive in good faith, the same way you gave me the pictures of Beth Harrell. All I want is my hard drive."

"And I'm supposed to believe that you don't have another copy of this stashed someplace?"

"I can't help it if you're not a believer. I'm a lawyer, not a rabbi."

Fiora studied Mason for a minute. "Come over here, Rabbi Mason. I want to show you something."

Mason joined Fiora at the window. The light from inside the office and the lack of light outside made the view opaque.

"Is there something I should be looking at?"

"You might find this interesting." There were two switches next to the window. Fiora hit one, and the office went dark. He hit the other, and the prow of the boat where Mason had celebrated New Year's Eve was bathed in a spotlight. "Nice view, don't you think?"

Mason repressed an involuntary shudder. "It's terrific. What's your point?"

"Every public area of this boat is under constant video surveillance. I want to know everything that happens on my boat. That prow is a very popular spot. Lovers like to make out there. Losers like to jump off. We got to watch it all the time."

"It must be tough to get good video in the dark."

"Nah! We got these low-light cameras make it practically like your living room. The technology is fantastic. This case of yours works out okay, you come back and we'll watch some home movies. What do you say?"

Fiora was giving Mason a mixed message. He was telling Mason that he knew what had happened on New Year's Eve and still had the proof. Maybe it was an offer to tell him who had tried to kill him, and maybe it was a not-so-subtle threat.

"You serve popcorn?"

Fiora laughed once without conviction. "You're good with the jokes. Don't be too funny, Rabbi Mason. You and your altar boy have a seat, make yourselves comfortable. I got to check with my computer people and see what they've done with your hard drive. It may be they already wiped it clean. In the meantime, why don't you give me that flash drive of yours so I can have them check it out?"

Mason grinned at Fiora and tossed the drive to him. "This one is blank. Bring me my hard drive and a computer. Mickey will check it out. If everything is on it but your records, Mickey will get you the real flash drive."

Fiora chuckled. "Careful you don't hit on sixteen and go bust."

CHAPTER SIXTY-THREE

Fiora left Mason and Mickey in his office. Mason picked up Fiora's deck of cards and looked at Mickey.

"Gin rummy. A buck a point. I'll charge your losses as an advance against your salary."

"That's really generous of you. I haven't played cards since I was a kid. You'll have to remind me of the rules."

Mason sat at the poker table and motioned Mickey to do the same, wondering how many scams Mickey could run at one time. "Am I about to get cleaned out?"

"Right down to your socks, boss. Deal."

By the time Fiora and Manzerio returned an hour later, Mason was down two hundred and fifty dollars. They watched while Mickey shuffled the cards as if he'd been born with them in his hands, fanning them, making bridges, palming top cards and bottom cards, and marking the corners of other cards with his thumbnail.

"Hey, kid," Fiora said, "you get tired of working for this stiff, I got a place for you at one of our tables."

"He can't quit," Mason said. "He's got to give me a chance to win my money back."

"Those words are the secret of my success," Fiora said. "That, and never trusting anybody, especially a schmuck lawyer who thinks he can come into my place and flimflam me like I was a refugee from a Shriners convention."

"I told you the flash drive was blank and that I'd get you the real one. I'm not trying to con you."

"Then you are a dumber cocksucker than I gave you credit for." Fiora stuck his hand out to Manzerio, who gave him a stack of papers. "Tony took another tour of your office. Seems you forgot to mention the copy of my bank records you printed out, you stupid fuck! I ought to have Tony beat you right up to the limit!"

Fiora's face turned purple as he bit off each word, casting flecks of spittle like confetti at a parade. Mason hung his head sheepishly, letting Fiora's outburst pass.

"Well, what the fuck do you have to tell me now, Rabbi Bullshit?"

"Look, I'm sorry," Mason began. "I'm out of my league here. It was my insurance policy, but that's it. You've got everything now. Let's finish our business and I'll get out of here."

"You'll be carried out of here! Why should I trade you anything but your fucking life?"

"Because you don't kill people, that's why. You said so yourself. I've got to have my files back or I'm out of business. You need your files back or you're out of business. It's not very complicated."

Fiora's natural color seeped back into his face as he rolled the papers into a cylinder and thumped them against his palm. "Don't fuck with me, Mason. I'm telling you, do not fuck with me. You got that, Rabbi?"

He smacked Mason's head with the rolled papers. Mason grabbed Fiora's wrist and pulled his arm down to the table, Fiora wincing, as much in shock as in pain. Manzerio took a step toward Mason, who released his grip. Fiora yanked his wrist from Mason's hand while motioning Manzerio to stay where he was with his other.

"I got it, Ed," Mason said so softly that Manzerio couldn't hear him. "Now you get this. You hit me again, and you can spend the rest of your fucking life wondering who's going to end up with that flash drive."

Fiora held Mason's sharp stare. "You got balls, Mason. I give you that. I give you that. Tony, have that four-eyed geek bring the computer in here. Let's get this over with."

A short time later, Mickey booted up the computer and

searched the hard drive for its contents. "It's got everything but the bank records, boss. You want me to remove the hard drive?"

"Give Fiora the other flash drive first, and let him see what's on it."

Mickey un-tucked his shirt and reached behind to the small of his back where he had taped the drive. He popped it into the computer and stood back as Fiora's bank accounts flashed across the screen.

"Good enough?" Mason asked.

"Good enough," Fiora said. "You can pull the hard drive out. Tony, give the kid the tools."

Mason said, "I'm glad we were able to work this out."

"Don't press your luck," Fiora told him.

"There is one other thing," Mason said.

"It better not be another flash drive."

"It's not. It's a favor. The one you said you owed me for stopping Beth Harrell from shooting you."

"Mason, you are too much. You bust my balls on this bank account shit, and then you got even more balls to ask me for a favor."

"I saved your life last night. That was a favor. This was business. You owe me the favor."

Fiora sighed, trapped by his own curious ethics. "What is it?"

"I want my client released on bail."

"Sorry, I can't do it."

"I don't believe you. You're wired into the prosecutor's office. That's how you knew they were going to offer Blues a plea bargain. Hell, it may have been your idea to begin with. I think I may know who has Cullan's files. I can't get to them myself and it's just as risky for you. Blues can get them. If there's nothing in your file that links you to Cullan's murder, you can have it. No copies and no questions. My client is innocent. I need those files to prove it."

"You aren't asking for much, are you?"

"I need an edge, I take it," Mason said. "The assistant prosecutor and I are meeting with Judge Carter on Monday morning at eight o'clock. I want Blues released on bail before ten. Make it happen."

CHAPTER SIXTY-FOUR

"That was extremely cool, dude," Mickey said.

They had just pulled away from the curb at the casino, and Mickey was fiddling with the radio, looking for some celebration tunes.

"Maybe. I just conspired with Ed Fiora to improperly influence a judge to get Blues out on bail. Fiora probably has the whole thing on tape. That doesn't sound so cool to me."

"Then why did you make the play?"

"It's the only one I had."

"That's bad public relations, man."

"What's that supposed to mean?"

"Let me tell you a story. I was conceived on the Fourth of July under a lucky star. My mother, Libby, spotted it over my father's shoulder from the backseat of his ragtop Firebird."

"I like the car better than the story."

"Dude! Chill and pay attention. My mother said the star was Altair and that it was found in the wing of the constellation Aquila the Eagle. Aquila was the mythical bird who helped Jupiter crush the Titans and seize control of the universe."

"So you're Aquila and I'm Jupiter?"

"You tell me. Anyway, Altair was a shepherd in love with another star, Vega, who was stranded on the western side of the Milky Way. Once a year, on the seventh night of the seventh moon, the lovers united across the heavens."

"So are you the son of a shepherd or the son of a star?"

"Libby was always a little vague about whether Altair started out as an eagle's wing and ended up a shepherd or vice versa. I figured he was an early cross-dresser, kind of a mythological RuPaul."

"No doubt the kind of role model that made you what you are today," Mason said.

"My mother told me the story the first time I asked about my father. I may have been a kid, but I knew the difference between an answer and a story. So I asked again. She told me I had two choices. Either my mother got knocked up in the backseat of a Firebird on a hot July night sticky enough to melt bugs together, and my father, who had great shoulders but no spine, ran out on us. Or I was conceived under a lucky star and I was destined for great deeds and greater love."

"Which one did you choose?"

"Adventure and babes. Either you just conspired with Ed Fiora to improperly influence a judge to get Blues out of jail, or you simply asked a friend if he'd put in a good word with the prosecutor to consider a reasonable bail for Blues. That's public relations."

Mason shook his head. "Don't ever run for office, Mickey."

"Why not, man?"

"You just might win."

CHAPTER SIXTY-FIVE

Monday morning was bleak. The sun's weekend cameo appearance had not been renewed for an extended run. Heavy clouds, thick and dusky, had rolled in from the north overnight, limiting the day's light to the perpetual gray of dawn. A cold front swept along at ground level, driving a gnawing, eroding wind.

Mason huddled in his Jeep, waiting for a stoplight to change and wondering whether the heater would kick in before he got to the courthouse. The day matched the mood of dark desperation that had gripped him since his fall from grace at Ed Fiora's feet.

Mickey's flexible ethic hadn't soothed his wounded conscience. He knew where the line was drawn between zealous advocacy for his client and the dark side. Even so, he'd stepped over it. It wasn't a movable line, one that could be redrawn in the sand or one over which he could hop back and forth with a moral pogo stick.

He'd replayed Blues's case a thousand times in the last thirty-six hours, each time he'd come to the same fork in the road, and each time he'd made the same choice. Not that it gave him much comfort. Neither did the replays that he often watched with his mind's eye of the man he'd killed more than a year ago. Then he'd been cornered, left without a choice. This time, there may have been another way out, but he hadn't been able to find it.

Mason knew that Ed Fiora wouldn't treat Mason's favor as a balancing of the books. Instead, he would record it as an investment with an interest rate that would make a loan shark blush. Fiora would come to collect one day unless Mason could wipe the ledger clean once and for all.

Icy pellets peppered Mason's windshield as he parked in the lot across the street from the courthouse. He cursed the weather and his own weakness as he cautiously made his way across the slick pavement.

Patrick Ortiz was waiting in the hallway outside Judge Carter's chambers when Mason arrived, sipping a cup of coffee, studying notes on his legal pad. Mason had decided to let Ortiz raise the issue of bail, not wanting to be too obvious with his knowledge that the fix was in. He knew that Ortiz wouldn't be happy, and he didn't want to rub his face in it.

"Morning, Patrick."

"Lou."

Ortiz greeted him with equal neutrality. They stood like two commuters waiting for the train, strangers avoiding eye contact and conversation, until the outer door to the judge's chambers opened and her secretary summoned them inside.

Judge Carter was waiting for them in her chambers, seated behind her desk, signing orders from the previous day's hearings. Her black robe was hanging on a coat hook. A half-eaten bagel and a plastic container of yogurt sat on the edge of her desk next to an empty coffee cup.

Judge Carter was fastidious in appearance and demeanor, impatient with the unprepared, and unsympathetic toward the guilty. Female African American judges were no longer a novelty, but a conservative Republican female African American state court judge who was on a short list for appointment to the federal bench was a rare phenomenon.

She had dark circles under her eyes, made darker by the contrast with her own rich coffee-colored skin. Mason had the sense that she'd either worked late the night before or gotten an early start this morning. Either way, she didn't look like she was having a good day and he didn't expect a warm reception.

"Sit down, Counselors," she instructed, waving them into the leather chairs opposite her desk. Floor-to-ceiling bookshelves crammed with statutes, appellate decisions, and treatises rose behind her, accenting her own imposing style. "Let's talk about your case. You're set for trial on Monday, March fourth. Tell me now if you'll be ready for trial. I don't like last-minute requests for continuances."

"The people will be ready," Ortiz said.

"The defense will be ready as well, Your Honor."

"There's been an awful lot of pretrial publicity. Are you going to ask for a change of venue?" she asked Mason.

"No. Hopefully, the press coverage will die down and we can get a fair jury."

Mason had been pleased with the press coverage so far and was counting on the jury to have read and remembered the stories that cast doubt on the police investigation and Blues's guilt.

"When we get to jury selection, you'll both ask the jurors if they've read anything about the case, if they've made up their minds already, and if they can be fair. The ones who want to serve will answer no, no, and yes. The ones who want to go home or go to work will answer yes, yes, and no."

Judge Carter had recited the truth about jury selection that every lawyer and judge wrestled with in every case. She said it with more resignation than humor, and the lawyers nodded their own understanding of the dilemma.

"Any other problems lurking out there on either side?" she asked them.

Mason kept silent, waiting for Ortiz to raise the question of bail.

"There is one issue," Ortiz said. "Defense counsel is a suspect in an arson and a homicide that took place last Thursday night. In the event that he's charged with either of those crimes, it could affect the trial date."

Ortiz dropped his bombshell with a routine matter-of-factness that underscored its crippling impact. Mason's stomach nose-dived as he stared at Ortiz, unable to contain his utter amazement. Ortiz looked straight ahead at the judge like someone who'd farted in a crowd and pretended not to notice. Judge Carter continued the exercise in understatement.

"I can see how that would be a problem. When does your office expect to make a decision whether to charge Mr. Mason? I'm certain he is as interested in knowing that as I am."

"It's a complicated case, Your Honor. The fire marshal is still investigating the cause and origin of the fire. The autopsy of the victim has been completed, but I don't have the final report. The investigation is ongoing. It's hard to know for sure when we'll be ready to present something to the grand jury. Maybe Mr. Mason will withdraw as counsel and the defendant will hire somebody else so that we can stay on track for trial."

Mason felt as if he were having an out-of-body experience, as if he'd left the room completely and crossed over to the twilight zone. Fiora had returned Mason's lifesaving favor with his own life-threatening ploy. That was the only thing Mason could conclude. Either that, or Fiora had only had inside information from the prosecutor's office, and not the juice to make Leonard Campbell give up his opposition to bail for Blues. Mason hated that he had compromised himself with Fiora. He hated it even more that his tactic had blown up in his face.

"Mr. Mason," Judge Carter said, "I assume you are aware of the ongoing investigation. Have you discussed with your client the possibility that you may have to withdraw as his attorney?"

Mason breathed deeply, collecting himself. "No, I haven't, Your Honor. I will speak to him today, but I doubt that he will want me to withdraw. I'm confident that I won't be charged with either of those crimes. My client will consider the threat to charge me as just another part of the prosecutor's strategy to pressure him into pleading guilty to a crime he didn't commit and will insist that I remain his counsel. That's how he and I view the prosecutor's opposition to bail and that's how I view these threatened charges."

"What about that, Mr. Ortiz? Why has the state taken such a hard line on bail? I've reviewed the court file on this case. You're relying on circumstantial evidence and one fingerprint for a capital murder case against a man with long-standing ties to the community and the financial ability to post a considerable bond. I've routinely granted bail in such cases. Why shouldn't I do that now?"

Ortiz clenched the sides of his legal pad, frustrated at the change in direction Judge Carter had taken. "The defendant has a history of violent behavior. He's a threat to the community, he's—"

"Getting released on bail. Mr. Bluestone has never been convicted of a crime. He served his country in the military. He served this community as a police officer. I hope you are devoting as much time to proving your case against him as you are the one against his lawyer. I'm setting bond at $250,000. That will be all, gentlemen."

Ortiz exploded out of his seat, nearly running over Judge Carter's secretary on his way out. Mason rose more slowly, making certain that his legs weren't shaking before he stood up. Judge Carter took a pack of cigarettes and a lighter from her desk drawer, leaned deeply into the back of her chair, and lit up. She blew the smoke out her nose, ignoring the *No Smoking* sign that hung on her wall.

"You know something, Mr. Mason?" she said. "You wasted a very expensive favor. I would have granted your client bail anyway."

CHAPTER SIXTY-SIX

Mason found the men's room, bent over a sink, and splashed his face with cold water until his skin stung. He wiped his face with paper towels, scrubbing at invisible stains. He challenged his image in the mirror for an explanation but found no answers in his own bewilderment.

He had wasted more than an expensive favor. Fiora hadn't gone through the prosecutor's office. He'd gone straight to Judge Carter, and now Mason had wasted her career, laid her bare to whatever hold Fiora had on her. If he didn't find a way to unring this bell, he would have wasted his own career as well.

At least Blues would be out of jail in a few hours and together they could try to find a way out of the wilderness. Mason found a room reserved for lawyers to meet with their witnesses, locked the door, and called Mickey, unable to stop the flutter in his voice.

"The judge ordered Blues released on bail."

"You want me to cancel the e-mail to Rachel Firestone?"

"Immediately. Copy Fiora's bank records on two different flash drives. I've got a safe-deposit box at City Bank. The key is in the top drawer of my desk. Put the drives in the box. I'll call the bank and tell them that you are coming over to use the box. Then wait for me at the office."

"What are you going to do?"

"Arrange for the bail and wait for them to process Blues's release."

"You don't sound so good, boss. You okay?"

"Yeah, I'm fine. I'm just trying to figure out the part where

Jupiter crushes the Titans."

"Don't forget your wingman, boss. You don't have to go it alone."

Mason paused, realizing Mickey was right about that. He didn't have to go it alone, but he didn't want to take anyone else down with him.

"Thanks. I'll talk to you later."

Mason's next call was to Carlos Guiterriz, his favorite bail bondsman. Carlos ran a one-man shop and took it personally when the prosecutor's office opposed bond for a defendant, claiming they were conspiring against him in his effort to support three ex-wives and five children.

"Guiterriz Bail Bonds," he said when Mason called.

"Carlos, it's Lou Mason. I need a bond for a quarter of million this morning. Can you do that?"

"Who's it for?"

"Wilson Bluestone, Jr., and let's keep it our secret. The press will pick it up soon enough."

"Holy shit, Lou! That is too sweet! How in the hell did you swing that?"

Mason had anticipated the question and knew that Carlos would repeat the answer a hundred times before the day was out.

"Judge Carter ordered the bail. She said she'd granted bail to other defendants in cases like Blues and that she wouldn't treat him any differently."

"I'll bet that tight-ass Patrick Ortiz shit sideways!"

"It was a thing of wonder." Guiterriz's enthusiasm took the rough edge off Mason's mood. "Blues will put up his bar as collateral, and I've got stocks worth fifty thousand bucks if you need more than that. Get the bond to the courthouse right away."

Guiterriz laughed loudly enough that Mason had to hold his phone away from his ear. "A thing of wonder," he quoted Mason when he stopped laughing. "I would have put up the bond myself to see Ortiz take it in the shorts like that. Give me an hour."

Mason wandered downstairs to the first-floor lobby of the

courthouse, undecided how to kill time until Guiterriz showed up. He stood at the glass doors that fronted Twelfth Street and watched pedestrians and drivers fight to keep their balance as a new coating of ice descended on the city.

City hall was across the street. Mason hadn't heard from Amy White since their meeting in the parking lot of the Hyatt Hotel. If Carl Zimmerman had been keeping her informed about the status of the homicide investigation, she might know something about Zimmerman's whereabouts the night Shirley Parker was killed.

Clutching his topcoat around his collar, Mason made the crossing from the courthouse to city hall, shook the ice from his shoulders, and rode the elevator to the twenty-ninth floor in the hope that he would catch Amy in her office, finding her waiting for the elevator when it opened on her floor. She stepped onto the elevator and pushed the button for the first floor.

"Perfect timing," Mason told her as he kept his finger on the button to open the elevator door. "I hoped that I would catch you in the office."

"Lousy timing. Whatever it is, I don't have time unless you have a hundred thousand tons of salt and a fleet of trucks to spread it. The weather service says we're going to get two inches of ice and ten inches of snow in the next twelve hours."

"I need to talk with you about something. It's important."

"What is it?"

"Carl Zimmerman."

Amy's mouth tightened as if a sudden pain had struck her. "You've got as long as the elevator takes to get downstairs."

Mason punched the buttons for all twenty-eight floors. "This may take a while," he said.

CHAPTER SIXTY-SEVEN

Mason and Amy eyed each other as the ancient elevator lurched to a halt at each of the next three floors. Amy broke off their eye contact with a nervous glance at her watch. The illuminated buttons on the elevator panel promised another twenty-five sea-sickening stops. Mason waited for Amy to speak first and set the course for his questions. The door opened on the twenty-fifth floor. Amy took a step toward the open door when Mason blocked her path.

"I'm getting off," she insisted.

"Nope. A deal is a deal. All the questions I can ask until we hit bottom."

Mason pushed the button to close the elevator door.

"Okay, fine," she said without meaning either. "What about Carl Zimmerman?"

"You know him?"

"He's a cop. Good enough?"

"Easy, Amy. How much snow can fall before we finish stopping at the next twenty-four floors? How do you know that he's a cop?"

"The chief brought him to the mayor's office after Jack Cullan was found dead. He and another detective—I think the other one was named Harry Ryman—were investigating the case and the mayor wanted some answers. The chief told Zimmerman to keep me updated on the case."

Mason listened, his silence prompting her to continue.

"You know all that already or you wouldn't be asking me," she said. "And you can't be so stupid to think I would lie about something you could so easily prove that I did know. So get to the point. You're running out of floors."

A barely operable ceiling fan wheezed and sucked warm, greasy air from the elevator shaft into the elevator, filling the car with the metallic taste of friction-heated oil. The odor combined with each ball-bouncing stop, turning their ride into a stomach-churning descent. Amy took off her knee-length navy wool coat and Burberry scarf and unbuttoned the high-necked collar of her dress. Her face was taking on a pasty, alien hue. Mason couldn't tell if her suddenly green-gilled complexion was due to their rocky ride or his questions.

"When was the last time he checked in with you?"

"I didn't log him into my PalmPilot. What difference does it make?"

"These are my floors, Amy," Mason said, pointing to the glowing buttons. "I get to use them any way I want. When was the last time you talked to Carl Zimmerman?"

"Last week. I don't remember the day, the time, or what we talked about."

"The conversation I want to know about is one that I think you'd remember. It was about Jack Cullan's files."

"That's a conversation I would have remembered, and I don't. You've got three floors left. Make them count."

"Where were you last Thursday night between six and ten o'clock?"

"Probably eating rubber chicken at a civic award dinner with the mayor, or home wishing I was."

"Did Zimmerman call you that night?"

The elevator stopped at the first floor, the doors opened, and they stepped out into the lobby. Amy steadied herself with one hand against a pillar, gulping cleaner air. They could see the snow tumbling from the sky like feathers from a billion ruptured pillows.

"My God!" Amy said. "This is going to be the rush hour from hell." Turning to Mason, she asked, "Do you have any idea how many complaints we will get by noon tomorrow that somebody's street hasn't been plowed?" Mason shook his head. "Everyone but the mayor will call. His street always gets plowed." She touched her forehead with the back of her hand, wiping away sweat she must have imagined. "I'm sorry, Lou. What did you ask me?"

Mason smiled. He'd questioned too many witnesses too many times to be pushed off track.

"Did Carl Zimmerman call you last Thursday night?"

Amy drew on her reserves of exasperation. "Yes, no, maybe. I don't remember. Should I?"

"That depends on whether Zimmerman needs an alibi for Shirley Parker's murder."

Amy studied Mason as she tied her scarf around her neck, cinching it securely under her chin, pulled her coat back on, and took her time carefully buttoning each button. She cocked her head to one side in a thoughtful pose and clasped her hands together.

"No," she said at last. "I'm quite certain I didn't talk to Detective Zimmerman at all that night."

CHAPTER SIXTY-EIGHT

Mason took seriously Patrick Ortiz's announcement that he was a suspect in the arson at Pendergast's office and in the murder of Shirley Parker. While the jailhouse bureaucrats processed Blues's release on bail, he spent the rest of the morning waiting for the police department's records clerk to make him a copy of the investigative reports on both crimes. He pushed her limited tolerance for defense lawyers when he asked for two sets of the reports as well as another set of the reports on the Cullan murder, knowing that Blues would want his own set.

Shortly after one o'clock, Blues emerged from the jail wearing the same clothes as the day he had been arrested. The suit he'd worn for his preliminary hearing was crammed into a grocery bag. Mason embraced him, Blues balking, more comfortable with a fist tap.

"Do I want to know how you pulled this off?" Blues asked.

"No. You hungry?"

"Is a bluebird blue? My tribal ancestors ate better on the reservation than I ate in that jail."

"Let's get out of here. I'm buying lunch."

The snow already had covered the streets and sidewalks, obliterating where one began and the other stopped. The only clues were the cars stacked bumper-to-bumper on every street, many of them stuck on the sheet of ice that lay beneath the snow, tires spinning in a futile effort to get traction. Other drivers had made the mistake of trying to go around those cars, only to slide into someone else attempting the same maneuver. The result was automotive gridlock accompanied by blaring horns, screaming commuters, and ecstatic tow-truck drivers.

Blues pointed to a bar a block west of the courthouse. "Let's try Rossi's. He never closes."

Rossi's Bar & Grill lived off of the traffic from city hall, the county courthouse, and police headquarters. Judges, lawyers, and bureaucrats provided the lunch traffic. Cops owned the place after hours. DeWayne Rossi was a retired deputy sheriff who heard everything, repeated nothing, and spent his days and nights parked on a stool behind the cash register chewing cigars. Rossi tipped the scales at more than three hundred pounds, limiting his exercise to making change for a twenty. Regular patrons had a secret pool picking the date he would stroke out. Rossi liked the action enough to have placed his own bet.

Rossi's had eight tables and was decorated in late-twentieth-century dark and dingy. A pair of canned spotlights washed the bar in weak light. Short lamps with green shades barely illuminated each table. A splash of daylight filtered in through dirty windows. A color TV hung from the ceiling above the bar and was permanently tuned to ESPN Classic. Rossi kept a .357 Magnum under the bar in case anyone tried to rob the place or change the channel.

There were two waitresses. Donna worked days and Savannah worked nights. They had both worked the street until they'd had too many johns and too many busts. The cops who used to arrest them now overtipped them to balance the books. A fry cook whose name no one knew hustled burgers and pork tenderloins from a tiny kitchen in the back.

"I haven't been in here since I quit the force," Blues said as he and Mason stamped the snow from their shoes.

"You didn't miss the atmosphere?"

"I didn't miss the company. I'm as welcome in a cops' bar as a whore is in church."

One table was occupied, as was one seat at the bar. Rossi turned away from the TV screen long enough to look at them, giving Blues an imperceptible nod that may just have been his jowls catching up with the rest of his head. Donna, a lanky, washed-out blonde with slack skin and a downturned mouth, was sitting at one of the tables reading *USA Today* and smoking a cigarette.

Mason and Blues chose a table against the wall that gave them a view out the windows. Donna materialized, setting glasses of water in front of them and laying her hand on Blues's shoulder.

"Long time, darling. How you been?"

"No complaints that count, Donna. How's life treating you?"

"Same way I treat it. Neither one of us gives a shit about the other. What'll you have on this lovely day?"

"Bring us a couple of burgers and the coldest beer you've got in a bottle."

Donna wandered back toward the kitchen to turn in their order. Mason unzipped the black satchel he used as a briefcase and handed Blues his copies of the reports.

"I thought you'd want your own set."

Blues left the reports on the table. "Did Leonard Campbell find religion and decide to let me out?"

Mason shook his head.

"I know Ortiz didn't do it on his own."

"It wasn't the prosecutor's office. It was the judge."

"Judge Carter? You're shitting me!"

Mason shook his head again, watching the replay of Kordell Stewart's Hail Mary miracle pass against Michigan, instead of meeting Blues head-on.

Blues asked him, "You think that game is going to end differently this time?"

Mason gave up and faced his friend. "No, sorry."

"How much trouble are we in?"

"It depends on whether we can prove that you didn't kill Jack Cullan and I didn't kill Shirley Parker."

"What about Judge Carter and my bail?"

"Small potatoes compared to capital murder."

CHAPTER SIXTY-NINE

Mason filled Blues in on his evening out with Beth Harrell that ended with him saving Ed Fiora's life. He described how Mickey had hacked into Fiora's bank records and been rewarded with a beating by Tony Manzerio. He explained his theory of how Beth could have hiked to Cullan's house, killed him, and returned to her apartment undetected. He detailed his suspicions of Carl Zimmerman and James Toland, making light of his failed surveillance of Zimmerman. He finished with a broad-brush recitation of the scam he'd run on Fiora with the bank records and the favor he'd unnecessarily cashed in to get Blues released on bail.

"You need a keeper, you know that?" Blues told him when Mason had completed his report.

"Well, at least you're out. Now we can sort this mess out."

Blues picked up the reports and began reading. Mason waited, hoping for the insight that a fresh look often brings. Donna returned with their burgers and beer. They ate in silence.

"Look at this," Blues said.

He placed the initial report on Cullan's murder in front of Mason. It was dated December 10, the day the housekeeper had discovered Cullan's body.

"Okay, what am I looking for?"

"The report is routine. It covers all the bases, including the location from which every fingerprint was lifted."

Mason read the index of fingerprints. "Damn! There's no record of any fingerprints found on the desk in Mason's office. Terrence Dawson testified at the preliminary hearing that's where he found your fingerprint."

"Now, look at this," Blues said, and handed Mason a supplemental report dated December 12, the day Blues was arrested.

"Dawson went back to the scene for a second look. That's when he found your fingerprint."

"Read the first sentence of Dawson's report on that inspection," Blues instructed.

Mason read it aloud. "At the request of Detective Carl Zimmerman, this examiner returned to the scene to determine if any other identifiable fingerprints were present."

"Zimmerman was a busy boy."

"How could Zimmerman have planted your fingerprint?"

"It's not as hard as it sounds. Zimmerman could have made a photocopy of a fingerprint of mine. While the photocopy was still hot, he could have put fingerprint tape down on it and lifted the print. Powdered photocopier toner can be used as fingerprint powder. Then Zimmerman went back to the scene and put the tape down wherever he wanted Dawson to find my fingerprint."

"So where did Zimmerman get your fingerprint?"

"From my personnel file."

"Isn't access to those files restricted? How did Zimmerman get ahold of it?"

"Once Harry started looking at me for the murder, they would have gotten my file without any problem."

"How can we prove your fingerprint was forged?"

"Identification points are the same on all prints from the same finger. That's why fingerprints are so reliable. But no two prints themselves should ever be identical since there's always a difference in position or pressure when the print is put down. If the print Dawson found is identical to the print in my personnel file, Dawson will have to admit it was forged."

"Unless Zimmerman was smart enough to get rid of the original print from your personnel file."

"That would have been too risky. If that set of prints turned up missing, there would be a separate investigation of everyone who touched the file. Zimmerman was banking that no one would compare the prints since they had made a new set of my prints when they booked me."

"Which gets us back to the real question. Why would Zimmerman take the risk of framing you?"

"It fits with your theory. Zimmerman and Toland were tired of working for Cullan. They wanted to go into business for themselves, so they killed Cullan. I was a convenient fall guy. Harry already hated me. The mayor wanted a quick arrest. No one wanted Cullan's files to be found. It should have worked."

Mason took the final swallow from his bottle of beer. "I'm going to talk to Harry."

"No way. He'll cover for Zimmerman. That's what cops do."

"Not this time. You find Cullan's files and I'll talk to Harry."

Blues grabbed Mason's wrists with both hands. "You're taking a hell of a risk for both of us. If Harry tips him off, Zimmerman will come after both of us. He won't have any choice. Are you carrying that gun I gave you?"

"No, and you can't carry one either without violating the conditions of your bail."

"Small potatoes compared to capital murder."

CHAPTER SEVENTY

Twelfth Street had become a frozen parking lot. Cars on the intersecting streets of Oak and Locust squirmed more than they moved. No one was any closer to home than when Mason and Blues had walked into Rossi's for lunch. The snow poured from the sky in thick, wet flakes heavy enough to reduce vision to a single block. Some drivers surrendered to the storm, abandoning their cars in the middle of the street to take refuge in city hall or the courthouse.

Mason and Blues waded through the drifting, blowing snow to Mason's Jeep. They waited for the car to warm up and melt the ice on the windows while they considered their options.

"You giving any thought to just waiting this out?" Blues asked.

"Nope."

"You expecting a sudden heat wave to melt this shit and clear up this traffic just so we can go home?"

"Nope. And we're not going home. We're going to my office. By the way, how long has Mickey Shanahan been living in his office?"

"Since the day I rented it to him."

"Does he know that you know that?"

"I never asked him. He seems like a good kid."

"He's a con artist, cardsharp, and computer hacker who doesn't have a pot to piss in."

"You hired him. He must fit in. How are you going to get us out of here?"

"Don't try this at home, boys and girls," Mason said.

He engaged the Jeep's four-wheel drive and rolled over the

concrete stop that separated the parking lot from the sidewalk. Dodging parking meters, he stayed on the sidewalk until he was clear of the downtown traffic.

The normally fifteen-minute drive to his office took an hour as he slalomed and cursed his way around one trapped driver after another. The streets were so slick, and the ice and snow so impenetrable, that the slightest incline had become an impossible vertical ascent for any car that didn't have four-wheel drive. Mickey was waiting for them when they made it back to Blues on Broadway.

"This is the homecoming crowd?" Blues asked.

"The cook and the bartender called in well," Mickey answered. "They said they were staying home because of sick weather. We're as good as closed anyway in this snow. The mailman is the only one who has come through the door all day."

Blues picked up a stack of mail that Mickey had left sitting on the bar and leafed through it, tearing open the last envelope.

"Son of a bitch!" he said, holding up the contents of the envelope. "The director of liquor control has suspended my liquor license pending the outcome of my case."

"Who's the director of liquor control?" Mason asked.

"Howard Trimble. I've got to go see him today."

"In this storm?" Mason asked. "He's probably stuck in traffic somewhere."

Blues dialed the phone number on the letter and listened as it rang for two minutes. He slammed the phone down, cursing Trimble and his ancestors in a Shawnee Indian dialect Blues reserved for special occasions.

"Dude!" Mickey said. "What's that mean?"

"Something about fire ants building a nest in your scrotum," Mason told him. "Trimble will have to wait until tomorrow. If this storm keeps up, everything will have to wait until tomorrow."

"We may not have that long," Blues said. "Once Zimmerman knows I'm out, he'll bury those files where no one will ever find them."

Mason and Mickey followed Blues upstairs to his office. Blues opened the floor safe and removed a .45-caliber Baer Stinger pistol and holster. He loaded the pistol, slid it into the holster he'd attached to his belt, and dumped two extra ammunition clips into his jacket pocket.

"Are you going to talk to Zimmerman or just shoot him?" Mason asked.

"Depends on my mood. If Toland and Zimmerman stole Cullan's files, they had to have a new hiding place. It's got to be someplace secure that won't attract attention. Zimmerman wouldn't leave it up to Toland, so it's got to be someplace Zimmerman picked. I'm a lot better at watching without being seen than you are."

"Where do you start watching? You don't even know where Zimmerman is. What makes you think he's going to go look at those files in the middle of a blizzard?"

"You are going to find out where Zimmerman is when you call Harry to tell him about my fingerprint. I'd ask where Zimmerman is first, since Harry will probably stop talking after you tell him about the fingerprint. Then I'll go sit on Zimmerman while you go visit Ed Fiora."

Mason asked, "What for?"

"Fiora said he's got videotape to show you. Odds are he has the person who shot at you on that tape. Tell him you think you know who killed Cullan, but you need to see the videotape to be certain."

"You think Zimmerman was the shooter?"

"Probably not. My money is on Beth Harrell, but it doesn't matter. The videotape is just a pretext for your meeting. Remind Fiora that you promised to give him his file if you found it. Tell him that Zimmerman has his file. Tell him to call Zimmerman and offer to buy the file and make Zimmerman a highly paid security consultant."

"Why can't I just do that over the phone?"

"Because you've got to make certain that Fiora actually calls Zimmerman. You can't take his word for it."

"Why do you think Fiora will be able to flush Zimmerman out on a day like this?"

"Because Fiora will also tell Zimmerman that his offer expires at midnight. After that, Fiora will put Zimmerman out of business himself."

Mickey said, "It's a cross-ruff. You figure Fiora won't wait for us to bring him the file. He'll go after Zimmerman. This way, you can take down both of them and get Fiora off of Lou's back."

"Not me," Blues said. "Harry will take them all down. He'll be the hero. I'll go back to being the bartender. Can you set it up with Harry and Fiora?" Blues asked Mason.

"Small potatoes. Where will you be while I'm running the snowstorm shuttle?"

Blues smiled. "Right here, nice and warm. Waiting for your call so I can go out and save our asses. You better take that gun I gave you. I didn't see it in the safe. Where is it?"

"My office, and you're right."

CHAPTER SEVENTY-ONE

Mason's phone rang as he stuck his pistol in his jacket pocket. "Lou Mason."

Rachel Firestone barked at him. "How did you do it?"

"How did I do what?"

"Don't give me that crap, Lou! How did you get Judge Carter to order bail for Blues?"

Mason wasn't surprised that Rachel had learned of Blues's release. He couldn't guess at the number of sources she'd cultivated over the years. Her sharp tone carried the unspoken complaint that he hadn't tipped her off.

"Off the record?"

"Not a chance."

"Fine. Judge Carter ordered Patrick Ortiz and me to appear for a status conference at eight o'clock this morning. I mentioned the prosecutor's opposition to bail. She said that she'd routinely granted bail in similar cases and saw no reason to treat Blues any differently."

"Didn't it strike you as odd that there was no formal hearing on bail, no opportunity for Ortiz to object on the record or present evidence?"

It was obvious that Rachel had already talked with Ortiz and gotten a taste of the prosecutor's fury.

"Judges have a lot of discretion. You'll have to ask Judge Carter why she handled it that way."

"No can do. Right after your conference, she turned in her resignation to the presiding judge and left the courthouse. No one answers the phone at her home and no one has seen her. She's disappeared. What's happening?"

Mason dropped into his desk chair and stared out the window at the blizzard. He'd been trying to navigate his way through a storm that had turned into an avalanche, an out-of-control cascading disaster.

"Lou!" Rachel demanded again. "What's going on?"

"I'll call you later," he said, and hung up.

Mason called Harry's cell. "Harry?" The urgency in Mason's voice was unmistakable.

"What's the matter?" Harry asked.

"Nothing," Mason lied, gathering himself. "I need to talk to you."

"I thought that's what we were doing."

"No. Not on the phone. Where are you?"

"Same place as the rest of the world. Stuck in traffic behind some moron with rear-wheel drive."

"Where?"

"On Main Street, between Thirty-Fifth and Thirty-Sixth."

"You alone?"

"Yeah. Lou, what's the matter?"

"Pull over and park. I'll be there in ten minutes."

Main was the next major thoroughfare east of Broadway. Though only four side streets separated them, Mason knew that he would make better time on foot than in his Jeep. Traffic was light on the side streets since most drivers had gotten stuck on the main roads before they could try alternate routes.

As he walked, Mason got a new perspective on the power of the storm. Tree limbs sagged under the heavy weight of ice and snow, some of the heavier ones fracturing and tumbling to the ground. He passed one house where a huge limb had broken and crashed through the roof. Mason gauged the strain on overhead power lines as they too bent in the wind. It wouldn't take much more for them to start snapping, adding another deadly special effect to the storm.

Mason found Harry's car in the middle of Main Street,

surrounded by a flotilla of stranded drivers.

"Nice day for a drive," Mason said as he slid into the passenger seat.

"Thanks for dropping by. We're always open."

"How'd you get stuck on duty? Where's your partner?"

"He got lucky and had some personal stuff to take care of at home. He never made it in today," Harry said as he turned down the radio.

"Any updates on the storm?"

"It's gone past blizzard. It's now officially a whiteout, whatever that is. The expected accumulation is a guess. The real problems are the ice and the wind. A lot of people won't get home tonight. So what's so important?"

"I need a favor."

"So ask."

"I want you to compare Blues's fingerprint that was found on Cullan's desk to the print for the same finger in his personnel file."

Harry didn't respond. The wipers squeaked as they brushed back and forth, moving snow from one side of the windshield to the other.

"What would I be looking for if I was to do that?" Harry asked, not looking at Mason.

"To see if the two prints were identical."

"You mean to see if someone forged Blues's print and planted it at Cullan's house."

Mason lowered his head and studied his gloved hands. "Yeah."

"You've read the reports?"

"I've read them. I know that Carl Zimmerman asked Terrence Dawson to take a second look at the scene and that's when Blues's fingerprint was found."

"So you know what you're saying? You know what you're asking me to do?" Harry turned and met Mason's eyes.

"I know, Harry. It's like you always told me. Knowing the right thing to do is the easy part. I'll see you later."

CHAPTER SEVENTY-TWO

Mason stopped at the bar long enough to tell Blues that Zimmerman was sitting out the storm at home. They agreed to keep in touch and Mason left again. He had almost finished scraping the newest layer of snow and ice from his car when Mickey opened the passenger door and climbed aboard.

"Damn, this weather blows!" he said when Mason finished scraping and joined him.

"What are you doing here?"

"Dude! Wingman riding shotgun."

"Any point in telling you to stay here?"

"None."

Mason put his gun in the glove compartment. "Did Blues give you a gun too, or are you just glad to see me?"

Mickey reached under his jacket and sheepishly removed a .44-caliber pistol that he added to the glove compartment. "He didn't exactly give it to me."

"Does he know, exactly, that you took it?"

"Not exactly."

"Then you'll want to return it when we get back and hope Blues doesn't find out, or he'll break both your legs above the knees."

"Exactly."

"If you've got any more toys hidden in your pants or stuck up your ass, get them out now. We'll never get next to Fiora without being searched. If we get to the point that we need weapons, it'll be too late to use them."

Mickey put a switchblade knife and a lead sap in the glove

compartment and closed it.

"Where did you get those?" Mason asked.

"Home Shopping Network."

Mason called the Dream Casino, leaving a message with Fiora's administrative assistant that he was on his way to watch Fiora's home movies. The drive to the casino was an adventure in urban off-road driving. Mason used side streets whenever he could, and sidewalks when he had to. Cops he passed shook their heads and fists at him, but they were too busy with car wrecks and traffic jams to chase him down.

Mason couldn't get the image of Judge Carter sitting behind her desk, frazzled and distracted, out of his mind. Now he understood why she had looked frayed at the edges. On the one hand, she had made herself vulnerable to Ed Fiora and paid the price. On the other, Mason had shoved her over the edge. It was another IOU that Mason would have to carry until he could find a way to pay it back.

The clanging, whistling, siren-sounding slot machines were getting a workout in spite of the weather, gamblers thankful for the storm that gave them the perfect excuse for getting home late. Tony Manzerio escorted Mason and Mickey to Fiora's office.

"This weather is killing my business!" Fiora complained when Mason walked through the door.

"The storm's like a kidney stone. It'll pass—painfully—but it will pass."

"Is that the kind of legal advice you give? 'Cause if it is, I'd seriously consider another line of work."

"I'm close to figuring out who killed Jack Cullan. I need one more piece of the puzzle. It may be in the videotape you told me I should come see after this case ends. I need to see the tape now. If it shows what I think it does, it may help me close the loop on a suspect."

"Mason, you're starting to act like I'm your fairy godmother with all the favors you've been asking. You haven't even thanked me for the last one I did for you."

"As long as I'm asking, I want Judge Carter's account marked paid in full. Take her off your books."

"This is no time to get a conscience, Mason. Everybody's a player at some level. She played, she lost. What's the big deal?"

"If you've got a marker with Judge Carter's name on it, I'd like to see it."

"It has her son's name on it. She keeps him from getting a beating when he comes up short, which happens with some regularity."

"How much does the kid owe?"

"Doesn't matter. He pays up one week, he's down the next. We send him postcards about Gamblers Anonymous; makes us feel better."

"Clear the kid's marker and don't let him back in the casino. That's my deal."

"In return for which I get what?"

"Jack Cullan's file on you."

"You're squeezing an awful lot of mileage out of that file."

"Just show me the videotape, and then I'll get you the file. You've probably got me on tape asking you to get Blues released. You can keep that, but I want the judge off the books."

Fiora shrugged. "That will work. Trade a judge for a lawyer. Too bad you can't throw in a player to be named later."

Fiora opened a cabinet behind his desk, revealing a television and DVD player. He popped a disk into the DVD player and pushed a button, and the screen came to life.

"Like I told you before," Fiora reminded Mason, "anyone comes into the casino, they are picked up on video before they've lost their first quarter. They move out of range of one camera, another camera picks them up. We can even create a video of any one person from the minute they set foot in the parking lot to the minute they leave."

"So whose video are you going to show me?"

"Watch."

He sat down in his desk chair and aimed a remote control at

the DVD player. Beth Harrell materialized on the screen. The day and date were printed in the bottom right-hand corner. It was New Year's Eve. Even with the camera's grainy, long-distance perspective, she flowed across the casino floor, drawing stares and envy. The absence of sound added a surreal note to her movements.

"I'll jump ahead to the good part," Fiora said as he punched another button on his remote control.

Mason watched as the camera followed Beth to the rear of the casino, where she found him, then out to the prow of the boat, where they had embraced. Mickey poked Mason in the ribs when the video showed Mason pushing Beth away. Mason winced at the memory of that moment, seeing the bitterness in Beth's expression as she had walked away.

The video jerked a bit as a different camera picked her up when she returned to the deck. Her face became indistinct as she slipped into shadows that made it impossible to see what she was doing or even to be certain that she was still the person on the video.

Mason recoiled as small flashes erupted from the darkness where the shooter was hidden. Then he saw his own image fill the screen, cowering in the prow and dodging bullets that ricocheted around him, shattering pale blue Christmas lights. He grimaced with sharp memory when he saw a bullet singe his side, touching the still healing wound, holding his breath as his video self vaulted into the river.

CHAPTER SEVENTY-THREE

"I love happy endings," Fiora said when the screen went blank.

"I want a copy," Mason said.

He was past understanding or explaining Beth. She had fallen out of first place in the Jack Cullan murder sweepstakes, but she was ahead of the pack in the psycho competition. Mason didn't know what he would do about her, only that he would do something.

"This is strictly pay-per-view. No more party favors. You get me the file; then we'll talk."

"You know a homicide detective named Carl Zimmerman?"

"Sure. He was one of Cullan's guys. Cullan called him and that other cop, Toland, his golden retrievers. Any time some bigwig or his kid stepped in the bucket, those two guys fetched the bad news to Cullan."

"I think they killed Cullan and went into business for themselves. They made Shirley Parker tell them where Cullan kept the files and then they stole the files and killed her."

"They don't call this the land of opportunity for nothing. Now you're going to go up against two rogue cops and put them out of business while stealing my file back for me. Is that it?"

"I've got help."

"Must be your client that I sprang from the county jail. That might even be a fair fight from what I understand. Are you keeping the good cops out of this?"

"We've got to until we get the files. After that, the good cops can have the bad cops."

"Why tell me all of this?"

"We don't know where Zimmerman and Toland have hidden the files. I want you to call Zimmerman and offer to buy your file and hire him as a security consultant. The only catch is that your offer expires at midnight. Tell him if you don't have the file by then, you'll send Tony to get it."

"Your partner figures to follow Zimmerman to the files, pop him, and bring me my file. Then you have a come-to-Jesus meeting with the prosecutor, Blues pleads guilty to some bullshit misdemeanor, and the whole thing goes away."

"You're not the only one who loves happy endings."

Fiora thought a minute, drumming his fingers on his desk, calculating the odds for the house.

"You got a phone number for this bum Zimmerman?"

Mason handed Fiora a slip of paper, and Fiora dialed Zimmerman's number, putting the call on speaker. Zimmerman went through the stages of grief, denying that he had Cullan's files, angrily accusing Fiora of blackmail, asking if Mason was in on the deal, and unsuccessfully negotiating better terms before accepting Fiora's offer, agreeing to a meeting at nine o'clock in Swope Park at the shelter next to the lagoon and hanging up.

Fiora spread his arms wide. "As you heard, Detective Zimmerman is seriously pissed off and seriously suspicious."

"Thanks. We're out of here."

"I don't think so. You and junior are going to keep me company until tonight. We'll go to the meeting together."

"Ed, that's not a good idea. This could get ugly. I don't think you want to be anywhere near the park."

"I don't like the odds if I'm sitting here fat and unhappy hoping you keep up your end of the deal. I figure Tony gives us an edge, and I always take the edge. So sit down and sit tight."

"Zimmerman has killed two people already. You don't kill people, remember?"

"I don't kill people. Tony kills people."

Mason looked at Tony, who had planted himself in front of the door to Fiora's office.

"I need to make a phone call."

"I thought you might."

Mason called Blues. "Nine o'clock at the shelter next to the lagoon in Swope Park."

"Good. Meet me at the office. We'll get ready."

"Can't do it."

"Fiora got you on a leash?"

"You got it."

"He and Tony figuring on coming along?"

"All the way."

"Make for a helluva party," Blues said, and hung up.

Mason closed his cell phone. "You got an unmarked deck of cards? I'm into Mickey for two hundred and fifty bucks. I might as well try and get my money back."

CHAPTER SEVENTY-FOUR

Tony remained at the door, moving only to allow Fiora to go in or out. Mason and Blues had not discussed the possibility that Fiora would hold him and Mickey hostage and insist on coming along. Though unexpected, Fiora's intervention would bring all the bad guys together. The combination would be volatile, unstable, and uncontrollable.

Fiora came back at six o'clock. "Let's get going," he said. "The roads are still a mess and I want to get there ahead of Zimmerman and Toland. What are you driving?"

"I've got my Jeep. It has four-wheel drive."

"Perfect. You drive."

The snow was still falling when they left the casino. Though city crews had been working for seven hours to clear the streets, they were fighting a losing battle. Fresh snow blanketed every plowed surface, erasing tire tracks and hiding the ice beneath like a land mine.

Tony sat in front next to Mason, leaving Mickey and Fiora in the back. Road conditions were treacherous, even for the Jeep. The wind blew snow across the roads in ground-level clouds, making it nearly impossible to see headlights or taillights.

Salt trucks outfitted with snowplows plodded along, clearing lanes while depositing a layer of salt in their wake. Mason crept steadily along, occasionally reaching speeds of thirty-five or forty miles per hour when he hit a stretch of clear tire tracks.

Mason entered Swope Park on Gregory Boulevard. The two-lane road ran ahead of them flanked by snow-laden trees looming like ghostly sentinels in the darkness. Irregularly spaced streetlights pointed the way, adding a halo to the falling and blowing snow. A concrete railroad bridge arched overhead as the boulevard funneled them into the park.

Colonel Tom Swope had donated Swope Park to the city in the early 1900s. The largest green space in the city, it was home to the zoo, an outdoor theater, two golf courses, and enough trails for anyone to get lost in. The lagoon was near the center of the park along Gregory Boulevard. Over the years it had been stocked with fish by the city and, occasionally, dead bodies by the less civic minded.

Mason eased to a stop along the curb where a bike path intersected with the road, and turned off his lights.

"Why are we stopping?" Fiora asked.

"The lagoon is around the next curve. If we go all the way in and Zimmerman is already in place, he'll see us."

"Tony." Fiora spoke his name as a command.

Tony grunted as he opened the door and disappeared without a backward glance.

"Where's he going?" Mickey asked.

"For a walk, Junior," Fiora answered.

Mason turned onto the bike path, keeping the Jeep at a slow crawl and his headlights off, the automotive version of blindman's bluff. The bike path emptied onto an unmarked service road that Mason followed another half mile before picking up the bike path again. This time, he backed the Jeep a hundred yards down the bike path and turned off the engine. If he was lucky, they hadn't been seen. Mason looked at his watch. It was seven thirty.

"What now?" Mickey asked. "It's cold enough to freeze-dry my nuts."

Mason handed him the keys. "You can turn the heat on if you have to. Just remember, Zimmerman can find you a lot easier when the engine is running."

"Hey, where are you going?" Fiora demanded.

Mason took his gun from the glove compartment. "For a walk."

"That's not our deal!"

"Mickey will keep you company, but don't play gin with him. He cheats."

"Like hell I'm waiting here. Zimmerman is expecting me, and if I don't show, you guys shoot craps."

"Suit yourself," Mason said, knowing there was no way to make Fiora wait in the Jeep.

"Wingman on your flank," Mickey said to Mason as he climbed into the front seat, grabbed his gun, and joined Mason and Fiora.

"Give me that," Mason said to Mickey, pointing to the gun.

"Are you kidding me?"

"You don't know how to use a gun. You'll shoot yourself or one of us. Give me the gun."

Mickey held the pistol up with both hands, and before Mason could reach for it, he unloaded it, disassembled it, and put it back together.

"Oh, ye of little faith," he said.

"That's pretty good, kid," Fiora said. "Where'd you learn to do that?"

"Video games—the perfect home-school curriculum."

CHAPTER SEVENTY-FIVE

They hugged the edge of the woods, walking briskly and single file along the service road, the storm concealing them. Before reaching the lagoon, they stepped into the woods. Mason took off his gloves and wrapped his fingers around his gun. The steel was icy and refused to warm against his hand. He found the safety with his thumb and switched it off.

"Let the games begin," Mickey whispered.

If Fiora had insisted on being early, Mason had to assume that Zimmerman and Toland would do the same and that Blues would not be the last one to arrive. Tony had gotten out of the Jeep twenty minutes ago. No one was going to be late for this party. Everyone was probably already there, each man fighting off the wind chill, waiting for someone else to make the first move.

"Why in the hell would Zimmerman set the meeting out here?" Fiora asked.

"Look around," Mason answered. "It makes sense. The interior of the park is isolated but accessible. There's not much chance of other traffic on a night like this. The shelter is out in the open. The nearest woods are far enough away that you'd have to be an incredible marksman to shoot someone from the trees."

Fiora wasn't convinced. "You think Zimmerman had that all figured out. How would he know about this place?"

"He's a cop who knows where bodies are dumped. Plus, he's a Cub Scout den leader. He's probably brought his troop here."

"You're shitting me? This hump is a Cub Scout leader? I'd pop him myself except I don't kill people."

Mason studied the wind-driven waves breaking along the snow-packed shoreline of the lagoon, moving his gaze outward to the road. There were no tire tracks, meaning that everyone else had walked in.

The shelter stood twenty-five feet from the southern edge of the lagoon. There was a streetlight close enough to outline it, but too far away to illuminate what was beneath it. The shelter was little more than a roof supported by four stout poles, a shelter from sun and gentle rain, but no port in a snowstorm. A bright light came on at the center of the shelter's ceiling, startling Mason and the others. Neither Zimmerman nor Toland was camped out beneath the shelter.

The light turned off a few minutes later, only to come on again in an irregular cycle. Mason could make out an electrical line that ran from the roof of the shelter to a utility pole to the west. The line bowed, heavy with ice.

"It's a motion light," Mason said. "It's for security. Any movement near the light turns it on for a preset period. Then it goes off. If the wind blows hard enough, that will turn it on. We'll be able to see Zimmerman and Toland when they get close enough to activate the sensor."

"Then what do we do, Counselor?" Fiora asked.

"I don't know."

"In the meantime," Fiora complained, "I'm freezing my ass off. Where the hell is Tony?"

Mason ignored Fiora's complaint and his question. Fiora was used to running the show and didn't like being a spectator. Though Mason wondered where both Tony and Blues were waiting. Fiora had been standing on Mason's left. Mason turned to his right to talk to Mickey only to discover that Mickey was gone.

Mason hissed Mickey's name, but the sound died in the wind. Mason remembered Mickey's announcement as he got out of the car—*Wingman on your flank*. Mason silently cursed himself for getting Mickey involved.

A moment later, he cursed aloud when he saw Mickey emerge

from the woods closest to the shelter, being pushed ahead by a tall figure poking Mickey in the back with a shotgun. Mickey stumbled and fell. The gunman prodded him with the barrel of the shotgun until Mickey got to his feet.

As the pair reached the shelter, the light came on again. In the instant before the gunman smashed the light, Mason saw Mickey's panicked face and the block-cut jawline of James Toland.

Fiora started toward the shelter, but Mason grabbed him by the arm. "Don't. "That's exactly what they want us to do. They'll try to take us one at a time. Mickey can handle himself."

Mason knew that he was right about everything except Mickey. The kid could deal cards, field strip a pistol, and hustle a rent-free pad, but Mason knew he was out of his league against Toland. Besides, sending Fiora to rescue Mickey was like telling the Dutch boy to put a bigger finger in the dike. Without Tony to back him up, Fiora was just a street-wise punk. Toland wouldn't be impressed. Fiora puffed himself up, as if sensing Mason's dismissive appraisal.

"Why not? I'm the guy they're expecting. If I don't go, they'll know they're being set up. I'll tell Toland that the kid is my driver and that he wandered off. You go find Tony and Blues."

Mason couldn't argue with Fiora's reasoning or stop him. Fiora chose a slow, casual walk, raising his right hand in greeting as he neared the shelter. Mickey and Toland were hidden in plain sight under the shelter, swallowed by the dark. When Fiora reached the edge of the shelter, he suddenly collapsed to the ground. Mason couldn't tell whether he'd been shot or struck, but Fiora didn't move as the snow gathered around him. In the same instant, Mason felt the icy sting of cold steel against his neck.

"I had a feeling you were in on this, Mason." Carl Zimmerman pressed the barrel of his gun tightly against the base of Mason's skull. "You should have told your client to take the plea."

CHAPTER SEVENTY-SIX

Zimmerman jammed his gun hard against Mason's neck. "Hands behind your back."

Mason knew that Zimmerman was going to cuff him, taking him out of the game. He had size on Zimmerman, but Zimmerman had a gun on Mason's brain stem. Mason obeyed and winced when Zimmerman caught his flesh in the cuffs.

"Stand real still," Zimmerman instructed. Keeping his gun in place, Zimmerman patted the pockets on Mason's coat and found his pistol. "Hope you've got a permit for this concealed weapon, Counselor. Otherwise, I'll have to issue you a citation."

"You shouldn't have lied about the body in Swope Park. Otherwise, you might have gotten away with it."

"I'm getting away with it now."

"You killed Cullan, forged Blues's fingerprint, stole Cullan's secret files, and killed Shirley Parker. That's a lot to get away with."

"You don't know shit. And I didn't kill anybody. At least not yet."

"It doesn't matter what I know. Harry knows you used Blues's fingerprint in his personnel file to forge the one on Cullan's desk. That will be enough for him. He'll hunt you down like a dog. You won't be able to use Cullan's files to wipe your ass."

Zimmerman spat into the snow. "Ryman's too old and too slow."

"We'll put that on your tombstone."

Zimmerman gave Mason a sharp shove in the small of the back. "Move it!"

Mason marched toward the shelter, squinting against the snow. There was no sign of Tony or Blues. Fiora was still down. Zimmerman shoved Mason again as they stepped beneath the shelter, knocking him into Mickey, who was handcuffed and sitting cross-legged on the floor.

Toland pressed the barrel of his shotgun under Mason's chin, dragging it down to Mason's chest until Mason joined Mickey. Toland crouched down to Mason's eye level, keeping the shotgun flush against Mason. Mason smiled at the trickle of blood frozen on the side of Toland's face.

"Cut yourself shaving?" he asked Toland.

"That big moose you had chasing us in the woods scratches like a girl. I had to damn near kill him just so I could tie him to a tree. Don't make me tie you to a tree."

Zimmerman said, "We've got these three. Tony is out of commission, which leaves Bluestone."

High-beam headlights flooded the shelter as a vehicle bore down on them, make and model invisible in the dark.

"Who in the hell is that?" Toland yelled.

The vehicle was aiming directly at them as it picked up speed over the fresh snow. The engine was revving hard as if the driver had floored the accelerator.

"Damn!" Zimmerman shouted as it got closer. "That's my Suburban!"

"It's got to be Bluestone," Toland said. "He's going to ram us. Shoot him!"

Toland fired his shotgun, pumped, and fired three more rounds while Zimmerman emptied his clip into the Suburban. Mason and Mickey jumped to their feet and ran to Fiora. Crouching down with their hands behind their backs, they each grabbed him by the shoulders and dragged him out of the path of the Suburban.

The windshield on the Suburban shattered, but the truck roared on like an enraged beast made angrier by the gunfire, crunching and packing the snow beneath its tires, oblivious of the barrage of firepower. Zimmerman and Toland leaped out of the way at the last moment as the Suburban crashed into one of the poles supporting the shelter, toppling the roof. The car flew past them, becoming airborne before plunging headfirst into the lagoon, sizzling and bubbling as it found the muddy bottom.

Harry and Blues were following on foot behind the Suburban. Blues ran low and straight at Toland, colliding with him and rolling across the snow. Toland managed to get to his feet first while Blues was on one knee. Toland launched a booted kick at Blues's head. Blues caught Toland's boot and sprang up, sending Toland tumbling onto his back.

The power line had snapped off the roof of the shelter with the impact from the Suburban, its deadly blue current dancing and writhing across the snow, measuring Toland like a cobra as he struggled to get to his feet. Toland slipped in the snow, clawed at the ground on all fours, and screamed as the power line stung him with a lethal jolt, the line lying across Toland's electrocuted body as the snow sizzled around him.

Zimmerman was in a shooter's crouch, knees bent, arms extended, aiming Mason's gun in a rapid arc, looking for a target. Harry tackled him from behind, flattening him against the pavement and pressing his face into the snow. He planted his knee in the middle of Zimmerman's back and wrapped his hand around Zimmerman's gun hand, forcing the barrel against Zimmerman's ear.

"Pull the trigger, you piece of garbage! Blow your fucking brains out!" Harry screamed. "Pull it, goddammit! Pull it!"

Blues ran to Harry's side, reached down, and covered Harry's hand with his own. "Let it go, Harry. You got him. Let it go."

Harry was heaving. "Okay," he said at last. "Okay." Harry cuffed Zimmerman. "Don't move, partner."

Mason looked at the lagoon, where the back end of the Suburban barely broke the surface. He staggered to his feet and made his way over to Blues and Harry.

"How did you do that?"

"I'll bet Blues hot-wired the Suburban, put a rock on the gas pedal, and steered with the door open while he ran alongside it," Mickey said.

"Good call, kid," Blues told him. "How'd you know?"

"That's exactly the way I would have done it," Mickey said.

"Next he'll tell people it was his idea," Mason said.

"That's public relations. Get us out of these cuffs."

CHAPTER SEVENTY-SEVEN

Harry unlocked their handcuffs.

"What's with Fiora? Did Toland clock him or shoot him or did the putz just have a heart attack?"

Fiora was still lying prone in the snow, not moving from the spot where Mason and Mickey had dragged him.

"I think he fainted," Mickey said. "When he walked up to the shelter, he raised his hand as if we were having a reunion. Next thing I knew, he took a dive. Toland didn't touch him."

They walked over to Fiora. Mason nudged him with his shoe. "Looks dead to me."

"It's a real shame," Mickey added. "He didn't live to see us kick the crap out of those guys."

"Weather like this," Harry said, "it could be hours before an ambulance gets here. Guess it doesn't matter since he's already gone."

Fiora stirred, groaned, and slowly rolled over on his back. He blinked the snow off his eyelids and groaned some more. "What happened?"

"How about that. Back from the dead. It's a miracle," Blues said. "I'll go find Tony. We may really need an ambulance for him."

Mason turned to Harry. "So I was right. Zimmerman forged Blues's fingerprint."

Harry hung his head for a moment. "Yeah. No one ever would have checked Blues's print against the ones in his personnel file if you hadn't asked me."

It was the first time in years that Mason had heard Harry refer to Blues by his nickname. Harry had always insisted on calling him Bluestone, rejecting any closer ties to their days as partners. Harry's face was drawn and he was shivering from more than the wind.

"Zimmerman counted on that. Don't be too hard on yourself."

Harry shook his head. "Carl counted on me wanting it to be Blues."

"Why'd you come out here with Blues?"

"I figured I owed him that. And I had to see Carl for myself. I had to be sure. If I was wrong, it would stay private."

"What happens now?"

"It's up to the prosecutor. The case against Blues is pretty weak without the fingerprint. Carl has a lot of explaining to do. I guess we're back to square one."

"Zimmerman told me that he didn't kill anybody. You think he's telling the truth?"

Harry thought for a moment. "I'm the wrong one to ask. I was his partner and I didn't see anything that made me think he was dirty."

"Toland was killed while he and Zimmerman were committing a felony. Under the felony-murder statute, Zimmerman will be charged with Toland's death. That's a capital-murder charge. Zimmerman is looking at the needle. He'll talk."

"That's not what worries me. It's who's going to be listening."

"Zimmerman will use Cullan's files. Instead of getting the bum's rush like Blues did, he'll put it all on Toland and offer to keep his mouth shut in return for a citation. He'll probably claim that he was investigating Toland and that we stumbled into his sting operation and screwed it up. Before he's finished, we'll be charged with Toland's death."

"How's he going to explain working a sting operation behind my back?" Harry demanded.

"Simple. You were too close to me. That's why Ortiz didn't put you on the stand at the preliminary hearing. If there was enough dirt in those files to scare Leonard Campbell into going so hard after Blues, Campbell will make that deal in a heartbeat."

"You have any suggestions?"

"Just one. My Jeep is parked about a half mile down that service road. I'd appreciate it if you'd go get it for me." Mason handed Harry the keys. "Take your time. It's real slippery."

Harry nodded as they both looked at the sunken Suburban. "Glad to do it. You be careful not to get wet out here. Your aunt will raise hell if you end up with pneumonia. And don't let my prisoner get away while I'm gone."

Harry ambled away as Blues and Tony appeared from the far side of the lagoon. Tony helped Fiora to his feet, dusted the snow from Fiora's topcoat, and listened impassively as his boss berated him for getting coldcocked by Toland.

"Where's Harry going?" Blues asked.

"To get my Jeep."

"You have to tip him for valet service?"

"That depends on what we find in the Suburban. Let's have a look."

Mason and Blues found Mickey at the edge of the lagoon. The Suburban was twenty feet from shore in water that was at least half as deep. They looked at the truck, the water, and each other, none of them anxious to go for a swim.

"It's too dangerous," Mason said at last. "A man wouldn't last ten minutes in that water without getting hypothermia. We don't know if the files are in the truck, and even if they are, it would be too easy to get stuck inside."

Fiora and Tony joined them. "You think my file is in that truck?" he asked Mason.

"I'd bet the house on it. Trouble is, the odds of us getting it out are a little steep. The cops will have it towed out of there, and we'll never see the files until after the grand jury indictments are handed down."

Fiora pulled Tony aside. The massive man leaned down to hear Fiora's whispered instructions. Tony straightened up and walked over to Carl Zimmerman, who was still lying facedown in the snow. Tony grabbed Zimmerman by the collar of his coat, yanked him to his feet as if he were dusting off a rug, and spun him once around. Keeping his body between Zimmerman and the others, like a solar eclipse blocking the sun, Tony found Zimmerman's handcuff key and removed the cuffs from his wrists. He clamped his viselike hands on Zimmerman's shoulders and delivered the message Fiora had given him. Tony held on to Zimmerman's left arm as they returned to the edge of the lagoon.

Zimmerman stared at the water, then at each of them. Tony gave him a slight shove toward the water. Zimmerman shook off Tony's hand in a fainthearted protest before stripping down to a T-shirt and boxers. No one spoke as he disrobed or when he waded into the water.

"What'd you tell him, Tony?" Mickey asked.

"Hey, kid," Fiora answered. "It's like going to a fancy restaurant where they got menus without prices. If you got to ask, you got no business being there."

Zimmerman climbed onto the back of the truck, opened one side of the split rear door, and disappeared inside the Suburban. He emerged a few minutes later, carrying a hard plastic box under one arm. Bracing himself against the floor of the truck, Zimmerman heaved the box into the water, where it bobbed toward the shore. They all clambered to the water's edge, waiting eagerly for the box to arrive, not noticing as Zimmerman ducked back inside the Suburban.

In the same instant that the box reached Mason, Zimmerman leaned out the rear of the Suburban and opened fire with a pistol he'd hidden in the truck. The first two rounds caught Tony in the neck, spraying the others with warm blood. Tony grasped at his throat before collapsing into the water. Mason snatched the plastic box out of the water, holding it up as a shield against the next volley.

Fiora screamed at Zimmerman and struggled to pull his own gun from beneath his heavy coat. Bullets slapped into the snow at Fiora's feet, then traced a mortal path up his midsection, exploding inside his chest.

Mason, Mickey, and Blues scattered, and Zimmerman's next shots went wide in the dark. Blues dropped and rolled over, coming up on one knee, his gun drawn as Harry skidded to a stop with the Jeep's headlights spotlighted on Zimmerman, drops of water glistening like ice crystals against his dark skin.

Harry swung the door of the Jeep open and dropped to the ground, his own gun extended through the open driver's window.

"Put it down, Carl!" Harry demanded.

Zimmerman held one hand to his eyes, trying to block out the glare of the headlights. "Why, Harry? You got what you came for. I'm out of options, man. Either I kill all of you or you kill me. That's all that's left."

"No! That's not the way this is going to go down. Think about your family."

"Too late for that, Harry. You're gonna have to kill me!" he shouted, opening fire again.

Harry fired at the first flash from Zimmerman's gun, not stopping until Zimmerman fell face-forward out of the Suburban, folded over the open door at his waist, his arms and face dangling lifelessly in the black water.

CHAPTER SEVENTY-EIGHT

The blizzard suffocated the city for two days, keeping businesses, schools, and government in suspended animation, an emphatic reminder that nature's power to destroy was a match for man's worst instincts. The difference between nature and man was that nature looked good doing it. The city was draped in a thick white blanket that sparkled brilliantly under the cold rays of the sun. The snow reflected a painfully beautiful glare that polished the ice-blue sky with aching clarity.

Seventeen inches of snow had fallen on top of three inches of ice. One hundred thousand people had been left without power, and hundreds of electrical lines had gone down breaking the fall of limbs that had snapped off trees like matchsticks under the weight of ice and snow. Property damage had been estimated at close to eighty million dollars. Nineteen people had been killed in car accidents. Two men had suffered fatal heart attacks while shoveling snow over the vigorous objections of their wives. Four men—two of them cops and two of them hoods—had been killed at the lagoon in Swope Park.

The story of those last men had led every newscast, filled every front page, and clogged the phone lines of every radio call-in show, shoving the snowstorm of the century to the back page, proving that people preferred bloodshed to blizzards.

The chief of police suspended Harry the moment he got to the lagoon. He demanded Harry's gun and badge on the spot and came within a hairsbreadth of arresting Harry for something, anything. Every cop who shot someone to death was placed on administrative leave while the shooting was investigated. Almost all of them were ultimately welcomed back to duty with more thanks than reprimands.

Not one cop in the department's collective memory had killed his partner, let alone turned over crucial evidence to the FBI before summoning his brother officers to the scene. Not one, that is, until Harry Ryman.

Harry explained to the chief that the box containing Cullan's files was evidence of a federal crime of political corruption and that the bureau's jurisdiction was obvious. The chief explained to Harry that he was full of shit and would be lucky not to be fired and convicted of murder. The exchange between the two men had been hot enough to melt the snow at their feet.

"You were right to call the feds," Mason told Harry later as they sat in the Jeep waiting for the crime-scene techs to finish up. "Nobody does a good job cleaning their own house."

"I know that, but it won't make things any easier if they let me come back. Did you find what you were looking for in Cullan's files?"

Harry had let Mason examine the contents of the plastic box while they waited for the FBI to arrive. Zimmerman and Toland had kept only the best of Cullan's files, limiting themselves to the dirt on the mayor, Beth Harrell, Ed Fiora, the prosecuting attorney, and a handful of influential businesspeople. They could have released the files on a CD titled *Blackmail's Greatest Hits*.

Mason studied the pictures of Beth, this time focusing on her face, searching for, but not finding, a clue that would bring her into focus. True to form, Cullan had given a set of Beth's pictures to Fiora, saving his own copy for another time.

The mayor's file was surprisingly thin, nothing more than a few ledger sheets that may or may not have been a record of payoffs. Though he had had only a few minutes to study Fiora's file, Mason hadn't found proof of any links between Fiora and the mayor.

Mason's calculation of the destruction caused by his search for these files rivaled the storm's devastation. Four men were dead, as many families were ruined. Judge Carter's career was in shambles. Harry had been suspended. Blues was still accused of Cullan's murder, and Mason was still under suspicion for the death of Shirley Parker.

Harry had repeated his question, not certain whether Mason had heard. "Any luck with Cullan's files?"

Mason had shaken his head. "There should have been something more in those files, but it wasn't there. Maybe Zimmerman and Toland were holding back." He hadn't known what else to say.

By Friday morning, the city was crawling back to life. Streets had been cleared, creating minicanyons paved with asphalt and surrounded by curbside walls made of exhaust-blackened, plow-packed snow. Mason was in his office when he got a call from Patrick Ortiz.

"We're dropping the charges against your client," Ortiz said.

"Thanks. Was it Zimmerman and Toland?"

"Doubtful. Zimmerman's wife told us all about his deal with Cullan. They've got an autistic kid. She claims he did it because they needed the money to pay for a special school for the kid. Toland just liked the good life—big Harley, women by the hour, booze by the case. Zimmerman's wife and Toland's girlfriend of the week gave both of them alibis for Cullan's murder and they checked out."

"Any other leads?"

"The truth is we don't have shit on anybody, but tell your client not to get too comfortable. We may refile the charges if we come up with something."

"What about Shirley Parker?"

"You're off the hook too. She and Cullan are dead-end bookends."

Mason permitted himself a small sigh of relief and changed subjects. "What do you hear from the feds?"

"They skipped the investigation and started with the inquisition. Harry Ryman has as much chance of getting his shield back as I have of getting it on with Jennifer Lopez."

"I don't know. My guess is that the chief will end up begging Harry to come back."

"Right, and if Jennifer turns me down, I'll have her call you. See you around."

Mason found Blues in his office, adding up his losses over the last month.

"I'm going to have to hire strippers and give away whiskey if I get my liquor license back just to pay my mortgage," Blues said.

"Don't give up yet. Patrick Ortiz just called. They dropped the charges against you."

Blues leaned back in his chair and looked at Mason, then swiveled to get a look out the window. He stood up, scanning the view down Broadway, before turning back to Mason. He pursed his lips and nodded.

"Good."

"That's it? That's not the reaction of a client who's happy enough to pay his lawyer."

"I didn't belong in jail. Nighttime was the worst. My pillow felt like quicksand. Makes it hard to get excited when it never should have happened. Makes it harder to forget when I know how easily an innocent man can get put away."

"Man, you are one depressing son of a bitch when you get philosophical."

Blues laughed. "I'll tell you what will cheer me up. Let's go see Howard Trimble at Liquor Control and get my license reinstated so I can pay your bill or buy you lunch, whichever costs less."

CHAPTER SEVENTY-NINE

Howard Trimble's handshake was fleshy and moist when he greeted Mason and Blues. His office was a disorderly and disheveled, coffee cups and donuts competing for desk space with official business. Trimble gestured Mason and Blues to be seated in the two chairs opposite his desk.

Blues led off. "I'm Wilson Bluestone. This is my attorney, Lou Mason. You sent me this notice that my liquor license has been suspended," Blues added as he handed Trimble the notice he had received in the mail.

"That's because you violated our regulations. From what I've seen in the news, your liquor license is the least of your problems."

Trimble showed no interest in Blues's situation. He was simply reporting the news with the inevitable disinterest of civil servants.

"I haven't violated any of your regulations."

Mason heard the edge creeping into Blues's voice. Blues had less patience with regulations and regulators than Mason did.

"Well, now," Trimble said, sensing the rising tension. "Liquor control regulations require that a license holder be of good moral character. That generally excludes murder, don't you think?"

Mason stepped into the conversation between Trimble and Blues. "Mr. Trimble, all charges against my client have been dropped. The city is about to erupt in a major political scandal. You've got a chance to avoid getting caught up in that mess by reinstating my client's license."

Trimble considered Mason's advice. "You don't mind if I check your story, do you, Mr. Mason?"

"By all means. Call Patrick Ortiz at the prosecutor's office."

Trimble dismissed Mason's suggestion. "I don't mess with the middleman, gentlemen. I go right to the top floor of city hall. The mayor's chief of staff is a personal friend of mine."

Trimble called Amy White while Mason and Blues gazed around his office, examined their cuticles, and pretended not to eavesdrop. Trimble cupped his hand over the receiver and turned his head to muffle his end of the conversation.

"Good news, Mr. Bluestone," he said after hanging up the phone. "I'll reinstate your license just as soon as I can."

He spoke as cheerfully as a man could who had just lost the perk of giving bad news.

"What's that supposed to mean?"

Trimble's hands fluttered in a failed effort to be casual. "It's just a matter of completing the paperwork. It's all about forms, you know."

"Well, let's get it done right now. I've got to be open tonight and I can't take the chance that some overexcited cop busts me because he didn't get the word."

"Don't worry about it. I'll see to it myself."

Blues wasn't satisfied, and Mason didn't blame him.

"I want to see my file," Blues said.

A red stain began to creep up Trimble's neck as he tugged at his collar. He was devoted to the bureaucratic dodge but was running out of places to hide.

"I'm afraid that's not possible."

Mason interjected, "I'm afraid that's not possible. Mr. Bluestone's file is a public record and we have an absolute right to see it. My client has been held in jail for a month for a crime he didn't commit. You suspended his license and put him out of business. There's a lawsuit headed your way, Howard, if you don't come up with that file now."

Trimble hitched up his pants to untangle his underwear. "There's no need for threats, Mr. Mason. I'm not refusing to show you Mr. Bluestone's file. I just can't. Not right at this moment."

Blues asked, "And why not?"

Trimble shifted his weight and lifted his butt off his chair, grimacing as if he'd just given himself a wedgie. "Amy—Ms. White—has your file."

"Which regulation says it's okay to give my client's file to the mayor's chief of staff but not to my client?"

Trimble stuffed his hand down his pants, rearranged his balls, and wiped a thin film of sweat from above his lip.

"Listen to me," Trimble said. "I've known Amy White since she was a young girl. Her father, Donald Ray White, was the director of liquor control when I came to work here. Amy and her sister, Cheryl, used to come down here to visit their daddy. They took to me like I was some kind of an uncle. Then things turned bad for them. Amy had a hard road and has come a long way. I'm real proud of her, and I don't want her to get into any trouble."

Mason's gut tightened as he wondered what Trimble was getting at. He chose a conciliatory tone, hoping it would keep Trimble talking.

"How could she get in any trouble over my client's liquor license? The file is a public record."

Trimble let out a sigh. "Her having the file isn't a problem. I mean, I know you want it right now, Mr. Bluestone. And I don't blame you."

"Mr. Trimble, you sure sound like a man who's trying to tell us something without saying it. Like I told you, the charges against my client have been dropped. If that's what this is all about, you'll help yourself and Amy if you just tell me why she has the file."

Trimble hesitated, struggling with his answer, uncertain whether he should give it up but not strong enough to hold it in.

"I hope you're right. Amy called me at home late one night last month. It was a Friday night."

Blues looked at Mason, silently telling him to take the lead as he got up from his chair and took a slow tour of Trimble's office.

"You remember the date?" Mason asked.

"December seventh," Trimble said. "Pearl Harbor Day. I

remember because my grandfather was killed at Pearl Harbor." He kept his eyes firmly on the floor.

It was also the night of Blues's confrontation with Cullan at the bar, Mason thought to himself.

"Did she tell you why she wanted the file?"

Trimble shrugged, kneading his hands like a kid who'd been caught shoplifting. "She only told me who wanted it, not why. She said Jack Cullan wanted it. It was late. I asked her why it couldn't wait until Monday morning. She said that Mr. Cullan wanted it right away. So, I met her down here and gave it to her."

"What time was that?"

"Around midnight, a little after."

Amy had told Mason that Cullan had called her that night and demanded that she get him Blues's liquor license file. She had told Mason that she had put Cullan off until the following Monday. Trimble's version could put Amy in Cullan's house the night he was killed if she had picked up Blues's file and taken it to Cullan. Yet that didn't square with Amy still having the file.

"Do you know what she did with the file?"

Trimble shook his head. "I didn't talk to her about it again until today."

"What did you mean that Amy had a hard road?"

Trimble looked up at Mason, uncomfortable with answering but more uncomfortable with being pushed.

"Amy's father died when she was fifteen. A tough time for a girl to lose her father even if he wasn't much of a father. That's when I took over this job. That was eighteen years ago."

"How did he die?"

Trimble sighed again. Mason thought Trimble would hyperventilate and pass out if he did it one more time.

"Amy's sister, Cheryl, shot him to death."

Mason had been trying to keep his interrogation casual. Blues was roaming around Trimble's small office, reading the diplomas and certificates that traced Trimble's career. Both of them came to attention at Trimble's explanation.

"What happened?" Mason asked.

"Cheryl was three years younger than Amy. Their father was arrested for abusing Cheryl. His lawyer got the charges dismissed and hushed the whole thing up so Donald could keep his job as director of this department."

Trimble tilted his head back as if trying to expel his memory of Donald Ray White. He continued the story, biting off each word.

"When Donald Ray was released from jail, he beat Cheryl so severely that she was permanently brain-damaged. Somehow, Cheryl managed to get ahold of Donald Ray's pistol and killed her father. Amy's mother hired the same lawyer who got her husband off to get her daughter off. Cheryl wasn't prosecuted because she was a brain-damaged child. Their mother drank herself to death a few years later, and Amy has taken care of Cheryl ever since."

"Who was the lawyer?"

"Jack Cullan," Trimble answered, aiming his words at a blank spot on the wall.

Mason put his hand on Trimble's shoulder. He wanted to thank Trimble for telling him the truth, but from the broken expression on Trimble's face, Mason knew that he didn't want any thanks.

290

CHAPTER EIGHTY

Mason pushed the button for an elevator going up as Blues pushed another button for one going down.

"I'm going to see Amy White," Mason said. "Don't you want to come along?"

"My guess is that she bolted right after Trimble called her. I'll wait in the lobby just in case she decided to clean her desk out first. I'll follow her if I get the chance. You can call Mickey for a ride back to the bar."

Mason stepped off the elevator on the twenty-ninth floor and into the mayor's suite of offices. Though the city was officially open, many people had taken another day off, leaving the office with a skeleton staff.

The one secretary who had come to work confirmed Blues's guess. Amy White had left without saying when or if she would be back. Mason was composing a lie he hoped would convince the secretary to give him Amy's home address when the mayor opened the door to his office.

"Your car is ready, Mr. Mayor," the secretary told him.

"Thank you," he said.

Though the mayor was known for his unflappable good humor and insistence on shaking every hand, he walked past Mason, his face cold, his smile buried in a snowdrift, his hands jammed in his coat pockets.

"I don't have time today, Mr. Mason," he said over his shoulder.

Mason caught up with him at the elevator. "Thanks all the same, Mr. Mayor. Actually, I was looking for Amy White, not you."

A panel on the wall with columns for each elevator and numbers for each floor kept track of the vertical routes of the four elevators that serviced city hall. As each elevator passed a floor, the number for that floor was illuminated so that anyone waiting for an elevator could watch with growing frustration the tortoise-paced progress of the cars. The mayor gave his full attention to the flashing lights, shutting Mason out.

"Amy asked me to find the file Jack Cullan kept on you," Mason said as if he and the mayor hung out together all the time. "Ah, but she probably didn't bother you with stuff like that."

The mayor chose not to hear Mason until he cleared his throat as if he were about to cough up a lung.

"Sorry about that. It's this damn weather. Makes me drain like a leaky faucet," Mason explained. "Anyway. I came by to tell her that I did find your file, but the FBI snagged it before I did. Man, you should have been at the lagoon when that cluster fuck broke out. I'll bet the chief of police, the prosecuting attorney, and Amy tripped all over each other to deliver that piece of good news to you. Luckily, I did get a chance to read your file. So tell Amy to give me a call and I'll tell her what's in it."

The mayor turned to Mason, his mouth and eyes fighting over which could open wider. "You read my file?"

"Cover to cover, Mayor Sunshine. Though I have to tell you, it was a disappointment. I mean, I was expecting more than some lousy ledger sheets that a pencil-necked bean counter will probably weave into a money-laundering and bribery indictment. Still, it was almost like someone had taken the good stuff out of the file and left just enough behind to chap your ass."

The mayor glared at Mason. "What do you want?"

"Not much. At this point, I'd settle for Amy's home address."

"Go fuck yourself."

"Is that an apartment or a house?"

An elevator arrived. Mason stepped in, turned around, and waved good-bye to the mayor as the doors closed. Blues wasn't in the lobby, and Mason assumed that he was following Amy White.

He tried Blues's cell but didn't get an answer, then called Harry with the same result. His next call was to Claire, and she answered.

"How's Harry doing?"

"Everybody takes their turn in the barrel. This is his turn," she said. "He went to see Carl Zimmerman's wife. She wouldn't let him in. He's out roaming and he doesn't want company."

"Have him call me on my cell as soon as he surfaces. It's important."

"It always is," Claire said.

CHAPTER EIGHTY-ONE

City hall had an ancient boiler that generated too much heat and an unbalanced ventilation system that created a worldwide array of climates throughout the building. The lobby felt like the tropics cooled with bursts of cold air drawn inside each time the revolving doors spun around.

Mason called Mickey, promising him lunch in return for a ride, lingering next to a cool marble column near the entrance. His cell phone rang, rupturing his fantasy of lying on a beach next to a suddenly heterosexual Rachel Firestone.

"You looking for me?" Harry asked.

"Yeah. Do you have any friends left in the department who would do you a favor?"

Harry snorted. "Like what? Box up the stuff in my desk and mail it to me, postage due?"

"That's an option. Would they do you a favor that might make them unpack your box?"

"Talk to me."

Mason explained to Harry what he wanted. "Is that doable?"

"It's a long shot on a good day, and this ain't a good day. I'll see what I can do, but don't be in a hurry. This may take a while."

Mason and Mickey stopped at Winsteads, home of the steakburger, and fortified themselves against the cold with double cheeseburgers with everything and grilled onions, crispy French fries, and chocolate shakes. They dipped their last fry into a pool of ketchup before navigating back to the office.

Mason tried returning some of the calls from lawyers on other cases he was handling but gave up when he realized they were using those cases as an excuse to talk about the shoot-out at the lagoon. Instead, he called Rachel and asked her to check the *Star's* clipping file for stories about the death of Donald Ray White.

"Who was Donald Ray White and why are you interested in that story?"

"Because."

"Because it has something to do with the mayhem epidemic you started, or just because?"

"Donald Ray White was the director of liquor control until he was killed eighteen years ago."

"If I ask you who killed him, will you tell me?"

"According to Howard Trimble, who inherited Donald Ray's job, he was killed by his brain-damaged daughter, Cheryl White."

"Why aren't you convinced? Do you have another suspect in mind?"

"Yeah. Amy White."

"Mayor Billy Sunshine's Amy White? Get out of town! Give it to me!"

"Do your homework first. I'm at the office."

Mason sorted through his mail, the volume of which had doubled. Much of it was from cranks and kooks who wanted to hire him. One writer even asked Mason to sue the planet Zircon for bombarding him with radiation.

His phone rang so often, he let his answering machine screen calls. When Beth Harrell called, he nearly succumbed to the sound of her voice and picked up the phone. She sounded distant, almost as if she were adrift.

"Lou," she said, "it's Beth. I know things are crazy for you right now. They sure are crazy for me. Call me when you can. There's something I have to tell you."

Mason ran down a mental list of what that could possibly be and didn't come up with anything he was anxious to find out. The sun was making its late afternoon exit, carpeting Broadway with shadows, when Mason's cell phone rang.

"Do you make house calls?" Blues asked.

"Depends on the patient's condition. Is it critical?"

"Could be. I followed Amy from city hall. She stopped at the Goodwill Industries sheltered workshop and picked up a woman who must be her sister. They went out to lunch, did some shopping, and came home."

"Sounds very suspicious."

"Wait till you hear about the snowman. The two of them came back outside and built a snowman and had a snowball fight. Then they got back in the car and went sledding on Suicide Hill on Brookside Boulevard, which isn't far from her house. Amy acted like she didn't have a care in the world. Her sister was a little slow. Amy had to help her with her mittens and show her how to steer the sled, things like that. They just got home."

"Give me the address," Mason said, jotting it down. "Keep an eye on them. I'm waiting to hear from Harry on something. As soon as he calls, I'll be there."

Mason stacked and unstacked the papers on his desk, rearranged the pencils in his drawer, and shot baskets with Mickey using wadded-up crank letters as basketballs and his trash can as a hoop. Mickey let him win the first two games before suggesting they play for money. Mason knew he was being set up but didn't mind. Mickey ran his scams with good humor, even making Mason feel charitable as the money changed hands.

Rachel rocketed into Mason's office at four o'clock with a set of clippings under her arm and high color in her cheeks. Mickey was bent over backward, making the winning basket in a game of H-O-R-S-E.

"Who's the contortionist?" Rachel asked.

Mickey looked up, sprang forward on one hand, and extended the other. "Mickey Shanahan."

"Beat it, Mickey," Rachel told him in a sharp tone that left no room for argument. "And close the door behind you."

Mickey looked at Mason, who nodded and pointed at the door. "She's usually a lot meaner. She's having a good day."

After Mickey closed the door, Rachel and Mason had a staring contest. Mason caught a merry glint in her eye and a fragment of a smile that turned the corner of her mouth slightly upward.

"First one to smile is a weenie," Mason said.

"Stand up and get over here."

Mason did as he was told, stopping well inside her territorial imperative while he tried to decipher the mixed message that was scrambling his hormonal network. Before he was able to crack Rachel's code, she grasped the back of his neck with both of her hands, pulled his mouth to hers, and crushed him with a kiss that nearly sucked the life out of him. Mason couldn't decide whether to hold on or beg for mercy. He settled for the Issac Newton kissing principle of equal and opposite reaction.

CHAPTER EIGHTY-TWO

"Damn it!" she said when she released him and came up for air. "Nothing!"

"What's the matter?" he gasped.

"It's not your fault," she said. "You're just not a woman. What a waste!"

"Could I have a translation here or at least a reverse-angle replay?"

Rachel stroked the side of his face with excruciating tenderness. "I'm sorry, Lou. I told you not to get a crush on me because I'd break your heart. I should have listened to my own advice. You're cute, funny, and you give great tips. Today's was a megatip. I guess it all overwhelmed me, and I had to find out if it was you or the tips that were making me wet."

"Shouldn't we at least have sex just to be certain?"

"Further proof that you'll never be a woman. You'll have to settle for the clippings on Donald Ray White. Why didn't you tell me that Jack Cullan was the family's lawyer?"

Rachel handed Mason the clippings and sat down on his couch as he leafed through them. "And take all the fun out of your job?"

She joined him on the couch. "Okay, give me the rest of it." Mason started to protest, and Rachel interrupted him. "I know. It's all off the record until you tell me otherwise."

"Jack Cullan and Blues had an argument in the bar the Friday night that Cullan was killed."

"I know. That was the key to the prosecutor's case," Rachel said.

"Cullan threatened to shut Blues down. Later than night, he

called Amy White and demanded that she bring him Blues's liquor control file."

"That night?"

"Cullan lived for immediate gratification. Amy told me about the call from Cullan but said that she told him that he'd have to wait until Monday morning, but Howard Trimble told me that Amy called him that night and he met her at his office and gave her Blues's file."

Rachel whistled. "So you think Amy took the file to Cullan and killed him for making her come out late at night?"

Mason shook his head. "Not exactly. According to Howard Trimble, Donald Ray was a child abuser. He'd been arrested for abusing Amy's sister, Cheryl. Amy was fifteen and Cheryl was twelve. Cullan got him off and kept it quiet and, in the process, added Donald Ray to his stable of indebted city officials. After Donald Ray got out of jail, he took his frustrations out on Cheryl, leaving her brain damaged. Then Cheryl shot her father with his own gun. Cullan made that case go away too."

"How does a brain-damaged twelve-year-old kill her father?"

"I don't think Cheryl shot her father. I think Amy did, and Cullan pinned it on Cheryl because nothing would happen to her. He made a long-term investment in Amy and was collecting—again—when he told her to get Blues's file."

"Maybe Amy decided her account was already paid in full."

"More likely that she decided to cancel the debt."

"The newspaper reported it as an accidental shooting, a tragic accident. The story says that Donald Ray had just cleaned the gun and set it down for a moment. The wife said Cheryl thought it was a toy and was playing with it when the gun went off accidentally. Everybody said how sad, and that was it. What now?"

"Harry Ryman is doing a ballistics check to see if Donald Ray and Cullan were killed with the same gun."

"Where's Amy?"

"Blues is babysitting her—from a distance. As soon as I hear from Harry, I'm going to go see her."

"Why not just send the cops to pick her up?"

"They already arrested the wrong person once. I'd like to be sure this time."

"You're better than I thought for someone with the wrong chromosomes. Keep me posted," she added before kissing him lightly on the cheek in the best tradition of sisters everywhere.

Harry called shortly after six o'clock. "You were right. But there's more there than even you thought."

Mason listened as Harry outlined what he had found. "How do you want to play this?" Harry asked him.

"Carefully. She's the last witness."

CHAPTER EIGHTY-THREE

Fifteen minutes later, Mason turned onto Amy's street. It was a neighborhood where garages were used for storage or spare bedrooms and people parked on the street. Every car had been plowed in, sandwiched between a three-foot snow wall and the curb. Some people had dug out, and others had given up and gone back to bed until spring.

Amy's house was the third one in from the corner. It was dark. There was no car parked in the driveway or on the street in front of the house. Nor was Blues anywhere in sight. He wasn't parked on the street or around the corner, and he wasn't hiding behind a shrub next to Amy's front porch.

Mason opened his cell phone and realized it was off. He turned it on and saw the digital readout informing him that he'd missed a call. He punched in the code for his voice mail. The message was from Blues. Amy was running.

Mason banged his fists on the steering wheel, nearly sending the Jeep into a figure-eight spin before he pulled it back to the center of Amy's street. He drove out of her neighborhood, parked in front of a Circle K convenience store, and called Blues.

"Where the hell have you been?" Blues demanded.

"Don't turn codependent on me! What happened?"

"I lost her."

"I hope the story is better than the ending."

"About an hour ago, Amy started turning out the lights in her house. A little while later, she started loading suitcases into the trunk of her car. She drives a black Honda, probably a couple of years old."

"What? You were hiding in the garage?"

"No, boy genius. I was hiding in my car at the back of a driveway across the street. Amy's house has a detached garage. I had a clear shot."

"You don't think she noticed you sitting in her neighbor's driveway?"

"It's like this. The driveway had been plowed down to the concrete. That meant the people who lived there used a service. Newspapers from the last three days were lying on the driveway. That meant those people were out of town. The driveway curves around to a side-entrance garage that is blocked off by tall evergreens. That meant I could see Amy but she couldn't see me. I waited until it got dark and drove up with my lights off. She never saw me."

"You are too good for words and you are my hero. So how did you lose her?"

"I was following her from a distance, about half a block, with a few cars in between us. I was in an intersection when one of the cars in front of me stopped suddenly and we had a chain-reaction collision. My new truck got sandwiched, and then I got T-boned by a car coming through the intersection."

"Are you all right?"

"I'm all right but we're fucked. Amy's in the wind, man."

Mason had brought Rachel's newspaper clippings with him. He fanned out the articles on the passenger seat, looking for the one he'd scanned a few hours ago without paying any real attention to it.

"Maybe not. I'll call you later."

The Jeep's heater couldn't keep up with the cold, and Mason's breath crystallized and evaporated in quick gray puffs as he studied the article. It was a human-interest piece on Memorial Day observances that featured a picture of Amy and Cheryl visiting their parents' graves at Forest Park Cemetery. The accompanying story recounted that Cheryl had suffered brain damage in a fall at home, that their father had been killed in an accidental shooting, and that their mother had passed away a short time later.

Amy was quoted as saying that they always visited their parents' graves on Memorial Day. She had added that they also visited before going away for a long trip, in keeping with a tradition started by Cheryl's guardian, Jack Cullan.

Mason couldn't imagine Cullan as a guardian of anything except a junkyard where he dumped people after he had used them up like rusted-out, stripped-down cars sitting up on blocks, their guts scattered to the four corners. He also couldn't picture Cullan taking the time to honor the dead, with the obvious exception of Tom Pendergast. Mason hoped that Amy had kept alive Cullan's curious tradition of visiting the dead before hitting the road.

The black wrought-iron gate that barred access to Forest Park Cemetery after dark hung open, tapping against a stone wall with each gust of wind when Mason pulled up to the entrance. His headlights shot bright streamers into the cemetery, which spread out like buckshot before disappearing in the distance. Mason blocked the entrance with his jeep and got out.

The padlock for the gate hung from a chain, smashed and broken, the scratches fresh. There were also fresh scrapes on the rails of the gate, as if the assailant hadn't been able to stop after simply breaking the lock. A woman's white cotton glove lay in the snow at the foot of the gate, stained with fresh blood. He got the message. Whoever had opened the gate was out of control, and anyone that got in the way was going to take a beating.

The main road through the cemetery had been scraped, leaving a bottom layer of packed snow and ice harder than the underlying asphalt. Mason stayed on foot, following tire tracks illuminated by the moon. Snow had drifted against many of the tombstones, all but burying them. Some heirs and mourners had erected taller monuments to the deceased, capped by crosses that broke through the snow toward heaven.

Mason's footsteps slapped against the packed snow, a hollow sound in a silent theater, his shadow a poor accompaniment to a night owl passing overhead, its moonlit silhouette leading Mason deeper into the cemetery. A rasping, grating, fractious noise drew Mason off the main road along a winding path among the dead, until he crested a small rise and looked down on a pair of graves.

Amy White was bent over one of the headstones, her back to Mason, flailing at it with a hammer, cursing the rock, the ground, and the bones beneath. Her car was stuck nose down in the snow on an embankment opposite where Mason stood, its engine running, headlights glowing beneath the snow. A woman he assumed was Cheryl lay nearby on her back, making angel wings in the snow with her arms.

"Amy," Mason called to her.

She wheeled around, her face twisted with exhumed rage, her movement revealing Donald Ray White's name engraved on the stone. Her cold skin was paler than the moon, colored only by flecks of blood at the corners of her mouth.

Amy raised the hammer above her head as if to throw it at Mason, then spun back to her mad work, striking another blow against her dead father. The head of the hammer flew off, knifing into the snow as the handle shattered, spearing her hand with a jagged splinter. She clamped the splinter with her teeth, yanked it from her fleshy palm, and spat it out.

"I knew it would be you!" she screamed.

CHAPTER EIGHTY-FOUR

Mason walked down the hill toward Amy, keeping his hands in plain view in an effort to calm her down.

"How could you know it would be me?"

Amy gulped air and wiped her bloody hand against her jeans. "That day in the parking garage, when I asked for your help—I knew you wouldn't do it. I knew you thought I was just Billy Sunshine's toady. That I just wanted to protect his precious goddamn career."

"You're right. That is what I thought. But I was wrong, wasn't I? You wanted me to find your file, not the mayor's."

Amy heaved, gradually catching her breath, forcing her madness back into a genie's bottle.

"If you had told me where the mayor's file was, I would have found mine. Then everything would have been fine, except I knew you wouldn't do it. I knew you wouldn't let it rest until you found out."

"Until I found out that you killed your father, not Cheryl; that you used the same gun to kill Jack Cullan."

Amy threw her head back. "How did you know about the gun?"

"You told me that Cullan had wanted Blues's liquor license brought to him on the Friday night he and Blues argued at the bar but that you put him off until Monday. Howard Trimble told me that he gave you the file that same night. Yet you didn't give the file to Cullan, and I couldn't figure out why. Then Trimble told me what your father had done to Cheryl, how your mother had hired Cullan to defend your father and then to defend your sister."

"My father was a hell-born bastard that deserved to die!"

"That's probably what a jury would have said. Especially since the police reports showed that you shot him in self- defense. The cops found a gun in your father's hand. Your mother said that he'd fired a shot and threatened to kill all of you. Her mistake was calling Jack Cullan before she called the police."

Amy slumped to the ground, her back against her father's tombstone. "I don't remember very much after I shot him. My mother and I were screaming. We didn't know what to do."

"Cullan must have convinced your mother that the only way to save you was to blame Cheryl since she would never be prosecuted. Cullan had the juice to make everyone look the other way. Your mother even got to keep the guns. Instead of a fee, Cullan got you, just like a future draft choice."

"Jack Cullan was as rotten as my father. When he called me that night, I did what he told me, but I couldn't stand it anymore. I couldn't stand that he was going to ruin someone else. I had found the gun in my mother's things when she died. I took it with me to Jack's house. I was going to make him stop."

"What did Cullan say?"

Amy pawed the snow at her sides as her face slackened into a dull, exhausted gaze. "He laughed at me and told me to give him the file. I took the gun out and he kept laughing, so I shot him. Then I turned off the heat, opened the windows, and went home."

Mason studied her, searched her suddenly detached face for a hint of meaning. She leaned against her father's headstone, reaching idly toward her mother's to dust the snow from the channels of her mother's engraved name.

"What did you do with the gun?"

Amy stood, brushed the snow from her jeans, and gave Mason a sly look. "I threw it into the Missouri River on New Year's Eve. By the way, you're quite the swimmer."

Mason flashed back to New Year's Eve. He remembered seeing Amy in the mayor's entourage just before Beth found him at the back of the Dream Casino. In the video Ed Fiora had shown him, Beth had left him on the prow of the boat. The next thing he'd seen was the flash from a gun. Though the shooter's face was obscured, he and Fiora had assumed that the shooter had been Beth.

"If it makes you feel any better, you didn't miss."

"Actually, that makes me feel worse. I didn't know what to do about you. I just knew I couldn't let you find out about me. I saw you and Beth Harrell go outside and I took a chance. You should have bled to death and drowned."

"Sorry to disappoint you."

"That's all right," she answered as she reached into her coat pocket and pulled out a gun. "I get a second chance."

"Your father's other gun. The one you used to kill Shirley Parker. Harry Ryman matched the ballistics reports. I told Carl Zimmerman where Cullan's files were, and he told you. You knew about the tunnel to Pendergast's office from when you worked at the mayor's campaign headquarters on the other side of the alley behind the barbershop."

"Jack even gave me the tour."

"You ran into Shirley in the tunnel and killed her."

"Kind of makes it your fault, don't you think?"

"Except I didn't pull the trigger. You did."

"Shirley was hysterical. She came at me with a pair of scissors."

Mason shook his head. "Self-defense would have worked when you were fifteen. That story won't sell. There were no scissors where you left Shirley's body. You got your file and part of the mayor's, but you left enough behind to convict him. Why?"

"I just took the parts about me."

"Carl Zimmerman and James Toland were late to the party. They stole the files they wanted and booby-trapped the rest. Did you know about that?"

"No, but I would have helped them if I had known."

"Blaming all this on dear old Dad won't work anymore, Amy. Killing me won't save you. Your car is stuck in the snow. You'll have to leave my body on your parents' graves. That's a pretty big clue. And your sister is an eyewitness. Are you going to kill her too?"

"Amy, I wanna go home," Cheryl said. "I'm cold."

Cheryl had given up making snow angels and was standing only a few feet from Amy. She spoke with a thick-tongued child's singsong whine. Though she was nearly thirty, her mind was trapped in those last moments when she'd been an innocent child, before her father had beaten her future out of her. Her labored speech was a lasting reminder.

"In a minute, Cheryl," Amy said, keeping her eyes and gun firmly on Mason.

"Now! I wanna go now!" Cheryl stomped her feet and hammered her sides with her fists.

"In a minute, I told you!"

Cheryl began to cry, softly at first, then building to a wail that convulsed her. "Now! Right now!"

Cheryl ran toward Amy like a child grabbing for her mother. Mason bolted at Amy in the same instant, knocking the gun from her hand as the three of them collided. Mason and Amy rolled into the headstones, with Amy on top of him howling and scratching his face. He gripped her wrists, and she crashed her forehead into his nose. Mason felt the cartilage crumble and tasted the blood that ran into his mouth. He pulled her toward him, cocked his arms like springs, and threw her off of him.

A shot rang out, stopping Amy for an instant in midflight, before she tumbled to the ground at Mason's side. Cheryl sat on the snow, the gun in her lap.

"I just wanna go home."

CHAPTER EIGHTY-FIVE

Mason always found April a soothing month. Its cool breezes and sun-painted skies made promises the rest of the year could never keep. Though the life cycle continued unaltered, April convinced his soul that life had an edge over death. He thought about that perpetual scorecard as he stood at the foot of Amy White's grave, the sun warming his neck without penetrating to the chilled memories he carried of the past winter.

Patrick Ortiz had ruled that Amy White's death was accidental. It had been his first official act after Leonard Campbell resigned and he was appointed to serve out Campbell's term as prosecuting attorney. Campbell had gone on the offensive, quitting and denying any wrongdoing before he was indicted.

"What happens to Cheryl White?" Mason had asked Ortiz.

"She's a ward of the state for now, but Howard Trimble has started adoption proceedings. What about you? I hear that Campbell tried to hire you."

Mason had laughed. "I took a pass. He and the mayor have been leaving me messages every day. I hear that Donovan Jenkins made a deal for immunity with the U.S. attorney that will put the mayor away."

"So why not defend one of them?"

"I'm too close to what happened. I'll probably be a witness."

Mason hadn't told Ortiz that he was waiting for his own visit from the feds. Galaxy Gaming Company had bought the Dream Casino. Mason figured it was just a matter of time before some Galaxy employee found the tape recording he was certain Fiora had made of Mason conspiring to gain Blues's release. He figured that Galaxy would either turn him in or book a favor. He couldn't decide which alternative he dreaded more—the visit from the feds or the visit from Galaxy.

Beth Harrell had visited him first. He was studying notes he had written on his dry-erase board about his newest case. Mason had agreed to defend a professional wrestler who'd been indicted for involuntary manslaughter when he'd killed his archrival during a match.

"From the ridiculous to the sublime," Beth had said from the open doorway.

Mason had looked up and pointed to the board. "My case or your life?"

"Fair question. I suppose an explanation is in order."

"No. I'd say it's out of order. You don't owe me an explanation. You just need to quit blaming your weaknesses on your past and move on. You may be kinky or just fucked up. I don't know which and it doesn't matter."

Mason cringed inwardly at his coldness toward Beth but shook it off with the realization that it was the only way he could break from her. She had a toxic allure that he couldn't risk.

"Meaning you don't care?"

"Meaning it doesn't matter. I can't help you either way."

Mason had picked up the wrestler's file and started reading. When he looked up a moment later, Beth had gone.

That had been a month ago, when winter was just releasing its grip. Mason bent down and pulled a dandelion from the sod covering Amy's grave. When he stood up, he saw Harry Ryman walking toward him.

"Blues said I might find you here," Harry told him.

"Yeah. I just thought I'd stop by and pull the weeds. What's up?"

"The chief wants to know if I'm coming back to work." Harry had declined a commendation for solving the murders of Jack Cullan and Shirley Parker and had been using up his accumulated vacation and sick leave. "There's a lot of outside pressure on him to bring me back, and a lot of inside pressure the other way."

"What are you going to do?"

"Carl was six months shy of a full pension. The department lets you buy out the time so you can retire, and still collect your full pension. I told the chief if he'd let me buy out Carl's time, I'd retire. What do you think?"

"I think we're both pulling weeds. Maybe that's the best we can do."

Harry looked out over the acres of grave sites. "I suppose so."

"Listen, I'm on my way to a rugby game. You should come along. I promised Rachel I'd take her to a game. You can keep her company while I get beat up."

"Sounds great. I'll pick up Claire and meet you at the game."

Mason thought about Amy's father and his own father, whom he scarcely remembered, as Harry walked away. Mason had pictures of his father, but little else. Jonathan Mason had been a tall, sturdily built man who his aunt Claire said had an easy laugh.

He couldn't remember the scrape of his father's unshaved cheek against his own. He couldn't summon his father's smell after he'd worked in the yard on a dusty, hot afternoon, nor after he'd slapped cologne on his neck on Saturday night. He couldn't remember the view from atop his father's shoulders. He had never caught a ball his father had thrown, nor measured his own strength against the man who'd given him life. He couldn't repeat the stories his father must have read to him. Nor could he conjure the fear he must have felt at his father's raised voice, or the comfort he surely had found in its softer tones. He examined his hands, searching without success for the memory of his father's touch.

There were times when Mason would have killed for memories of his father, though he knew the depth of his longing was metaphorical. Amy White's memories of her father had made the metaphor murderous.

He bent down to pull another young dandelion. Casting it aside, he placed a small rock on Amy's tombstone in the Jewish tradition of remembering the dead, certain that no one else would remember Amy White.

THANKS

Thank you for adding *The Last Witness* to your library. This is an exciting time to be a writer and a reader. The indie revolution has given writers the chance to connect with readers in ways that were never imagined before.

The next novel in the Lou Mason series, *Cold Truth*, will be available soon as an e-book and POD. Enjoy the opening chapters I've included beginning on the next page and stay in touch.

Find out more about me at www.joelgoldman.com.

Follow my blog at http://www.joelgoldman.blogspot.com.

Sign up for my newsletter at http://www.joelgoldman.com/newsletter.php.

Follow me on Twitter http://twitter.com/#!/JoelGoldman1.

Follow me on Facebook at http://www.facebook.com/joel.goldman.

JOEL GOLDMAN

ACKNOWLEDGMENTS

Writing is not always a solitary pursuit. Thanks to the following people who helped with this book the first time around: Stuart Jaffe, my honest reader; Josh Garry and Dan Cofran, my political consultants; John Fraise, my private cop; Karen Haas and Ann LaFarge, my editors at Kensington Publishing Co., when this book was first published in 2003; and Meredith Bernstein, my agent. Special thanks to my loving wife, Hildy, who keeps my feet on the ground when my head is in the clouds.

The e-book revolution is about a lot of things, including more choices for readers and new opportunities for writers. One of the best things is the chance to share my books with people who, in spite of my late mother's best efforts, had somehow missed them when they were first published. I think of her with an ebook reader and smile.

**ENJOY THIS EXCERPT FROM *MOTION TO KILL*,
THE THRILLING FIRST NOVEL IN JOEL GOLDMAN'S
SERIES FEATURING LOU MASON**

CHAPTER ONE

A dead partner is bad for business, even if he dies in his sleep. But when he washes ashore on one side of a lake and his boat is found abandoned on the other side, it's worse. When the sheriff tells the coroner to "cut him open and see what we've got," it's time to dust off the résumé. And the ink was barely dry on Lou Mason's.

The time was seven thirty on Sunday morning, July 12. It was too early for dead bodies, too humid for the smell, and just right for the flies and mosquitoes. And it was rotten for identifying the body of a dead partner. These were the moments to remember.

Mason's dead partner was Richard Sullivan, senior partner in Sullivan & Christenson, his law firm for the last three months. Sullivan was the firm's rainmaker. He was a sawed-off, in-your-face, thump-your-chest ballbuster. His clients and partners loved the money he made for them, but none of them ever confessed to liking him. Though in his late fifties, he had one of those perpetually mid forties faces. Except that now he was dead, as gray as a Minneapolis winter and bloated from a night in the water.

Sullivan & Christenson was a Kansas City law firm that employed forty lawyers to merge and acquire clients' assets so they could protect them from taxation before and after death. When bare-knuckled bargaining didn't get the deal done, they'd sue the bastards. Or defend the firm's bastard if he was sued first. Mason's job was to win regardless of which bastard won the race to the courthouse.

The U.S. attorney, Franklin St. John, had been preparing a special invitation to the courthouse for Sullivan's biggest client, a banker named Victor O'Malley. The RSVP would be sent to the grand jury that had been investigating O'Malley for two years. Sullivan asked Mason to defend O'Malley the day Mason joined the firm as its twelfth partner. Mason accepted and Sullivan spoonfed him the details of O'Malley's complex business deals.

Mason figured out that O'Malley had stolen a lot of money from the bank he owned. He was having a harder time figuring out how to defend him. Fifty million dollars was a lot to blame on a bookkeeping mistake.

Two days earlier, Sullivan took Mason to lunch and, over a couple of grilled chicken Caesar salads, casually inquired what would happen to O'Malley's defense if certain documents disappeared.

"Which documents?" Mason asked.

Sullivan studied Mason for a moment before answering. "Let's assume that there are records that show O'Malley and one of his business associates received favorable treatment from his bank."

Mason didn't hesitate. "That's what the whole case is about. There are too many of those documents to lose even if I didn't mind going to jail with O'Malley. Which I do."

"Lou, I only care about the documents with my name on them. Do you understand?"

Mason nodded slowly, wiping his hands with a white cloth napkin more than was needed to clean them.

"I'm not going to jail for you either. Show me the documents, and we'll figure something out."

Sullivan gave him the pained look of a disappointed parent and changed the subject. Mason knew then that he'd never see the documents. In the same instant, he also knew that his career at Sullivan & Christenson was over. He had failed Sullivan's test but passed his own. He decided to think it over during the firm's annual retreat that weekend, but he knew what he would do come Monday morning. Quit.

The retreat was at Buckhorn resort at the Lake of the Ozarks in southern Missouri. It was a long weekend of golf, drinking, and leering for the lawyers and staff.

Mason went for a walk after the Saturday night poker game, stopping at the beach, a kidney-shaped plot filled with sand along a retaining wall at the water's edge. A slight breeze rolled off the water, just enough to push the air around. A young couple was braided together at one end of the beach. He lay down at a discreet distance on the only lounge chair, turned his back to them, and felt the loneliness of the voyeur.

He didn't realize that he'd fallen asleep until a voice interrupted the recurring dream of his last trial before he joined Sullivan & Christenson. Tommy Douchant, his client and best friend, looked up at him from his wheelchair, eyes wild, tears beading on his cheeks, as the jury announced its verdict against them. Mason begged the jury to come back, to listen to him, as they filed out of the courtroom, their faces dissolving as a voice sliced through his dream.

"Excuse me . . . are you Lou Mason?"

Tommy rolled back into Mason's subconscious as he opened his eyes. The voice belonged to a woman standing over him, backlit by the glare of the morning sun. The glistening effect was a mixture of a Madonna halo and a Star Trek transporter. He thought about asking her to beam him up while he rubbed any leftover drool from his chin stubble.

The best he could do was a slightly sleep-slurred, "Yeah, I'm Mason."

Snappy repartee after spending the night on a bed of vinyl was sometimes the beginning and end of his charm.

"I'm Sheriff Kelly Holt. We need to talk."

"It's okay, Officer, I paid for the room."

Drumroll, please, he silently requested, satisfied that he was really hitting his stride.

"I'm sure you did, Mr. Mason. I'm more interested in whether you know Richard Sullivan."

Fully awake now, he stood so that he could see her clearly. Khaki uniform, Caribbean blue eyes, Pope County sheriff's badge, natural, no-sweat beauty, pistol on her hip. A shade shorter than his six feet, with honey-colored hair that draped the shoulders of a tanned, athletic body. She was a slap-on-the-cuffs dream come true, but her question flattened the fantasy.

"He's my law partner. Is there a problem?"

"I'd appreciate it if you would come with me. I'll meet you in the lobby in fifteen minutes. You may want to change first."

Mason looked down at his beer-stained T-shirt and gym shorts with a hole where the pocket used to be. He realized he was losing on banter and style points.

Doctors, lawyers, and cops all use the same technique when they give bad news. They tell you a little at a time. Knowledge is power—give it away all at once and the power is gone. Having done the same thing, Mason knew better than to press.

He was ten minutes late but smelled better and looked better in tan chinos, a green polo shirt, and deck shoes. The rest of him fit the clean clothes. Dark, closely trimmed hair and steel gray eyes that his aunt Claire always claimed darkened like thunderheads whenever he was angry. An anonymous flying elbow thrown during a muddy rugby scrum had left him with a speed bump on his nose just below eye level. He was clean shaven at seven a.m. but could expect a five-o'clock shadow an hour early. Good orthodontics bred a sincere smile that juries had found persuasive through ten years of practice in his first firm. It had yet to be tested in his new one.

Mason had had some luck and notable failures—his ex-wife, Kate, being foremost—with women. He knew it wasn't politically correct to immediately appraise Kelly as a social prospect, but it filled the time while he waited for her to tell him what was going on.

She showed no more interest in him than in any other out-of-towner she'd awakened on the beach, and she wasn't talking. So Mason took the first shot as they pulled away from the resort in her pickup truck.

"Listen, we can play twenty questions or you can just tell me what this is all about."

She shifted gears as she kept her eyes on the curving road

317

that snaked away from the lake. A two-way radio crackled with background static. He rested his head against the butt of a shotgun mounted on the rear window.

Kelly chose questions over answers. "When did you last see Mr. Sullivan?"

Mason rolled the window down and let the truck fill with the muggy morning air. The smell of summer flowers and long grass was a welcome change from midtown traffic.

Mason had sat across from Sullivan at last night's poker game, his first with his future former partners. For a ten-dollar buy-in, he spent the evening with a good cigar, a cold beer, and an open window into their psyches. Mason believed that poker made you win with your strengths and fold with your weaknesses. Luck always plays a part, but even the luckiest lousy card player will eventually lose it all if he gives the cards enough time. Sullivan was a good card player, but it sounded like he'd hit a losing streak that would spread to the other partners, who depended on the business he brought in.

"Last night around eleven. We'd been playing poker."

"Who else played?"

"Snow White and the seven dwarfs. All the regulars."

"You were better company before you woke up. Or is this just a phase of your arrested adolescence?"

"Tell me what happened to Sullivan. After that and eight hours of sleep on something besides vinyl, I'll charm your socks off."

She answered without a sideways glance or a hint of humor.

"One of the locals found a body this morning. It's been in the water overnight. The ID belongs to your partner. I want you to tell me if the body belongs to the ID."

CHAPTER TWO

Her voice was pure matter-of-fact, as if she had told him to check the tires and the oil. He caught a quick dip in her shoulders, as if she was dropping her burden of bad news in his lap. Still, she said it with a practiced weariness that convinced Mason she was used to violent death. He wasn't. He was accustomed to family deaths, natural causes, and ritualized grieving. Floating bodies were not part of Mason's life-cycle résumé.

Barring a freakish case of mistaken identity, Mason knew that Sullivan was dead. The odds of his ID being mismatched with a stranger were slim. Mason didn't know him well enough to grieve honestly. Partners are harder to get to know than spouses or friends. Agendas overlap only on narrow ground.

His emotions were a mixed bag that didn't include grief. He was more relieved than sorry. Sullivan's suggestion that Mason destroy evidence in the O'Malley case would be buried with him. Mason could stay at the firm if he chose. Yet he couldn't muster any enthusiasm for reversing his decision to leave. There was no glory in defending Victor O'Malley. His aunt Claire's warning that he wasn't cut out to fight over other people's money, especially when the money was dirty, echoed in his mind.

His recurring dream of Tommy Douchant's trial reminded him of unfinished business that he would have to complete on his own. Sullivan's death may have shown him the way out instead of the way back in.

The sheriff would have told him if Sullivan's death was accidental since there would be no reason to withhold that information. The likelihood that Sullivan's murder was tied to the O'Malley case and perhaps to the documents Sullivan had asked him to lose swept through him like a convulsion.

He was shaken by the twin possibilities that the killer might want to eliminate O'Malley's other lawyer and that the sheriff might suspect him in the crime if she knew what Sullivan had asked him to do. He felt his color drain and hoped the sheriff would attribute it to the grief he couldn't summon. It occurred to him that he was probably the least likely person to identify Sullivan's body.

"Why did you choose me?"

At last she surrendered a small smile.

"You weren't my first choice. We found a key to a room at Buckhorn. It belonged to Mr. Sullivan. The hotel manager gave us a list of the rest of the guests from your firm. You were third on the list. The first two checked out at dawn."

"Harlan Christenson and Scott Daniels."

Harlan Christenson sat next to Mason at the poker table. A shock of white hair hung loosely over his forehead, accenting his coal black caterpillar eyebrows. Shaped like a badly stuffed pillow, he filled his chair to capacity and grunted his bets with a Scotch-scratched voice. Only his head and hands had moved as he'd peeled back the corners of his first three cards, praying for aces.

He was a grandfatherly patrician of Kansas City society, opening doors that Sullivan never could have knocked on. Where Sullivan was brusque and kept everyone at arm's length, Harlan touched everyone. He shook their hands warmly and guided them to his office with his arm comfortably around their shoulders. Together they had built a powerful practice.

He was widowed and Mason was divorced, so he invited Mason to his farmhouse for dinner every couple of weeks after he'd joined the firm. They cooked out and tossed fishing lines in his pond, never really trying to catch anything.

Mason's other best friend and law school classmate, Scott Daniels, had sat on his other side at the card game. Scott and Tommy Douchant had flipped a coin to decide which one would be best man at Mason's wedding. Scott had called heads and won. Tommy claimed he'd used a two-headed coin, a charge Scott never denied.

Scott had started with the firm when they graduated and was now second in command in the business department, which Sullivan ran. Ten years after graduation, he still carried 175 pounds rationed along a swimmer's V-shaped frame. His eyes were robin's-egg blue with the shell's dull finish. Fine dark blond hair, slicked back, etched an undulating hairline along an angular, sallow-cheeked face.

Kelly asked, "Any idea why they left so early?"

"Scott had to get ready for a closing on Monday. Harlan said he had a noon wedding."

"And that left you, Mr. Mason. What were you and your partners doing at the lake?"

"Having our annual retreat. Lawyers, legal assistants, and administrative staff getting away from it all but not each other."

She pulled in at a marina called Jerry's Port. The water rolled with a slight chop stirred by the steady boat traffic of the lake patrol.

Mason's chest tightened along with his throat as he wondered if he'd recognize Sullivan's body. He remembered a wrongful death case he'd handled in which the victim had drowned. A body left in water long enough swells up like an inflatable doll, stretching the features into a macabre mask. The pictures of the deceased in that case had led to a rash of tasteless jokes in his office, none of which he could recall.

Mason followed Kelly to a sheriff's department patrol boat. She drove, while he hoped the spray off the lake would help him keep his cool. Soon she turned toward shore, aiming at a sign that read *Crabtree Cove*. The sides of the cove were lined with private docks. Modest lake homes sat above the docks, away from the water, which fed a shallow marsh at the heel of the inlet. Two other patrol boats were anchored across the back of the cove, forming a floating barricade. Kelly cut the motor to idle, and they coasted past the sentries until the bottom of the boat slid into the soft mud.

Knee-high grass had been tramped down into a rough carpet leading from the water's edge to a short, squat, rumpled man wearing dirty brown coveralls. He could have been half man, half stump, sitting on a log next to a tarp-covered shape that was roughly the size of a body.

"Mr. Mason, say hello to Doc Eddy, Pope County coroner," Kelly said.

"Damn shame, Mason, too bad."

He wiped his hands on his pants before pulling back a corner of the tarp. Sullivan's lifeless eyes stared unblinking into the still rising sun. Heat, water, and death had stolen his attraction and intimidation. Oily engine exhaust mixed with the swampy smell of brackish water and the sickly sweet odor of decomposing flesh. Mason's stomach pitched and yawed as he lost last night's dinner.

He stumbled a few yards away while the aftershocks rocked his belly, and his head slowly stopped spinning. Kelly appeared at his side and pushed a towel into his clammy hand. He was surprised at the softness of her skin when their hands brushed against each other.

"Listen, I'm sorry. There just isn't an easy way to do this. Is it Sullivan?"

The metamorphosis from "him" to "it" suddenly seemed natural. "Yeah, probably—don't know. You better ask his wife."

He was fresh out of smart-ass. Dead bodies, Mason realized, are hell on humor.

"We tried to reach her in Kansas City. No one answered."

"That's because she's here—at the lake. They have a place in Kinchelow Hollow near Shangri-La. We're having brunch over there at eleven this morning."

Kelly turned back toward the coroner. "Doc, we'll meet you at Listrom's Mortuary in an hour. Tell Malcolm to hold the body for identification. Counselor, you come with me to see Mrs. Sullivan."

Kelly aimed him toward the boat with a slight shove. He didn't need the help, but he got the point.

CHAPTER THREE

The path from Sullivan's private dock to the deck on the back of his house followed a switchback route up a slope landscaped with descending terraces set off by railroad ties and planted with a multihued variety of annuals and perennials. If Matisse had been from the Ozarks instead of France, he'd have painted Sullivan's backyard instead of all those gardens.

Kelly and Mason climbed the path while Pamela Sullivan watched them ascend toward her from the protective shade of a moss green canopy suspended over the deck. Mason had met her only once in the last three months. She was cordial but disinterested, a well-cared-for woman accustomed to the role of professional wife.

Mason wanted to protect her from the news that Kelly carried, even though there was no avoiding it. Protecting people when they were in trouble. That's what the law is for, his aunt Claire had taught him. She was his father's sister and the first lawyer, liberal, and hell-raiser in his family.

She wielded the law like a club for her clients, who were usually poor, disadvantaged, or just outnumbered. "There, that one," she would tell him when he was a child and she read the paper to him about the day's injustices. Then she'd be off on another mission.

She raised him after his parents were killed in a car wreck when Mason was only three. She tried talking him out of going to law school, telling him that he wasn't cut out for the only kind of law worth practicing. Her kind. He'd gone anyway, suspecting that she was right. He enjoyed the battle but didn't care enough about the war she never stopped fighting. When he graduated, he joined a small firm that specialized in representing injured people.

"It's the kind of practice where I can do good and do well at the same time," he told her.

"Go sell your slogans to someone else," she said.

Mason thought of Claire as the sun rose at their backs. She called Kelly the intrusive arm of the law—investigating, accusing, and punishing. She taught him that it's the lawyer's duty to shield the individual from that power. That duty drew her to the law. He understood the duty, but it had never held the allure for him that it had for Claire. Still, as they reached Pamela, he could hear Claire's voice telling him, "There, that one."

Pamela had the look of a handsome woman who did not miss the untarnished beauty of her youth. She carried herself with the confident assurance of someone who understood that age brings its own luster.

This morning, a lavender sweatband held back her chin-length chestnut hair. Her face was lightly made up, but not enough to cover the glow from a just-finished morning run. A trace of sweat darkened the scoop neckline of the yellow T-shirt that hung over her matching shorts. She stood with her hands on her hips, her full chest rising and falling with still settling breath, giving them a quizzical look as they topped the stairs.

"Oh my, excuse me. It's Lou, isn't it?" she asked him with sudden recognition.

"Yes, Pamela. I'm one of your husband's partners. We met a couple of months ago."

"Of course. Please excuse me. I wasn't expecting you or the police," she added, turning toward Kelly and extending her hand. "I'm Pamela Sullivan. But I expect you know that or you wouldn't be here. What can I do for you, Officer?"

Kelly shook her hand quickly and firmly. "Mrs. Sullivan, I'm Sheriff Kelly Holt. Would you mind if we spoke inside?"

"My, this is starting to sound quite official." Kelly didn't reply and Pamela's refined control showed the first sign of fraying as she held her arms folded across her chest. "Yes, it is a bit cool this morning, isn't it?"

It wasn't close to being cool, but Mason understood Pamela's sudden chill. There was no possible explanation for their visit that could include good news. As if she sensed their purpose, Pamela led them through a sliding door, taking her time to delay the inevitable a few seconds longer.

They followed Pamela through a sliding glass door and into the den. She eased herself onto a sofa, her careful movement underscoring the fragility of the moment. Uncertain of his status, Mason stood near the sliding door. Kelly sat on the edge of a chair next to Pamela.

"I'm sorry to intrude on you, Mrs. Sullivan," Kelly began in a soothing voice that quickly gave way to a crisp matter-of-factness. "A man's body was found this morning in a cove not far from here. A wallet was also found with your husband's driver's license and credit cards. The man generally matches your husband's physical description. Mr. Mason thinks it may be your husband."

Pamela held fast as her jaw tightened and her eyes widened at the implications. She shook her head in response to the inevitable question of whether she knew where her husband was. Kelly's request that she identify the body left Pamela mute and renewed Mason's protective instincts.

"Sheriff, I'll bring Mrs. Sullivan, but I would think my identification is sufficient."

Kelly acknowledged his offer without taking her eyes from Pamela. "You're welcome to come along, Counselor, but identification has to be made by next of kin if possible." Her soothing tone was reserved for the newly widowed. He was entitled only to her official voice. "You can bring Mrs. Sullivan in her car."

"I'm not a native, Sheriff. I'll need directions."

"I'm certain of that," she replied. "Take County Road F to Lake Road 5-47 and pick up Highway 5 south. Go across Hurricane Deck Bridge and take the highway all the way to Starlight. Listrom's Mortuary is on the square. I've got to return the boat, and I'll meet you there."

ENJOY THIS EXCERPT FROM *COLD TRUTH*,
THE THRILLING THIRD NOVEL IN JOEL GOLDMAN'S
SERIES
FEATURING LOU MASON

CHAPTER ONE

Ted Phillips, the Channel 6 cameraman, watched Earl Luke Fisher sit cross-legged on the sidewalk answering Sherri Thomas's questions. He listened on his headphones, filming Sherri and Earl Luke's "live from the street" duet for the ten o'clock news.

Earl Luke was a homeless panhandler still prospecting for donations on a hot night in a deserted downtown. Sherri was a Channel 6 television news reporter filling her slot on a slow-news Labor Day. They were both desperate optimists, hands outstretched—his for money, hers for ratings.

Locked into his camera and headgear, Phillips didn't hear the window shatter eight stories above or a woman scream as she jackknifed through the glass. Earl Luke saw it happen and popped his toothless mouth open as if he'd just seen a naked Madonna.

Phillips swung his camera in a quick arc from Earl Luke past Sherri's raised hemline, past her breathtaking chest and upturned slack-jawed face, not stopping until he caught the falling woman in his lens, pinwheeling in a fatal tumble, pancaking onto the pavement, one side of her head flattened like a splintered melon.

"Hold the shot," Phillips said to himself, keeping the camera on the woman's body.

He aimed his camera at the broken window, zooming in for a tight shot of the ragged outline left by the remaining glass. A shadow flickered in the window frame, or so he thought. He blinked, uncertain of what he'd seen, but confident that the camera had a steadier eye than he did.

Phillips put his camera down, wiping away flecks of blood that had hung in the air like ruby raindrops before chasing the dead woman to the ground. Earl Luke was gone. Sherri was panting, pounding Phillips on the arm, and shouting.

"Son of a bitch! Tell me you got that, Ted! Son of a fucking bitch! If you got that, we're golden!"

"And we're still live on the air."

CHAPTER TWO

Lou Mason rewound the tape of the dead woman's plunge and replayed it for the tenth time, forcing himself to focus on the TV screen sitting next to the dry-erase board in his office.

"Too bad you can't ask Dr. Gina one last question," Mickey Shanahan said as he came in and sat down on the sofa across the room from the TV.

"Like who shoved her through that window?"

"For starters. Better yet, tell me how she got such a cushy gig giving advice for the lovelorn and sleep deprived."

"Sleep deprived?"

"Yeah. You know, I'm deprived of sleeping with my good-looking neighbor because my wife doesn't understand me."

"Her cushy gig was the highest-rated radio program in town and one of the biggest in national syndication."

Mickey picked up a hardcover book on Mason's coffee table titled *The Way You Do the Things You Do* by Dr. Gina Davenport.

"Best seller?"

"*New York Times* best seller. Twenty-six weeks on the list. Same for the audio version. Psychotherapy the easy way. People loved her."

"Not everybody. Not whoever kicked her ass out the window. You gonna take the case?"

"There's no case yet. Dr. Gina's office and the radio station are both in the Cable Depot Building in the garment district downtown. Arthur and Carol Hackett own the radio station and the building. They want me to represent their daughter if she's charged with the murder."

"Who's the daughter?"

The tape ended with Sherri Thomas covering her mouth, realizing that her ecstatic outburst had been broadcast throughout Channel 6's two-state viewing area. Mason punched rewind on the remote control.

"Jordan Hackett. She was a patient of Dr. Gina's and a twenty-one-year-old head case. The cops interviewed her, took fingerprints and hair samples, and they took fiber samples from her clothes. Her parents waited to call a lawyer until the cops were through. Said they didn't want to treat her like a criminal."

"Good thinking. If she's not a criminal, why are the cops checking her out and why are her parents scared she'll be charged with murder?"

Mason pulled a bottle of water from the small refrigerator beneath the bay window that looked out on the street from his second-story digs above Blues on Broadway, taking a quick pulse of the traffic as he drank. Broadway hummed with people heading home, back in the groove after a three-day weekend.

Yesterday was Labor Day and most people hadn't worked, but Sherri Thomas and her cameraman put in a full day. Earl Luke Fisher never worked or never stopped, depending on your view of panhandling. Gina Davenport was in her office at ten p.m., probably catching up. Her killer worked overtime. It had been some holiday.

"Don't forget which side we're on, Mickey. She's not a criminal unless she's convicted."

"Even if she did it?"

It was an argument he and Mickey had been having since Mickey started working for Mason. Mickey claimed that public relations was his true destiny and that he was working for Mason only until he got the gig he really wanted working on big political campaigns.

Spin was everything for Mickey, who could shape an issue for any audience, except for Mason's criminal-defense clients. Mickey had to know they were innocent. Mason accepted that he only had to make the state prove they were guilty.

"It's not that simple, even if she killed Gina Davenport. Jordan Hackett could be guilty of first- or second-degree murder, voluntary or involuntary manslaughter, or innocent by reason of insanity. Or she may have killed Dr. Gina in self-defense. Our job is to make the state do its job and prove she's a criminal. Otherwise, no one is safe, especially the innocent."

"I hear you, but working the angles in a PR campaign is a lot cleaner than massaging a murder."

"You need to bring your nothing-is-black-and-white-when-you-spin-it-right morality to criminal-defense work."

Mickey chuckled. "You're the best spin-meister I've seen, boss, but you haven't answered my question. Why do the cops want Jordan Hackett?"

"And you're getting better at cross-examination. I met with her parents this afternoon. They said that Jordan didn't do it. They think the police are checking out all of Dr. Gina's patients. I'll know more after I talk with Jordan tomorrow."

"How did they get the videotape? Did the cops hand them out as party favors to the suspects?"

"The Hacketts are plugged into the local media. They arranged for me to pick up the tape from Channel 6."

"I read in the paper that Samantha Greer is the lead homicide detective on the case. You guys still dancing between the sheets?"

Mason shook his head, more at Mickey than at the question. "Not for a while. She told me she's not a car battery I can jump-start whenever I feel too lonely for another night alone."

"That in Dr. Gina's book?"

"Page 210, under bad analogies used to answer stupid questions."

Mason fast-forwarded the videotape to the moment when the cameraman retraced Dr. Gina's flight back to the window. He used the freeze-frame function of his VCR to break down that segment frame by frame so he could study each image.

"You see anything unusual in the window?" Mason asked Mickey.

"What's to see? It's dark; the picture is fuzzy. I can barely tell it's a window."

"Maybe you're right. When he gave me the tape, the cameraman told me he thought he saw a shadow, like someone standing close enough to look out the window without being seen."

"The killer?"

"Or a witness."

"Why was Dr. Gina treating Jordan Hackett?"

Mason turned off the tape. "Her parents said she had a problem with anger management. When we got past the shrink-speak, they told me that Jordan is too violent to live at home."

"Swell. Where does she live?"

"Safe House. It's a residential facility for teenagers and young adults with emotional problems."

"So there's no case yet, but there's gonna be a case. Are you gonna take it now or when it gets ripe?"

"You want to get paid this week?"

"Dude! You know I do," Mickey said as he got up from the sofa. "Hey, doesn't Centurion Johnson own Safe House?"

Mason nodded. "Centurion gave up a promising career as a drug and thug entrepreneur for the not-for-profit world of social services. Harry busted him a few times and sent him to jail for a long stretch. Soon as he got out, he was back in the game until Blues helped him find religion."

"I'll bet that was a painful conversion."

"You can count on that."

Mason opened the dry-erase board on the wall and began—as he always began—by writing down what he knew and what he had to learn to keep Jordan Hackett off of death row. He wrote Gina Davenport's name, circled it, and labeled her *victim*. Moving from left to right, Mason drew a line and wrote Jordan's name, giving her a casting list of roles: *patient, witness,* and *killer.*

In the upper right-hand corner, he drew a circle around

Centurion Johnson's name and labeled it *trouble*—then added a capital *T*.

Returning to Gina Davenport, he drew a vertical line straight down, capping it with a horizontal bar, like a family tree.

He labeled the next branch *winners* and *losers*. That's where he would find the killer.

About The Author

Joel Goldman is an Edgar and Shamus nominated author who was a trial lawyer for twenty-eight years. He wrote his first thriller after one of his partners complained about another partner and he decided to write a mystery, kill the son-of-a-bitch off in the first chapter and spend the rest of the book figuring out who did it. No longer practicing law, he offices at Starbucks and lives in Kansas City with his wife and two dogs.

NOVELS BY JOEL GOLDMAN

Motion to Kill

The Last Witness

Cold Truth

Deadlocked

Shakedown

The Dead Man

No Way Out

PRAISE FOR JOEL GOLDMAN'S NOVELS

Motion to Kill

"Admirable . . . high tension . . . fierce action scenes carry the reader toward an electrifying dénouement."
—*Publishers Weekly*

"Lou is a fascinating protagonist . . . fans will set in motion a plea for more Lou Mason thrillers."
—*Midwest Book Review*

"The plot races forward."
—*Amarillo Globe News*

"Lots of suspense and a dandy surprise ending."
—*Romantic Times*

The Last Witness

"Fast, furious and thoroughly enjoyable, *The Last Witness* is classic, and classy, noir for our time, filled with great characters and sharp, stylish writing. We better see more Lou Mason in the future."
—Jeffery Deaver, author of *The Vanished Man* and *The Stone Monkey*

"*The Last Witness* is an old-fashioned, '40s, tough-guy detective story set in modern times and starring a lawyer named Lou Mason instead of a private eye named Sam Spade. There's a lot of action, loads of suspects, and plenty of snappy dialogue. It's a fun read from beginning to end."
—Phillip Margolin, author of *The Associate* and *Wild Justice*

Cold Truth

"Wanted for good writing: Joel Goldman strikes again with *Cold Truth*. Kansas City trial lawyer Lou Mason doesn't shy away from the hard cases. Always working close to the edge, he worries that he 'was taking the dive just to see if he could make it back to the surface, gulping for air, beating the odds, wishing he had a reason to play it safe.'"
—*Kansas City Star*

"Joel Goldman is the real deal. In *Cold Truth*, Lou Mason goes his namesake Perry one better, and ought to make Kansas City a must-stop on the lawyer/thriller map."
—John Lescroart, best-selling author of *The First Law*

Deadlocked

"In his fourth novel, attorney-turned-author Joel Goldman delivers a well-plotted legal thriller that takes an insightful look at capital punishment and questions of guilt. *Deadlocked*'s brisk pace is augmented by Goldman's skill at creating realistic characters and believable situations. Goldman is among the legion of strong paperback writers whose novels often rival those in hardcover."
—Oline H. Cogdill, *Orlando Sun Sentinel*

"A certain death penalty case and execution is the catalyst in Joel Goldman's legal thriller *Deadlocked*. The fourth Lou Mason case is

the best and most thought provoking and when the action starts it is a real page turner delivered by a pro."
—*Mystery Scene Magazine*

"Lou Mason's best outing . . . very satisfying and highly recommended."
—Lee Child, *New York Times* best-selling author

Shakedown

"Here's why . . . mystery lovers should put *Shakedown* on their nightstands: Goldman, a 'nuthin' fancy' kind of writer, tells a story at a breakneck pace."
—*Kansas City Star*

"Goldman's surefooted plotting and Jack Davis's courage under fire make this a fascinating, compelling read."
—*Publishers Weekly*

"*Shakedown* is a really fine novel. Joel Goldman has got it locked and loaded and full of the blood of character and the gritty details that make up the truth. Page for page, I loved it."
—Michael Connelly

"*Shakedown* is a chillingly realistic crime novel—it's fast-paced, smartly plotted, and a gripping read to the very last page. Joel Goldman explores—with an insider's eye—a dark tale of murder and betrayal."
—Linda Fairstein

The Dead Man

"A masterful blend of rock-solid detective work and escalating dread. *The Dead Man* is both a top-notch thriller, and a heart-

rending story of loss, courage, and second chances. I loved it."
—Robert Crais, *New York Times* best-selling author

"*The Dead Man* by Kansas Citian Joel Goldman is a rock-solid mystery with likable, flawed characters. I would have enjoyed it even if it had not been set in Kansas City, but scenes such as Harper looking out over Brush Creek or eating in the Country Club Plaza added to the pleasure."
—*Kansas City Star*

"*The Dead Man* is one of those rare novels you will be tempted to read twice: the first time to enjoy, and the second to appreciate how Goldman puts the pieces together. The hours spent on both will be more than worth it."
—Joe Hartlaub, Bookreporter.com

No Way Out

"Sleek and sassy, *No Way Out* is a page-turner that keeps going full speed until the very end."
—Faye Kellerman, *New York Times* best-selling author

"Goldman spins his latest yarn into a clever, complex tangle of chain reactions between six families of characters whose lives are intertwined by blood, grief, lust, desperation and even love. The fun, of course, lies in the untangling . . . If you like to blink, you may want to skip this novel."
—*435 South* magazine

JOEL GOLDMAN

THE LAST WITNESS

CPSIA information can be obtained at www.ICGtesting.com
Printed in the USA
LVOW071421030613

336707LV00002B/19/P